Seamstress Daria Dembrowski must find a historically-minded killer before the fabric of her peaceful town rips wide open...

When the reality show *My House in History* comes to Laurel Springs, Pennsylvania, savvy seamstress Daria Dembrowski sees a business opportunity. The show follows two elderly sisters' quest to restore their colonial mansion, and that means a heap of work for a seamstress who specializes in historical textiles. Although one of the old women is a bit of a grump, Daria loves the job—until she discovers one of the researchers dead, and the whole project threatens to unwind.

As a series of historical crimes pile up, from a stolen Paul Revere platter to a chilling incident of arson, Daria must find the killer quickly, for her life is hanging by a thread.

Also by Greta McKennan

The Stitch in Time Mystery series
Uniformly Dead
Historically Dead

Historically Dead

Greta McKennan

LYRICAL UNDERGROUND
Kensington Publishing Corp.
www.kensingtonbooks.com

LYRICAL UNDERGROUND BOOKS are published by

Kensington Publishing Corp.
119 West 40th Street
New York, NY 10018

All Kensington titles, imprints, and distributed lines are available at special quantity discounts for bulk purchases for sales promotion, premiums, fund-raising, educational, or institutional use.

Special book excerpts or customized printings can also be created to fit specific needs. For details, write or phone the office of the Kensington Sales Manager: Kensington Publishing Corp., 119 West 40th Street, New York, NY 10018. Attn. Sales Department. Phone: 1-800-221-2647.

Lyrical Underground and Lyrical Underground logo Reg. US Pat. & TM Off.

First Electronic Edition: December 2017
eISBN-13: 978-1-5161-0169-6
eISBN-10: 1-5161-0169-3

First Print Edition: December 2017
ISBN-13: 978-1-5161-0172-6
ISBN-10: 1-5161-0172-3

Printed in the United States of America

For Mom, who inspires me.

Acknowledgments

I want to thank my editor, Martin Biro, for being patient with me throughout the writing process, and my agent, Jessica Faust, for her unfailing encouragement. Thanks to all the folks at Kensington who work their magic to transform a story into a published book and then send it out there for people to find and read.

Thanks to Laura Lippman and her Double LL Ranch workshop group from Eckerd College's Writers in Paradise conference for helpful comments on the first twenty-five pages, especially Jami Deise, fellow workshop participant and copy editor of my first novel.

Thanks to Tim Barnhill for giving me tips on how the film industry works in Pennsylvania.

Finally, thanks to my family: Mike, Jamie, Laura, and Johnny, for supporting me throughout this ongoing journey. I couldn't do it without you!

Chapter One

"What do you think? Do I look like an eighteenth-century lady?"

I stepped back to survey my client's gown and overall appearance. Straight sleeves ending in a cascade of white organdy and lace—check. Flowered lavender petticoat falling over a hoopskirt stiffened with real whalebone—check. White linen fichu covering the stooped shoulders—check.

Orthopedic athletic shoes—not so much.

"You look gorgeous, Miss Priscilla," I said. "General Washington himself would bow and kiss your hand if he could see you."

She inclined her head and dropped a deep curtsy, no mean feat for a woman of eighty-odd years. "Of course, General Washington would never see this dress, my dear. This is only a house dress, after all." She straightened up and held herself still and erect as I knelt at her feet and pinned up the endless hem.

A sigh escaped my lips at the thought of the hours of hand sewing ahead of me. I contemplated breaking my cardinal rule and running the hem up by machine instead of setting it in by hand, but I knew I wouldn't. I wasn't willing to sacrifice those little touches of craftsmanship that set my work apart. My historical sewing business, A Stitch in Time, was taking off nicely, and I wasn't about to let any shoddy shortcuts drag me down.

My pins slid into the silky fabric. I'd stepped back in time on this job. The wooden floorboards I knelt on dated from the mid-1700s. Their lustrous surface was wavy from the passage of years and many a booted foot. The spacious living room had been emptied of its twentieth-century furnishings, leaving only a few graceful antiques. A drop-leaf table balanced the two tall windows, which were still covered by nothing but mini-blinds. A small arrangement of wingback chairs grouped around an occasional table stood before the cozy hearth. A tall chest of drawers in dark mahogany wood stood on spindly legs against the opposite wall.

Priscilla Compton, the quiet, reclusive mistress of this estate, was a tiny woman in her eighties. Content to sit knitting on her front porch, dressed in long calico gowns, she'd been a fixture in our small Pennsylvania town for a quarter of a century, almost the entirety of my lifetime. As a child, I'd always thought of her as the crazy old lady in the haunted house on the hill, practically a ghost herself. Nobody bothered much with old Priscilla Compton, until she gained notoriety through the reality TV show *My House in History*. Now the whole town watched while she transformed her home to its original eighteenth-century condition.

"When you get the hem pinned up, my dear, shall we talk about the curtains?"

I bit back a smile. Priscilla always called me "my dear," as if I were her beloved granddaughter rather than a hired seamstress. She probably didn't even know that my name was Daria.

"Yes, curtains. Were you thinking heavy, or light and airy?" I slid in the final pin and scrambled to my feet. I paced around her, checking the drape of the skirt. Perfect. "You can slip that off now, and I'll have it hemmed up by tomorrow." I moved to unfasten the row of hooks and eyes on the back of the bodice, and helped Priscilla ease the gown off her shoulders.

She pulled on her everyday clothing, a simple gown of sprigged muslin that fell to her ankles. "Light and airy for the parlor, I believe. Professor Burbridge has the drawings we're working off of. Such a delight to have a learned historian on our team, isn't it, my dear?"

Her enthusiasm for the project was what delighted me the most. "I'll check in with the professor later."

"Will you be around this evening, my dear? The new attorney is coming to meet all of us. He's a delightful young man who Ruth has hired to tell us what all the lovely things in this house are worth."

I glanced around the living room, noting the silver tea service arranged on the antique side table, and the framed coat of arms above it that proclaimed the honor of the Compton line. They were only a few of the "lovely things" that filled Compton Hall. The newly hired attorney would have plenty of work to occupy himself in this house.

I smiled at Priscilla. "I'll probably leave around dinnertime. Maybe I'll get the chance to meet the new attorney tomorrow."

I bundled up her gown, gathered up my pincushion and sewing gauge, and turned to leave the room when an insistent knocking sounded on the front door.

"Oh, dear, the door must be locked. Poor Ruth gets so upset when she can't get in." Priscilla gathered up the flowing folds of her skirt in her knobby hands and made her slow way toward the door. She paused with a hand to her chest as the knocking continued. "Just open the door for her, would you, my dear?"

I hastened to the door, still clutching my sewing implements. The wood shivered under the force of the knocking outside. I opened it to reveal a tall and very thin old woman on the step, gold-tipped cane poised to assault the door again. She wore a fur coat on this muggy August afternoon. Straight, blunt-cut gray hair fell just below her long earlobes, which were dragged down by heavy pearl earrings. Those oversized earlobes were the only resemblance I could see between Ruth Ellis, widow of the late philanthropist Thurman Ellis, and her older sister Priscilla. She drew herself up to a formidable height and frowned down at me.

"I could have finished one of Tolstoy's novels standing out here." She brushed past me into the foyer, pulling tight brown gloves from her hands. "Where is my sister?"

I felt an absurd urge to curtsy and say, "Follow me." Instead, I indicated the living room with a wave of the hand. "She's just in there. She's waiting for you."

She shot me a sharp glance. "And getting older every wasted minute." She headed across the foyer, leaning heavily upon her elegant cane. I was dismissed.

I shrugged, and headed for the stairs. Priscilla had set me up in the sewing room on the third floor to do her historical sewing, so I could do all my work on-site. It was certainly more convenient for fittings, and I could get my cardio workout from all my trips up and down the curving staircase. I felt a sense of self-importance at being a seamstress-in-residence.

The sewing room was lovely. A small room compared to the rest of the mansion, it still eclipsed my fitting room back home. Faded floral wallpaper covered the walls, and a white-painted chair rail encircled the entire room. A small oak side table held a large bowl that was probably silver under its layer of brassy tarnish. An antique treadle sewing machine occupied the place of honor opposite the door. The head was incredibly well preserved, despite the layer of dust that had coated it when I first arrived two weeks earlier. I'd cleaned and oiled the whole machine, replaced a belt or two, and adjusted the tension until the needle rose and fell smoothly with the tap of a foot. I'd made a deal with Priscilla that I could use the treadle machine for any seams that wouldn't show, reserving the hand stitching for hems and other details on the outside of each garment. It was a compromise between her desire for authentic details in the process of refurbishing her life to reflect an eighteenth-century way of life, and the need for speed in the transformation. The TV show's schedule dictated the frenzied pace of the work.

I settled down to my hemming, my needle flashing through the silky fabric. The time sped by as I toyed with the idea of making myself a quick homespun gown to wear while working at Compton Hall. I was wondering what sort of sandal one would wear with an eighteenth-century gown and apron when my phone rang. Welcoming the break, I scooped up the phone. It was my renter and roommate, Aileen.

"Hey, your four o'clock appointment is here, wondering why you ran off with her wedding gown."

Fiona! I couldn't believe I forgot about her fitting. I could hear Fiona's soft voice protesting in the background, seemingly ignored by Aileen.

"So, are you on your way home, or what?" Aileen said.

I gathered up the silken gown with one hand and stuffed it into my spacious shoulder bag. "Yes, yes. Tell Fiona I—"

"Tell her yourself," she cut in. I could hear fumbling, and then Fiona came on the line.

"I never said you ran off with my wedding gown, Daria."

I chuckled. "Of course you didn't. That's Aileen for you. Fiona, I'm so sorry I forgot your fitting. I can be home in twenty minutes, unless you want to reschedule."

"No, I can wait. Don't worry, I've got hours of reading to get through, so it's no trouble."

I was already out the door and hurrying down the stairs. "Bless you. I'll be there as soon as I can."

I heard the shouting as soon as I hit the first floor. Despite my haste, I paused in front of the living room door, my heartbeats accelerating like they always did at the sound of raised voices. Could Priscilla be in the middle of an argument? I couldn't picture it, any more than I could picture the First Lady yelling at her children in public. I could hear the querulous tones of Ruth Ellis, ridden over by a man's deep voice.

"I won't be silenced!"

No chance of that—he was shouting loud enough to disturb the next-door neighbors. I jumped out of the way as the door flung open and Professor Burbridge stormed out.

Burbridge's face was mottled with anger. A tall, thin man save for his prominent paunch, full of boundless, caffeinated energy, he slammed past me without acknowledging my existence. His sparse black hair shot with gray stuck out in all directions, churned up by a frustrated hand. His ever-present tweed coat with the leather elbow patches was flung over his shoulder, and he clutched a bulging leather briefcase in one hand. I could hear him muttering, "I have every right—they can't stop me...." He stormed up the stairs and disappeared down the second floor hallway.

Obviously not a time to ask him for historical drawings.

I hesitated in the front hall, wondering if I should check to make sure Priscilla was okay. But with Fiona waiting at home, I couldn't risk the delay. I hurried out the door, checking the lock to make sure the door was unlocked this time.

I halted on the doorstep when I saw what was happening outside. Priscilla's Japanese maple trees were famous in town, rising fifteen feet to frame the front of the house around the living room windows with their scarlet leaves. But not today. I watched in horror as Jamison Royce from Laurel Landscape Arts, who had been hired to renovate the gardens and landscaping, tossed an uprooted maple tree onto a growing pile. He was tearing out every one of Priscilla's prized Japanese maples!

"What are you doing?" I gasped.

A big man in his middle fifties, Royce looked me over with a shrug. "What does it look like I'm doing? I'm pulling up these plants." He wiped his hands on his dirt-covered jeans, adjusted his odd-looking work cap with flaps that covered his ears, and turned to tackle the one remaining maple tree.

"Why?"

Royce leaned on his shovel, pushing the blade into the ground at the root of the tree. He scratched his chin, which was covered by an unfashionably long beard. "Japanese maples didn't exist in Pennsylvania gardens in 1770. We're going back in time here, remember? Out with the new, in with the old." He spaded up a load of dirt. "Seems a shame, but it's all about the money, now isn't it? Money and fame, fame and money. Can't get enough of either, can we?"

The Japanese maple appeared to shiver as he laid hands on it to rip it out of the ground. Fragile red leaves showered down by my feet. The soft murmur of voices drifted out the open window around the corner of the house. Ruth and Priscilla seemed to be talking earnestly. For an instant I wondered if Priscilla really knew what was happening to her beloved maples. But I didn't have time to find out. I only had two minutes to make it to the bus. "What's going to happen to these trees?"

"I'm hauling them off to the dump. You want one?"

"Yes! I have to run—can you save me one or two? I can collect them this evening."

He nodded with a shrug. "Suit yourself. I'll leave you a couple by the side door. If they're still there in the morning, they're history."

I called my thanks over my shoulder and sprinted for the bus stop. I made it in time for the 4:05 bus and got home barely within the twenty minutes I'd promised. It was only a five-minute drive from the Highlands where Compton Hall overlooked the Schuylkill River valley to the tree-lined downtown neighborhood where I lived, but the bus took much longer. It was the price I had to pay for my enduring fear of driving. True, I'd saved my life in a wild car chase through the streets of Laurel Springs not one month earlier, but I still hated driving with a passion. Me behind the wheel of two tons of steel was an accident waiting to happen, and I knew it. Best to simply say, "I don't drive," and deal with the consequences. In this case, they weren't severe—merely a few extra minutes of studying for a forgiving client, and a little more egg on the face for me. I could live with that.

As I dashed up the cockeyed concrete steps to my front porch, I could hear the heavy bass beat of the band coming from the basement. Aileen and the Twisted Armpits must be in full swing. Poor Fiona; I'd forgotten to warn her about the noise. I hurried into my fitting room, the formal dining room of my nineteenth-century three-story house.

I paused on the threshold. Despite the muffled booms from beneath the floorboards, Fiona had fallen fast asleep in one of my comfy chairs, her book open on her chest. During a pause in the band's clamor I could hear Fiona's soft breathing. With her smooth brown curls swept back from a broad forehead and her mouth slightly open in sleep, she looked far too young and innocent to be an honors law student, much less a bride-to-be. She exuded peace and serenity. Not wanting to catch her in such a vulnerable state, I backed out of the doorway and stepped right onto the tail of my long-suffering cat. Mohair yowled and streaked off into the kitchen in an orange blur, and I jumped and dropped my shoulder bag with a clatter. No worries about having to wake Fiona now! I gathered up the spilled contents of my bag and entered the room with a cheery hello.

Fiona got to her feet and greeted me with a smile. "I must have dozed off there. So much for catching up on my reading."

"So sorry for forgetting about you." I rummaged through the rack of wedding gowns hanging in the corner, and pulled out the plastic-wrapped hanger labeled "Fiona Tuckerman." "It's a big day—you get to put this on for the first time." I pointed her to the curtained-off corner reserved for changing. "Don't worry about the back—I'll fit it for the buttons today."

While Fiona changed I took a minute to set some hot cider to bubbling on the sideboard, breathing in its spicy aroma. In my experience, brides-to-be were happier with my work when they felt relaxed, a neat trick to achieve between the normal stresses of wedding preparations combined with a metal band rehearsing in the basement. I hoped to scale back on my wedding gowns as the historical sewing increased, but I had yet to achieve that level of specialization.

Fiona emerged from the changing area, clutching the bodice of her dress so the whole thing wouldn't fall right off her. I quickly pinned up the back and steered her to the three-way mirror. She turned and swayed and admired the shining folds of her wedding gown. She'd chosen a custom-made design based on drawings I'd done from her specifications. The gown featured a striking strapless neckline with diagonal shirring through the bodice to provide the only ornamentation. The wide, flowing skirt trailed on the floor in just a hint of a train. The heavy satin glowed with a luster of its own, needing no adornment of lace or sequins. It was a sophisticated, lovely look that well suited this professional young woman.

I gave Fiona a few minutes to admire the possibilities, and then instructed her to stand still while I marked the back for the line of satin-covered buttons. When she winced, I nearly dropped the whole pincushion.

"Oh, no, did I poke you?"

She gave me a puzzled glance over her shoulder. "No, I'm good."

A second later she flinched again. I wasn't even touching her. "Is everything all right, Fiona?"

"It's just, that noise. How can you stand it?"

It was my turn to look puzzled, until I registered the howling emanating from the basement where the Twisted Armpits held sway. The unrelenting bass of the band had become such a backdrop to my daily life that it didn't bother me anymore. "I guess I've gotten used to it. I'll ask Aileen to knock it off for a few minutes."

"No, no, it's okay. We're just about done, right?" She checked her watch. "I'm meeting Randy in half an hour for dinner." She held her arms out obediently for me to finish with the back. "I hope you'll get a chance to meet Randy soon. He's starting work for a client here in Laurel Springs, so we'll be able to see each other every day instead of just on the weekends."

She checked her watch again, and I instinctively tried to speed up my work. So much for the relaxing effect of the cider aroma.

"He lives out of town, then?"

"Philly. You wouldn't think that would be too far, but between my studies and his caseload, we can only get together on the weekends. I usually go into the city, so it's a treat to have him come live with me for a bit. He used to live here, so it won't be such a shock for him to hang out in the backwoods for a while."

Fiona jumped as the basement door slammed against the wall, letting loose the cacophony of a truly colossal drum solo. Aileen appeared in the doorway, having characteristically neglected to shut the basement door behind her. Her skintight purple leather short-shorts and red lace-covered corset suited the sultry August day. Her ever-changing pixie hairdo sported streaks of fluorescent red, yellow, and purple today, on a base of jet black. Brass chains looped over her shoulder, snaked around her waist, and twined down her right thigh. A pair of black cracked-leather platform boots added a good seven inches to her over-six-foot frame. If you wanted to sum up Aileen in one word, "intimidating" would work nicely.

"We're calling out for pizza, Daria. Do you want to go in on it?"

After the peanut butter incident, in which Aileen slathered a perfectly good pepperoni pizza with crunchy peanut butter topped with hot sauce and dried mango slices, I'd learned to never, never share food with her, of any description. Whatever she was planning to top her pizza with today, I wanted no part of it. "No, thanks, I'll pass."

She shrugged and said, "Your loss," before clomping into the kitchen.

I turned back to Fiona, who was checking her watch yet again. "Two more pins and we're done." I set the pins, marked the center back line with dressmaking chalk, and quickly unpinned her.

While Fiona changed, I flipped through my planner, taking stock of my projects. With Fiona's wedding in a little over two weeks, I needed to have her in for another fitting to pin up the hem, and then one final time when she would collect her gown and make her last payment. Just in time, with my mortgage payment coming due at the end of the month. For the umpteenth time I prayed for success with my historical sewing business, so I could gain some financial security after all these years. I had also assured Priscilla that her gown would be hemmed by tomorrow—looked like a long night for me. But I still needed to eat, right? My finger ran down the page for today, coming to rest on the entry "Sean M—dinner (?)." I didn't know where he planned to take me, but it had been three weeks since I'd seen McCarthy and I wasn't about to forgo that date in favor of an endless hem!

I sent Fiona on her way with an appointment for the following week for the final fitting of her gown, then ran upstairs to change for dinner.

My bedroom was on the second floor of my Federal-style house, the only thing left of my failed relationship with my former fiancé. It boasted three stories and a total of six bedrooms complete with fireplaces in every one. Despite my bitter memories of Randall, I loved the house with my whole heart. Its quirky closets, unexpected stained-glass window in the sole bathroom, and promise of hidey-holes behind the eaves gave it a charm that new construction could never offer. The price for charm was felt in the exorbitant heating bills needed to keep the high-ceilinged rooms livable in the winter. I'd solved this problem by taking in Aileen as a renter, and then welcoming my brother Pete to the mix when he returned to Laurel Springs after his disastrous attempt to make it big in Hollywood. Pete got the big third-floor bedroom, Aileen had one on the second floor as well as her band's practice space in the basement, and I had a bedroom and sewing workroom on the second floor. Technically we had two empty bedrooms, but I resisted Aileen's suggestion that her four bandmates could move in with us. One crazy guitarist in the household was enough!

My cozy bedroom, furnished in collegiate style with bricks and boards bookcases and a desk and chair scavenged from yard sales, suited me just fine. I kept a padded rocking chair in front of the hearth. Even though the fireplace was bricked over, it was a comfy place to read a novel. Of course, I usually spent my late evenings at the sewing machine, but I could always dream. But tonight, at least my early evening would be spent in stimulating company.

I slipped on a pale blue cotton blouse and a swingy skirt that fell just above the knee, paired with my favorite strappy sandals. Not too dressy, but ready for dancing if that was what McCarthy had in mind. I shook out the bobby pins holding back my flyaway brown hair, and studied the possibilities in the mirror. No matter how much I brushed and coaxed, my unruly mop was not so much smooth and shiny as rough and ready. I remember standing in the girls' bathroom with my high school buddies, the three of us brushing and primping before fourth period math class. Suzanne had poked me and said, "It doesn't matter if you brush your hair or not, it looks the same either way." I'd sulked over that statement for weeks afterward, but now at the wise old age of twenty-nine I had to admit she'd been right. No sense wasting time over it! I swept up the sides into two carved bamboo combs and let the back fall free. I smiled at my reflection: wide brown eyes, teeth a titch crooked through lack of middle school braces, cheeks soft and rounded. Standing tall at five foot three, I was repeatedly cast as the young ingénue in high school drama productions. "You've got that fresh-faced look we want," was the mantra. Fair enough. I scooped up a light cotton sweater and headed down the stairs to meet McCarthy.

He was waiting for me on the front porch. Any other man would be sitting on the porch swing, or leaning on the rail checking messages on his phone. Not McCarthy! He lay on his stomach on the floorboards, his camera lens trained on some point off the corner of the porch. He didn't notice me in the doorway. He scootched along on his belly, heedless of his white shirt, murmuring, "Come on now, you've got this." He chuckled softly, his camera clicking away.

The familiar sight of his comfortably worn jeans, customary white button-down shirt with the sleeves rolled up, and dark blond ponytail tied back with a thick rubber band made me smile. I hadn't admitted to myself how much I'd missed him while he was away these past three weeks.

Sean McCarthy took pictures for the local newspaper, the Laurel Springs *Daily Chronicle.* I'd met him a month earlier, when he was covering a Civil War reenactment for which I was sewing uniforms. The heady mix of romantic historical reenacting and violent death at the encampment threw us together into an intense relationship. I'd welcomed McCarthy's recent absence as a chance to sort out my feelings for him. Now, faced with the man himself, I knew I had come to no conclusion. Would it be so bad if I just went along for the ride?

I must have made some noise coming out the door, for McCarthy rolled onto his left shoulder and peered up at me. His camera caught a quick image of my face, and then he scrambled to his feet. "Spidey's got a wasp in his web. It's struggling like crazy, but it hasn't got a chance. Look, you can see him ejecting the poison." He fiddled with the buttons on the back of his camera and held it out to me. Indeed, his magnificent close-up shots revealed a showy black-and-yellow spider locked in a death dance with a half-wrapped wasp. A rapid-fire series of photos caught a strand of the web separating from the whole, falling away from the struggle. As always, I marveled at the magical world that McCarthy's lens unveiled.

"Are you rooting for the spider, you bloodthirsty voyeur?"

He grinned, and brushed some dust off his shirt. "This is a story of survival, and I'm on the spider's side all the way. I was ambushed by wasps once, when I was eight. True, I had just trampled on their nest, but they shouldn't have taken that so personally. It left me scarred for life."

I laughed and gave him a quick hug. "It's good to see you."

With the awkwardness averted, we hopped in his car and drove across town to the Commons to find a place to eat. As usual, the street parking was full, but McCarthy managed to find a place to park in a sketchy-looking alley. I watched my step until we reached the brick pavement of the Commons.

McCarthy chatted about his trip to the Catskills to photograph a local Boy Scout troop's high adventure white-water rafting excursion. "They hope to get a feature in *Boys' Life* magazine. It's hardly the Pulitzer, but they're pretty pumped." He took my hand and swung our arms between us as we walked. "I hear you're working on the historical makeover of the old Compton house. Do you suppose those TV folks will let me hang around and take some photos?"

I gently disengaged my hand. "Would it stop you if they said no?"

His eyes crinkled at the edges when he smiled at me. "There is that."

We settled on Fortni's Pizzeria, a cozy storefront with round tables covered in red-checkered tablecloths and decorated with candles planted in wine bottles dripping with multicolored wax. We ordered spinach and mushroom pizza, paired with a pitcher of sangria garnished with peaches.

"So, what's it like to work on a reality TV show set?" McCarthy pulled out his notebook, but only to doodle on a blank page while we talked.

"It's kind of cool, and kind of creepy at the same time. You never know when someone's going to start filming you and asking a bunch of questions about what you're doing. Everyone's hyped up about the money."

"Money?"

"What, you don't know how this whole thing works?"

He laughed. "I've been in the wilds of upstate New York, camping on the banks of a raging river. I'm a bit out of touch."

"Okay, I'll give you that. Priscilla's house was chosen by *My House in History* to compete with maybe a dozen other historic houses. They're all challenged to restore the houses to the time period in which they were built, which in this case was 1770. Film crews are documenting the work along the way, and when it's all done the TV viewers get to vote on their favorite historic house. The winner gets a million dollars and the chance to be on the sequel show, *My Life in History*. In this one they have to live in their historical time period, with film crews documenting their daily activities."

I stared at McCarthy's paper, watching in fascination as he doodled a series of complex snowflakes radiating out from a central point. He caught me looking, and started drawing a line of dollar signs. "A million dollars is a lot of money."

"Sure. It might be worth all the upheaval at Compton Hall. But there's always the chance that someone else will win, and Priscilla will be left with an eighteenth-century house with no running water or electricity."

"Poor old lady. It's hard to imagine her being motivated by a million dollars. She's always seemed so unsophisticated."

"She's a darling." I moved the salt and pepper shakers out of the way so the waitress could set down our pizza. "Do you know her?"

McCarthy snagged a piece of pizza and picked off a big slice of mushroom to pop into his mouth. "I photographed her last year during the Laurel Springs House Tour. It was the first time she'd put Compton Hall on the tour in thirty years, or so the organizers told me. They were stoked to offer tours of a house on the National Register of Historic Places. Priscilla suffered the onslaught of visitors with quiet dignity."

"How did she deal with an obnoxious photographer pestering her for yet another close up?"

He grinned. "I was on my best behavior, I'll have you know. She reminded me of my grandmother, who died when I was eleven years old. Sweet lady."

I wasn't sure if the sweet lady was Priscilla or his grandmother, but either way, I enjoyed the tender tone in McCarthy's voice. It vanished in an instant.

"So, can you get me in for a story on the reality show? The *Daily Chronicle* would love to run a feature, and I imagine the TV folks would welcome some free publicity."

I took a drink of sangria, surprised to find that the sweet, fruity wine was giving me a buzz. "What's in it for me?"

"For you...a page one photo, in color, of the town's premier historical seamstress at work."

I laughed, and drained my glass. "I'm the town's only historical seamstress, who has to get back to finish setting in the biggest hem in history. But let's walk down the Commons and back before we head home."

The evening air was cooling down, making for quite a pleasant walk. I loved window-shopping on the Commons, a pedestrian mall created by closing off a two-block section of downtown, paving the street over with bricks, and installing decorative lampposts to shine outside the quaint, artsy shops. I never spent much money on the Commons, as neither my lifestyle nor my budget allowed for stained-glass hanging candelabras or fairy statues for garden paths, but I always enjoyed looking.

We strolled past the equestrian statue of Major Samuel Compton, Revolutionary War hero and ancestor to Priscilla and Ruth. Compton Hall had been his home before he was killed in the famous Battle of Laurel Springs. Famous to us in this town, I guess. I stopped to glance at the plaque at the base of the statue.

"'Dedicated to the heroism of Major Samuel F. Compton, savior of the town of Laurel Springs at cost of his own life.' I always love that line."

McCarthy trained the lens of his camera on the plaque. "I don't know, it seems like it would make a better story if he could have made it out alive."

"Hey, don't go criticizing our town hero. You didn't grow up here. You can't possibly understand the devotion of the born and bred Laurel Springsian for our own Major Samuel Compton."

He laughed, and I laughed with him. But I was partly serious about the sense of pride that I felt for the town hero.

We strolled on down the Commons.

"Look, Sean, the new Italian restaurant is open."

"La Trattoria," McCarthy proclaimed, eyeing the elegant script letters on the hand-painted sign. "Looks pretty ritzy."

Indeed, the dining room looked opulent, with its white linen tablecloths set with shining gold silverware and bud vases with a single rose in each. Well-dressed couples out for a special evening filled the small space, the waiting line spilling over to the sidewalk outside. As McCarthy and I lingered outside, appraising this new addition to our small town, Fiona emerged from the crowded restaurant arm in arm with a tall, dark-haired man sporting a charcoal-gray suit and red power tie. In passing a full table, he leaned over the shoulders of two of the men, tossing out a comment that set them all to laughing. When he turned his head to speak to Fiona, I got a better look at him. I knew that face! Sharp nose, thick bushy eyebrows, and a wide, sensuous mouth—once the face of my dreams.

Fiona spotted me and weaved through the crowd. "Daria! I'd like you to meet Randy—Randall Flint, my fiancé." Fiona squeezed his arm lightly and beamed at him. "This is Daria Dembrowski. She's making my wedding gown."

I held my head high as Randall's eyes fell on me. A wide smile curved his lips as he extended a hand to me. "How nice."

His fingers scarcely grazed mine before I pulled my hand away. I could feel my cheeks flaming, but I tried not to lose my cool. "Do you know Sean McCarthy? He's a photographer for the Laurel Springs *Daily Chronicle*."

McCarthy seized Randall's hand with a sure grip. "Pleasure." He glanced down at me, clearly sensing my discomfort. "Daria and I were just scoping out the new restaurant. Hot entertainment in a small town."

I laughed a shade too loudly. "You should have seen the crowds that turned out to tour the new post office downtown last month. Stamp sales spiked at their highest level since the Forever Stamp was created."

"Hmm." Randall twined his fingers in Fiona's and drew her hand close to his chest. "Well, I wouldn't worry about any spike in Italian food consumption. Dinner was mediocre at best, and the service was extremely slow." He caught Fiona's eye. "Shall we, darling?"

She threw me a bright smile. "Gotta go!" She waved as the two departed.

McCarthy took my hand and twined his fingers around mine in an obvious imitation of Randall. He pulled me in close, his eyes twinkling. "So?"

I snatched my hand away and shoved both fists into my sweater pockets. "So, I hoped I would never see him again." I stalked off down the brick walkway, with McCarthy trotting along to keep up. "I used to date him. We split up." Or rather, he split, taking the balance of our joint bank account with him, leaving me with a broken heart and a pile of debt. But I didn't feel like hashing through the whole sordid tale with McCarthy.

Surprisingly, his journalistic instincts did not kick in at this point. He refrained from putting me through the "who, what, where, when, why" litany. Instead, he just eased my hand out of my pocket and held it lightly as we walked through the Commons. "Next time, let's give La Trattoria a try. I think I just heard a positive review, considering the source."

I squeezed his hand gratefully.

* * * *

McCarthy dropped me off at home and then took off so I could get to work on Priscilla's hem. I settled in on the couch in the living room for the long haul. Several yards of hand stitching later, Pete wandered in and turned on the TV. "Phillies game is on tonight." He sank down on the couch next to me and offered me an open bag of potato chips.

I swept the voluminous skirt away from him. "Don't get your greasy fingerprints all over my handiwork here."

He grinned and wiped his hands on his jeans. He wore a soft flannel shirt covering a nondescript T-shirt, with a Phillies cap proclaiming his passion. My brother read baseball statistics books for fun when he was twelve years old, and he never outgrew his love for the game. "Nuts!

They're losing seven to three to the Reds." He slouched down in his seat and scowled at the TV.

"How's the filming going for that new movie you're working on?"

Pete shoved a fistful of chips into his mouth. "We spent all day at the arboretum today, shooting thirty-seven takes of cardinals landing on tree branches. Pretty cool, actually."

I dropped my needle with a start. "Oh, that reminds me. I need to pick up one of those Japanese maples before Royce throws them all away."

On the TV, one of the Reds players hit a triple, and two runs scored. Pete groaned.

It seemed like a good time to ask, "Could you give me a ride in your truck? Just up to Compton Hall in the Highlands."

He stood up and snapped off the TV in disgust. "Sure, why not?"

* * * *

Pete drove with his eyes fixed on the road, his hands drumming meditatively on the steering wheel. I watched him in silence for a few minutes. He looked a lot better than he did a month ago when he had just come home from Hollywood, fresh out of jail on drug charges. He'd gained a healthy amount of weight and the hollow look had just about left his eyes. There was nothing he could do about his broken nose at this point, but still, it felt like the old Pete was nearly back, as if he'd really closed the door on that chapter in his life.

He caught me looking, and threw me a smile. "Checking up on me?"

"You'll pass. Except for those potato chip crumbs all over your shirt. Disgusting."

He laughed and swiped at his flannel shirt. "What's the deal with these maple trees?" He pulled into the sweeping driveway of Compton Hall.

"Royce was pulling them all out to make way for historically correct plantings. He was going to leave them on the side of the house for me to take whatever I want. They're Priscilla's prize-winning Japanese maples—I can't believe she's letting them go."

We picked our way through the darkness to the side of the house. I pulled out my phone to light the way. Royce had left an obstacle course of tools and cuttings strewn across the path. The light from my phone illuminated a large pile where he must have left the maple trees for me to root through. I bent over the pile, checking the bases for a healthy root ball that might survive replanting. I shifted around to the back side of the heap, searching. Something brushed against my foot, and I jumped with a gasp. I shined the light down to catch the tail of a mouse disappearing into the tangled pile. I sprang backward, and collided with Pete standing behind me.

"Not scared of an itty-bitty mouse, are we?" The light from his phone revealed two or three more roaming through the pile.

I tried to play off a shudder. "Who, me?" I shifted a few more branches to uncover a passable specimen. "Gimme a hand with this one."

Between the two of us we were able to extricate the tree from the pile and load it into the back of Pete's truck. I would have stopped there, but the vision of twin Japanese maples arching over my front stoop led me back to the pile, despite the ever-present threat of mice. I circled around the pile, scanning for a matching tree. I kept shining the light at the ground by my feet, in case another mouse wanted to get too close. All I saw was an old red brick lying on top of a tangle of maple branches.

I found a second Japanese maple that I thought would work, although it was a good two feet taller than the first. It wouldn't make a completely balanced pair, but the distinctive red leaves would definitely brighten up my front yard. I got Pete to help me load it into the truck, and called it good. I still had a marathon hem to finish.

* * * *

It took me until two thirty in the morning to get through the entire hem. Then I slept fitfully, dreaming of a needle flashing through flowered silk all night long. Morning came much too soon.

The sun was shining as I waited for the bus up to the Highlands. I hoped the good weather would hold, so I could get my new Japanese maples planted when I got back home.

Priscilla's house sparkled in the morning sunshine. The staff was already hard at work. Jamison Royce was working on the side of the house, loading the rest of the Japanese maples into the back of a pickup truck. I knew I had no room for any more, but the thought of those prize-winning trees headed for the dump just about broke my heart. I averted my eyes and hurried up the walkway to the house.

I heard a commotion when I entered the hall. I peeked into the kitchen, now the domain of Carl Harper, the contractor who had been tasked with the removal of all the modern appliances from the kitchen. He was perched atop a ladder, his head and shoulders hidden inside the stainless steel hood over the stovetop. A big, powerful man, clad in dirty brown work pants and heavy army boots, Harper was a force to be reckoned with. A steady stream of swearing emanated from inside the oven hood, amplified by the gleaming metal. As I watched, he smacked the inside of the hood with a heavy hand, cursing all the while. An industrial-sized wrench slammed to the floor, and I backed away from the door, leaving him to struggle with his work.

I sought out Priscilla in her sitting room at the back of the house. She sat at a tiny writing table by the window, a pile of papers spread out in front of her. Her long white hair was caught up in a chignon at the base of her neck. She greeted me with a sweet smile.

"Good morning, my dear. Such a lovely day, isn't it? Did you see the fairy footprints in the garden on your way in?" She winked at me. "I think it was a night of magic last night."

I stood rooted in the doorway, not sure what to say. But I didn't get a chance to reply. Ruth Ellis entered the room, a massive frown distorting her features. "Don't encourage her," she growled at me. "Priscilla, the seamstress is here with your new dress." She glared at me. "Show her."

I pulled out the flowered gown with a flourish. "It's all finished and ready for you to wear."

Priscilla gazed at the dress in delight. "How lovely! I'll put it on right away." She stood up and gathered the soft garment into her arms. "Please ask Louise to meet me in my bedroom."

"Of course." I hurried out of the room, pursued by Ruth's baleful glare.

I searched throughout the house, finally locating Priscilla's caregiver, Louise Pritchard, on the back patio enjoying a cigarette. Late middle age had fallen heavy on her, exacerbated by a two-pack-a-day habit. Her thinning black hair was overtaken by gray, and her leathery skin was seamed by fine wrinkles. Bent on resisting the changes in the household, she wore an oversized cotton T-shirt and elastic waist pants with dark blue tennis shoes. I'd offered to make her a period dress and apron, but she'd refused me flat out. "I won't wear no maid's mobcap, and that's final."

I put as much cheeriness as I could into my voice. "Hi, Louise. Miss Priscilla asked if you could help her dress in her bedroom."

"She already got dressed once." She took a last drag on her cigarette and threw the butt into the flower bed. "Next time, bring the new clothes first thing, so I don't have to dress her twice." She turned without another word and disappeared inside.

I bent to locate the still smoldering cigarette butt among the goldenrod and ground it out with my foot. I found a large leaf to shield my fingers so I could pick it up without touching it. I ducked into the kitchen to drop the nasty butt in the trash.

Carl Harper had succeeded in dismantling the shiny oven hood, which now lay in a heap of metal on the kitchen floor. He leaned his elbow on the counter, deep in conversation on his cell phone. I heard him say, "The job's done, dammit! It's too late to change that now," before I nipped back out the door. I figured I could take a few minutes while Priscilla dressed to check in with Professor Burbridge about the curtains.

Priscilla had set the professor up in the private library on the second floor. This small room was distinguished from the main library on the first floor in that it held the personal volumes of the Compton family. Diaries, business ledgers, family Bibles, and the like filled the shelves of the private library. Priscilla told me there was a portfolio of drawings of butterflies made by her great-great-grandmother, and a series of books of limericks collected by her great-great-great-uncle, who had penciled in an explicit set of definitions for each one. I envied the professor his access to such quirky documents.

The library door was closed, with a small wooden sign hung over the door handle that read "Interruption-free zone." I lingered outside, wondering how serious he was about his desire to be undisturbed. I fingered the sign, which read "Enter at your own risk" on the flip side. I laid my ear to the door, but didn't hear any sounds at all coming from within. Finally I decided to risk the professor's wrath, and knocked softly on the door. No answer.

I knocked a bit louder, but no one answered. After a few more tries, I jiggled the door handle. It turned stiffly, and the door creaked open. I slipped inside.

"Excuse me, Professor Bur..." My words died on my lips. No worries about interrupting Professor Burbridge. He lay sprawled facedown on the floor, clutching a pile of papers in one hand. A patch of blood stained his cheek.

Chapter Two

I stood in the doorway staring for what seemed like hours, although it was probably no more than seconds. The ticking of the clock on the wall over the bookcase snapped me out of my stupor. I advanced into the room, circling around the professor without getting too close. With both hands pressed to my mouth, I leaned closer, hoping to find signs of breathing. There were none. I backed away, pulling my phone out of my back pocket. With shaking fingers, I dialed 911. In a few quick words, I told the dispatcher I was in the presence of a dead person. I couldn't remember the exact address of the house. I thought "Compton Hall" would give sufficient information, but the dispatcher didn't seem familiar with the historic landmark. "Hold on, hold on," I shouted as I ran through the hall and burst out the front door to look at the numbers above the lintel. I saw Jamison Royce puttering about with the uprooted maple trees. He watched me openly as I concluded my 911 call.

He leaned on his hoe. "What's all the fuss there?"

I ran over to him, and barely resisted clutching his arm with both hands. "I just found Professor Burbridge on the floor in the library. He's dead."

Royce dropped his hoe. He took off in the direction of the library with me close behind.

"We can't let Priscilla see this," I panted. "The ambulance should be here soon." Indeed, I could already hear sirens approaching.

Royce walked around the professor, scanning the body just as I had. Even in the presence of a dead man, he did not remove his cap. "Heart attack, do you think?" He squatted down to peer at the thin line of dried blood from a cut on the professor's right cheek. "He must have hit the corner of the desk on his way down."

I heard the tapping of a cane outside the door, and ran out into the hall. Royce followed me out, slipping out the front door as I faced Ruth and Priscilla standing in the hall.

"What is all this hullabaloo?" Ruth frowned at me, clearly thinking I was the source of upheaval in the household.

"Professor Burbridge is dead," I blurted out. Then I took a long breath, willing myself to slow down to try to spare these two old ladies a terrible shock. I didn't want any fainting or heart attacks on top of everything else. But the two women surprised me.

"Poor, dear man," Priscilla said, her face twisting in compassion. "I didn't think he was that old. Was he ill, do you know?" she appealed to her sister.

Ruth scowled at me. "Have you called the proper authorities?" She pushed past me to enter the library. Her eyes widened and she fell back a pace at the sight of the body. She backed out of the room, blocking the doorway so Priscilla couldn't enter. "Priscilla, please go with this young lady to the living room and ring for Louise. There's going to be a lot of unseemly activity around here shortly." She gave me a look that said, "Do what I say and do it now."

I offered my arm to Priscilla and walked with her to the living room. I sat her down on one of the wingback chairs. "Let me get you a glass of water and call for Louise."

She nodded without a word.

I could hear the sirens screaming up the winding drive. I ran upstairs to try to find Louise. When I didn't find her in her room, I simply stood in the middle of the hallway and hollered her name. I knew Ruth would abhor the unseemly noise, but it worked. Louise popped out of Priscilla's bedroom, clutching a duster in one hand.

"What are you carrying on about? You know the old lady doesn't like a lot of noise in the house."

"Priscilla needs you downstairs." I sucked in my breath, and then told her the bad news. "Professor Burbridge is dead."

Louise dropped her duster. "What, murdered?" she whispered.

"What?" I stared at her, shocked at that suggestion. "No, it looks like he had a heart attack. Could you bring a glass of water down for Priscilla? I'm sure she'll want you to sit with her."

Louise bent down to retrieve her fallen duster. I was already running back down the stairs as she turned back to Priscilla's bedroom.

The paramedics were entering the front hall when I descended. I ducked back into the living room to find Priscilla still sitting on the chair where I left her. I knelt down at her side.

"All right?"

She turned her sweet, vacant smile to me. "Such a lot of hubbub in the hall. I hope they show the proper respect for the poor, dear man." She shook her head sadly. "Poor man, Ruth was so hard on him. Now they'll never get the chance to talk it over and make things right."

"What do you mean?"

But Priscilla didn't get a chance to answer.

A tall police officer entered the room. "Who found the body?"

I stood up, feeling the blood rush to my cheeks. "I did."

"Please follow me."

He led me up the stairs to a small sitting room across the hall from the library. He left the door open, so I could see the backs of the paramedics as they bent over the professor's body on the floor. I fixed my eyes on the police officer's face, trying to shut out the noises from across the hall.

The policeman looked like he was nearing retirement age, with a well-lined face that evoked images of a kindly grandfather rather than a stern officer of the law. "My name is Officer Travis, from the Laurel Springs Police Department. I have a series of routine questions to ask about this unattended death."

I nodded, and answered automatically as he took down my name and other identifying information. The police had all this information on file from earlier this summer, when I was questioned in a murder case. I hoped they wouldn't flag me as a dead body magnet or something. At least this was merely an "unattended death" and not a homicide. Still, I didn't see the need to bring up my previous encounter with the police.

"What is your relationship to the deceased?"

"I don't know him very well, really. He and I are—or were—both working on the Compton Hall renovation for the TV reality show. I'm a seamstress. Professor Burbridge had done some research for me on eighteenth-century embroidered curtains. I went in today to ask him for the drawings, and there he was on the floor." I clasped my hands together in my lap. "I didn't touch him. I called 911."

Officer Travis wrote down all my responses in a small notebook, and finally dismissed me with a brief "Thank you for your time. I'll be in touch if I need more information."

I returned to the living room to see that a newcomer had joined Priscilla. A large man in his fifties, with cropped gray hair that highlighted his prominent ears and long earlobes similar to those of the Compton sisters, he leaned over one arm of Priscilla's chair and listened while she talked softly. I didn't see Ruth in the room, and wondered where she'd gone.

Priscilla noticed me entering the room. She extended one hand to me, while the other kept hold of the newcomer's left hand. "My dear, come meet my nephew, Johnny. He's Ruth's younger son, you know. He lives just down the street, such a good boy. Not like Robby, not at all."

I took Priscilla's outstretched hand. Her fingers were cold, and trembled a bit. "Nice to meet you," I said to Johnny.

His sharp brown eyes took me in from head to toe as he shook my hand firmly. "It's John. And you are?"

"Daria Dembrowski. I'm the owner of A Stitch in Time, which provides historical sewing services. I'm working with Priscilla to transform herself into the mistress of an eighteenth-century house for the TV show."

He nodded, his attention already diverted from me as Louise Pritchard entered the room.

"Miss Ruth would like to see Miss Priscilla in the dining room," she announced, sounding like the grand butler from a forgotten era.

I watched in silence as Priscilla rose and shuffled out of the room with Louise.

"Is there anything else I can do?" I asked John once the door closed behind the two of them.

He was scrolling through his phone. "You don't know of a good cleaning service, do you?"

I shook my head, somewhat shocked at his callousness. "I guess I'll be leaving, then. I don't suppose Priscilla will want to think about curtains at a time like this."

He just shrugged, deep in his research. I gathered up my sewing things and left the room.

On the way out the door I saw yet another newcomer passing through the hall. I recognized his broad shoulders and trim build encased in an expensive pinstriped suit. Of course, the new attorney. It figured. I would have ducked into a room, any room, to avoid meeting him, but he heard my step and turned around.

"Ah, Daria. We meet again."

"Randall. I was just leaving." I tried to slip past him, but he sidestepped so that he blocked my path. I refused to let him see that I noticed. "You must be the new attorney."

He inclined his head. "I've been retained to oversee the appraisal of the contents of the house, in my capacity as a wills and estates lawyer for the law firm of Flint, Perkinson and Hubbard. It looks like we'll be seeing a lot of each other, especially since you're making my fiancée's wedding gown." He smiled lazily down at me, daring me to cross him. "She's a lovely girl, my Fiona. Deserves nothing but the best. I trust that's what she'll receive from you."

I drew myself up as tall as I could manage, which was hardly impressive given my short stature. "I take pride in my work. Fiona has nothing to worry about...from me." I left those last two words hanging in the air between us and took a step forward, inviting him to move aside and let me pass. He complied with a chuckle.

The bus was practically empty on my ride home. I stared out the window, scarcely noticing the profusion of mountain laurel bushes throughout the upscale neighborhood. All I could think about was Randall, reappearing in my life when I'd finally succeeded in moving on.

I seized my unexpected afternoon off to work on Fiona's wedding gown. I spent almost three hours assembling the buttons for the back of the gown. Rather than using ready-made satin buttons, I was using fabric from Fiona's dress, so the buttons would match perfectly. This process involved cutting a small circle of satin, placing it over the metal button head, and snapping it into the shank to form a custom-made button. The thickness of Fiona's satin made it hard to stretch such a small piece over the tiny bit of metal with no wrinkles. Every single one of the fourteen buttons took two or three tries to get right. By the end of the afternoon my fingers tingled with the effort. But I was glad of the need to concentrate, so I couldn't dwell on the sight of Professor Burbridge sprawled on the floor of the library, dead.

The late afternoon sun was flooding into my workroom by the time I finished up the final button. I piled them all into a small box on my worktable and headed downstairs to look into dinner.

Pete, Aileen, and I tried to eat together at least once a week, just to foster a sense of community in the house. Often we found ourselves at the table at the same time on other nights, but Fridays were the official "family meal" nights of the week. It was a little inconvenient for Pete and me, but Aileen insisted on Friday so she could have a decent meal before her inevitable gig. Whatever Aileen wanted, Aileen got. We didn't have a formal schedule as to whose turn it was to cook, but Pete and I always tried to get to the kitchen before Aileen. Last time she cooked we had to eat gefilte fish on freezer waffles slathered with chocolate marshmallow sauce and topped with carrot shavings. Thanks, but no thanks.

I served up a perfectly ordinary meal of sautéed chicken and vegetables with a hint of curry. I refused to let Aileen get a rise out of me when she dumped a massive pile of curry powder on her plate.

She shoved a huge forkful into her mouth and mumbled through the food, "Either of you two know a guy with dark hair, tall and slim, who goes around in a fancy three-piece suit and carries a brown leather briefcase that's too big for him?"

I almost choked on my chicken. I remembered that briefcase. I'd given it to Randall on his graduation from law school, after saving for six months to be able to afford the real leather model. He'd scoffed at the unstylish size of the thing, and refused to carry it to the office. What surprised me most was the fact that he still had it, if indeed he were the one Aileen was describing.

"Why do you ask?"

She narrowed her eyes at me. "Is he a friend of yours? Or should I say, 'was'? He came poking around the house today. Jerk tried the door, even. I hollered out the window and ran him off. He won't be back anytime soon."

My hands went cold at the thought of Randall trying the door. He wouldn't know that I had changed the locks after he left me, disappearing with the balance of our joint bank account. What made him think he could come back now?

"He tried the door?" Pete frowned. "Do you think he was trying to break in?"

Aileen snorted. "Either that or he was the rudest jackass alive." She snagged the bottle of curry powder and dumped on a fresh layer.

"Did he say anything when you hollered at him out the window?" I asked.

"Yeah, sure. He professed his undying love for you while strumming on a mandolin. What do you think?" Aileen stopped in midstream, noticing the blush on my face, no doubt. "Wait—you know this guy?"

I nodded. "I'm guessing it was Randall Flint, a guy I used to know."

"Randall, as in the guy you were going to marry?" Pete said.

"Yeah, that guy." I glared at Pete. Nothing like a big brother to blurt out all the painful details of one's life.

"So the 'undying love' wasn't so far off." Aileen couldn't resist. "What, the wedding seamstress was a jilted bride?" She turned to Pete, "Did you run him off, Moron?"

Pete shrugged, unfazed by Aileen's habitual nickname for him. "I never met the guy. I understand he was a jerk, though."

"Of the highest order." I sighed. It looked like Randall was back in my life. I needed to fill Aileen in. "I met him at a wedding, when he was in law school. We went out. He moved in. Then he ditched me. Anything else you want to know?"

"Touchy, aren't we?" Aileen scowled at me. "Yeah, there's a lot I want to know. If this jerk's gonna be coming around trying to get into the house, I want to know what he's after. I want to know if he'll be sneaking into my bedroom in the middle of the night, or setting fires in the basement. I want to know if you're planning to get back together with him or if I should keep running him off. I think I have a right to know."

I got up from the table. "Okay, you made your point. I went out with him for four years. He lived with me here in this house while he was in law school, to save money. I thought he loved me, but he was just using me for free rent. While I was making my wedding dress, he was making sure we had a joint bank account, which he then cleaned out before he split. As a matter of fact, Aileen, you can thank Randall for your opportunity to live here, because I wouldn't have had to take in a renter if he hadn't stolen all my money."

I didn't mention the fact that I had missed the classic signs of manipulation as Randall distanced me from my friends and family and surrounded me with his unrelenting attention that morphed from showering me with flowers and candy to demanding to know exactly where I was at all times of the day or night. And through it all, I had loved him, fool that I was. I didn't need to mention that, either.

"So, no, Aileen, I don't intend to get back together with him, especially since he happens to be engaged to marry my lovely client, Fiona."

Pete let out a low whistle. "You never told me all that stuff."

"Well, what good would it have done me? You didn't have any money to help me pay the bills. Plus I didn't want you to judge me for getting sucked in by such a con artist."

He smiled at me. "I wouldn't do that. You didn't judge me for getting sent to jail for drugs."

I smiled back. "Yes, I did. That's what sisters do."

Aileen rolled her eyes. "Okay, so what you're saying is, this Randall jerk is going to be hanging around our house while you make his fiancée's expensive wedding gown." She grimaced at me. "I have the feeling that the band is going to need a lot of extra rehearsals. Too bad they might happen whenever that jackass is around."

Pete laughed. "He'll probably want to call the whole thing off by the time you get done with him."

"You got something to say about the band, Moron?"

"No way! I love the Twisted Armpits, as long as I have my trusty earplugs handy. Without them, the noise might make me want to end it all." I gasped, catching Aileen in midsnort. She and Pete stared at me.

"All this talk about Randall—I forgot to tell you. Professor Burbridge died today. I found his body in the library."

If I were trying to rival Aileen in the shock category, I hit the jackpot. Pete dropped his fork with a clatter, and Aileen swore, "What the hell?"

"You know Professor Burbridge is working with Priscilla to catalog the historical books in her collection. I needed to talk with him about the curtains for Compton Hall, and when I went in he was on the floor, dead. It was horrible."

"What is it with you? Are you trying to break the world record for most dead bodies discovered by one person?"

"Yeah, Aileen, that's my life's ambition."

* * * *

I settled in to do some research on eighteenth-century draperies after supper. Without the professor's drawings, I would have to come up with my own design for Priscilla's curtains. I felt guilty for focusing on my own mundane needs when the man lay dead, but there was nothing I could do for him now. I was coming to the conclusion that I wouldn't find anything useful on the Internet when the doorbell jangled. I jumped. If it was Randall, I intended to give him what for.

Aileen obviously had the same thought. She beat me to the front door, which she flung open to crash against the wall. I was thankful that the leaded-glass window in the door survived the impact.

"What are you after now? Oh, it's you." She stepped aside to let the new arrival in. "It's your newspaperman, Daria."

"Hello, Aileen." McCarthy stepped across the threshold, filling the hall with his boundless energy. He turned his attention to me. "I heard you discovered a death up at Compton Hall. Are you all right?" News travels fast in a small town, and even faster at a small-town newspaper. McCarthy always seemed to know everything that happened before anyone else did.

"Yeah, I'm okay." I led him into the kitchen, the heart of my home. "Want some tea?" I fussed with getting the water cold and filling up the kettle while he sat down and watched. "What did you hear about the professor's death?"

He pulled out his ever-present little spiral notebook, and poked a tiny pencil out of the wire. "I heard the professor died of an apparent heart attack." He looked at me quizzically. "Anything you can add to that?"

I got out two mugs and pulled out an assortment of teas. He chose Earl Grey, and I went with my favorite, green tea with ginger. "Not really. There was some dried blood on his face, but Jamison Royce thinks he probably hit the corner of the desk when he fell." I poured the hot water into the mugs.

McCarthy frowned as he dunked his tea bag in the water. "Professor Burbridge was only forty-three years old—kind of young for a heart attack. I understand the coroner's ordered an autopsy, routine in the event of an unattended death. I hope they don't discover anything suspicious." He winked at me. "Wouldn't want you to get mixed up in another murder investigation."

I rolled my eyes. "I'm not mixed up in anything."

McCarthy stayed just long enough to finish his tea and cajole a favorite song from Aileen. The fact that he had a favorite Twisted Armpits song never ceased to amaze me.

I struggled online for another hour or so before calling it quits. I could not find enough information about eighteenth-century draperies to make a historically accurate decision about the embroidery design for the curtains for Compton Hall. If only I could get my hands on the drawings Professor Burbridge had located. But the professor wasn't going to be able to help me, or anyone else, ever again.

Chapter Three

I stood before the door to the library the next morning, and hesitated with my hand on the doorknob. I didn't really believe in ghosts, but a man had recently died in that room, and I was about to go through his belongings. It seemed somehow sacrilegious, even if Professor Burbridge was not noted for his piety. Still, I needed the drawings to continue my work on the curtains. The professor was dead, but the rest of us were still alive. Life goes on, and all that. I pushed the door open and crept inside.

The cleaning crew had done good work. The room smelled fresh and piney, with overtones of bleach. The only evidence of death was a noticeably lighter spot on the faded carpet. The mess of papers on the desk had been neatly stacked into a pile. I gritted my teeth and began sifting through them.

I was surprised to see so many handwritten pages in the pile. Evidently the professor was slow to embrace modern technology. I tried not to pay attention to the content—if I read every page on his desk I'd be there for three weeks. All I needed were a set of drawings, or maybe a description of the drawings—I wasn't sure exactly what I was looking for. When I'd gone through all the papers on his desk without finding anything about curtains, I turned my attention to the file boxes stacked on the floor.

The top box was titled "Summer Term." I knew the professor was teaching a class called American Myths for Oliphant University's summer term, so I doubted I would find anything useful in this box. Sure enough, it contained files on lecture topics and a section with names of students. Nothing about the house, furnishings, or curtains.

I replaced the lid and shifted the box to get to the next one. This one was titled "Library," and held files corresponding to the various bookshelves in the room where Professor Burbridge died. Again, no curtains.

The last box on the bottom of the pile was titled "Major Samuel Compton." It didn't surprise me that Professor Burbridge was researching Laurel Springs's hometown Revolutionary War hero and esteemed ancestor of Priscilla and Ruth. It was possible that the professor's research on the original furnishings of the house could be in this box. I popped off the lid and scanned the bulging file folders within. Their labels read things like "Sources," "Letters," "Battle of Laurel Springs," and "Treason." I didn't find anything having to do with the renovation project.

I replaced the stack of boxes and heaved a sigh. Where would the professor have squirreled away the important drawings I needed to produce authentic eighteenth-century curtains?

I checked the desk drawers, but they were filled with office supplies and boxes of old family photographs that looked like they belonged to the Compton sisters rather than Professor Burbridge. I would have loved to spend all afternoon going through those pictures with Priscilla, hearing her tell family stories. Unfortunately, I really didn't have time for that. I did spare a few minutes to shuffle through a few of the boxes, just to get a glimpse of the old ladies back when they weren't old. I found a shot from Ruth's wedding, back in the late 1950s by the look of the style of the gown and bridesmaids' dresses. Priscilla was maid of honor, wearing a stiff taffeta dress with an off-the-shoulder neckline and a full gathered skirt that fell just below her knees. Her youthful face was almost unrecognizable, except for her sweet smile, which had never changed.

Another photo showed Priscilla standing next to Ruth and her husband in the front yard of Compton Hall. Ruth held a baby in her arms, and a young boy snuggled up beside her. Priscilla wore a tight sweater and a tweed skirt, with her long hair curled up in a bun. She couldn't have been more than thirty, but she already looked like the maiden aunt. I shuffled through more photos, watching the two boys grow older and their father grow stouter, while in them all Priscilla stood by their side, serene and alone.

I slipped the stack of photos back into the small box. I didn't know a whole lot about the Compton family, but I did know that Priscilla never married. Ruth married a Philadelphia lawyer some years older than herself. I had a vague memory that he had died seven or eight years ago, while I was in college in Ohio. There was some scandal about his death, but I was in the midst of writing a thesis on the impact of French couture on American fashion throughout the twentieth century, and had no time or inclination to follow the society news from Laurel Springs. The couple evidently had two children. I'd met one of them yesterday, John Ellis. I wondered what the other son was up to.

I replaced the photo box in the desk drawer and slid the drawer shut. This little glimpse of Priscilla's family history was all very well, but I had curtains to make. I stood up and scanned the room, looking for a place to stow historical drawings. Of course! A long credenza stood along the wall next to the door, overshadowed by deep hanging bookcases built into the wall. Another tall pile of papers on the credenza finally yielded the drawings I needed. Two photocopies of the actual drawings showed a set of dimity curtains framing a mullioned window, done from several different angles. The light curtains were looped up with a set of ruffled tiebacks with tassels at the ends. The professor's notes in the margins read "Master Bedroom, The Hampton Estate, 1760s."

I hugged the pages to my chest, happy to have them at last. As I turned to leave I saw Randall, once more blocking my way. He lounged on the doorjamb as if he'd been there awhile. "Checking out the professor's personal papers, are we?"

I felt my face get hot. "Professor Burbridge didn't get the chance to give me the drawings he had located for me. I needed them to finish the curtains for the living room."

Randall slowly straightened up from the doorjamb and advanced into the room. "So you found them? Anything else of interest?"

I shrugged, trying to look unconcerned by his insinuation that I was snooping. "All I needed were the drawings." I slipped past him, and headed upstairs for the sewing room.

I spent the next hour measuring and cutting the filmy curtain fabric, all the while kicking myself for feeling like I had to explain myself to Randall. I resolved to avoid him as much as possible. Good thing I liked Fiona so much, or I might be tempted to sabotage her wedding gown or charge her double to try to get back a little of what Randall stole from me. I pushed aside thoughts of revenge, and considered whether I needed to warn Fiona about Randall's questionable character. I'd hate to see him take advantage of her like he did to me. Of course, Fiona was a bright law student who could probably deal with Randall in court if she had to. I hoped, for her sake, that she never would.

I was just about to start hemming the curtains, resigned to the prospect of setting in each hem by hand, when Louise Pritchard appeared in my doorway.

"You're wanted in the living room," she proclaimed, clearly put out by the indignity of having to come upstairs to fetch the seamstress.

I followed her down to find the entire household gathered in the living room. The two elderly sisters sat in the wingback chairs by the hearth, leaving the rest of the assembled people to stand. Randall leaned an elbow on the mantel, looking like he owned the place. Jamison Royce stood on the other side of the hearth, his jeans grimy from the soil in the garden, his work hat pulled low over his eyes. Carl Harper, the contractor, stood near the door, a nail gun dangling from his hand. Louise walked across the room to stand behind Priscilla's chair. Two imposing figures faced this group: the producers of the TV show, *My House in History.*

A petite woman in her early thirties with brown hair cropped close to her head, dressed in multicolored pastel leggings and a clingy tunic blouse, Cherry Stamford radiated nervous energy. Next to her stood Stillman Dertz, a giant of a man who gnawed on the stub of a cigar and avoided eye contact with anyone. I had met the two of them a week and a half ago, when they had invaded my sewing room and taken footage of me cutting out Priscilla's gown. They had caught me kneeling down with the fabric spread out on the floor—not the most flattering pose. I hoped they would minimize that segment in the final broadcast.

Cherry held a clipboard in her hand and addressed the group. "We've fallen behind schedule, folks. We lost an entire day due to paramedics, coroners, and whatnot tramping through the house. We did take footage of the disturbances, and I don't know if we'll use them or not, but the fact remains that we're woefully behind at this point. The renovations are slated to be finished by next Wednesday so we can wrap up filming on the finished product."

Stillman shifted his weight beside her and removed the cigar stub from his mouth. "Tell them about the new arrangements."

Cherry barely paused for breath. "We've decided to take hour-by-hour footage of the run to the finish. Everyone will need to accelerate their work accordingly." She clapped her hands. "It's settled. We'll be following each of you with cameras from now on. Back to work, folks!"

I stood up with the rest, intrigued by this new development. It would be interesting, and maybe a bit daunting, to have cameras following my every move.

Randall sidled up to me on his way out of the living room. "Do you have a minute, Daria? I have some things I'd like to talk over with you." He ran his fingertips lightly up my arm in a caressing gesture that I used to love.

I flinched away from his touch, my mind racing. Who did he think he was? He was engaged to be married, for goodness' sake!

He didn't notice anything amiss. "Can you join me in the library?"

I shoved my hands in my pockets and drew myself up. My five feet three inches were hardly impressive, but the gesture helped me calm my frazzled nerves. "I'm sorry, I have to get back to my sewing. Maybe some other time?"

As soon as I said it I knew it was a mistake. The gleam in Randall's eye as he turned away with a polite "Fine, some other time" told me I was in for a prolonged tussle with the master of manipulation.

* * * *

I spent the rest of the afternoon handstitching the hems in the living room curtains. The filmy fabric frayed terribly. Normally I would have finished the edge with my serger and then set in the hem, but such modern methods would be glaringly obvious in this attempt for historical accuracy. I reminded myself of the romance involved in recreating a lost era, and soldiered on with the hems.

Hemming doesn't take any kind of mental attention, which left my mind free to wander. I tried to focus on the seamstresses who might have made such curtains in the olden days, wondering what they would have thought about their work. But my mind kept returning to the image of Professor Burbridge sprawled on the faded library carpet.

I clipped the end of one thread and threaded another long length onto my needle. It took me another forty-five minutes to finish the last hem on one set of curtains. I stood up and stretched, shaking out both hands to alleviate the cramps from the repetitive work of hand stitching. I still had one more set to go. Feeling the need for company, I gathered up fabric, needle, and thread, and zipped downstairs in the hopes of finding Priscilla at leisure to engage in a good gossip.

I dodged past the open door to the library. I had no desire to "talk things over" with Randall, either now or at any other time. Luckily he was intent on his work at the desk and didn't notice my passing.

Priscilla sat on the front porch, rocking slowly in her maple rocker just as she did when I was a child. She wasn't knitting—her knotted hands lay still in her lap. She just sat, watching a trio of little girls across the street setting out leaves and sticks for their dolls to have tea. I sat down beside her.

"Mind if I join you? Hems get tedious after a while with no one to take my mind off them."

She smiled, looking genuinely pleased to see me. "Of course, my dear. Are those the curtains? They look lovely. You asked the professor for his drawings, then?"

"Well, I didn't get the chance before he died. I found the drawings in the library." I looked over at Priscilla, gently rocking in her porch chair.

Priscilla's rocking never slackened. "Poor, dear man. Such a sad day it was. It's always a tragedy when the young go before their time." She picked up a small photo album that had been lying on the doily-covered side table next to her. Her bony fingers caressed the cracked spine, and then she laid the album open flat on her lap. One gnarled finger pointed to the studio portraits within. I saw two black-and-white pictures of young men, so similar in appearance that at first I thought they were two pictures of the same person. Both had crew cuts and wore suit and tie to pose for what looked like their high school graduation pictures.

Priscilla tapped the photo on the right. "Robby was gone too young. This is the last picture I have of him."

I leaned over her shoulder to gaze at the clean-shaven young man. "Robby?"

"Johnny's big brother." She shook her head sadly. "I gave him some homemade fudge for Christmas that year. I told him to save some for his father, but he ate the whole batch that very night." She closed the book and replaced it on the table. "You never could tell Robby anything."

I thought of the family pictures I'd seen in the library. "What happened to him?"

Ruth came out onto the porch as I spoke. She frowned at me. "So you're the one detaining my sister." She held out a lightweight shawl to Priscilla. "John is taking us out for dinner. We obviously can't eat in that construction zone of a kitchen."

Priscilla pulled herself to her feet. "Have a good evening, my dear." As she exited with Ruth, I could hear her saying, "Did you borrow my silver candlesticks, by any chance? They weren't on my mantel this morning. You know I light them every morning to welcome the daylight. It would be a shame to lose Great-Aunt Millie's candlesticks, after all these years."

I never did find out what happened to Robby.

* * * *

I finished the last hem and shook out the filmy curtain. Next came the embroidery along the bottom hem, as well as the tailored valances that would top the window treatment. But first I needed to wash the sateen fabric for the valances. I bundled up the curtain and headed up to my sewing room to get the sateen.

The door to my sewing room was closed, even though I always left it open to dispel the mustiness of the ancient carpeting. I paused in front of the door, frowning. Maybe Louise had closed it in a fit of tidiness, although she truly didn't seem like a tidy person to me. I reached for the door handle, hoping that Randall wasn't waiting inside to "talk things over" with me.

I threw open the door and scanned the room from the doorway. Nothing seemed to be amiss. Maybe I had closed the door, and just forgotten. I gathered up the sateen and headed down the three floors to the basement.

I ran into Cherry on the way down.

She thrust a microphone in my face and signed the silent man following her to begin filming. "What are you doing now"—she consulted a paper on her clipboard that had a series of head shots on it—"Daria?"

I held up my fabric. "I'm headed to the basement to wash this fabric. It's always important to launder any machine-washable fabric before sewing. If you neglect this step, the seams could pucker if the fabric shrinks when the finished garment is washed." I smiled at the camera, sure that no one could possibly care about my laundry endeavors.

Cherry must have come to the same conclusion, for she flashed a hand sign to her cameraman that could only mean "cut." "Very good," she said to me, and hurried on her way.

I marveled all the way down to the basement. I'd never been involved in filming a TV show before, so this was all eye opening to me. Cherry and her crew were taking hours and hours of footage, which would then be distilled down to one hour-long episode. It seemed like a monumental task.

I located the washer and dryer in the basement, along with a slimy bottle of liquid detergent. Either Carl Harper hadn't gotten to these modern appliances yet, or the show's producers decided that renovating the main floor was good enough. I shoved the fabric into the washer and started it up.

I noticed a kitty litter box in the corner, although I hadn't seen any cats since I'd been working in the house. They were probably spooked by all the commotion of the renovations, not to mention the chaos surrounding Professor Burbridge's death. I started searching around the corners, calling, "Here, kitty, kitty" in my most persuasive voice. I didn't flush out any kitty cats, but I did notice a strong smell of smoke when I approached the boiler. Worried about the possibility of fire, I poked around, trying to discover the source of the smell. A thin stream of smoke drifted up from a fresh pile of ashes in a metal bucket next to the boiler. Next to the bucket a manila folder lay discarded on the floor. I picked it up and turned it over to read the label: "Treason."

Chapter Four

I stared at the empty file folder. Last time I'd seen it, it was in a box in the library along with other files that Professor Burbridge had compiled. But it had been full to bursting then. I stirred the smoldering ashes in the metal bucket. It didn't take a detective to deduce that the contents of Professor Burbridge's file were right here in front of me. What I didn't know was, why had someone burned them?

I looked all around the basement, but I didn't see any other manila folders, either empty or full. The ashes in the bucket were so thoroughly burned that it was impossible to tell what had been written on them. I frowned at the folder in my hand, wondering if Randall was culling the professor's files in this fashion. What right did he have to mess with the dead man's research? I laid the folder on the dryer and searched for a sink to wash my hands before transferring the fabric into the dryer. I didn't know if I was going to confront Randall or not, but I did want to peek into that file box once more and see if any other files were missing.

* * * *

The library's open door invited me in. Randall was nowhere to be seen. He was probably at dinner with Fiona, turning up his nose at another beloved Laurel Springs restaurant. I slipped into the library and eased the door closed behind me. The stack of file boxes appeared to be untouched on the floor. I shifted the top two boxes to get to the bottom one, the one marked "Summer Term." But that wasn't right. That box had been on the top of the stack. Obviously Randall hadn't put them back correctly. I checked the other two boxes. The "Library" box was on the top, and the box labeled

"Major Samuel Compton" came second. I lifted off that lid and peered inside. There were only two files remaining: the ones labeled "Sources" and "Letters." Wasn't there something about a battle? I thumbed through the two file folders. "Sources" contained a pile of handwritten pages listing books, magazine articles, and various websites having to do with Major Compton. "Letters" contained just that: pages of photocopied letters written either to or by the major in flowing, old-fashioned handwriting. At the back of that file I found a sheaf of notebook paper covered with more modern, indecipherable handwriting. It looked to be an outline. I could just make out the title, "The Hero Exposed." I was fanning through the pages, trying to make sense of the handwriting, when I heard a step just outside the door. I whirled around, clutching the pages behind my back, trying to think of some excuse as to why I was trespassing on Randall's domain. But it wasn't Randall who came through the door.

A tall, thin young man with an outdated haircut and black horn-rimmed glasses stood on the threshold and gazed at me. He wore a short-sleeved white dress shirt and khaki slacks with green tennis shoes and no socks. He looked too clean for one of Carl Harper's construction crew, and too casually dressed to be a member of Randall's law firm. I stared at him at a loss.

"You must be Mrs. Pritchard," he said, entering the room and giving me a tentative smile. "I just needed to know where I could find some boxes or even plastic bags to pack up the professor's things."

For an instant I thought about impersonating the housekeeper, but then I thought better of it. As McCarthy pointed out to me once, "Unless there's a good reason to lie, it's always safest to tell the truth."

"I'm not Mrs. Pritchard. I'm Daria Dembrowski, the seamstress." I kept the professor's papers concealed behind my back, trying to think of some convincing reason why I might be holding them. "Maybe I could help you find some boxes."

The young man started shuffling through the piles of papers on the desk. "That would be great. I'm Noah. Noah Webster." He shot me a glance, half-sheepish, half-defiant, clearly expecting me to comment on his name. After years of enduring chants of "Hairy Daria, Dumb Brewsky" in school, I had zero interest in ribbing anyone about a funny name. I settled for the mild query. "Are you a colleague of the professor's?"

Noah smiled widely, in relief, no doubt. "I'm one of Burbridge's grad students. Or was." His face clouded. "I'm working on my PhD in history. Burbridge was my adviser. I don't know what will happen to my chances, now that he's dead."

I bent over the Major Compton box and slipped the pages I held back into their place without him noticing. "This box seems to have a lot of room in it. Could you put some other things in here?"

Noah glanced at the box and nodded. "I suppose there's no use in trying to preserve Burbridge's system." He flashed me that wide smile again. "He was an incredibly disorganized person. Veritably the absentminded professor, in fact." He sat down heavily in the desk chair. "God, I'm going to miss him!"

I hovered by the file box, not quite sure what to say. I was touched by the young man's expression of emotion. I hadn't experienced Professor Burbridge as anything other than a bossy academic, so I appreciated the chance to see him in a new light.

"I didn't really know him very well, but he was helpful to me by researching historical curtain styles." I didn't see the need to mention the fact that he'd insisted on doing the research for me and had spurned any suggestion that I could take responsibility for the curtain design myself. "You must have worked very closely with him in your PhD studies."

Noah nodded, passed a hand over his face, and resumed sorting through the papers on the desk. "I've worked with him for six years now. I know, that's a long time to be in school. I'm ABD by now, of course." He looked at my blank face and kindly added, "All But Dissertation." He sighed. "Who knows when I'll finish now."

I picked up the file box and moved it closer to the desk. "What's your dissertation on, if I can ask?"

"I've been researching the Battle of Laurel Springs with Professor Burbridge, focusing on the nighttime events that led up to the decisive defeat of the British forces. I hope to write a narrative nonfiction account of the battle from the perspective of the D Company, the foot soldiers who discovered the ambushing troops before it was too late." He gave me that tentative smile again. "You're familiar with the details of the battle?"

"Sure, we learned about it in fifth grade, sixth grade, and every grade after that. Major Compton has more five-paragraph essays written about him than all other citizens of Laurel Springs combined."

Noah laughed. "I'm only touching on him in my research, since I'm focusing on the foot soldiers. Burbridge was the source of cutting-edge research on the major." He indicated the file box lid labeled "Major Samuel Compton." "He's got this explosive new theory that will shatter our understanding of the battle for all time. I'm still trying to wrap my head around it." He fell silent.

I tried to remember what I'd learned about the battle, which had taken place in the middle years of the Revolutionary War. British troops had surprised Major Compton's forces at night by adopting the Continental Army's tactic of concealment rather than marching openly to battle. Many Continental soldiers died, including the major, but the British were finally defeated and the town was saved. Major Samuel Compton was hailed as a hero, with his statue on the Commons as proof. "What was this new theory?"

"Well, well, what have we here?" Randall advanced into the room, a wide smile on his face. Bypassing me, he held out a hand to Noah. "Randall Flint, Esquire. You look like you're on a mission."

They shook hands. "I'm packing up Professor Burbridge's things to take back to the university." He glanced sidelong at me. "I'm Noah Webster, one of Burbridge's grad students."

"Noah Webster, as in the dictionary?" Randall chuckled. "For real? I'll bet you get a lot of comments on that."

Noah flinched, as if he were ducking a blow. "People don't even use dictionaries anymore."

A surge of anger shot through me at Randall's insensitivity. I turned to Noah with a big smile. "I'd love to talk to you more about all this. Could we get together sometime?"

"Sure, you can catch me at the university," Noah said. "I'm usually around the history department." He gathered up the rest of the papers on the desk and shoved them into the half-empty file box. "I'll just get out of your way here." He hurried out the door, hugging the box to his chest.

I went to follow him out, but Randall blocked my way without actually touching me. "Do you have a minute for a little chat, Daria?"

I didn't want to waste even one minute on Randall, but I could see that he wasn't going to leave me alone until he had his chance to talk. "What is it?"

He took my hand and drew me far enough into the library so that he could close the door behind me.

I wiggled my fingers free from his grasp. "What do you want?"

"I have a proposition for you." He smiled down at me, evidently sure that I would jump at anything he proposed. "I passed by the old house, and had a hankering to live there once more."

My jaw dropped. Live in my house? The two unoccupied bedrooms on my second floor popped into my mind. Did Randall seriously think he was going to move in with us? Not in this lifetime!

Randall didn't notice my shock. "I was wondering if you've ever thought about selling the old place." He favored me with his most winning smile. "If you haven't, maybe I could convince you to think about it now."

I couldn't keep the incredulity out of my voice. "You want to buy my house?"

"I do. I'm thinking of settling in Laurel Springs after the wedding. It would be a fine place to bring a new bride home to."

I managed to refrain from either slapping him in the face or laughing myself silly. "The house isn't for sale. Sorry." I checked my watch. "I need to get back to my curtains."

Randall opened the door to allow me to pass. "Just think about it." He touched my shoulder lightly as I passed him. "I could make it worth your while."

I hustled down to the basement to retrieve my fabric from the dryer. Just what was he suggesting to make it worth my while? He could surely afford to pay for the house, but it sounded like he had something else in mind. If he thought I was pining after our broken relationship, he needed to have his head examined. But it didn't matter anyway. The last thing I would ever do was to sell my beloved house to Randall.

I checked the time and then pulled out my phone to call Pete. "Can you come pick me up at Compton Hall? It's getting late for the bus."

He groaned. "The ball game just came on. You'll make me miss the first inning."

"Listen to it on the radio." I hung up before he could protest any more.

Pete texted me barely five minutes later, "Here." I grabbed my shoulder bag and hurried down the stairs. I ran out to his truck idling on the front drive and hopped into the passenger seat.

"Thanks for the ride. I owe you."

He grinned at me. "I'm keeping a tab." On the radio the excited voice of the baseball announcer celebrated a double.

I looked out the window, noticing that Pete was driving along the river rather than heading straight home. A nice drive to take us to the end of the inning, I supposed. I leaned back in my seat and watched the mountain laurels flash by. Their pink-and-white blossoms were spent now, but the hardy green shrub that gave our town its name still dominated the roadsides here along the river. The sight relaxed me so that I jumped when Pete spoke.

"So I wanted to ask you, what do you think about Ruth Ellis?"

"That old witch? Every time she so much as looks at me, she criticizes me. She and her sister couldn't be more different."

"That's not what I meant." Pete glanced at me sideways. "She's a shady character. You remember she was accused of killing her husband in that fire seven years ago?"

"I remember some scandal about her husband's death, but not the details. What was the deal?"

"I looked it up last night when you told me about the professor's death. The Ellis house in Philadelphia caught fire and burned to the ground with her husband inside. It was ruled arson. Everyone thought she had died in the fire as well, but it turned out that she had unexpectedly spent the night at a hotel outside the city. Well, that looked suspicious. It didn't help her case when she said they'd had a fight and she couldn't stand to sleep under the same roof as him." He turned off the river road at last and headed toward home. "She hired an expensive law firm and ended up being exonerated for the crime. But they never did find out who set the fire."

"That expensive law firm didn't have Flint in its name, did it?"

Pete grimaced. "Actually, it did. Flint, Perkinson and Hubbard. Randall's dad did most of the work on the case. I'm guessing that's how Randall got connected with his current job at Compton Hall." He pulled up in front of the house and shut off the car. "Sounds like the band's all here."

Indeed, the howling of the Twisted Armpits assailed us as we walked up the front sidewalk. It was a constant wonder to me that the neighbors didn't call the police two or three times a week with noise complaints. Of course, they may have feared to tangle with the formidable Aileen.

I chuckled to myself as I walked up the steps to the porch. But the smile faded at the feel of a slimy crunch underfoot. I looked down and saw a mess of raw eggs splattered all over the porch.

"What the heck?" Pete said.

One well-placed egg dripped from the door handle, and a bunch of ants investigated a pile of smashed eggshells on the doorstep.

"Kids think they're so cool," Pete fumed.

"Maybe that's the neighbors' way of telling the band to settle down." I pulled a tissue pack out of my purse and gingerly cleaned off the door handle.

"It's not even late! They can just chill out." He walked around the side of the house and dragged out the garden hose. "Go on in, I'll clean up this mess."

I didn't argue.

Chapter Five

After a relaxing day on Sunday in which I did nothing more strenuous than transplant my new Japanese maples on either side of the front porch, I was ready for a new week. Still, I was unprepared for what I saw when I got off the bus the next morning and walked down the street to Compton Hall.

It was obvious that something was wrong. A couple of police cars sat in the circular drive, lights off but still ominous in the bright sunshine. The front door hung slightly ajar, a sin in the eyes of Ruth, who abhorred any thought of flies getting into the house. Suddenly fear gripped me—had something happened to Priscilla? Only slightly reassured by the absence of an ambulance, I hurried into the front hall.

The house was uncharacteristically quiet, with no noise of construction coming from the kitchen. Since I didn't think Carl Harper had finished tearing out the kitchen appliances, the calm made me even more apprehensive. A man's measured tones emanated from the living room. I paused outside the closed door, engaging in the time-honored tradition of all stately homes: listening at keyholes. I could only catch scraps of the discourse, which sounded like one person lecturing the rest of those present. I heard the phrase "blunt force trauma," followed by "death." Priscilla? I abandoned any effort to be discreet, and pushed open the door.

I gasped at the blur of faces gaping at me. The only one my brain registered was Priscilla, sitting quietly in her chair next to Ruth. She looked to be free of any blunt force trauma and as far away from death as usual. I ran across the room, refraining from enveloping her in a huge hug. Instead I knelt on the floor by her side and patted the gnarled hand lying on the chair arm.

She held a finger to her lips as if I were a student coming in late to class. "Officer Travis wasn't finished, my dear."

The tall, kindly-looking police officer stood in front of the fireplace, commanding the attention of the entire room. He looked pointedly at me. "Ms. Dembrowski."

"I'm sorry to interrupt." I glanced around at the people gathered there. Carl Harper, Jamison Royce, Louise Pritchard, John Ellis, and the TV producers Cherry Stamford and Stillman Dertz joined Ruth and Priscilla.

Office Travis nodded. "To fill you in, Ms. Dembrowski, Eric Burbridge did not die of natural causes. Preliminary autopsy results indicate that he died of blunt force trauma to the back of the head. He'd been dead for a good twelve hours before his body was found on Friday morning." He paused.

Both hands flew to my mouth. "Somebody killed him?" I croaked. "Here, in this house?"

The officer watched me closely, gauging my reaction. "Precisely."

He didn't get any further. Ruth stood up, leaning heavily on her gold-tipped cane. "That's just it, isn't it? Someone committed murder in this house." She glared around the room. "Who?"

Travis indicated her seat. "Ma'am, please have a seat. The LSPD will get to the bottom of this." He continued talking about the professor's physical condition when his body was discovered, but I couldn't make sense of his words through the roaring in my ears. I looked around the room like Ruth had, with her imperious "Who?" echoing in my brain. She thought it was one of us!

Slowly Officer Travis's words came back into focus. "...sorry for the inconvenience, but we are now in the midst of a murder investigation." He plucked the radio from his utility belt and spoke into it, "Ready to question the witnesses." He replaced the radio and stood silent in front of the crowd.

I sat back on my heels, stunned. A murder investigation. That was the last thing I wanted to be in the midst of. I'd been involved in a murder investigation during the Civil War reenactment in June, when my friend Chris found the body and was suspected of being the killer. My hands went cold. I had discovered Professor Burbridge's body. Would I be the number one suspect?

"How long a delay can we expect?" Cherry Stamford appealed to Officer Travis. "We have a very tight production schedule here." She swept her arm to encompass Jamison Royce and Carl Harper. "These contractors are far behind schedule as it is. We cannot tolerate an extended delay."

"I understand your concerns, but our investigation is paramount." Officer Travis turned away, indicating the end of that conversation. He spoke quietly to a pair of police officers who entered the room, and then they began to take one or the other of us off for questioning. A young officer with dark hair and snapping black eyes led me off to the library, of all places.

"I'm Officer Maureen Franklin." She ushered me in to the library and shut the door behind us. "And you're Daria Dembrowski, the seamstress. I understand you found the professor...here, as a matter of fact." She watched me closely.

"Yes."

Officer Franklin grimaced at my curt answer, and pulled out a small notebook. "Let's start at the beginning. How did you know the deceased?"

"I'm working on fabric arts for the remodeling of Compton Hall, so that means dresses and curtains, mostly. Professor Burbridge had done some research for me on historical curtains, and he had found some drawings of embroidered curtains. When I came in on Friday I was going to ask him for those drawings. But he was dead." I shuddered at the thought of the professor lying huddled on the floor right in front of where I now sat. Someone had hit him on the head and killed him! He had been lying here, dead, the whole time I was rooting around the pile of Japanese maples just outside the library window on Thursday night. If I had peeked in the window, could I have saved him?

Officer Franklin's voice pulled me back to the present. "Can you describe what you saw when you entered the room?"

"The professor was lying on the floor by the desk." I indicated the spot by my feet. "There was some blood on his face. I didn't see anything on the back of his head."

"Did you touch the body?"

"No. I couldn't see any breathing, so I guess I assumed he was dead. I called 911."

I watched Officer Franklin taking down what I said, and then consulting another small notebook that she pulled from her pocket. A sidelong glance showed me that it was notes from my first interview with the police just after Professor Burbridge died. My heart sank at the realization that Franklin was comparing today's answers to the ones I'd given two days ago. Was she trying to catch me out in an inconsistency, a lie? I closed my eyes and took a deep breath, trying for a calm, matter-of-fact demeanor. I might be a murder suspect, but I wasn't guilty, so I had nothing to hide.

Officer Franklin questioned me for over an hour, focusing on the position of the professor's body and my actions upon finding it. She pointed to the expanse of floor at my feet and conjured up the image of the dead man so many times that I began to feel nauseous. I could feel beads of sweat forming on my forehead, but hesitated to wipe them away for fear of looking guilty. I was sure she had brought me to this room and conducted her inquiry the way she did in an effort to prompt me to give myself away as a murderer. I could only hope that she knew that anyone being questioned in a murder investigation was bound to be nervous.

Finally it was over. Officer Franklin never spoke the words "You are a suspect." I certainly wasn't going to ask. She preceded me out of the library and led me back to the living room. The crowd had dwindled to Priscilla, Ruth, and John Ellis. Franklin surveyed the group and said, "I'd like to speak with Priscilla Compton now."

Priscilla leaned heavily on the arms of her chair to get to her feet. She adjusted the full skirt of the period gown I'd made her, and accepted the offer of her nephew John's arm to steady herself. "How can I help you?"

Ruth elbowed her son aside and settled Priscilla's hand on her own arm. "I will accompany my sister while you question her."

"There's no need," Officer Franklin soothed. "I can assure you, we will be careful not to upset Miss Compton."

Ruth didn't budge. "My sister has moments of diminishing lucidity. She cannot be considered a reliable witness. You may question her in my presence, or you may wait until our lawyer arrives. There are no other options."

"Actually..." Officer Franklin bit back the rest of her retort, evidently coming to the conclusion that it was fruitless to argue with Ruth, the human dragon. "Very well. Come with me, please."

She marched out of the room, followed by Ruth supporting Priscilla. "John, I want you here when we get back," Ruth admonished on her way out the door.

I stood in the middle of the room, staring after them. I noticed my hands were shaking, and quickly stuffed them in my pockets. I turned to see John watching me.

"You were a long time with the cops. What did they say to you?"

"Officer Franklin just asked about Professor Burbridge's body when I found it...." My words died on my lips at the look on John's face: not mere curiosity or commiserating over a distressing experience that we both shared, but a look of calculation, of discovery. Ruth's fierce "Who?" echoed in my mind once more. Could it have been John? Did John think it was me?

"Um, I should go get to work," I stammered, and fled for the stairs.

But I couldn't focus on historical embroidery. I kept getting up and going to the head of the stairs, listening for the tap of Ruth's cane, wondering what Officer Franklin was learning from Priscilla. I shared Ruth's concern about the usefulness of Priscilla as a witness, given her sweet vagueness. I didn't really know if she suffered from dementia or was just delightfully quirky, but she did have a way of distorting reality that could be disconcerting, especially when it came to a murder investigation. I hoped Officer Franklin really was taking it easy on Priscilla.

I looked out my window to see a couple of officers pacing around the exterior of the house, examining the ground around the windows and checking the walls and windowsills. I shivered at the thought of a murderer creeping in the library window to bludgeon poor Professor Burbridge to death.

Finally I couldn't stand it anymore. I threw down my curtains, having only succeeded in adding two inches of embroidery to the hemline, and strode out of the room and down the stairs. I paused in the great hall, listening. A clatter came from the kitchen, so Carl Harper must have finished with the police and gotten back to work. I turned toward the living room to find the door closed and Louise Pritchard standing outside, ear pressed to the keyhole. I chuckled at the picture she presented, far less subtle than I had been. But she could probably hear much better than I had. I walked over and tapped her on the shoulder.

Louise reared back as if I'd hit her over the head with the murder weapon. She let out a yell you could have heard all the way in Philly. Carl Harper popped out of the kitchen brandishing a massive wrench at the same instant that Officer Franklin hustled out of the living room.

"What's the matter?"

"It was a mouse," I cried, willing Louise to keep her mouth shut. "It ran right along the baseboard. It scared us both." I took Louise's hand and pulled her away from the door. "Come sit down in my sewing room to get over your fright." I propelled her to the stairs, catching a glimpse out of the corner of my eye of Carl Harper trying to hide the oversized wrench behind his back, while Officer Franklin's bright black eyes took everything in.

I dragged Louise up the stairs and led her to my sewing room. I pushed her into the only chair, and perched myself on the corner of the sewing table. "So?"

She rubbed her mouth sullenly. "What'd you have to go poking me like that for? Scared the bejesus out of me." She shuffled her feet and rubbed her hands on her blue twill pants. "You didn't really see a mouse, did you?"

"No, of course not. I didn't think you'd holler like that, or I would have called your name or something."

"Well, don't go judging me for listening at keyholes."

I rolled my eyes. "I'm not judging you. I want to know what was going on inside. What did they say?"

She stared at me, and then started to laugh, an ugly sound with a hint of hysteria just below the surface. I waited as patiently as I could until she settled down.

"That lady cop, she's asking Miss Priscilla all kinds of questions. See, there was an argument with the professor, the night before you found his body. The two old ladies were going at it with him, I don't know why. Somehow the cops found out, and now they think the old ladies bumped him off."

I bit my lip, remembering the shouting I'd heard coming from the living room right before Professor Burbridge stormed out, muttering something about not wanting to be silenced. If he had something to say that the two old ladies wanted kept quiet, then they'd gotten their way in the end, hadn't they? Could they have threatened him? Could they have actually killed him?

"That's ridiculous," I said out loud. "Neither Ruth nor Priscilla could have hit Professor Burbridge over the head hard enough to kill him."

"Miss Ruth could have done it in a heartbeat," Louise retorted. "That cane of hers could drop an ox. You know she murdered her husband. What makes you think she'd never do it again?"

I stared at her. "She murdered her husband? I heard she was acquitted at trial."

"Maybe that's what you heard, but I'm telling you, she was guilty. She had a fight with him, she stormed out of the house, and then the house burned to the ground in the wee hours of the night with him in it. Who else wanted that man dead? People loved him. He was always donating to worthy causes. She was probably just mad that he was giving away all her money." She leaned in to whisper in my face, "I'll bet that professor found out something about the old man's murder, so Ruth had to shut his mouth for good." She sat back with satisfaction, no doubt enjoying the dumbfounded look on my face. "I hope the cops get to the bottom of this before anyone else gets clonked over the head!"

I shook off the mental picture of Ruth creeping up behind Professor Burbridge and whacking him over the head with her gold-tipped cane. "Did you hear anything else just now?"

Louise stood up and dusted off her pants. "The cops said there was no evidence of forced entry into the house. The murderer didn't need to break in. The professor was killed by someone who was already in the house."

Chapter Six

I mulled over Louise's bombshell long after she left to return to her duties. Someone inside the house had killed the professor. Unless the murderer had snuck in, an unlikely prospect given the fact that the doors were usually kept locked as a safety precaution, then it was a member of the household, or someone involved with the remodeling for the TV show. Chances were, it was someone present in the room when Ruth stood up and demanded, "Who?"—unless it was Ruth herself, with her shady past and cantankerous nature. The only one I could be sure of, besides myself, of course, was Priscilla. There was no way that Priscilla could be a murderer!

My hands trembled as I passed the needle back and forth through my curtain fabric, mindlessly embroidering a winding vine along the hemline. I couldn't let sweet Priscilla suffer under any hint of suspicion of murder. At her age, she'd earned the right to be left in peace, regardless of her unorthodox ways. My resolve hardened with each prick of the needle. I had to look into the professor's death myself, to make sure that Priscilla didn't become the focus of the Laurel Springs Police Department's murder investigation.

Why would someone want to murder Professor Burbridge? He was bossy and sometimes disagreeable, but that didn't seem like a motive for murder. Maybe it was time for me to get together with Noah Webster.

I made myself finish the embroidery along one of the six curtain panels before knocking off for lunch. If I was going to meet this tight deadline, I had to be sure to put in the time on my sewing, even if my mind was distracted. The embroidered vine had a few unexpected trailing tendrils, but the TV cameras were unlikely to pick up on them, so I called it good. I packed up my sewing bag and hurried down the stairs.

I popped my head into the living room to see Priscilla dozing in her wingback chair, and Ruth sitting bolt upright reading the newspaper. "I'm taking off for lunch," I said softly, so as not to disturb Priscilla. My heart ached at the thought of that sweet old lady undergoing a rigorous police questioning and feeling herself to be suspected of murder.

Ruth didn't even look up. She turned the page of the newspaper deliberately and continued reading. I didn't know if she was ignoring me or if she hadn't heard me, but I really didn't care. I headed out the front door and down the long driveway to the street.

Compton Hall presided over a street lined with maple trees, which had replaced the stately elms that had stretched a canopy over the road before they all died of Dutch elm disease in the 1960s. The picturesque road led past the Tremington estate to the outskirts of Oliphant University.

The imposing brick buildings of Oliphant University encircled a quad crisscrossed with cobbled paths. The academic quad was dominated by Old Main, the only original building still standing following the devastating fire of 1892. Ironically it was the simplest of the academic buildings, built of fieldstones with wide shutters framing the symmetrical windows on the four-story edifice. Numerous renovations had all spared the marble staircase in the front entry, which bore the imprint of generations of students' feet in the smooth indentations on each stair step.

The plaque next to the stairs listed the history department on the third floor. I hastened up the stairs, conscious of my fast disappearing lunch hour.

The third floor looked like it had last been renovated in the 1940s. Wooden doors overlooked by transom windows lined the plain white hall. Small brass plaques screwed into the wall identified classrooms and professors' offices. I looked for Noah Webster's name, on the off chance that he had an office to himself, but didn't see it. Professor Burbridge's office was easy to spot by the crime tape stretched across the door. I stood in front of it at a loss, wishing I'd gotten Noah's phone number before Randall had scared him off. I didn't consciously mean to do it, but all of a sudden my hand went out and jiggled the doorknob of Professor Burbridge's office. Surprisingly, it opened.

I checked the deserted hallway, and then ducked under the yellow police tape and slipped into the professor's office. I didn't know what I was looking for, since the police had obviously already been here, but the opportunity was too good to pass up.

As Noah had mentioned, the professor had been extremely untidy. Piles of paper covered the desk and spilled down into numerous mounds on the floor. An old green chalkboard covered one wall above an old plaid couch that had probably accompanied the professor from his own years in grad school several decades ago. The professor's spindly handwriting filled the chalkboard with some kind of outline under headings like "Early career," "Influences," "Maneuvers," and "Mr. X." I pulled out my phone and took a series of pictures of the chalkboard, certain that the police had done the same.

I longed to sift through the papers or rummage through the desk drawers, but I didn't want to leave my fingerprints all over the office of a dead man whose body I had been the first to find. I settled for easing open a few drawers with the folds of my skirt, hoping that I didn't leave any fibers behind. I didn't see anything interesting, beyond an extensive pile of replacement typewriter ribbons that presumably matched the shrouded machine perched on a rolling metal table in the far corner. A desktop computer sat on the wooden desk, indicating that the professor kept the typewriter for its historical value rather than as an everyday tool. I thought of my antique treadle sewing machine, which I did use on a semiregular basis, and felt a sudden affinity toward this pretentious academic who obviously loved a bygone way of life.

An uproar in the hallway outside the office startled me out of my reflections. I crept to the window in the door and peered out to see a flood of young men and women clutching thick textbooks to their chests as they chattered their way down the hall. I checked the clock above the chalkboard: 1:00. Class must have just gotten out. I waited until the hallway was quiet again, and slipped out of the office, softly closing the door behind me. Once I was on the correct side of the crime scene tape again, I paused to plan my next move.

"If you're looking for Burbridge, he's dead."

I turned to see a young woman dressed in overalls and an oversized bright purple T-shirt, balancing a heavy backpack on one shoulder. She couldn't have been older than nineteen. Her long brown hair was caught back in an untidy ponytail that swished whenever she moved her head. She regarded me steadily, waiting for me to make the next move.

"I know. Shocking, isn't it. You never expect your teacher to die on you."

She eyed me doubtfully. "He was your teacher? Are you a grad student, then?"

I smiled and held out my hand to her. "No, I was working with him on the historical renovations on Compton Hall. I'm Daria Dembrowski, a seamstress."

She shifted her backpack and shook my hand limply, as if unaccustomed to this social convention. "I'm Liselle. He was my American history prof for summer term. I didn't really know him that well—he would lecture once a week or so, but the grad students led all the discussion sections." She gazed at the crime tape blocking the door. "He was brilliant."

I paused a moment, touched by her matter-of-fact statement. "I heard he was researching Major Samuel Compton."

"I don't know about his research." She glanced at her watch. "I gotta get some lunch before my biology lab. Are you headed to Foraker?"

I knew enough about Oliphant University to know that Foraker was the student union, which presumably housed the cafeteria. "Yeah, I'll walk along with you." I abandoned all hope of returning to Compton Hall in time to satisfy Ruth, and fell in step with Liselle. "Do you know the history grad students?"

She shifted her loaded backpack long enough to brush a wisp of hair out of her face. "Sure. There's a history table at lunch on Mondays. We're already late, but I could introduce you, if you want."

"That would be awesome. Will Noah Webster be there?"

"Were you looking for him? He's leading a discussion section until two thirty, I think." She led me down a winding cobbled path that led to the edge of the academic quad, where it turned into a nondescript concrete sidewalk snaking off down a sloping lawn to the student union building. Built in the 1960s, all asymmetrical slate and glass, Foraker contrasted with the stately academic buildings encircling the quad. It hummed with activity as the summer term students foraged for lunch.

Liselle waited while I purchased a meal ticket, and then helped me navigate the various food stations. I bypassed the made-to-order items in favor of the premade cafeteria entrees that could be slapped on my plate without delay. I followed her to a large round table filled with about a dozen students. We plopped down our trays and pulled up a couple of chairs as other diners squeezed over to make room for us.

"This is Darla, she's a seamstress," Liselle announced, cutting into a spirited discussion on the New Deal. She took a big bite of her ham and cheese sandwich.

"It's Daria," I said, flashing a big smile. "I was working with Professor Burbridge on the historical renovations at Compton Hall. Such a sad thing, him dying suddenly like that."

A clamor arose at my artless statement. One voice rose above the rest, that of a clean-cut young man wearing a blue Oliphant University T-shirt and cheap sunglasses perched on his close-cropped head.

"You know he was murdered? Somebody shot him in the back at close range."

I merely nodded, uninterested in correcting his misinformation. I worked on my macaroni and eggplant casserole while the talk of murder swirled around the table. Then I threw out my next gambit. "I wish I'd known the professor better. I hear he's a brilliant researcher."

The serious-looking young woman sitting beside me heaved a sigh. "He might have been, no one knows. He was very secretive about his research. I think Lexicon's the only one who knows what he was working on."

"Lexicon?"

Liselle giggled. "You know, your friend Noah Webster. Like the dictionary. We call him Lexicon. He hates it."

Poor Noah. Obviously he was the one I needed to talk to. "I wonder why Professor Burbridge was so secretive about his research."

"Maybe he thought somebody would kill him over it." The clean-cut guy with the sunglasses took a big slurp of soda, relishing the thought of a murderer stalking the historian on account of research.

"Maybe he didn't want anyone to know how far behind he was, while at the same time giving his students points off for late work," another voice piped up.

"Oh, come on!" The painfully thin woman across the table from me twisted the gaudy rings covering her bony fingers. "Burbridge wanted to be the first to publish his research, just like any other historian. If he was behind in his research, it was because of all the other things he was involved in, in addition to teaching."

My ears perked up. "What other things was he involved in?"

She rolled her eyes. "He was your consummate conspiracy theorist. He had all these crusades he was working on—like historical investigative reporting or something. He was looking into a cheating scandal at the law school four years ago that got covered up by the administration. Then there was that story of corruption in the contractors' union that happened eight years ago. Burbridge wanted to find out if the city assembly was behind the corruption that it supposedly exposed."

"Hmm. I thought Professor Burbridge focused on Revolutionary War history. It's funny that he was spending a lot of energy on these kinds of modern-day causes."

She shrugged. "He wasn't a purist. He always said you could consider anything to be history as long as it didn't show up in the newspaper's New Year's recap of the biggest events of the past year."

Another voice piped up, this time coming from a petite young woman with oversized black glasses that made her look more owlish than sophisticated.

"I think he really enjoyed the thought of getting other people in trouble. I'm guessing there were lots of people who wanted him dead."

I gazed around the table at the serious faces of the students. "What about his students? What did you guys think about him?"

"What, you think we wanted him dead?" the clean-cut guy demanded.

His very defensiveness made me wonder. "No, of course not. I was just wondering if he was a well-loved professor, that's all."

"You either loved him or you hated him." The thin woman picked at her overly long nails. "He was notorious for giving tough grades. If he gave you a D, he'd look you in the face and say you earned it. But if you got an A, you'd know you earned that too." She looked at the watch dangling from her skinny wrist. "Time for class! Nice to meet you, Darla."

"It's Daria," I muttered, watching the students scrambling to gather up their trays, books, and backpacks. I followed them out of the student union, checking the time myself. My lunch hour was long ago over, and living room curtains weren't going to embroider themselves. I resolved to connect with Noah another day, and hustled down the street and back to Compton Hall.

I spent the afternoon stitching leaves and butterflies on an endless vine border along the hemline of the curtains. The fancy work was a delightful change from simple hemming, but at the same time it demanded a certain amount of concentration. More than once I let my mind wander and had to rip out a butterfly flying backward or a vine tendril pointing in the wrong direction. But I couldn't still my mind to focus solely on embroidery.

I thought about what I had learned from the students at Oliphant University. Professor Burbridge was a tough teacher, who enjoyed pointing out to students that they had earned a D. But some students loved him— that was obvious from the way Noah spoke about missing him. No one but Noah knew details of the professor's research, whether due to fear of being harmed (which I had a hard time believing) or because of some kind of paranoia about making sure no one else beat him to the publishing punch. One student had described him as a "conspiracy theorist" who was investigating cheating at the law school and corruption in the contractors' union. I wondered if those investigations had anything to do with his death. If I was going on the assumption that someone involved with the household or the renovations of Compton Hall was responsible for the professor's death, then disgruntled students were not suspects. But there was a lawyer associated with the household, and a contractor as well.

I thought back to Randall's time in law school at Oliphant University. He graduated with his JD degree two years ago at the age of twenty-seven.

Not a stellar student, he had barely managed to graduate in three years, and it had taken him three tries to pass the bar exam. If a cheating scandal had taken place four years ago, he would have been a 2L student at the time. When I first met Randall I had been drawn to his charming wit, but over the course of our time together he revealed his ugly side, railing against demanding professors and bright students who had eclipsed him in class discussions. Cutthroat competition between students characterized the culture at Oliphant Law School at the time. If Randall had known about widespread cheating, I was sure he would have exposed the perpetrators to be sure that they were disciplined, thus moving himself up in the ranks. Yet he had never mentioned a cheating scandal at the law school. I briefly considered the possibility that he simply didn't know, but that was unrealistic. Randall made it his business to know all about anything that could affect himself and his fortunes. If there were any cheating going on at Oliphant Law, Randall Flint would have been the first to know. I could only conclude that he had taken part in the cheating. In that case, his law degree, which conferred on him the honor of placing the title "Esquire" after his name, was a sham. If exposed, he could stand to lose his law license, and his partner-track position at his father's law firm. Was that enough to kill a man for?

I stabbed my forefinger with a needle that trembled, as I considered the possibility of my former fiancé being a murderer. It wasn't a far-fetched idea. I laid down the curtain and popped my finger in my mouth. Before rushing to conclusions, I needed to learn more about Professor Burbridge's involvement in exposing this cheating scandal. Plus, I needed to find out what Randall knew about the professor's activities.

I folded up the curtain and laid it aside for the day. I usually tried to take a break whenever I pricked my finger and drew blood. No client wanted to see a blood smear on their garment, especially if it was a wedding gown. Speaking of wedding gowns, I had a fitting scheduled with Fiona for Thursday. Maybe she could tell me about Randall's law school days. But I knew I wouldn't ask her. If I, who had lived with Randall at the time, didn't know about any cheating, I was sure Fiona wouldn't have anything to tell me. I had no interest in hurting this delightful young woman by disparaging her fiancé with baseless accusations. I would have to find another way to look into Randall's questionable past.

I was still friendly with one of Randall's former classmates, whom I had met at a law student party in the early days. Marlena Hernandez, one of the bright students who so infuriated Randall, worked at the legal aid clinic in town. She might be able to spare some time to talk to me about her law school days. I sent her a quick text, and we arranged to meet for lunch on the following day.

I packed up my sewing bag, leaving the curtains in a neat pile on the table. They could wait until tomorrow, at which point I could probably finish them with no trouble. As I turned to click off the light, something caused me to pause. The side table looked different. I walked closer to the little oak table sitting under the one window. An unremarkable candle sat atop the white lace doily covering the chipped surface of the table. I picked it up and breathed in its fresh piney scent. It was a new smell to the cozy old room. Void of the candle, the doily bore the faint outline of a larger item that no longer sat upon it—the tarnished bowl that I'd noticed the first time I had walked into the room. The silver bowl was missing.

Chapter Seven

I didn't know whether to make a big deal about this or not. Was the bowl stolen, or simply moved? It obviously needed polishing—maybe Louise had come in and taken it to clean it up. It would make a nice touch in the background for the filming. I shrugged and switched off the light.

I was passing the door to the kitchen on my way out when Carl Harper bolted out of the room and ran smack into me. I staggered backward, dropping my bag and scattering sewing implements on the floor. "Hey!"

Carl swore and hollered at me, "Get out of my way!" His face was red and his eyebrows were screwed up to where I thought he'd have a stroke. I flattened myself against the wall and watched him rage on down the hall. The man had an unbelievable temper. Sheesh!

I found Priscilla on the front porch, relaxing in her favorite rocking chair. I sat down next to her. "It's a lovely afternoon."

Her vacant eyes sharpened at the sight of me. "It certainly is, my dear. The pixies will be out soon with their twinkling lights."

I leaned over and patted her hand. "We always called them fireflies."

"What's in a name?" she quoted. "They say a rose by any other name would smell as sweet, which may in fact be true. But I'm not sure if the pixies appreciate being called flies or bugs. They can be formidable adversaries, you know, if you get on their bad side." She leaned forward to whisper in my ear, "Some even say they hold the power of life and death in their tiny little hands."

I drew back involuntarily. "Whose life or death are we talking about?"

"Why, no one's died around here, my dear, except for the poor professor. Do you suppose he got on the bad side of the pixies?" Her wizened face screwed up in anxiety.

I patted her hand again. "No, I don't think that's what happened to him. The pixies stay outdoors, right? The professor was inside when he died."

"Oh, yes, in the library. Not a bad way to go; surrounded by books, those old friends." Her face clouded. "But dear Eric wasn't ready, was he? He never got the chance to make things right with Ruth, after that unfortunate disagreement. They say you should never let the sun go down on your anger, my dear." She waggled her finger at me. "You never know what might happen next."

I nodded so she would feel like I was heeding her sage advice. "What did Ruth and the professor disagree about?"

"Well, I couldn't really—" Priscilla's words were interrupted by the imperious tapping of a gold-tipped cane. "Why, Ruth, were your ears burning? We were just talking about you."

"I trust you can come up with a more suitable topic of conversation," Ruth snapped. She lowered herself into the chair on the other side of Priscilla and glared at me. "If you will excuse us..."

"Of course." I stood up with as much grace as I could manage. "Nice to chat with you, Priscilla. I'll be back in the morning." I slung my bag over my shoulder and left the sisters to their own "more suitable" conversation.

I fumed all through my bus ride home. I had been on the brink of discovering the basis of Ruth's argument with Professor Burbridge, when that human dragon prevented Priscilla from talking. What did she have to hide? Ruth's interference only solidified my resolve to get Priscilla alone and find out the truth.

A warm evening breeze blew softly as I got off the bus a block from my house. I breathed deeply, letting the frustration flow out of me. Maybe I could take a break from worrying about murder long enough to enjoy a lovely evening. After all, the pixies, also known as fireflies, would be coming out soon.

My newfound serenity deepened at the sight of the twin Japanese maples framing the front porch. Their red leaves picked up the color of the red front door to present a lovely picture. I skipped up the steps leading to the porch, and almost stepped on the tiny body of a dead mouse. I stifled a scream. My cat Mohair didn't often leave such offerings for me, thank goodness. I stepped gingerly around the mouse and up onto the porch. An appalling sight met my eyes.

Dead mice lay scattered all across the porch. Everywhere I looked there were limp tails, tiny claws, or flies buzzing on a furry carcass.

I did scream this time. I stood rooted on the edge of the porch, unable to get inside my own house, surrounded by at least a dozen dead rodents.

There were far too many to think that they'd been left by Mohair—someone had unloaded a bag full of dead mice onto my porch!

The front door flew open to reveal Aileen, dressed in a solid black spandex jumpsuit that made her look like a cat bandit. "What the?" She slammed the door behind her and advanced onto the porch. "Your cat never did this?"

I shook my head wordlessly, afraid to speak for fear of my voice cracking.

She pulled out her phone and started snapping pictures of the corpses. "You should call McCarthy to come and get some professional shots."

I stared at her. "What for? It's not like I want to hang them on the wall or anything."

She snorted and held out her phone to me. "What, you don't want this hanging in the kitchen? You could think of it as a diet aid."

The image of the limp mouse repulsed me. I pushed her phone away. "I'm not on a diet. Who could have done this?"

She finished taking her ghoulish pictures and stashed her phone on the porch swing. "Same ones that did the eggs yesterday. You been making any enemies lately?"

I folded my arms, hoping that her next move would be to clean up the loathsome mice. "I figured those eggs were from neighbors fed up with the noise of the Twisted Armpits."

Aileen's head snapped up. "You think? That's a pretty cowardly way to ask us to turn down the volume."

I pulled out my own phone and snapped a picture of Aileen: black jumpsuit, black spiky hair, and thick black makeup. I held it out to her. "Would you ask her to turn down the volume?"

Aileen stared at the photo a minute and then met my eyes. "Hell, yeah. And you know what? If they asked me, I would turn it down. But I'm not gonna play nice after they make a total mess with raw eggs and then strew dead mice all over my porch. They better pull out their earplugs from now on, 'cause we're gonna crank it up a notch!"

I groaned as loud as I could. "So what is this, the battle over the band?"

She flashed me a wicked grin. "Why not?"

"Well, we could be wrong about the neighbors. They could be totally innocent. Maybe somebody else did this."

"Back to your enemies again. Got any ideas?"

"There was a murder at Compton Hall. Maybe the murderer's trying to intimidate us."

Aileen leaned against the door frame and contemplated the carnage. "Murderer, huh? Why would he be after us?"

"Why did he kill Professor Burbridge?" That was the question. But there was an even more ominous one—was he likely to strike again? Were my household and I in danger?

Aileen heaved herself up off the door frame and scooped up her phone. "Obviously you're going to make it your business to find out." She opened the door. "Just as obviously, you have no intention of cleaning up this mess." She grinned at me. "See ya!"

"Oh, come on Aileen," I called after her as she slammed the door behind her, leaving me stranded on the porch with a dozen dead mice. I waited for a few minutes, but when she didn't reappear I traipsed down the porch steps and around to the back of the house, only to find more dead mice on the back doorstep. I almost gagged at the sorry sight. I punched in Aileen's number on my phone as I walked back to the front porch.

"Help me out here. There's mice all over the back step too. I don't have anything to clean them up with."

She groaned and hung up. A minute later she burst out the front door once more, armed with broom and dustpan. "You owe me, big-time." She swept the bodies into the dustpan and went to throw them over the porch rail into the bushes.

"Wait, let me get a bag. They'll stink there." I ran inside and grabbed a couple of trash bags. I couldn't watch while she tipped the horrible load into the bag. The only thing that made it at all bearable was the fact that Aileen didn't laugh at me. She grunted, clearly grossed out by the whole episode just like I was. When the last carcass was double-bagged and safely in the garbage can, we both stood at the sink, taking turns washing our hands over and over.

"I'd rather go with the murderer than the neighbors," Aileen said finally. "It takes a pretty twisted person to collect dead mice like that. I hope it's not the people we live next door to."

I couldn't agree more. But the thought of a murderer leaving his calling card on my front porch sent shivers up my spine.

I spent the next half hour standing by the front windows, peering out at every sound or movement I detected. I alternated between watching the front door and the kitchen door, until I couldn't stand it anymore. If the murderer was trying to freak me out, he was doing a pretty good job of it. But I wasn't going to let him win. I turned my back on the front door and went to the kitchen to make some tea. Armed with the steaming mug, I forced myself to go out and sit on the porch. I pushed the image of dead mice aside and focused on the fireflies flitting in the evening light. They seemed to like my new Japanese maples—their little lights twinkled energetically among the scarlet leaves.

I sipped my tea and let the quiet evening calm my thoughts. Still, when McCarthy peeled up with a boisterous toot of the horn, I couldn't believe how happy I was to see him. He jumped out of his car, waving vigorously. I almost ran down the steps and threw myself into his arms. In the midst of all this uncertainty and doubt, he was completely above suspicion.

When I first met McCarthy he landed on my short list of murder suspects, and at one point I was convinced that he was the guilty party. Thankfully I had been wrong, and he was magnanimous enough to forgive me for calling him a murderer to his face. Not a great way to start a relationship, of whatever description! I was so glad to be able to trust him completely now.

He bounded up the porch steps. "I hear your professor was murdered. The cops said they're focusing on the people associated with Compton Hall. Do I have the pleasure of addressing the prime suspect?"

His mock solicitude took my breath away. "Me? Of course not!" I sat back down. "There was no indication that I was a suspect, any more than anyone else in the house."

He sat down in the chair next to me with a pointed glance at my tea mug. "Good to know. What else did you learn from the cops?"

I stood back up. "Let's go for a walk." I texted Aileen that I was out walking with McCarthy, so she wouldn't discover me gone and freak out. Of course, the thought of Aileen freaking out over anything so inconsequential as a missing housemate was so ridiculous that I couldn't help laughing out loud. McCarthy looked over at me, bemused.

"Sorry, I'm a little punchy this evening." I led him down the steps and along the walkway to the sidewalk. We turned toward the canal that wound its way through the artsy part of my neighborhood. We always called it a canal, but in reality it was merely a creek bed that had been reinforced with concrete where the water flowed past the historic houses. Not exactly Venice, but it was a peaceful place to walk in the evenings. We paused to watch a red-winged blackbird perch on a limb overhanging the water.

"What's making you punchy?" McCarthy finally asked. "The murder?"

"That, plus some jackass dumped a pile of dead mice on my porch for me to find when I got home. They were all over the back too—it was awful!" I was embarrassed to note that my voice was shaking.

"Wow." He picked up a small stone and lobbed it into the placid water. Ripples fanned out in ever-widening circles. "That's nasty. Any idea who did it?"

"Well, it was either the neighbors protesting the band, or a murderer deciding to harass me for some unknown reason."

"Your neighbors don't like the band?"

I laughed, and threw my own stone into the water. My ripples intersected with his to form a new pattern. "What do you think?"

"You know I love the Twisted Armpits, but I suppose I might think differently if I were a senior citizen and had to listen to them day and night when I preferred Frank Sinatra."

"Exactly!"

We resumed our walk past a property draped with lines of Buddhist prayer flags mingled with clotheslines full of tie-dyed T-shirts and shorts.

"If it was the murderer, why would he target you?"

I heaved a heavy sigh. "That's what I can't figure out."

"But you're moving heaven and earth to find out, aren't you. Nosy seamstress! What do you know that I don't know?"

"So much it would make your head spin."

He laughed and took my hand as we walked down the middle of the quiet street.

"I talked with some of Professor Burbridge's students today."

He nodded his approval. "Hot on the case, I see. I just found out the man was murdered a couple hours ago, and you've already interviewed his closest associates. It's a constant wonder to me why you don't just chuck the sewing and join the force."

"They'd probably make me mend their bulletproof vests or design new uniform shirts." I briefly enjoyed the mental picture of myself, measuring tape in hand, whipping the police force into style.

"So what did the students tell you?"

I pulled myself back to reality. "Professor Burbridge was doing Revolutionary War research into Major Samuel Compton. He had some files in the library at Compton Hall about that." I frowned, remembering that some of those files had disappeared between the time I'd first seen them and the news that the professor had been murdered. Was that Randall, or was the murderer interested in the professor's research? I resolved to find a chance to talk with Noah Webster without delay.

"They also told me that the professor was the kind of guy who liked to get other people in trouble. He had these projects he was working on, more current events than history, although I guess he was researching them as if they were history."

"What kind of projects?"

"One was a cheating scandal at the law school about four years ago. The other had something to do with corruption in the contractors' union eight years ago. Burbridge was looking into the city's possible involvement."

"Sounds like he should've chucked the academics and gone into investigative journalism. Too late for that, though."

"You don't know what was going on eight years ago, do you?"

He shook his head regretfully. "Before my time. I've only lived here for a few years. I can check into it for you, though. I've got the full resources of the Laurel Springs *Daily Chronicle* at your service."

He looked so excited to sink his teeth into a mystery that I decided to leave this piece of the puzzle to him. "Nosy photographer!" was all I said. He grinned.

We strolled back in the deepening twilight. It wasn't until we were within steps of my house that I realized that McCarthy hadn't taken a single photograph on our entire walk. I glanced over to see that, sure enough, he was without his ever-present camera. "You're missing your camera tonight, Sean."

He nodded. "It happened this afternoon, when I was trying to get a shot of a kid in the act of vandalizing the bridge. He sprayed me with spray paint and it got all over my camera. I had to take the whole thing apart to clean it up. It's a sorry sight, all in pieces on my kitchen table." He sounded like he was in mourning, grieving the loss of a loved one. "I missed it just now—that red-winged blackbird was magnificent."

"Bummer." I scanned the porch as we walked up the steps. Nothing out of place, thank goodness. I paused in the doorway, feeling McCarthy's close presence right beside me. I reached up and touched his face lightly. "Yeah, I can see a hint of purple there, by your left ear."

He laughed and rubbed the spot with his palm. "You should have seen me earlier. I think the camera will survive, but the shirt I was wearing is history." He bade me a cheery goodbye.

I hummed all the way upstairs. That invigorating walk with McCarthy chased the thought of an enemy right out of my head. I settled down for a long evening of embroidery. If I was going to spend my day tomorrow being nosy, as McCarthy put it, then I needed to get my work done tonight.

Aileen took off for a gig after nine, and Pete popped in to say hi when he got home well after ten o'clock. He'd started a run of sixteen-hour days working on filming, and warned me that I wouldn't be seeing much of him around for a while. He went straight to his room to crash. He seemed so tired out that I didn't even bother him with my tale of dead mice.

I sewed until almost midnight, at which point I gave up some seven inches shy of finishing my second border. I shook the cramps out of my hands and went downstairs to lock up the house.

Not for the first time, I wished for a deadbolt on the back door leading to the kitchen. Maybe I should hire Carl Harper to install one, once the Compton Hall renovations were complete. I thought about the volatile contractor, who seemed to be in a temper every time I saw him. What had he been talking about on the phone the other day? I remembered that when Louise Pritchard had shrieked, Carl had emerged from the kitchen with a heavy wrench clutched in one hand. He'd tried to hide it behind his back in front of the police investigators. Was that because he didn't want them to come to the wrong conclusions, or was he concealing the actual murder weapon? A big wrench like that could easily kill someone if wielded by a brawny man like Carl. Add to his muscular physique an explosive temper, and it wasn't hard to imagine Carl Harper in the role of impulsive murderer. I shuddered. Maybe I'd be better off seeking out a different contractor to install my deadbolt.

I checked both doors several times, and made sure that all the first-floor windows were closed. I would have preferred to keep them open to let in the cool night breeze, but paranoia overrode comfort. I enjoyed living in Laurel Springs precisely because you didn't need to worry about leaving windows open at night, or locking your house and car at every turn. I had a friend who didn't even know where her house keys were when she needed them to give to a house sitter. I never took things that far, but I always appreciated the sense of safety and community that comes with a small town. A murderer had destroyed that precious peace of mind for me.

I slept fitfully, hearing noises all night long. Night was the best time to hear an old house talking nonstop: creaking, settling, crackling with the temperature changes. Add to that the noise of two housemates, one who snored and the other who banged around at all hours, as well as a cat who did her best hunting after dark, and it was a wonder I ever got a good night's sleep. But tonight was different. Amid all the familiar noises, I felt like I heard something else, a sound of scratching outside. It was a faint sound, so faint that I wouldn't have noticed it except for the fact that I'd left my second-floor windows open to let the night air in. They let in the night sounds as well. I definitely heard something fishy outside, below my window along the back wall of the house.

I lay still for a few minutes, wondering if I could just ignore it and go back to sleep, but I soon realized that that was ridiculous. I crept out of bed and crawled along the floor to the window. I'd left the curtains open so the wind wouldn't flap them. The sound outside was louder now, but still stealthy. I raised my head up to the level of the windowsill and peered out. The moon was shining, casting silvery shadows on the backyard. Normally I loved to see the yard in the moonlight, dappled and serene. I hated the fact that I was seeking a threat this time.

I didn't see anything at first, but as my eyes adjusted to the light I did see a dark shape in the hydrangea bushes by the kitchen window. Incredibly it looked like a man, dressed all in black up to the black stocking cap on his head. He even wore black gloves, a detail that chilled me more than anything else about his nighttime actions. He appeared to be trying to break in through the kitchen window over the sink—the one window that had no latch to lock it. If he could get the right grip on it, he could simply slide it up and creep into the house, for whatever nefarious purpose he had in mind.

I watched him, my mind racing. I could call 911, but by the time the cops got here he would be inside the house. I could rouse Pete and Aileen, and the three of us should be a match for him, unless he had a gun. He looked like a professional cat burglar, but I couldn't guarantee that he was unarmed. I heard the faint but unmistakable sound of the window raising, and realized I needed to act immediately, on my own. I grabbed the nearest thing I could get my hands on, a decorative wooden box I kept on my dresser for knickknacks. I heaved it out the window, hollering in as deep a voice as I could muster, "Get out of my yard, you idiot!"

The response was overwhelmingly satisfying. The window slammed down with a crash loud enough to disturb my back door-neighbor Mrs. Hevla's dog, which started barking as if the redcoats were coming. The person cursed sharply. I hoped I'd beaned him with the box. He scrambled out of the bushes and darted past the side of the house. I ran down the hall, colliding with Pete at the top of the stairs.

"What's going on?" he mumbled, still half-asleep.

Aileen burst out of her room, her hair a wild tangle. "What's the ruckus?"

"He's getting away!" I ran down the stairs and fumbled with the back doorknob. By the time I got outside, I couldn't see any trace of the intruder. I heard a car revving several blocks away. "Shoot! We'll never catch him now."

Pete leaned on the open doorway, clearly uninterested in chasing after a thwarted burglar. "Who was it?"

I stood in the moonlight, staring at an empty street. "I don't know. Somebody trying to break into the house through the kitchen window—the one with no latch. He was wearing all black, like an art thief or something."

"Yeah, like he's going to steal all our priceless paintings," Aileen scoffed.

"Your band gear is probably worth a lot," Pete said. He held the door wide for me to come inside. But I wasn't done.

I scoped around the ground outside the kitchen window, looking for anything the intruder might have dropped in his flight. Pete and Aileen watched me in silence for a few minutes; then Aileen disappeared inside. She came out a moment later with a small flashlight that she shined along the foundation. "Look, a clue!" She trained the light on my decorative wooden box, lying ajar on the ground.

"That's mine." I scooped it up and brushed off some dirt. "I threw it out the window when I yelled."

"Did you hit him?" Aileen's eyes gleamed in the moonlight. More than anything else, she loved a good brawl.

"Maybe. I heard him swearing. I hope I hit him."

Pete finally followed Aileen out to peer at the ground as well. "You keep saying 'he.' Was it a man, then?"

I took Aileen's arm and pulled it up so the flashlight shone on the window frame. "I couldn't tell if it was a man or a woman. It was big enough to be an adult, though, not a kid. It sounds weird to call a person 'it,' so I said 'he.'" I glared at my brother. "Got a problem with that?"

He shrank back in mock horror. "I'm not getting into gender politics, of all things. I just wondered if you could tell who was trying to sneak into our house in the middle of the night."

I hugged the box to my chest and turned to go in. "Sorry. I'm a little freaked out by the whole thing, especially after the mice."

Pete locked the door behind us. "What mice?"

Aileen and I exchanged glances. I'd forgotten that Pete didn't even know about the most recent incident.

"Someone dumped a bunch of dead mice on the front porch this afternoon. It was horrible."

"I took a bunch of pictures if you want to see them, Moron."

Pete shook his head. "Dead mice at three thirty in the morning is more than I can handle." He rattled the kitchen window, shoving it down as far as it would go. "Do you think it was the same person as our mystery man? Should we call the cops?"

I groaned. "I don't want to hang around all night talking to cops when there's nothing for them to see. The guy wore gloves, so there's no fingerprints. I couldn't see anything that he left behind. He took off in a car, but we never saw it. What could we possibly tell the cops?"

"Well, do you think we're being targeted? First eggs, then dead mice, then a burglar in the middle of the night. Chances are those are all connected." I narrowed my eyes at him. "You're not being targeted, are you? By some riffraff from Hollywood?" Pete had gotten mixed up in drugs while trying to launch a film career. He'd served time in jail and been threatened in the past by thugs he owed money to. He'd borrowed money to pay them off, and we all assumed that that was the end of that sordid story.

Pete winced, and I instantly regretted voicing such suspicions with no proof whatsoever. He shook his head, and after a moment said, "Nobody from Hollywood is bothering me anymore. I promise."

Aileen poked him with an elbow to the ribs, eliciting another wince. "She told me the neighbors were probably pissed off about noise from the band. Can you imagine?"

We all laughed, just for a moment. I picked up the kettle, filled it with water, and set it on the stove. "I'm sorry, I don't mean to point fingers at anyone. No doubt it's just some murderer, coming here for who knows what reason and messing with our minds."

Pete took a box of tea bags out of the cupboard, and Aileen rooted out some cinnamon, curry, and strawberry jam to add to her cup. I sat down at the kitchen table and put my head in my hands. "That's the most terrifying possibility of all."

The three of us sat for the next hour or so, drinking tea and trying to summon up the courage to go back to bed for the rest of the night. Aileen brought a couple of wooden drumsticks up from the basement to wedge vertically into the window frame so the window could not be opened. "These are new drumsticks, I'll have you know. If they get broken, Pinker will have conniptions."

"I'll buy new ones." I tested the tautness of the drumsticks. "I don't think he'll be back tonight. Hopefully he's nursing a headache."

Finally fatigue drove us upstairs to finish out the night in bed. I was completely exhausted, but after a big cup of tea in the middle of the night, I couldn't fall asleep. I tossed and turned for hours, trying to banish the thought of a black-cloaked murderer creeping into my bedroom to discharge a passel of live mice to torment me. Just as I was about to give up and get up for the day, I drifted off to sleep.

I woke up so late that it wasn't even worth it to go to Compton Hall before lunch, so I simply lay in bed for another half hour before getting out of bed. I felt better after a shower. The house was quiet—both Aileen and Pete were gone by the time I got downstairs. I knew Pete had a busy filming schedule, but I had expected Aileen to be lounging around the house just like I was. I shrugged—who knew what motivated Aileen at any given moment?

The house was so quiet that it started to get on my nerves. I double-checked the doors and windows so many times that I could have earned an obsessive-compulsive merit badge. Every little sound outside sent me flying to the window, straining to see a dark form slipping around the corner. Finally I threw down my work in disgust, grabbed my bag, and ran for the bus. I'd be early for my lunch date with Marlena Hernandez, but I didn't care. I needed to get out of the house.

Marlena and I had agreed to meet at The Pig's Ear, a rainbow-colored food truck just off the Commons that sold deli sandwiches seasoned with a special sauce that kept customers lining up for more. I strolled along the Commons, watching the pigeons stalking a boy with an overflowing bag of popcorn, until it was time to meet Marlena.

She bustled up to the food truck line at precisely 12:00. A short woman who compensated by wearing four-inch stiletto heels with slacks or skirt alike, she wore her long black hair pulled back in a sweeping ponytail that reached to her waist. A navy straight skirt and a softly patterned blouse completed her professional ensemble. I waved and strolled over to join her, conscious of my unremarkable khaki pants and short-sleeved linen shirt. I suppose I could have tried a little harder, since I was going to have lunch with a lawyer.

We exchanged pleasantries while waiting in line for our roast beef sandwiches. We saw each other infrequently, but I always enjoyed spending time with this bundle of energy and passion. Her current project had to do with a dispute between the grocery store franchise and a group of four employees who had been fired for funneling day-old doughnuts to a day care center across town instead of throwing them away as instructed. As she liked to say, she was always looking out for the little guys.

We settled down on a park bench with our sandwiches, and Marlena came straight to the point. "I heard that Randall's back in town, with a beautiful fiancée." She took a dainty bite of roast beef and watched me closely.

"That's right. Have you met Fiona? I'm actually making her wedding gown. She's a lovely young woman."

Marlena choked on her iced tea. Evidently she hadn't heard this particular detail. "How can you say that? You don't hate her?"

I swiped up a dollop of sauce with my finger. "I didn't know her fiancé was Randall until the dress was designed and begun. I'm really glad I had a chance to get to know her before he showed up. He's working for the Compton family in the midst of the renovation of Compton Hall for the

TV show. I've actually bumped into him several times, since I'm doing the sewing for the renovation."

Marlena chewed in silence, mulling over this charged situation. "Then there was that murder at the Hall. I remember Burbridge from my law school days. He once taught a class on the intersection of law and society in presidential politics. I was the only one in the class who got an A." She chuckled. "There was a big stink about it, at the time."

"Everyone in your class was supercompetitive, weren't they? I remember Randall was always stressing about his grades."

She nodded, working on her sandwich. "That's law school for you."

I leaned closer. "I heard there was a lot of cheating at the law school when you guys were there. Do you know anything about that?"

Marlena took a big bite of sandwich, taking a moment to clear her mouth and perhaps collect her thoughts. "Randall told you that?"

I shook my head. "I heard that Professor Burbridge was doing a research project on widespread cheating that took place at the law school four years ago. It made me wonder if Randall was mixed up in that. He never said anything, but I have to wonder."

Marlena smoothed her napkin on her lap. "Cheating at law school is a very serious accusation."

"I'm not accusing anyone of anything. Certainly not you! I'm sure you earned that A in Burbridge's class."

She picked at some crumbs on her skirt. "As a matter of fact, everyone cheated, including me." She paused a moment to let that sink in. "We had one professor, Old Mossman, who required everyone to brief the case for each class, and we didn't know who would get called on to read that day. If it was your day, he would spend the entire class period grilling you about the case while everyone else watched. It was the most stressful experience of my life. One day a student who shall remain unnamed came to class without having written out a brief on the case. Bummer for him, Old Mossman called on him to read. He reached over to the desk next to him and swiped his classmate's brief, and read brilliantly for the next hour and a half. Mossman didn't see, but most of the class did. We all got together on the quad after class and talked about what had happened, and decided to share our briefs from then on. We each picked a day, prepared the brief, and distributed it to the rest of the class. It worked, only because Mossman didn't require us to turn in our papers at the end of class. I still did all the readings, because I couldn't trust someone else to get it right. But it took a ton of the stress out of the class to not have to write a brief from scratch every single day. We rationalized it with the thought that any other professor would tell his students in advance what day they were going to present, so we were simply putting ourselves on a level playing field with students in other schools across the country." She raised her eyes to my face. "We all swore to never reveal our deception. Now that I've told you about it, I'll have to kill you."

I jumped and dropped half of my sandwich on my lap.

Marlena laughed and passed me an extra napkin. "Wow, you're jumpy."

My hands shook as I cleaned up the spilled food. "Marlena, somebody did kill Professor Burbridge! What if it was one of the students who didn't want the story of cheating to come out? You could all lose your law licenses, couldn't you?"

She shook her head, still smiling at my reaction. "I doubt it. Oliphant Law School was striving for a culture of collaboration, where they encouraged students to work together outside of class. We spent a lot of time poring over the student handbook and parsing each sentence of the academic integrity code. We concluded that if we turned in someone else's work as our own, that would be an actionable offense, but merely reading someone else's work out loud would not be. Does that sound like splitting hairs?"

She paused, waiting for my answer, so I nodded.

"That's what lawyers do! That whole episode gave us invaluable skills into the practice of law." She folded up her napkin and stood up. "True, I wouldn't want the whole story to come out. You'll keep this to yourself, right? No running to the Laurel Springs *Daily Chronicle* with a hot tip!"

Yeah, McCarthy would have a field day with this. I nodded again. "People know, though. Professor Burbridge's students know what he was working on." I gathered up my trash and stood up as well. "Now that he's dead, they might talk to the police, and the police might want to pursue the story. Who knows, they might already know all about the professor's work." I sincerely hoped so, since I didn't want to find myself in the position of obstructing a police investigation by withholding evidence.

Marlena tossed her trash in a garbage can and checked her watch. "I need to get back to work. I'm going to assume that no one cares about some student collaboration from four years ago. At this point, I'm calling it water under the bridge. Some of my classmates have moved on to do some very important work in overseas development agencies as well as in the state legislature. Nobody cares whether or not they personally briefed the *Vandermeer v. Richmond* case for Old Mossman's class back in the day." She fixed me with a stern gaze. "Yes, Randall was part of the collaborative group. It wasn't his idea, but I'm sure he benefited from it. As did we all."

"Okay." I did a final scrub on the oily spot on my pants from that tasty special sauce. "Thanks for telling me about it, Marlena. Thanks for not killing me afterward."

She grinned and waved goodbye. "Have fun making that wedding dress for Randall's 'lovely' fiancée!" She bustled on back to the legal aid clinic to do her own version of important work in service of the community. I watched her until she was inside, and wondered if she was right. Did it really matter if a person cheated, if it didn't hurt anybody in the process?

Chapter Eight

I headed to Compton Hall after lunch, hoping I wouldn't be lectured for tardiness by Ruth the human dragon. But the Hall was quiet when I arrived. I peeked into the kitchen to see what Carl Harper was up to. If he was swearing and throwing tools around, I was prepared to hightail it out of there. But he wasn't even there. The metal and chrome fixtures had all vanished, and a magnificent open hearth was nearing completion. I paced through the kitchen, admiring the weathered red bricks making up the massive fireplace. They looked familiar, somehow. I was trying to remember where I might have seen similar bricks when Carl walked into the room. He was deep in conversation on his cell phone. "We've got to get this straight," he said. "We can't afford any slip-ups." He looked up and saw me standing there. "Listen, I gotta go. Keep it together." And he ended the call.

"Can I help you?"

I flashed him a big smile, my mind racing. I would have given the entire proceeds from Fiona's wedding dress to know who he was talking to on the phone and what it was that they needed to "get straight." I tried to keep my conversation neutral. "I see you've gotten all the modern appliances out of here. It really looks like an eighteenth-century kitchen now."

He beamed. "I'm almost done with the fireplace. I found these antique bricks at the site of the old clockworks factory that was torn down three years ago. See the mortar here." He indicated the joints between the bricks that had already been applied to form a façade covering up a sheet of drywall. "I can attach them to the drywall the regular way, but the TV folks told me whatever showed had to look old. I had to do a bunch of research about how stonemasons did their work in those times. That professor was going to find some tips for me, but he never came through." He stopped, as an ugly flush of red swept over his face. "That didn't sound good. I'm sure he would have, if he had enough time. I mean, he didn't die on purpose." I felt sorry for the man, struggling to correct the bad impression his words were creating. "Maybe he did find some tips, but he just didn't have time to tell you. Did you look through his papers to find out?"

It was an innocent suggestion, but I watched him closely to see how he would answer. I didn't care to judge, since I had looked through the professor's papers myself. But I did want to know who had torched Professor Burbridge's files in the basement after he died.

"No, I never looked through any papers. I expect they're all gone by now, between the cops and that lawyer the old girls hired to price out all the valuables in the house." He pushed back the paint cap on his head to scratch with both hands. He ran a finger over the masonry. "It'll be fine. The TV folks want the work all done by tomorrow morning."

I smiled my assent. "Yeah, I need to get going on my embroidery if I'm going to get the curtains hung by then. Thanks for showing me the bricks."

I ducked out of the kitchen and headed straight upstairs to closet myself in the sewing room with the final yard or so of embroidery. I resolved not to leave the house for the evening until the curtains were safely hung in the living room.

Vines, flowers, and butterflies merged together under my nimble fingers while I replayed this conversation in my mind. Carl's words were innocent enough, even though he did give the impression that he found the professor's death to be an inconvenience to him personally. What really piqued my interest was the phone conversation cautioning no room for "slip-ups." Did that have something to do with Professor Burbridge's research into the scandal with the contractors' union? I hoped McCarthy had come up with some information today.

But what had I learned today? Surprisingly, Marlena had told me the whole story about systematic cheating at the law school. Or had she? I frowned as I picked out some stray stitches that marred the soaring flight of a monarch butterfly. It was odd how readily she told me that tale, given the serious ramifications associated with cheating at the postgraduate level. I found it hard to believe that the students could have rationalized such behavior as being anything other than cheating. They must have really been stressed out!

I thought back to those days, when Randall was living with me in my house, struggling with the grueling classes in his second year in law school. He had often complained about Old Mossman, but he never mentioned anything about cheating, or collaborating to get the better of this curmudgeon of a professor. Either he knew that what they were doing was risky, or he didn't want to sully his integrity in my eyes. Or, he didn't trust me enough to even think of confiding in me. I felt the familiar flush of anger against my ex, and focused on the present instead. Professor Burbridge was looking into this story of widespread cheating. He was making no secret of his work, since his summer students knew about it. Had one of the former law students gotten word, and killed him just as Marlena jokingly threatened to do to me? I took a deep breath and moved to the next logical step. Was that student Randall? Had he discovered some notes in the professor's boxes that were left behind in the library where Randall was now working, and killed the professor to stifle the story? But that didn't make sense! Randall moved into the library after the professor was killed. If he saw any papers, it could only have been after the murder had taken place. Of course, he could have heard about Professor Burbridge's research earlier, and moved into the library to eliminate any evidence of his work after killing him.

I rubbed my forehead with both hands, and then stood up to work a kink out of my back. If I were to focus on motive, I would have to say that Randall had a strong motive for murder. Although he had a good job as an associate on a partner track in a prestigious law firm (headed up by his father, no less), he could lose it all if his law school degree were called into question on a serious matter of academic dishonesty. He could get disbarred, with his name published in the newspaper for all to see. A narcissistic person like Randall could never stand the shame.

I sat back down again and forced myself to continue with the endless vine, while I forced my mind to consider the next question. Was Randall the kind of person who could kill to protect his own interests? He had been increasingly controlling with me, but never violent or overtly threatening. He had always been charming, in a suave kind of way that originally made me feel like the luckiest woman alive. Toward the end I had wondered if the restrictions in my new life were worth the man who put them in place, but I had never once envisioned the depths to which Randall had been scamming me. But did that make him a potential murderer?

I rushed through the last few inches and thankfully tied off the final knot. I shook out the finished panel and gathered up the other three curtain panels. I carried them down to the living room, and then shuttled down my iron and ironing board. I needed to press them before hanging them in the windows.

The living room was deserted. Like the kitchen, it appeared to be almost ready for the final filming for the TV series. Completely furnished with period pieces, with the wood floor newly burnished but not waxed to a modern-day shine, it only lacked my hand-embroidered curtains to give it authenticity. I set up the ironing board and turned on the iron, and then checked the time, wondering what the other occupants of the house were doing. It was almost six thirty—they were probably finishing up with dinner by now. While the iron heated up, I paced around the spacious room, wrestling with one final question. Did some part of me *want* Randall to be the killer? It didn't really matter, since my feelings had nothing to do with what had happened or who had done it. But in the interest of self-awareness, if nothing else, I faced the reality that I really didn't hope that Randall turned out to be the murderer. I didn't even want him to be disbarred for cheating at law school. It wasn't just that I really liked Fiona and didn't want her future to be compromised. But I didn't want to have to admit that I had been taken in by a cheat and a murderer, instead of merely a con artist who had played on my emotions to finance his law school career. But it wasn't about me. A man was dead, and an eccentric old woman might be the prime suspect in his death. I owed it to them to try to uncover the truth. I didn't owe Randall anything.

I took extra care in pressing the four curtain panels, making sure to cushion the embroidered sections by placing a fluffy towel on the ironing board and running the iron along the back side of the fabric. I was in the middle of this painstaking task when Cherry Stamford walked into the living room, clutching her ever-present clipboard.

She licked her finger and flipped through a number of pages, finally settling on the one she wanted. "And what are you up to now?"

I indicated the ironed panel I'd carefully draped over the back of the settee. "I've finished the embroidered curtains for the living room. I'm just ironing them before I hang them up."

Cherry tapped a pencil to her red lips. "We should get minute-by-minute footage of this." She pulled out her phone and punched in some numbers. "Stillman, get a camera to the living room, pronto." She pocketed the phone and looked me over critically. "You'll need some makeup and perhaps a different hairdo. We'll go with your jeans, since this is an in-process segment. Can you freshen up your makeup, and brush your hair out over your shoulders?"

"No, and no." I said. Then I relented at the look of shock in her face. "I need to have my hair up while I'm working, or it'll get in my way. Sorry. I don't have any makeup with me, but if you have something you want me to put on, I will. Or I could just finish up my work and call it a day." I pulled out my phone to check the time, hoping she would conclude that I had better things to do than fuss with makeup in order to film a segment. But she didn't get the hint.

She pulled out her phone again, but before she could make the call, Stillman hurried into the room, camera in tow. "What have we got?"

"Oh, Stillman! We need makeup for"—she checked her papers again—"Daria, here."

Stillman looked me over just as Cherry had done. He flipped on the camera and peered through the lens at me, cocking his head from side to side. I stood quite still, not sure if he was testing or filming. He barked in his own phone, "We need lights and makeup in the living room."

"Should I keep ironing, or wait until the camera's rolling?"

Cherry blinked at me, surprised at being interrupted in the midst of her directing. "How much longer until you're done?"

"I have this piece, and then two more just like it. It might take another forty-five minutes or so." I took another look at the time for good measure.

"Yes, yes, keep working. You can always go over it again if you have to."

I sighed and turned back to my ironing, which was definitely not my favorite part about sewing. I had no intention of going over it again. If nothing else, I could save the last piece until they were ready to film.

It wasn't long before the lights and makeup arrived. A young woman wearing enough makeup to qualify her to take the stage with the Twisted Armpits pulled me aside and started brushing on foundation and eye shadow. When she was done with me, she started in on Cherry. A couple of technicians brought in huge lights on poles to illuminate the room. My iron steamed lightly on the ironing board.

Finally all was ready. Cherry signaled me to resume ironing. She nodded to Stillman, who hoisted the camera and clicked the Start button. "And what are you up to now, Daria?"

I indicated my ironing board, spread with the final curtain. "I'm finished with the embroidery for the living room curtains." I extended a hand to one of the pressed panels draped faceup over the settee. "This is all hand-embroidered, just as a woman would do in the 1770s. I used silk embroidery thread so as not to overburden the light fabric with worsted wool." I ran a finger lightly over the stitches. "This is a very simple design, to give the overall impression of elegant embroidery without spending the time needed for a more elaborate design."

Cherry's hand slashed across her neck in the "cut" sign. She glared at me. "Make no mention of the need to work quickly or give any indication that we are scrambling to catch up!" She blotted her forehead with her handkerchief. "Viewers don't need or want to know that we are cutting corners to make our deadline." She circled her hand to Stillman to start filming again. "Is there a particular reason that you're ironing the curtain upside down?"

I gulped, and pasted on a camera-worthy smile. "I don't want to squish the stitches. I've placed them on top of a towel so the stitching will fall down into the pile of the terry cloth and the fabric will get ironed." I peeled up a corner of the hem to display the result. "This technique gives the embroidery as much texture as possible, making it more noticeable." I passed the iron over the last few feet of curtain. "Now all I have to do is hang them up."

Cherry slashed the "cut" sign again. "How long will that take?"

"It would go faster if I had someone to give me a hand."

Cherry looked around the room, but the makeup and lights folks had stepped out, leaving only herself and Stillman. Clearly she had no intention of either helping me or wielding the camera so Stillman could help. She waved a hand at Stillman. "Get someone to help."

Stillman summoned the crew, and then there was another delay while the makeup gal touched up the lights wranglers, and then they were finally ready to film us hanging the curtains. With two strong guys to help me it was a matter of minutes to get the whole job done. The drape was lovely, and the curtains looked like Betsy Ross herself had made them. I beamed at the camera, barely resisting the urge to throw out my arms and cry, "Ta-da!"

Cherry twirled her hand and said aloud, "That's a wrap." She graced me with a smile. "Nicely done." She paged through her clipboard again. "So, what else do you have to finish up?"

"Priscilla's gown is finished, so I think I'm all done."

"What about the rest of the household?" Again she shuffled through the papers. "Louise Pritchard, the caregiver? Is Ruth Ellis's gown done as well?"

"I offered to make a dress for Louise, but she refused. There was never any talk of making anything for Ruth."

Cherry gasped like the damsel being tied to the railroad tracks in an old melodrama. "You haven't even begun to make a gown for Ruth?"

I shrugged and shook my head.

Cherry started pulling papers off her clipboard, searching through them as if they held the answers to all her problems. "That was the whole point—two sisters revamping their house and their lives back to 1770! How can we do this with only one sister?" I was afraid she was about to start hyperventilating.

"I'm sure I can whip up something for Ruth," I said in the soothing tone I'd perfected for dealing with stressed-out brides. "I'll talk to her as soon as I can. Maybe Louise would agree to wear a period costume if you told her how important it was for the filming. She absolutely refused when I asked her."

"Stillman!" Cherry infused the one word with all the imperiousness of command. He melted from the room without a word.

Cherry stood still for a moment, breathing deeply while watching the two guys packing up the pole lights. Then she snapped her papers down on her clipboard and bustled out of the room.

"I got this, no worries," I called out as she left. The reassurance was as much for me as it was for her.

I schlepped my ironing board back up the stairs, then ran back down and brought up the iron, towel, and the rest of my gear. I hoped that maybe the physical exertion would help me summon up the courage to approach Ruth and tell her I had to measure her for an eighteenth-century gown. From past experience with Ruth, I didn't hold out much hope of success.

I found the sisters on the porch, drinking iced tea and rocking in the early evening calm. Priscilla saw me first.

"Good evening, my dear. Lovely weather we're having, wouldn't you say? The clouds are high in the sky, so I'm looking for a lavender sunset tonight. The red ones are always so spectacular, but they can bring bad luck, you know. Lavender ones are the most peaceful."

"Peaceful is what we need, that's for sure," I said. "I finished the curtains for the living room. They're all hung and look great."

Priscilla clapped her hands like a five-year-old. "I can't wait to see them!"

I took a deep breath and forged on. "I thought I was all finished, but Cherry wants me to make a gown for you, Miss Ruth."

Ruth set her glass down with a snap. "Is that so? Well I have no intention of wearing a fancy dress costume, thank you very much."

Priscilla's face broke out in a smile. "Ruth, darling, you'll look so lovely in a period dress. A dark red one, to bring out the tint of your cheeks." She turned to me eagerly, "You can do a dark red one, can't you?"

"I can do whatever color you want." I let my answer fall somewhere between the two of them.

"Don't be ridiculous, Priscilla. My cheeks haven't had a tint to them since 1969."

"That was the year Robby broke his arm on the backyard swing." Priscilla's eyes took on a faraway look. "He had to miss swimming lessons that entire summer. He hated it that Johnny learned backstroke before he did."

"That was a long time ago." Some of the bluster had gone out of Ruth. "He always hated it when Johnny got the better of him. Remember I told you that? You do remember, don't you, Ruth?" Priscilla's voice took on an anxious tone that I'd never heard before. "Robby and Johnny, always fighting. How can we get them to stop fighting?"

Ruth leaned over and laid a hand on Priscilla's knee. "They don't fight anymore, Priscilla." She turned to me, the steel returning to her voice. "I trust you're not contemplating dressing my son John out in Revolutionary War garb as well?"

My mouth fell open. "I sincerely hope not! I can come up with a quick gown for you, but a man's coat is another matter."

Priscilla giggled. "John would look so handsome in a Revolutionary War coat. He'd be the spitting image of our famous ancestor, Major Samuel Compton."

I was relieved that she seemed to be returning to the present. "Shall we go with a dark red gown, then?" I knew I didn't have any red fabric on hand, so I'd need to make a quick trip to the fabric store before closing time.

Ruth heaved an exasperated sigh. "Very well." She pulled herself to her feet and preceded me into the house where she suffered me to take her measurements.

"My understanding is that all the renovations are to be completed by tomorrow morning, with final filming scheduled for Friday."

I nodded as I jotted down her back to waist measurement. "I'll do the best I can. This will be a very simple gown, so it shouldn't take too long." I tucked my notebook back into my sewing bag. "I'd better get started."

Ruth watched me silently as I hurried out of the room. I pulled out my phone and checked my messages. I'd gotten three texts from McCarthy in the past half hour: "Dinner?" "Not dinner?" and "Maybe dessert?" A fourth was coming in: "Want to know what I know?"

I typed back, "Yeah. Pick me up at C Hall."

McCarthy arrived a few minutes later and waved out the window of his snazzy new sports car. He had the sunroof open and the sleeves rolled up on his white button-down shirt.

When I hopped in the passenger seat, I glanced at the center console. "I see you've got your camera back."

He peeled out from the curb. "Good as new. Except for that one patch of purple that I couldn't get out of the strap. I'll forever be reminded of my vulnerability to spray paint."

I laughed, fingering the unmistakably purple spot on the camera strap. "Hey, can you take me to the fabric store? I've got a new eighteenth-century dress to make before tomorrow morning."

"Wow! The nosy seamstress has her nose to the grindstone. And here I thought you were accepting my invitation to have dinner and talk about corruption." He obligingly changed course and headed for the fabric store in the mall east of town.

"Maybe we could talk about corruption while searching for dark red fabric. Did you find out about the scandal with the contractors' union?"

He tapped his palms on the steering wheel and sang along to the oldies show on the radio.

I rolled my eyes. "What do the Beatles know about money buying love? Was the contractors' union scandal about money?"

"Well, it wasn't about love." He turned down the radio. "The contractors' union was trying to get the city assembly to lighten up on code violations. They said they didn't want to get the code requirements changed; they just wanted more properties grandfathered in to the old code requirements that weren't so strict. It wasn't an unreasonable suggestion, given the sheer number of older homes that were built in the dark ages, before city code required no more than four inches between balcony rail posts, for instance. But the city assembly wouldn't go for it. So the contractors' union hired a big-name lobbyist for an insane sum of money to try to change the minds of the assembly members. Said lobbyist wined and dined the assembly members, sent them Christmas hams and tickets to the Sixers' games, and guess what happened."

"Hmm, let me think. Did the city assembly cave and relax their code requirements?"

"Give the woman a cigar!" He turned into the mall parking lot and eased into a parking space.

"So what's the big deal? Is this some kind of secret information to make it worth Professor Burbridge's while to research it?" I gathered up my bag and hopped out of the car. We walked together into the mall.

McCarthy shrugged. "This is all public information, straight from the *Daily Chronicle* archives. There was a stink at the time about ethics and undue influence, but at the end of the day, the code regulations were more lenient than before friend lobbyist came to town." He gazed about him as we entered the fabric store and I made a beeline to the patterned calico fabric along the far wall. "I don't get to spend much time in here."

"It's my second home." I scanned along the rows of red calico, looking for a dark shade that might in fact bring out the tint in Ruth's cheeks.

"But here's the interesting part." McCarthy leaned in close and lowered his voice to give his next words a flavor of mystique. "The contractors' union got what they wanted, apparently. But they refused to pay the lobbyist their agreed upon amount. They claimed that he employed tactics that they couldn't condone, so they backed out of their contract. The lobbyist sued, the union stood firm, and more money has gone to the lawyers than was ever spent to either hire the lobbyist or to woo the assembly members. Guess who's representing the contractors' union in the dispute?"

I picked up a bolt of sprigged cotton in a deep red shade and held a fold of the fabric up to my face to study in the mirror. "Please say it isn't Flint, Perkinson and Hubbard."

"Bingo! It sounds like a simple matter of breach of contract, but the litigation has stretched out for almost eight years now." He pulled out a fold of geometric fabric in a hideous mix of green and purple. "How about this one?"

I shook my head, refraining from commenting on his lamentable taste. "So what's the mystery about this lawsuit?"

McCarthy shrugged. "No idea. That's what your professor was researching, I'm guessing. Do you suppose he uncovered a smoking gun?"

I cringed at his choice of words. True, Professor Burbridge was bludgeoned, not shot, but still...

I draped the deep red calico around my body to get an idea of the pattern on a larger scale. It looked fine, plus it complemented Priscilla's lavender gown, so the two sisters could sit side by side for the TV filming. I toted the bolt over to the cutting table to get it measured and cut.

McCarthy leaned an elbow on the counter, watching the saleslady measure out twelve yards of fabric for me. "So, my nosy seamstress friend, are you planning to complete the professor's research, or what?"

I picked up the thick bundle of fabric and the cutting slip to take to the cash register. "What. I'd say I've got my work cut out for me for the next twenty-four hours or so. Of course, I still have to cut it out."

He grinned at my lame joke. "So, no dinner tonight?"

I shook my head regretfully. We settled for a trip through the drive-through for burgers and fries, and then McCarthy dropped me off at my house. He walked me to the door instead of dropping me at the curb like he usually did. I wondered what was behind this unusual solicitude, until I saw him scanning the porch floor, looking for dead mice or raw eggs, no doubt. Thankfully there was nothing amiss, unless you counted the deafening noise of the band in full cry in the basement. I shouted my thanks to McCarthy for accompanying me to the fabric store, and he waved a cheery goodbye.

I almost headed straight upstairs to cut out Ruth's gown, but my conscience wouldn't let me skip the important step of washing the fabric to shrink it before cutting and sewing. I carted it down to the basement, sidestepping the band, and popped it in the washing machine.

While the wash cycle ran, I retrieved the bodice pattern from Priscilla's gown, and modified it to fit Ruth's measurements. The sisters were both thin, but Ruth was a good six inches taller, with longer arms and legs to match. I had to simplify the pattern as well as alter the size, since I didn't have time for fancy embellishments on the sleeves and neckline. I settled for a plain square neckline to be covered by a white batiste fichu, and white batiste ruffles at the end of each sleeve. While the red fabric tumbled in the dryer, I cut out the fichu and ruffles, and ran up their seams on my machine. Sorry, no painstaking hand stitching tonight!

I rushed through the hot work of ironing twelve yards of cotton fabric and laid it out on the floor of my workroom to cut out the dress. I glanced at the clock. It was almost eleven o'clock, and I was just now making the first cut. What possessed me to say I could finish an entire eighteenth-century gown in one evening? I pushed that thought to the back of my mind before I started to panic, and doggedly pinned and cut out the bodice, sleeves, and skirt.

What I hadn't told McCarthy was the fact that the act of cutting and sewing only occupied a portion of my concentration, leaving me ample opportunity to think. Maybe I wasn't snooping in the professor's business or interviewing his colleagues, but I was still working out the clues in my mind. Although I did need to talk to Noah Webster as soon as I could. I resolved to pay a visit to Oliphant University as soon as I finished Ruth's gown.

Once the bodice was all cut out, it was a fairly simple task to sew it together. The V-shaped panel in the front alleviated the need for darts, so any necessary alterations could take place in the side seams. Fitting the dress would go so much quicker in the morning.

I hummed and sewed and thought about McCarthy's revelations. I truly didn't know what to do with the information about the contractors' union, the lobbyist, and the city assembly. I snipped thread ends, and tried to picture how this story could intersect with the cast of characters at Compton Hall, where the professor was murdered. Carl Harper was a general contractor—surely he belonged to the contractors' union. Did he have some secret related to that litigation that he would kill to keep private?

Again I wondered who he'd been talking to on those two occasions, and what he and the caller had been talking about.

Then there was Jamison Royce, the landscape artist. Did he count as a contractor, and if so, was he a union member? If not, what union did he belong to, and where did they stand in relation to the litigation between the lobbyist and the contractors' union? I called up a mental image of Royce, with his head completely hidden under his peculiar work cap with the flaps that covered his ears, leaving only his beard to indicate the color of his hair. I remembered that he'd been second on the scene of finding the professor's body. He'd seemed concerned at the time, and was helpful in terms of keeping things matter of fact. But what did I really know about him, other than the fact that he was willing to destroy prize-winning Japanese maples on the whim of a TV show that would do their filming and then move on? Those maple trees could have lived another fifty years, easily. What did the gardeners' union think of someone who would tear up beautiful living plants like that, I wondered? But maybe that was just my own sensibilities. My sewing machine whirred as I fed the voluminous skirt under the presser foot. What would the historical seamstress union, if there was one, think of me planning to run up the hem in an eighteenth-century skirt by machine? I guess it was all a matter of perspective.

It wasn't until I went to bed exhausted, with aching back and cramped fingers, that I recalled where I had seen a weathered red brick before today. It was all by itself on top of a pile of Japanese maple branches on the side of Compton Hall, below the window of the library, where a man had died of blunt force trauma to the head. The murder weapon!

I was wide awake now. The presence of one of Carl Harper's bricks on the ground outside the library window didn't prove that he was the murderer, of course. Anyone in the house could have picked up a brick from the kitchen. But maybe the police could get some fingerprints off it, if they were able to find the brick. I resolved to call them in the morning. It was well after three in the morning before I finally fell asleep, to dream uneasily about clients owing me huge sums of money, which they paid off in miniature Japanese maples.

I woke up late to the sound of my phone dinging. I'd received a short text from Marlena. It read: "Speaking of Randall, I heard his law firm got broken into last night."

Chapter Nine

I called the police first thing, and told them about the brick on top of the maple branches. The officer who took my call listened to my description, but refused to tell me if the police already knew about this potential murder weapon. "Thank you for your information," was all she would say.

I called McCarthy next, to let him know about the break-in. He hadn't heard about it yet.

"Once again, the nosy seamstress gets the information first. So what's your plan of action?" he asked.

I groaned. "No plan. I have to fit Ruth's gown this morning so the filming can go ahead." I shifted the phone to my shoulder so I could pour myself a bowl of cereal. "They're breathing down my neck as it is."

"Oh, let 'em sweat. What are the chances that this break-in is related to the professor's murder? I'd say pretty darn good!"

I plopped the bowl down on the kitchen table. "Okay, I'll give you that. But I'm a seamstress, not an investigator, remember?"

He laughed. "A nosy seamstress, who loves to poke that nose in where it doesn't belong."

"Well, maybe not this time. But I think I know who I can count on to do it justice."

"All right, if you're sure you're okay with passing up this opportunity to do your own snooping. I'll go to Philly to the offices of Flint, Perkinson and Hubbard and take photos of the break-in scene, and see what I can find out. I'm tied up this morning, but I'll get there before they close for the day."

"I'm sure you'll charm them with your irresistible personality and they will tell you all about what the intruders were looking for."

He was still chuckling when I hung up.

I hurried through my breakfast and caught the 9:10 bus for the Highlands. The bus wasn't crowded—the office workers were already at their desks, and the shopping crowd had some time before the stores opened at 10:00. I didn't know how early Ruth got up in the morning, but I needed to fit her gown and get it finished before Cherry had conniptions.

Compton Hall gleamed in the morning sunlight, as if the entire façade had received a good wash. I cocked my head and studied the manor house as I walked up the drive. Something was different, aside from the lovely sunlight highlighting the cream-colored bricks. It's easy to see something out of place, but it's harder to notice something that should be there but isn't. It took me a few minutes to realize that I was missing the glorious Japanese maples that should have protected the front of the house. The exterior walls looked forlorn, denuded of their leafy ornamentation. Once again, I hoped that the rewards of participating in the reality show with the chance to win a million dollars warranted the destruction of those prize-winning Japanese maples.

I shook off a profound sense of sadness and loss, reminding myself that a man had died on the same day that the maple trees had been uprooted. Shame on me for mourning the plants more than the person!

The front door of Compton Hall was firmly shut. I tried the knob, but it was locked. I sighed and rang the bell, knowing that Louise Pritchard would chastise me for disturbing whatever she was doing at the time.

Surprisingly, she didn't say a word when she eventually opened the door. Her dust cloth told me that I'd interrupted her weekly dusting, and her scowl expressed her irritation better than words, while at the same time letting me know that she didn't consider me worth wasting her breath on. I threw her a cheery "good morning" nonetheless, rising to the challenge of getting Louise to smile in spite of herself. Not this time.

"Is Miss Ruth ready for her fitting? I've brought her new period gown."

Louise grumbled, clearly peeved at having to answer my direct question. "She's in the middle of breakfast. You're just going to have to wait."

"Okay." I abandoned Louise to her housework, and wandered into the living room to admire my curtains one more time. They looked so beautiful! The morning sunlight filtered through the filmy fabric, lighting up the colorful embroidered flowers and butterflies along the borders. I pulled out my phone and snapped a few pictures for future promotional materials. Too bad McCarthy wasn't here to take some professional shots—my phone camera didn't do them justice.

I drifted over to the side table, admiring the stoneware vase displayed there. It was in the shape of an urn, with a squat round base and a long, thin neck. John Keats's "Ode on a Grecian Urn" came to mind as I studied the whimsical figures painted on the base. One was a man wearing an overcoat and fedora—hardly the attire of an ancient Greek.

"Communing with the soul of my departed husband, are we?" a sour voice demanded.

I almost dropped the urn.

Ruth tapped her way into the living room and plucked the urn out of my hands.

"I'm so sorry," I stammered. "I didn't realize... I thought it was a vase that just didn't have any flowers in it yet."

Ruth replaced the urn on the side table and dusted her hands. "Well. Now you know that it is the repository of my late husband's mortal remains. I would mention that you've no call to handle any item in this house regardless of its origin, but I fear my words would be wasted." She fixed me with her sharp eye. "Have you brought my historical gown?"

"It's right here." I hastened to pull the gown out of my sewing bag. "I just need you to slip it on so I can pin up the back and the hem." I held the gown out to her.

At that moment, the TV crew swept into the room, camera rolling. Stillman focused in on Priscilla's face as she made her slow way into the living room. Cherry intoned, "The living room curtains are in place, as the final touch to the restored living room." She waved her hand to indicate a cut and instructed Priscilla, "Walk over to the curtains, take a fold in your hand, and tell the camera how much you love them."

Priscilla gave us a vague smile. "Why, Ruth. I wondered where you'd gone after breakfast. You didn't even finish your coffee and sweet roll."

"I haven't eaten a sweet roll since the Nixon administration, and I'm not likely to start today." Ruth glared at the camera crew. "Get on with it. We have other things to do right now."

Cherry didn't falter. "Just take a bit of curtain in your hand, Priscilla, and tell the camera how beautiful it is."

"Yes, of course." Priscilla meandered over to the window and fingered a fold of the curtain. "Such lovely embroidery." She looked right at me. "You did a beautiful job, my dear."

I felt my cheeks flush as the camera panned over to me. I had a moment when I didn't remember what I was wearing or if I would look okay on television, but it passed. "Thank you, Miss Priscilla. The curtains are hand-embroidered in a pattern that would have been commonly used in the 1770s. Thanks to Professor Burbridge's research, I feel sure that they are historically accurate." My voice faltered at the sight of Cherry's hand frantically waving "cut."

"Make no mention of Professor Burbridge or give any hint that anything out of the ordinary has happened here. We're not using the 'M' word on this production!"

The "M" word. Murder. Cherry could deny its existence, but I couldn't stop thinking about the professor's death and the almost certain presence of a murderer in our midst. I still didn't know why someone would want to kill Professor Burbridge. Until I figured that out, I couldn't ignore the shocking fact that a murder had taken place in this house. To censor any mention of the professor's name seemed to belittle the horror of his death.

Cherry carried on, unmoved. "Ruth, please tell us about that impressive vase on the table next to you." She waved for Stillman to continue filming.

I caught a glint of amusement in Ruth's eye as she picked up the urn and displayed it for the camera. "This vase is a mortuary urn containing human remains. The urn itself may be historic, although I strongly doubt it. The remains are quite recent, seven years old, to be exact. They are the ashes of my late husband, the philanthropist Thurman Ellis." She paused, clearly surprised that the camera was still rolling. Both Cherry and Stillman seemed to be listening in a trance. I hung on her every word, remembering Pete's story of Ruth's possible involvement in her husband's death, and Louise's adamant assertion that Ruth was a murderer. "What else would you care to know?"

Stillman blinked and glanced at Cherry. Before she could wave "cut" again I spoke up. "What happened to your husband?"

Ruth glared at me as if I were a hideous creature who had crawled out from under a rock. The camera kept rolling.

"He died in a house fire. You can find out all the sordid details from any newspaper at the time, to satisfy your voyeuristic desires."

I cringed as her words hit home.

"Poor Ruth. Your beautiful home all gone, and your love as well." A single tear rolled down Priscilla's withered cheek.

Ruth drew herself up to her full formidable height. "I keep this urn to remind myself of the dangers of marriage in general and marriage to a rich bastard in particular." Her fierce gaze impaled Stillman. "I fail to see how this is pertinent to a discussion of house renovation, but that is, as they say, your business. If you will excuse me, I have a gown to try on." She thumped the urn back onto the side table. "We can proceed with the fitting in my dressing room," she said to me, and gripped the gold-tipped handle of her cane. You couldn't say she swept out of the room, but the fierce tapping of her cane expressed her disdain in similar fashion.

I followed her down the hall, feeling like I'd been rightly chastised for my rude curiosity. Still, I privately resolved to find those newspaper articles and read all the "sordid details" on my own time.

Ruth donned the red gown in silence, and stood stiffly while I marked the back and pinned up the wide hem. I circled around her still form until I couldn't stand the silence any longer.

"I'm sorry I asked about your husband like that, Miss Ruth. I hope you'll forgive my rudeness."

She let out an exasperated sigh. "This entire reality TV experience is an exercise in relinquishing one's privacy in the name of entertainment. Whatever possessed my sister to embrace that, I will never know."

* * * *

I spent the next hour and a half working on Ruth's gown. I abandoned all pretense at authenticity, and ran the hem up on the treadle sewing machine. My legs were tired out by the end of it, but I shaved a good three hours off my sewing time. All I had left was the buttons in the back, which I could do this evening at home. I bundled up Ruth's gown and set out for Oliphant University for a second attempt at talking with Noah Webster.

I managed to slip out of the house without being accosted by Cherry and Stillman. I breathed a sigh of relief once I was out the door and walking briskly down the tree-lined street. I was surprised to note how glad I was to be out of that oppressive household. Murdered professors and dead husbands were starting to take their toll on my psyche.

At the university, the innocent chatter of college students bustling about their academic business made me feel like I'd stepped back in time to my own college days. I'd been unattached at the time, happy to be studying history and fashion design with no more pressing concern on my mind than the next exam.

I entered Old Main and made my way up the smooth marble steps to be met by a crowd of students in the third-floor hallway. They stood quietly, intent on the open door of Professor Burbridge's office. I jostled my way to the front of the crowd.

The first thing I saw in the professor's office were two police officers, holding camera and notebook, respectively. The second thing I noticed was the state of chaos, far greater than the general untidiness I'd observed the other day. I turned to the student closest to me. "What happened?"

"Burbridge's office got broken into." The student chewed on the end of his backpack strap. "The cops are trying to figure out if anything is missing."

I felt a momentary flush of guilt, remembering my own foray into Professor Burbridge's office. I hoped I hadn't left any incriminating evidence for forensic experts to find.

I didn't want to get caught up in witness questioning, so I wormed my way back out of the crowd. I caught a glimpse of Noah Webster on the outskirts, his arms full of books and notebooks. I hurried over to him. I touched his arm lightly, and he jumped like he'd been shot.

"Hi, Noah. I just learned that Professor Burbridge's office was broken into."

He gazed blankly at me, his face pale. "Yeah. Um, hi."

"I was hoping we could talk about the professor's research—unless you have to be here to talk to the police?"

He shook his head, knocking his horn-rimmed glasses askew. "I don't want to talk to any cops."

I took his arm and steered him away from the crowd, half wondering if he was experiencing some sort of shock. "Let's go get a cup of coffee and talk."

We walked in silence to Foraker, but when we reached the doors to the cafeteria, Noah pulled away from me. "We can't talk here, it's too crowded. Let's go to the Station."

He led me back outside the building, around the corner and down a short flight of mossy stairs to a small red door marked "Station." It opened to a wood-paneled coffee shop filled with small tables arranged in cozy nooks for a maximum of privacy. We ordered coffee and blueberry scones, and settled down at an empty table furthest from the door.

After a few bites of scone, a bit of color came back into Noah's cheeks. "I'm sorry, I don't remember your name."

"I'm Daria Dembrowski. We met at Compton Hall, remember? You were going to tell me about Professor Burbridge's research into Major Samuel Compton."

He nodded over a slurp of coffee. "Right. Sorry. It was a shock to see Burbridge's office all strewn about like that. Almost like he'd been killed all over again."

I made sympathetic noises, all the while chafing inside. I needed to find out about the professor's research! "I keep thinking about the professor's death, and wondering if his research had anything to do with it. Can you tell me what he'd learned about Major Compton?" I sipped my coffee, my eyes on him.

Noah ran a hand through his untidy hair. "Okay. So, you know the story of the Battle of Laurel Springs, right?"

"Sure. The rebels were camping on the outskirts of town, holding off the British troops. But the British attacked the camp at night, and a lot of American troops were killed before the British were finally defeated. Major Compton died as well, but he was hailed as a hero for holding off the British and saving the town from invasion."

He nodded, smiling slightly. "That's the abbreviated version. If you dig deeper you find out that there's more to the story. I don't know if you know that intimate details of the rebel camp, including the positions of sentries and outer defenses, as well as troop numbers and location of armaments, were found in the possession of the attacking British troops."

I nodded. I had heard about this, although these details weren't generally emphasized when teaching fifth graders about the heroic battle. Of course, this only made the kids want to know more. "Right. I did learn that there was a traitor among the American troops who was feeding information to the British."

Noah was grinning now. "And do you know the identity of said traitor?"

"No one ever knew. I learned that the survivors were all questioned, but no one confessed, so the authorities concluded that the traitor was killed in the battle. That was the end of it." I studied his face. "Wait—did Professor Burbridge find out who the traitor was?"

Noah clapped his hands, literally. A couple of students looked over at us, and he shrank down in his seat. In a lowered voice, he said, "That's exactly what Burbridge found out."

He didn't say any more for a full minute. I had to prompt him. "So, who was the traitor?"

But I wasn't going to find out that easily.

Noah glanced around, and then leaned forward to say, "Burbridge was a brilliant historical researcher. He combed through letters and diaries and other primary sources. He was obsessed with finding out the answer to this historical mystery. It was his life's work." He bowed his head for a moment, clearly moved. "I like to think that I helped him out through my own research. I've focused on the foot soldiers in D Company, like I told you. One of them, Eli Fuller, wrote daily letters home to his brother, which his descendants saved religiously. These letters were donated to the Laurel Springs Historical Society in the 1830s, and the Historical Society gave them to the Tremington Museum at the turn of the twentieth century. I was able to access them for my research. His letters were typical of soldiers at the time, detailing army life and the terrors of battle, and they gave me a fantastic glimpse into the daily life of a Continental soldier. Then I noticed that whenever Fuller named a fellow soldier, it was a name that didn't correspond to the roster of D Company members. I compiled all the names from Fuller's letters, and finally concluded that they were a code. Burbridge and I worked on the code for months. When we finally succeeded in breaking it, we discovered that Fuller was telling his brother what was really going on in D Company."

I was mesmerized. "What was going on?"

"Fuller painted a picture of widespread abuses by the officers against the men. Fuller was a little guy, a weaver's apprentice by trade, who didn't feel able to stand up to the injustice he was experiencing. All he could do was document it through his coded letters."

"Did his brother figure out the code?"

"We couldn't find any evidence that he ever did. The collection includes the brother's letters to Eli as well, and I couldn't see any reference to coded messages in his correspondence. There's absolutely no historical record of dissension or injustice within the ranks of D Company, other than Fuller's coded account."

I felt sorry for poor little Eli, trying to be a whistleblower with no success. "What happened to Eli Fuller?"

"He was mortally wounded in the battle. He died three days later, on October 14, 1778. He had time to write one last letter home to his brother."

Noah leaned back in his chair with his arms crossed behind his head. I stared at him. "And?"

"It's a sad letter. Fuller knew he was dying, and he wrote to say goodbye. He mentioned the names of numerous colleagues who had died in the battle." He leaned forward. "None of those soldiers were ever in D Company."

I gripped the edge of the table. "It was another code?"

He nodded. "When we analyzed it, we concluded that he was telling his brother the name of the traitor who sold out his company to the British. But his brother didn't get it, so historians never knew the identity of the traitor, until now."

I could scarcely contain my impatience. "Who did Fuller name?"

Noah glanced around him again and leaned in to within inches of my face. "Major Samuel Compton."

I goggled at him. "Major Compton was a traitor?"

"Shh!" Noah waved both hands as if trying to quiet an unruly crowd. "This is revolutionary original research! Burbridge was going to stun the history world with his discovery. He was on the cusp of fame and critical recognition."

I couldn't help thinking that the fame and recognition might actually belong to Noah Webster, but that was beside the point. "So, what now?"

He sat back in his chair with a sigh. "No one else knows about Burbridge's research besides me. He was very protective about his work, because he wanted to publish and he didn't want anyone else to beat him to the punch. He wanted to find corroborating evidence to back up Fuller's account, but so far neither one of us has found anything. So we could be dealing with a disgruntled foot soldier who wanted to stir up trouble in his unit, or we could be sitting on a historical bombshell." He lowered his voice once more. "Can you imagine the scandal this news would cause? Major Compton is our town hero. He saved Laurel Springs from invasion by the British at the cost of his own life. Was he the one to invite the British in to attack the men under his own command? It boggles the mind to think of it!"

"So, maybe Fuller made the whole thing up."

Noah shook his head gently. "No, I don't think so. I've been reading his letters for the past three and a half years. He's one of the good guys. Get this—he wrote home about a horse that got shot in a random skirmish. The horse was screaming, and nobody was doing anything about it, so Eli had to put it down. I could hardly read the words, because they were smudged so badly." Noah stopped talking, and looked intently at the wall above my left shoulder.

"Smudged?"

He nodded. "By his tears. He was a gentle soul—he couldn't stand seeing an animal in pain. His last letter was heartbreaking. It took me an entire week to get through it, and that was just the narrative, not the code. I kept hoping he would survive the battle, even when I knew that he didn't." He gave me a sheepish look. "That sounds crazy, doesn't it?"

I gave him an encouraging smile. "Not at all. You've obviously made a connection with poor Eli."

"Yeah. So I really want his account to be fact, not invention. As a historian, it's my job to ferret out the facts and discard the fabrications, no matter how compelling those fabrications might be." He sighed again. "I'm worried that my fondness for Eli Fuller might be clouding my judgment."

"Well, what did Professor Burbridge think?" I couldn't imagine him feeling a fondness for the object of his research.

Noah smiled slightly. "Burbridge was eager to believe Fuller's story. He loved the idea of exposing the town hero as a traitor. He was a dedicated historian, but I believe he was ready to publicly accuse the heroic Major Compton of treason."

A public accusation! I choked on my coffee. The day that he died, Professor Burbridge had engaged in a vocal disagreement with Ruth and possibly Priscilla. He had stormed out of the room shouting, "I will not be silenced." Had he just laid out his theory to them? Had he said to Ruth Ellis's face, "Your esteemed ancestor was a cowardly traitor, and I'm going to publish his story for all the world to read"? Had she tried to silence him? I set my cup down with trembling fingers. Whatever else I didn't know, it was clear to me that Professor Burbridge was permanently silent. Only one person could tell that damning story now.

I regarded the earnest grad student sitting across from me. His right forefinger was stained with ink, like a true academic. His dusky red T-shirt proclaimed, "I'm a historian. Don't make me repeat myself." His black horn-rimmed glasses shielded eyes moist from emotion. He had lost his beloved mentor, and held that man's life's work in his hands.

Suddenly I was afraid. Whoever killed Professor Burbridge had come here to the history department to ransack his office. Were they trying to suppress his research? Did they know that Noah could divulge the whole story? Was Noah in danger?

I gripped his forearm. "Noah, have you had any threats made against you, or any weird things happening to you?"

He screwed up his face in thought. "I have been getting a lot of phone calls, where someone calls and then hangs up without saying anything."

"When did these calls start? How many is 'a lot'? Do they ever say anything at all?"

He stared at me, perplexed. "I got the first one a couple days ago. It might have been after Burbridge died—I don't know. I didn't think much of it. I've got some friends who like to play practical jokes. There have been four more calls since then."

My heart was racing by now. "Did you tell the police?"

He shook his head. "Do you think I should?"

I nodded. "You need to take this seriously. This research could be a bombshell, as you say. I'm afraid that someone wanted to silence the professor so his research would never come to light. But you know everything Professor Burbridge knew. What if the murderer is after you as well?"

"Wow." He stared at me, stunned. "That never occurred to me. Wow." He picked up his almost empty cup and took a sip. "I guess I could call—"

His words were cut off by the sound of his phone ringing. He pulled it out of his pocket and stared at it fearfully. Then he swiped the screen to answer and handed the phone to me without a word.

I held the phone up to my ear. I could hear a faint whooshing sound in the background, and the soft, unmistakable sound of someone breathing. It wasn't heavy breathing or threatening in any way, but it chilled me nonetheless. Then the call disconnected.

"Were the other calls like that one?" I handed back the phone with fingers that trembled slightly.

He nodded. "You really think I should call the police?"

I could have laughed at the plaintive note in his voice, if this wasn't such a serious matter. "Go ahead and call now, Noah, and then we'll both feel better."

He fumbled with his phone, and then laid it down on the table. "I better get my facts straight before I call. I need to remember when the other phone calls came in, and I can keep data on any new ones that I get." He noted the time in the spiral notebook that he carried.

I tried one last time. "I really think you should call now, Noah. The police need to know that someone's threatening you."

"Yeah." He finished his coffee in a gulp. "Look, I need to think things over before I make the call. But I'll be really careful in the meantime, okay?" He stood up. "I need to get back to work."

I bit back my frustration and nodded. "Okay. Give me your phone number, so I can get in touch with you if something comes up."

I typed his number into my phone as he gathered up his pile of books and headed out the door. "Stay safe," I called out after him. At least he was warned.

Chapter Ten

I thought about having lunch at the student union on campus, but decided that the students I'd met previously might ask awkward questions. I sent a quick text to McCarthy.

"When are you going to Philly? Time for lunch first?"

He picked me up ten minutes later.

"How 'bout lunch in Philly? Kill two birds with one stone?"

I laughed and hopped in the car. "Am I going with you to Randall's law firm?"

He gunned the engine. "I never expected you to let me do this alone."

McCarthy drove with all his windows rolled down, exulting in the wind blasting in his face. I have this theory that the cars people own and the way they drive gives an invaluable peek into their personality. For instance, Pete still had the pickup truck he bought in high school with his paperboy earnings. He lovingly took it in for service right on schedule and drove conservatively like a little old grandma. Aileen owned a beat-up red Ford with black flames painted on the hood, which she drove way too fast and parked in spots that might possibly accommodate a motorcycle, but nothing bigger. She didn't actually have spikes protruding from her hubcaps, but I suspected that was only because she hadn't gotten around to welding them on yet. I didn't drive at all and had never owned a car, which did throw my theory off a bit. I liked to think that it made me mysterious and bewitching, but no one had ever used those adjectives in my hearing. McCarthy had collected the insurance money on his totaled BMW and bought a brand-new bright yellow Mustang that he drove like he was riding on an amusement park thrill ride. He swooped up the hills and zoomed down them as if he hoped to finally one day go airborne. I clutched the door handle with one hand and my wildly whipping hair with the other, praying that we would land on all four tires again if we ever did achieve his desire.

The relentless wind made conversation impossible, so I leaned back and tried to enjoy the scenery whipping past us. The road took us along the west bank of the Schuylkill River, past Fairmount Park, which was home to a number of historic mansions. I wondered if any of them had been candidates for *My House in History*.

Our progress slowed when we exited the highway and drove along the city streets. McCarthy finally maneuvered into a spot on the curb near Washington Square, and killed the engine. He led me around the block to a small storefront. "Franco's is my favorite lunch spot when I'm in the city."

He led me into the dimly lit room, filled with orange vinyl upholstered booths surrounding nondescript tables that all seemed to be full. Overflow customers gathered around a couple of pool tables along the far wall. Foreign currency papered the walls, which were hung with black-and-white photographs from various European countries. I wondered if any of the pictures were McCarthy's.

He led me to the one empty bar stool, and leaned over my shoulder to address the bartender. "Hey, Louie, this is my friend Daria. We'll each have a Philly cheesesteak." He gave me a quick glance. "You like Philly cheesesteak, right?"

I smiled politely, although this local specialty was one of my least favorite lunch choices. But I'd never eaten at Franco's before.

By the time our food was ready, a pretty waitress named Amelia had settled us into a booth by the front window and started us out on a delightful assortment of roasted olives. She called McCarthy by name and teased him about a game of pool he'd evidently lost the last time he'd been in.

"Her boyfriend's a pool shark," he said, filling me in when she'd gone back to the kitchen. "She dared me to challenge him, and of course he trounced me." He grinned. "All in good fun."

I smiled back, my mouth full of my first bite of Philly cheesesteak. The fresh Amoroso roll was lightly toasted, the beefsteak was practically sizzling, and the provolone cheese beautifully melted over all. That was it, no onions or mushrooms to dull the taste of the meat and cheese. "This is the best Philly cheesesteak I've ever had."

McCarthy took a huge bite, mumbling, "I thought you'd like it. Nothing but the best at Franco's."

We ate in silence for a few minutes, the better to appreciate the tasty food. Then McCarthy wiped his fingers on a napkin and leaned back in his seat. "So, my nosy seamstress friend, what did you find out from your most recent interviews at the university?"

I knew he'd ask me, and I felt funny about wanting to keep Noah's revelations from him. But I knew Sean McCarthy loved a scoop as much as any other newspaperman. I just didn't feel like I could trust him to keep quiet about a story as potentially explosive as the prospect of Major Compton being a traitor. "When I got to the university, I found that Professor Burbridge's office had been broken into. The cops were still going over the scene. I talked with Noah Webster, a grad student who worked closely with Professor Burbridge. He told me the professor was working on some secret research, and he wondered if that could have had some bearing on his murder." I saw McCarthy pull out his little notebook, and hurried to steer the conversation away from the topic of that research. "Noah was afraid he might be in danger as well, since he knows about the professor's research."

McCarthy jotted down a few notes. "What kind of research could get a guy murdered? Does this have to do with the contractors' union or the law school cheating?"

I shrugged and took a big bite of cheesesteak. "Noah didn't tell me all the details." I wasn't technically lying, since I was sure there were lots of details from those bulging file boxes that we hadn't talked about.

McCarthy's pencil scratched away. "How much do you know about Noah Webster? Maybe he's the murderer, who killed his professor to take credit for this secret research for himself?"

I hadn't considered that possibility, but it was certainly true that Noah was the only one left who knew about Professor Burbridge's insight into Major Compton's treason. He had done much of the research for his own thesis. Was he seeking fame and recognition for himself at the cost of his mentor's life? And if he was a murderer, did he now have his sights trained on me, after telling me about this historical bombshell?

No, I couldn't believe that. I thought of Noah Webster, his voice filled with emotion as he talked about his fondness for little Eli Fuller. I didn't often make unerring snap judgments about people, but in this case I knew, without a shadow of a doubt, that Noah Webster was one of the good guys.

"No, Noah's not a murderer. I'm sure of it."

McCarthy eyed me skeptically. "Sounds like he's got a pretty good motive, if this research is as important as he says it is."

"Sean, he's a sweetheart. He's a goofy history nerd who knows all the secrets of a somewhat paranoid professor who is now dead. He's terrified.

Plus he told me he's been getting hang-up phone calls. He got one while we were talking."

"Did he tell the cops?"

"He said he didn't want to talk to the cops. He was freaked out about the professor's office being broken into."

McCarthy frowned, and made another note. "He doesn't want to talk to the cops? That doesn't sound suspicious to you?"

I stood up. "It does not. Let's go see what we can learn from the law office."

He paid for our meal and we walked out the door. "So, what's your plan to get us in the confidences of the good folks at Flint, Perkinson and Hubbard?"

I patted his camera, hanging around his neck as usual. "You tell them you've been sent by the newspaper to take photos to cover the story of the break-in. We're interested in Laurel Springs because Randall is associated with the historical renovation at Compton Hall, which is big news in our small town. I'm along as your 'assistant,' and as such I can go anywhere and ask all kinds of nosy questions."

He grinned. "I've never had an assistant before. This should be fun."

Randall's father's law firm was located in a red brick row house in the Society Hill neighborhood. White shutters framed the windows, and a hundred years' worth of ivy twined up the walls. A brass doorplate with the name "Flint, Perkinson and Hubbard" was the only indication that a prosperous business resided within. I knew immediately that this law firm was not one to advertise on late-night TV with a catchy phone number like 1-800-LAW-SUIT.

A middle-aged woman sitting at a heavy cherry reception desk met us when we walked in the door. Everything about her radiated professional perfection: her platinum-blond hair brushing her shoulders in a smooth bob, her beautifully manicured nails that clicked the keys of her keyboard, and the tasteful turquoise earrings that matched her turquoise bead necklace. She greeted us with a professional smile and said, "How can I help you?"

I felt immediately intimidated, but I'd forgotten that I was in the presence of a different kind of professional. McCarthy's disarming smile as he introduced us looked suspiciously like a grin to me, but it worked, like it usually did. "We're here to take some shots of the office and staff, to run with a short sidebar on the break-in." He pulled out his notebook and pressed it into my hands. "Daria will make sure that the names of the staff are correctly spelled."

I took my cue from him. "How do you spell your name, ma'am?"

She spelled out "J-O-A-N M-I-L-L-E-R," and I bit the inside of my cheek to keep from laughing out loud. But the ice was broken. Joan showed us around the office and introduced us to a couple of junior partners. "Mr. Flint is not in the office, and Mr. Hubbard is preparing for a deposition in an hour and a half, so you won't be able to see him."

"What about Mr. Perkinson?" I asked.

She gave me a pitying look. "Mr. Perkinson passed on some twenty-seven years ago. He was one of the founding partners, so the firm still bears his name."

I just nodded, making a note in McCarthy's notebook so it looked like I knew what I was doing.

McCarthy snapped some random photos of the reception area. "Can you show us where the burglar got in?"

Joan led us to a corner office with windows on the two outer walls. A large cherry wood conference table surrounded by matching chairs dominated the room. Original artwork hung on the wall, and a delightful set of driftwood carvings depicting seagulls in flight formed a centerpiece on the table. One window was ajar, with the frame bent in such a way that it could no longer close completely.

McCarthy zoomed in on the twisted window frame, snapping a series of photos. "How did the burglar access this third-story window?"

I wandered around the periphery of the room while Joan pointed to the fire escape. I couldn't discern anything out of place in the immaculate space. I passed behind Joan and gave McCarthy a surreptitious shrug.

He nodded, and asked Joan to stand next to the window for a couple of shots. "I see the burglar didn't touch the artwork. Was anything taken from this room?"

Joan shook her head, and then rearranged her pristine hairdo for McCarthy's next photo. "He came in here and then snooped around in the partners' offices. As far as we can tell, the only files he accessed were in Mr. Flint's office."

"Can you show us?"

She led us down the hall past more original artwork, and into a lavishly decorated private office. The cherry desk matched the other furniture in the office, and the wood shone from vigorous polishing. On the desk a black-and-white photograph in a silver frame depicted a young blond woman holding a toddler, their cheeks pressed together in a beautiful pose of love. I recognized Randall's wide mouth in the face of the laughing little boy. I felt a pang at the sight of his joyful innocence. Some people would benefit from never growing into adulthood.

Joan caught me looking at the photograph. "Mr. Flint's first wife died shortly after that photo was taken. He's been married twice since then, but he refuses to take that photo off his desk."

McCarthy's eyes twinkled at me as he snapped a picture of the office. I turned away so he wouldn't pick up on the confusing mix of emotions surging through me. Randall had never told me about his mother. In the four years we'd been together I had never even met his father. I hadn't made a big deal of it at the time, since I didn't want to introduce Randall to my overbearing father, either. We'd been two people without a past, who turned out to be devoid of a future together as well. I wrote a few random words in the notebook, and tried to focus on the task at hand.

"Which files did the burglar seem interested in?" McCarthy asked.

Joan indicated a wood file cabinet whose drawers were splintered as if they had been pried open with a crowbar. "This is where Mr. Flint keeps files on the wills and estates of the most prominent families in the Philadelphia area." She pulled a drawer open, with a palm wave worthy of a game show hostess. "The burglar tore through the files on the Compton family in your hometown of Laurel Springs." McCarthy's camera clicked away, documenting the mess of papers hastily stuffed back into manila folders. Joan's voice dropped to a dramatic whisper. "The original wills of Priscilla Compton and Ruth Ellis were taken."

Chapter Eleven

"Were any other wills—" McCarthy started to say, when a voice boomed from the doorway, "Joan! What are you doing in my office?"

Richard Flint, Esq. stood in the doorway, gazing at us with revulsion.

Joan turned a remarkable shade of red and stammered, "Newspaper photographers."

McCarthy shot me the barest glance, possibly wondering what my relationship to the father of my ex-fiancé consisted of. Then he plunged right in, as usual. He held out his hand. "Sean McCarthy, from the Laurel Springs *Daily Chronicle*." Another quick glance in my direction. "This is my assistant, Daria. We heard about your recent break-in, and realized that your firm represents the folks at Compton Hall. The whole town is fascinated with the reality show filming there, so the paper sent us here to get some pictures of your offices. Your lovely receptionist has been so kind as to show us all around." He beamed at Joan, whose cheeks were gradually returning to their original shade. "You must be Richard Flint."

Flint nodded, and slowly advanced into the room. The spitting image of Randall, with a couple of decades added on, Flint exuded the same cold superiority as his son. He set his briefcase down on the desk. His eyes flicked over the open file drawer. "Did you see everything you needed to see?"

McCarthy glanced at the silent figure of Joan Miller, caught with her hand almost literally in her boss's files. "Could I get a shot of you here in your office, Mr. Flint, with the file cabinet that was broken into in the background?" Without waiting for consent, he snapped a few pictures of Flint standing by his desk, frowning. McCarthy chattered away. "Please forgive me for intruding like this; I'm like a kid in a candy store when it comes to photographing break-ins. I imagine you've been through the whole rigmarole with the police photographers, as well. Us newspaper photogs are always the last to hear the news." He circled around Flint to snap another photo. "How would you like your name to appear in the newspaper?"

If McCarthy expected Flint to warm up at the prospect of his name and picture appearing in the newspaper, he was disappointed. This ploy had the opposite effect. Flint took a swift step toward McCarthy and held up his hand over the camera lens.

"Enough! Let's get one thing straight, young man. Flint, Perkinson and Hubbard is a prestigious law firm with an illustrious seventy-seven-year history. We are uninterested in the negative publicity that could be generated by publishing photographs showing the vulnerability of our offices. If you must report on the break-in, you will not include any images of myself or any other senior staff. A police report has been filed, and you may request access to that as a member of the press." He held out his hand, indicating the camera. "Kindly delete the photographs of myself that you just took."

McCarthy took a step backward. "Delete?" He pulled the camera to one side, out of reach of Flint's hand. "Oh, no, I never delete an image. Rule number one in the photographers' manual: never press Delete, because as soon your picture is gone, you're going to want it." He flashed a charming smile at Flint. "That actually happened to me once, early in my career when I was doing wedding photography to make ends meet. I was in the middle of a perfectly ordinary series of photographs of the bride dancing with her father when the brawl erupted. I got some fantastic action shots of the groom busting the heads of three of his guests. Those pictures could have launched my journalistic career the very next day, but the bride's father forced me to delete them all." He paused, waiting for Flint to respond. He was not disappointed.

Flint crossed his arms on his chest and frowned at McCarthy. "And how did the father of the bride convince you to delete the photos?"

McCarthy grinned. "You probably wouldn't believe me if I told you that the entire wedding party was made up of Mafia hit men who had Uzis stuffed in their cummerbunds, so let's just say he persuaded me with all the weapons at his disposal."

I stared at the two men, wondering what exactly McCarthy was hoping to gain by stalling Flint off with this ridiculous story.

Incredibly, Flint started to chuckle. "Fine. The weapons at my disposal are dry, legal ones, but I am very skilled at wielding them. I would much prefer to come to an amicable arrangement."

"Ah. Well said. I can almost hear the bailiff calling the court to order." McCarthy turned the camera over and scrolled through the pictures he'd just taken. He held it out to Flint while he highlighted the four images that included the senior partner, and pressed Delete. He held out his hand. "No hard feelings?"

Flint shook hands like a gentleman.

McCarthy held out his hand to Joan as well. "It's been a pleasure. I do apologize for coming in here and running rampant all over you." He winked at me. "Daria's favorite name for me is 'obnoxious photographer,' after all." He retrieved the notebook from my hand. "Time for us to go."

Both Flint and Joan accompanied us to the outer door of the office. As it closed behind us I punched McCarthy in the arm. "What was that all about? That stupid story of Mafia hit men in the wedding party, of all things? You obviously didn't care about those pictures of Flint, or you would never have deleted them."

He grinned at me. "You're very perceptive, my nosy seamstress." His grin faded. "Did you see the way Flint looked at poor Joan, who was in the middle of sharing his confidential legal files with us? He could have fired her on the spot for breach of confidentiality. But he got a taste of how obnoxious and persistent I could be, and then he got to win in his conflict with me. I'm hoping his taste of victory will allow him to overlook her lapse in judgment and let her keep her job."

"Wow, the obnoxious photographer saves the day!"

He laughed. "My cape is at the dry cleaner's."

He preceded me out the door and down the sidewalk to his car. "Anyplace else you want to go while we're in the city?"

I shook my head. "I should get back to work." I had just enough time to buckle myself in before McCarthy eased out of his parking spot and headed down the road. He waited until we were back on the highway to ask, "What do you make of our visit to the illustrious law firm?"

I swiped a strand of hair out of my mouth and hollered above the noise of traffic, "Lots to think about."

He gave me a swift glance, and hit the buttons to roll up the car windows. "I've got a bunch of questions. First one is for you. I thought you dated this guy Randall for a long time, but his dad didn't seem to recognize you."

"Was there a question there?" With the windows now closed, my voice came out overloud, sounding even more belligerent than I felt.

He chuckled. "Who, what, where, when, and why, huh? Okay, was I right in my observation that Richard Flint, Esquire did not recognize you after you went out with his son for a long time? That's a yes or no question. Then there's a follow-up: If I was right, why didn't he recognize you?"

"That's better." It wasn't really, but at least the stalling gave me a chance to ponder this uncomfortable fact of my recent relationship. "No, he did not recognize me, so yes, you are correct in your observation. He did not recognize me because we, in fact, had never met before."

McCarthy rolled his eyes at my evasion. "I met the dads of all the girls I ever went out with. One of them came with a waiver outlining my rights to any photographs I took of his daughter. Another one skipped the niceties and invited me into his living room for a chat while he was sorting out his ammunition. He made sure I knew he had seven different types of bullets, for a variety of weapons."

I couldn't come up with a light and witty response to this comment, as my brain went into overdrive wondering how many girls we were talking about here. McCarthy and I had never really talked about former boyfriends or girlfriends. Not that it mattered to me anyway, right? I settled for a somewhat strained laugh and a lame remark. "You must present a more threatening picture than I do."

"No doubt." He grinned, obviously waiting for something more. I had nothing. After a minute I asked, "What were the other questions you had?"

Traffic slowed in front of him, and he turned his attention to the road. "Aside from the obvious, 'who broke into the law office,' I'd really like to know what they wanted with Priscilla Compton's and Ruth Ellis's wills, and how that ties in to the murder of Professor Burbridge."

"You think the two are related?"

"They have to be. Well, they don't *have* to be, but chances are they're connected." He maneuvered into the left lane to bypass whatever was holding up traffic. I could practically see him champing at the bit to get back to flying down the road. "What do we know about Burbridge in relation to the Compton sisters?"

I leaned back in my seat, freed for the moment of my worry about spinning out of control on the freeway. "He was hired to go through the library at Compton Hall. I don't know if he had any prior connection to Priscilla or Ruth. I don't even know if they hired him or if it was the TV people."

McCarthy looked at me thoughtfully. "That's an interesting point. Who is paying for all the work going on at the Hall? It's for the TV show and the chance to win a million dollars, but if they don't win they'll have a lot of renovations to do just to get the house back to a livable condition."

I nodded. "It's like what Pete has told me about moviemaking in this area. The film company will scope out a house or neighborhood that looks like what they have in mind for their movie, and then they might gut the house to turn it into a restaurant or something. Pete says the production company would pay to return the house to its original condition. But in this case, I don't know if the production company would pay all the construction costs, or if Priscilla would be on the hook for some of them. It must be an expensive TV show."

"So who's paying you, Priscilla or the TV folks?"

I busied myself with my seat belt, which was pulling on my shoulder. I didn't want him to see my face. "Priscilla's paying me. She'll give me her final payment after the TV show airs and the vote is taken."

"How much is she counting on winning that million dollars, Daria?"

I shrugged. "You know Priscilla. She doesn't have a good grasp on reality. I'm sure she has no idea how much a million dollars is worth, or what all this work is costing her, or how much money is in her bank account." And if she didn't win the million dollars and couldn't afford to pay me, I'd just write it off as a business expense on my taxes. No way was I going to take that sweet, daft old lady to small-claims court.

Traffic finally let up, and McCarthy resumed speeding down the highway. He hit the button to roll down his window, then reconsidered and rolled it back up again.

"So who takes care of her accounts for her? Does someone have power of attorney?"

I hadn't given this question any thought. "I don't know, it could be Ruth, or maybe John, Ruth's son. That wouldn't surprise me."

"John, Ruth's son? Presumably the heir to Compton Hall? What's he all about?"

I tried to call up a mental image of John, whom I had met that one time after finding Professor Burbridge's body. A portly man in his fifties, professional looking, who had inquired about a cleaning service while a man lay dead in the library. He had been in the group three days later when the police revealed that the professor had been murdered. I remembered his sharp eyes evaluating me, as if I were a suspect in the killing. "I've only seen him twice. I don't even know what he does for a living. He lives down the street from Compton Hall."

McCarthy dodged past a car that was driving too slow for his liking. "Want me to check him out?"

"Sure, if you want." McCarthy had all the resources of the newspaper at his disposal. But I intended to check out John Ellis as well. All of a sudden I had a renewed interest in learning about the Ellis family, from Ruth's husband, the victim of arson, to the two sons, one of whom lived right down the road from the location of another unexplained death.

We heard the sirens as we neared downtown Laurel Springs. I almost expected McCarthy to speed up to get out of their way, but he pulled over like all the other law-abiding citizens to let the fire engines pass.

"It looks like they're heading for your neighborhood." He eased back onto the road and followed the fire engine.

A flash of fear swept over me at the sight of a thick plume of smoke rising from the direction of my street. I had witnessed a house fire once as a child, and it had made a deep impression on me. In high school chemistry I made my lab partners light the Bunsen burners, afraid that I might somehow start a conflagration that would burn down the building.

My fear intensified as we rounded the corner to see the fire trucks parked on the street in front of my house. I gripped McCarthy's arm. "Hurry!"

He angled into a spot on the street two houses down, and I was out of the car before the wheels stopped turning. I sprinted down the sidewalk, pushing past a firefighter unrolling a hose, to stop in front of my house.

The smoke and flames were coming from a pile of brush strewn across the front porch steps. It didn't look like any part of the porch structure had caught fire yet. Through the thick smoke I saw Aileen, barefoot in a black trench coat with a towel wrapped around her head, wielding a wimpy fire extinguisher on the blaze. There was no sign of Pete.

The firefighter instructed Aileen to go back into the house and come out the back door. When she disappeared, he turned his hose on the flaming pile. The volume of water quickly knocked down the flames, to my vast relief.

McCarthy came and stood next to me, an arm around my shoulder. "Looks like they'll get this under control pretty quickly." He squeezed me tight for a moment, and then pulled out his camera to document the scene in his own particular fashion.

I couldn't say a word. As the flames receded, I could see the pile of brush more clearly. Clearly enough to recognize my new Japanese maples that had been uprooted, thrown onto my porch steps and set on fire.

Chapter Twelve

It felt like a violation. I registered that Aileen had come out of the house to stand next to me, but I couldn't see her clearly through my tears.

Aileen, of course, did not indulge in tears. "What the hell is going on here, Daria? Who in this town is out to get us?"

I shook my head, swiping at my eyes. "Where's Pete?"

She pulled the towel off her wet hair. "He's not home from work yet. He's doing sixteen-hour days, remember?" She shook her head like a dog, sprinkling me with droplets of water. "I was having a shower before my gig tonight. Good thing I had the window open, or I'd have missed all the excitement."

We stood watching McCarthy circling around the porch, capturing every angle of my poor burnt-up Japanese maples. I pressed my lips together so I wouldn't start crying again. Pete and I had worked so hard to save those little trees from the dump, giving them a new lease on life in my front yard. It killed me to see them destroyed after all that.

A police cruiser drove up, and a middle-aged officer with a gleaming bald head got out and came over to me. I recognized him as Officer Carson, whom I had encountered at another crime scene a month ago.

"Daria Dembrowski," he said by way of greeting. He pulled out a small notebook and looked at me expectantly. "What happened here?"

I took a deep breath. "I don't know. I just got home to find the fire trucks here and my Japanese maples torn up and set on fire on my porch steps." I bit my lip and pointed at Aileen. "Aileen was home; maybe she saw something."

Aileen shook her head. "I was in the shower. I heard the fire crackling and smelled the smoke and ran out. Damn—I left the shower running!" She darted back into the house.

"The thing is, this isn't the first thing that's happened." I took another deep breath, and told Carson all about the eggs and the dead mice and the dark figure who tried to break into my house in the middle of the night. "I feel like someone is targeting us—but I don't know why. It could have something to do with Professor Burbridge's murder. I don't know."

Officer Carson took down everything I told him, and went on to interview Aileen when she came back outside. McCarthy finished photographing the smoldering pile and snapped a few shots of Aileen and me being questioned.

Carson clicked his notebook closed. "I'll be in touch."

"Wait!" I clutched him by the arm. "Do you think we're safe here in the house? What if something else happens?"

"Your brother still live here with you?" He glanced over at Aileen, who had slipped on combat boots when she came back outside. Her jet-black hair hung limp on her shoulders, not yet gelled into spikes all over her head. Carson gave a satisfied nod. "I'm guessing between the three of you, you can deal with this. The perp's not going for violence so much as intimidation."

"I'll intimidate him," Aileen growled.

I gave a somewhat shaky sigh. "Okay. We'll let you know if anything else happens." I watched Carson walk down the sidewalk and get back into his car. I was reassured by his faith that we could handle the situation, while at the same time I wished he had volunteered to stand watch over our house for the night.

"What time is it?" Aileen grabbed my wrist to look at my watch. "I gotta get ready for my gig!" She disappeared inside again, leaving McCarthy and me alone on the front porch.

"So when does Pete get back?" McCarthy poked at the pile of brush, turning over the sodden branches and spreading out some still smoldering spots.

"I don't know. He'll be late. They're in the middle of filming so he's looking at sixteen-hour days." I peered at the porch roof, noting some scorching on the red trim under the eaves.

"Do you have a shovel? It would be good to get this stuff off the porch steps and a little farther away from the house."

I went down to the basement and rousted out a shovel for him. Aileen was hauling her gear up from the basement. I liked to joke that it was her regular weight-lifting routine, but I stopped saying that when she suggested that the band could just take over the living room and then they wouldn't have to carry their amps and things up and down the basement stairs. I had no intention of sacrificing my living room to the Twisted Armpits. A little exercise was good for her, right?

"I'll be at Wexman's all evening," Aileen grunted, swinging a guitar in each hand. "You should get McCarthy to hang around until your brother gets home."

I'd had the same thought. I didn't relish the idea of being all alone in the big, creaky house for hours, and at the same time I didn't want to leave it vacant for some jerk of an arsonist to have another crack at it. But asking McCarthy to hang out at my house all evening had overtones of taking our relationship to a new level, one that I wasn't sure I was ready to explore. I shifted the shovel in my hand and turned to go outside, not at all sure what I was going to say to him.

I was saved by the unexpected sight of McCarthy greeting Fiona and Randall as they walked up to the front porch. I stared at them at a loss. I was pretty sure Fiona's fitting wasn't until tomorrow. I handed the shovel to McCarthy without a word.

Fiona threw me a smile. "Randy wanted to come along for my fitting. I told him he couldn't have even a peek at my wedding gown. Still, it was sweet of him to want to come along."

Randall stood by her side, the very picture of the solicitous bridegroom. He smiled lazily at me. "I'll be good." He watched McCarthy shoveling up the remains of the Japanese maples and tossing them into the front yard. "Funny place for a bonfire." He reached for the door handle.

I beat him to it. Bowing to the inevitable, I held the door wide and ushered the two of them inside. I truly didn't know if Fiona's fitting was scheduled for today or tomorrow, but after forgetting about her last one and making her wait for me, I decided to just go with it. Luckily I had done the work on her gown, so I was actually ready for her.

I hovered in the doorway for a minute. "Thanks for moving that stuff, Sean. I forgot that I've got this fitting this evening. Let me know what you find out about John Ellis."

He leaned on the shovel like a farmer spading his garden. "You gonna be okay here?"

I nodded with a quick glance over my shoulder. Fiona and Randall had disappeared inside the house. "I better get to work. Thanks again!" I ducked inside, both relieved and sorry that he wouldn't be hanging out at my house all evening.

I hastened to my fitting room, to find the couple examining the dolls I had displayed on the mantel. Every now and then I got to sew period doll clothes for a local church guild's fund-raiser auction, and I kept a few dolls to display sample dresses. Randall handled one of them, my favorite brunette with the soft curls, turning her around to examine the back of the dress. I could scarcely restrain myself from snatching her out of his hands.

"Randall, you can wait in the living room while we're working on Fiona's dress."

He bent to give Fiona a lingering kiss. "Have fun, my dear." He walked out of the room with a smirk on his lips.

The last thing I wanted was to have Randall on the loose in my house. I quickly pulled out Fiona's dress and pressed it into her hands. "Go ahead and get dressed. I'll be right back."

I walked noiselessly out to the living room, half hoping and half fearing to catch Randall snooping through the house. He had strayed into the hall, where he checked out the corners and lifted up the window bench to look inside. He eased the lid down slowly, so it wouldn't bang, no doubt. His eyes roved around the hall, resting on the framed photograph on the mantel. It was a close-up of a white rose that I'd taken with McCarthy's camera. It replaced a series of photos of Randall and me, laughing together on ice skates. They were taken several years ago by a college friend, back when Randall still allowed me to have friends. Without turning his head, he said, "I see you've changed the photos on the mantel."

I held my head high, wondering how long he'd known that I was watching him. "Those old photos? I couldn't relate to them anymore."

He turned to face me, crossing his arms and leaning against the door as if he had nothing to do all day but harass me. "You've changed, Daria."

Darn right I've changed! He wasn't going to find a submissive, starry-eyed pushover in this house anymore. "What do you want, Randall?"

He opened his eyes wide in a parody of innocence. "I'm not supposed to see my bride in her wedding gown before the wedding. You've banished me. I'm simply passing the time until her fitting is over." He turned his superior gaze on me. "Is her fitting over?"

I bit back a retort, and gritted my teeth under a smile. "Not yet. Please have a seat in the living room to wait for her." I held out my hand to indicate the living room, which he knew perfectly well how to find.

For an instant I thought he was going to refuse, and then we would be at an impasse. But he merely stood up and proceeded to the living room, where he lounged in an easy chair and pulled out his phone. Hoping that he would become immersed in the news, social media, or an addictive app, I hurried back to Fiona.

She had donned her dress and the white satin shoes she would wear at the ceremony, but she was unable to button up the back by herself. She clutched the strapless bodice to her chest, unable to move, no doubt, for fear that the weight of the flowing skirt would pull the whole thing off her.

I bit back a smile at her predicament, and buttoned up the back. "You'll need to have a bridesmaid help you dress on the big day." I checked the drape of the skirt in the front. Perfect! "Okay, here comes the hard part. You have to stand up straight and still while I pin up the hem." I surveyed the shining folds of satin. Actually, it would be a lot easier than Priscilla's period gown, because I only had to make sure that the front was the right length. The train could be off by as much as an inch without spoiling the look of anything.

Still, I anticipated that it would take a good half hour to get the hem pinned up. I couldn't leave Randall to his own devices for that long. I set the first panel's worth of pins and then scrambled to my feet. "It'll be just a minute, Fiona, I just need to run up to my workroom to get something."

"Okay. Could you check on Randy for me? I don't want him dying of boredom."

"Sure thing." I bustled out of the room, glad for Fiona's permission to do what I intended to do anyway. Slowing my steps so as not to make any noise, I slunk up to the door of the living room. It was empty.

I whirled to check the hall, but he had already cased that area of the house. After a quick check of the kitchen, I determined that he was not on the first floor of the house. Where would he go, upstairs or to the basement? I hesitated an instant, then ran up the stairs, trying not to make too much noise on their creaky treads. I had this horrible thought that he might be checking out my bedroom for some twisted old time's sake or something. If I found him in my bed, I was going to call the cops!

I scouted the hallway that ran down the middle of the second floor with bedrooms opening off it on both sides. No sign of Randall. I ran into my bedroom, which was Randall-free, and peeked out the window to see if Aileen had already left. Her red Ford with the flames painted on the hood was absent from its usual parking spot along the curb. McCarthy's bright yellow Mustang was also gone. A sleek dark blue sedan parked further down the street probably belonged to Fiona, unless Randall had gotten a new car since he ditched me. Either way, he wasn't outside getting something from the car. What could he possibly be doing sneaking around my house?

I practically ran out of my room, and collided with Randall in the narrow hallway. I gasped and staggered backward. He was emerging from the back stairs that led from the kitchen. He was so startled that he stepped backward as well, and would have fallen down the back stairs if I hadn't reached out and grabbed his forearm. I gripped his arm hard, resisting the temptation to dig in my fingernails.

"What are you doing up here?" I cried.

He shook off my hand and smoothed his rumpled shirt. "I was just looking for the bathroom." He turned as if to head down the hall to the bathroom.

I drew myself up as tall as possible, blocking his way. "I'm sorry, Randall, but I can't have clients ranging through my house while I'm in a fitting. In case you hadn't noticed in your prior inspection of the downstairs, there is a new powder room under the stairs for the use of my clients and their guests. I have to ask you to return downstairs and use those facilities."

Randall smiled down at me, clearly amused by my attempt to throw my petite weight around. "Your request is duly noted. But I don't think it should apply to me. I'm not a client or a guest, but former owner of this house." He took a step closer, backing me up against the wall. "If I want to use the upstairs bathroom like I used to do, I think I have a right to do so."

I ducked past him while still blocking his way to the bathroom. "You have no rights to this house or anything in it! You never owned this house—you moved in with *me*. I agreed to open a joint bank account with you, and look where that got me. But your name was never on the lease of this house, which is mine! If you don't want me to start screaming bloody murder for your fiancée to hear, you will turn around and walk down the main stairs and sit down in the living room and stay there until Fiona's fitting is finished." I glared at him, heart pounding, daring him to make a move so I could start hollering.

He must have believed I would do it, because he turned and stalked down the stairs without another word. I watched him go, then collapsed against the wall, breathing heavily. I wanted nothing more than to curl up in my bed and hide, but Fiona was downstairs waiting for me to quickly fetch something, and Randall was down there too, up to who knew what. I grabbed a random tape measure and hurried down the stairs.

A quick glance into the living room reassured me that Randall had complied with my demands. I hurried into my fitting room.

"I'm sorry, Fiona, I couldn't find my tape measure." I made a show of measuring the hem to the floor, while adding the rest of the pins as fast as I could.

"Perfect! I'll have the dress finished and ready for you to pick up next week." I unbuttoned each of the fourteen buttons in the back and steered Fiona to the curtained-off corner of my fitting room. "Go ahead and get changed. I'll be right back."

I stole out into the hall and peeked in the living room. Randall lounged in an easy chair, his eyes on his phone. I breathed a sigh of relief.

Fiona emerged a few minutes later, dressed in her street clothes. She entered the living room unnoticed by Randall, and leaned over his shoulder to hug him around the neck and drop a kiss on the top of his head. I looked away.

"The gown is so lovely, dear. You'll be amazed at what Daria can do."

He stowed his phone in his pocket and stood up. "We'd best be going." He linked his arm in hers and propelled her out the door without even a goodbye. Fiona waved over her shoulder, "See you next time!"

I closed the door behind them, locking it securely. I ran to the back door and checked the lock there as well. Then I climbed the back stairs to the second floor, retracing Randall's steps to make sure he hadn't set any booby traps or anything.

A loud grumble from my stomach reminded me that I hadn't had anything to eat since that delicious Philly cheesesteak at Franco's. I headed to the kitchen and rooted through the fridge, coming up with nothing better than some scrambled eggs and toast for supper. I filled Mohair's food bowl, and talked to her while she ate. Pete used to laugh at me for holding a conversation with my cat, but sometimes I felt like she was the only one I could be completely honest with. I wished she could talk back to me. Maybe she had seen where Randall went and what he was doing in my house.

"What do you think he wants, Mohair? Why did he come here today? He couldn't watch what Fiona and I were doing, so he obviously had some ulterior motive for accompanying her here. He wanted to see something in the house—something upstairs. The bathroom was a ruse. What could he have wanted to see?" I scratched behind her ears, and Mohair meowed appreciatively. But she had no answers to offer me. When she finished eating I scooped her up and carried her upstairs. I hid my face in her soft fur and whispered, "Fiona is such a sweet girl. Do you think she even knows about me and Randall? I can't stand seeing her in love with him. Remind me not to go to their wedding." Mohair purred in my arms.

I kept her with me the rest of the evening while I worked on the buttons on the back of Ruth's gown. I should have made button loops by hand, out of red thread to match the dress, but I didn't. Instead, I made regular buttonholes using my Bernina sewing machine. Definitely not authentic in any way, but I rationalized it with the thought that the filmmakers wouldn't be focusing on her back.

I had a hard time concentrating. First I turned the radio up loud to cover any noise from the creaky house; then I switched it off so I could hear if anything out of the ordinary was happening. I got up to check the door locks and peer into the darkening yard so many times that I probably walked five miles up and down the stairs.

Finally Ruth's eighteenth-century gown was finished. I hung it up in my fitting room as if it were a wedding dress, and pulled out my planner to take stock of my projects.

Once the hem was done, Fiona's gown would be finished. She hadn't talked to me about a veil or other headpiece. I didn't know if I wanted to bring it up or just leave her to figure that out for herself. Veils were always fun to make, with more room for creativity than most gowns. But I really wasn't interested in Randall accompanying Fiona again to hang around my house and snoop. I dropped the planner for another surreptitious scan of the yard. Nothing.

I shook myself and picked up the planner again. Priscilla's everyday gown was finished, as were the living room curtains at Compton Hall. Ruth's simple gown was done—all I had to do was deliver it. Cherry had talked of making a gown for Louise Pritchard. I was game, but I doubted if Louise was. I could check in with her tomorrow when I went to deliver Ruth's gown.

I plucked Fiona's wedding gown off the rack. I carried it into the living room and settled into an armchair to hem it while watching an old Fred Astaire movie. I needed some pleasant background entertainment while I worked on the mindless hem. I didn't want anything dramatic or suspenseful for tonight.

* * * *

I woke with a start, with Fiona's gown draped over me like a blanket. I had fallen asleep to the sound of Fred and Ginger dancing, and the movie was now over. Some noise had jerked me awake.

I kept perfectly still, listening. Just when I was about to write it off as nothing but nerves, I heard it again. It was a stealthy creaking, just outside the front door—the unmistakable sound of footsteps on the front porch.

I slid the dress off me and got up from the armchair. I crept to the kitchen doorway, where I could see the front door. The doorknob rattled. He was trying the front door! I slipped into the kitchen to pull a cast-iron skillet out of a bottom cupboard. I held it with both hands, hoping that the sight of it would be enough of a deterrent that I wouldn't have to really whack the intruder with it. I lurked in the kitchen doorway with beating heart as the handle turned and the front door swung slowly inward.

The intruder shined a flashlight in front of him, making it hard to see him clearly. He was tall, clearly a man. I couldn't tell if he wore a mask or gloves. He closed the door softly behind him, clicking the lock closed. I seized my chance while his back was turned, and jumped out of my hiding place, hollering at the top of my lungs, hoping to scare him off.

I scared him, all right. He yelled in response, spinning around and dropping his light with a clatter. With his back to the door he fumbled behind him and hit the light switch, to illuminate me advancing on him with upraised skillet.

"Back off, Daria!"

It was Pete.

The skillet fell to the floor with a loud thud. I doubled over in hysterical laughter, tears streaming down my face. Pete collapsed against the door, breathing hard. Then he slowly approached me, leaned down, and snatched up the cast-iron skillet to get it out of my reach. I laughed harder.

"What the hell was that? You almost gave me a heart attack."

I sank down to sit on the floor, trying to stop laughing. He stared down at me for a few minutes, then squatted down to my level. "Do you need a glass of water or a cup of coffee?"

I waved a hand in front of my face, struggling to get myself under control. "No, just... Yeah, water."

He disappeared into the kitchen, and came back with a glass of water and no skillet.

I gulped down a swallow, coughed and sputtered when it went down wrong, and wiped my eyes with my sleeve. "I heard you coming in.... I thought you were a burglar."

"I come in every night. I live here." Pete peered at me, clearly thinking I was cracking up in front of his eyes.

I took another swallow of water, and leaned back against the wall. "It's all these crazy things happening to the house. I came home this evening to find my new Japanese maples on fire on the front porch." Tears started to fall again as I thought of those lovely trees reduced to ashes on the lawn. "Then Randall came with Fiona for her fitting, and he was snooping around upstairs. I don't know why." I started shivering, and hugged my arms around my body. "What if somebody tries to break in tonight, while we're sleeping?"

"Well, they better run, 'cause you'll bean them with a honking big frying pan! What were you planning to do with that thing? If you hit me over the head with that, I'd be as dead as your professor."

I dropped my head in my hands. "I'm sorry, Pete. I'm kinda freaking out. It was so sad to see those Japanese maples all burned up."

He pulled a sweater off the coatrack hanging on the wall and draped it over my shoulders. He sat down on the floor next to me and leaned back against the wall. "Who set them on fire, do you think?"

I shook my head. "The murderer? I don't know."

"Do you think it was Randall?"

"Randall, a murderer? I just don't know. I'm starting to wonder if it's all connected. Ruth's husband died in an arson fire seven years ago. Is that where this was heading tonight?"

Pete leaned his head back against the wall. "I am so tired. The fire's out, the house didn't burn down, and you didn't kill me with a frying pan. I say we go to bed and figure it all out in the morning."

"I won't sleep a wink."

He heaved himself to his feet. "Fine. I will." He reached out his hand and pulled me to my feet. Then we both froze at the sound of a number of cars roaring up the street to stop in front of our house. Doors slammed and people called out, despite the late hour. Several people stomped up the porch steps and milled about on the porch.

I looked at Pete, wide-eyed. He rolled his own eyes heavenward. "It's Aileen, Daria. She lives here too. Try not to freak out on me, okay?"

Aileen flung open the door to admit her bandmates, all four of them, at going on one o'clock in the morning. She took in the sight of Pete and me in a glance. "You guys are still up? Scared of the bogeyman, aren't you?"

"I'm just scared of the big black frying pan, but that's beside the point." Pete greeted Pinker and Corgi and the gang. "How was the gig?"

Aileen spoke for the band, as usual. "The sound system sucked and the crowd petered out by ten thirty, but that's what you get with a midweek gig." She frowned at Pete. "Don't you have to be at work by six a.m., Moron?"

He nodded toward me. "Daria was worrying about intruders."

I glared at him. But for once, Aileen didn't scoff at me.

"Yeah, that's what the guys are here for." She indicated the band members, who seemed to be unpacking their gear in the hall and living room. "We're gonna keep watch all night. Don't worry, we'll mute the amps."

I started to laugh, mercifully without hysteria. "Thanks, Aileen. Nobody's going to break in to the middle of a metal band rehearsal."

"Damn straight!"

I chuckled all the way upstairs. Mute or no mute, I could still hear the band wailing away downstairs. For once it was music to my ears. I snuggled into bed and fell right to sleep.

I slept late the next morning. By the time I straggled downstairs for breakfast, both Pete and the Twisted Armpits had gone. Aileen sat at the kitchen table hunched over a supersized cup of coffee and a bowl of yogurt topped with bacon bits and jalapeño peppers. I stifled a gag and poured my own coffee. "Did you guys play all night?"

"Nah, we quit about five thirty. Then we played poker till seven, so I guess you could say we played all night." She yawned and took a huge slurp of coffee. "No funny business, as far as I could tell."

"Good." I sat down next to her with a bowl of oatmeal, studiously avoiding the sight of her so-called breakfast. "I'm going to be out and about today. Do you think everything will be okay here?"

She shrugged and scratched her spiky head with both hands. "I'm gonna hang out, but I might go to bed at some point. We could set up some booby traps, if you want."

"What, like tossing a bunch of dead mice across the front porch to keep the bad guys out?"

She grinned. "It's worth a shot."

"There is no way I'm throwing dead mice all over my own porch, Aileen!"

She laughed at me. "Careful not to lose your sense of humor over this, Daria."

I glared at her for a beat. "Whatever."

She got up and threw her bowl into the sink. "That's my line."

Chapter Thirteen

I left Aileen to hang out or go to sleep, although I doubted she'd ever sleep again after I watched her refill her gigantic coffee cup.

Whatever.

I knew I should head straight for Compton Hall to deliver Ruth's gown, but I had one stop to make first. I set out on foot for the public library.

The Laurel Springs Public Library, built on Main Street in the 1820s, was one of the oldest surviving buildings in the downtown area. Its massive front steps flanked by Corinthian columns led to a surprisingly small interior, most notable for its domed ceiling. The bookshelves were arranged in a curve to mirror that impressive dome. The original building had been added on to, as had most buildings in the area. Small alcoves rayed out from the center like arms on a starfish, each one housing a different collection of books. I sought out the local history section.

I had browsed through some articles about the Compton family that I'd found online, but I felt like I needed more information. I knew the library had an extensive collection of materials on Major Samuel Compton and his illustrious descendants. I wasn't sure exactly what I was looking for, but I had a feeling I would recognize it when I saw it.

I spent a good hour searching through books, maps, and newspaper articles on the Compton line, but nothing jumped out at me. I laid my head down on the table like I used to do at college when I needed a quick nap before an exam. What question was I trying to answer here?

I thought about the smoldering pile of maple branches on my front porch, and the bucket of warm ashes in the basement at Compton Hall. I had handled the mortuary urn containing the ashes of the late Thurman Ellis, who had died in a house fire that was deliberately set. I didn't know why, but I had the feeling that his death was part of the story that was unfolding even now. I needed to find out what happened at the Ellis home in Philadelphia seven years ago.

I raised my head to see Mrs. Wirdle advancing on me. Mrs. Wirdle had been the librarian at the Laurel Springs Public Library for the past three hundred years, or so my friends and I thought when we were kids. We called her Mrs. Birdie, and took care to keep her from overhearing our conversations or seeing anything we wrote. She knew everything that went on in our small town, and she wasn't shy about passing this information on to our parents when she thought the kids of Laurel Springs were out of control. Even now, the sight of Mrs. Wirdle approaching was enough to make me sit up and hastily close all the books surrounding me.

"There's no sleeping in the library," she announced in that stern voice I remembered from seventh grade. Her beady eyes took in the books I'd collected. "Interested in the Compton family's history, are we?"

I stacked the books into one tidy pile. "I am. I'm also interested in the Ellis family, specifically Thurman Ellis. He met a terrible fate, didn't he?"

She pursed her lips, no doubt trying to decide if she should throw me out or help me with my research. I could almost see the scholar and the disciplinarian warring within her. I tried to help her out.

"I was looking for pictures of his house, both before the fire and pictures of the blaze. But I'm having a hard time figuring out how to access the newspaper archives."

Mrs. Wirdle frowned at the laptop I held out to her. She rummaged through the bookshelf and pulled out a thin volume titled *Notable Homes in Philadelphia: From the 1700s to the Present*. A quick glance told me that the "present" was 1960 or so. Mrs. Wirdle leafed through the book until she found the page she wanted. She held it out to me, pointing a bony finger at "Fig. 37: 'Delphos,' home of the investment banker Charles Ellis." The black-and-white photograph taken in 1924 showed a stately three-story mansion built of light-colored bricks, with fanciful turrets framing the roofline. Graceful elms arched over the grand front entrance. The photograph showed both carriages and vintage cars pulled up in the circular drive.

"Delphos was among the notable mansions in the Fairmount Park area of Philadelphia," Mrs. Wirdle recited. "It belonged to Thurman Ellis's grandfather Charles. It passed down to Charles's son Robert, and then to Thurman after him. Thurman's eldest son, also named Robert, normally would have inherited the mansion upon Thurman's death, but after everything that happened, the legacy passed on to John, the second son. Although John was unable to inherit, of course, due to the complete destruction of the structure in the fire seven years ago."

She flipped through the pages, showing me pictures of the interior of Delphos. "The house was renovated in 1957, when the north turret was removed in favor of a gabled roof. Then in 1989 the entire house was rewired to reduce the risk of fire by removing outdated electrical connections. Of course, no rewiring could protect the house from arson." She turned a final page, a look of profound sadness on her face at the thought of such beauty destroyed by fire. I could sympathize with her feelings on that one.

I skimmed the captions accompanying the photos. There was no mention of any renovations to the house, and of course any work that was done in 1989 would not have been included in this volume from the sixties. I looked up at Mrs. Wirdle's wrinkled face leaning over my shoulder. "How do you know about the different renovations on the house?"

She clicked her tongue. "I am a librarian, young lady. Knowledge is my calling." She reached for my laptop. "The library has online access to the archives of the Philadelphia *Inquirer*. You can read the news articles about the fire there." She pulled up the *Inquirer* website and keyed in a password with fingers too fast for me to follow. She returned the laptop to me. "If you need anything else, feel free to inquire." Leaving me with that play on words, she bustled off to poke another sleeping library patron.

I scrolled through the first article on the fire, which featured a full-color photograph of Delphos completely engulfed by flames. The news story detailed the discovery of the fire in the middle of the night. By the time a neighbor called for help, the entire mansion was involved. Seventy-three firefighters battled in the predawn hours to check the blaze, but it wasn't until after noon the following day before the fire was sufficiently out to allow them to enter the residence. They found the remains of Thurman Ellis in his bedroom, overcome by smoke and subsequently buried by falling debris. They searched the entire house for Ruth, finally giving her up for dead as well. Then she appeared on the scene, alive and well and telling a story about having an argument with her husband and leaving in the middle of the night to stay in a hotel.

As alibis go, this was pretty lame, which is one reason that the jury acquitted her of her husband's death in the end. I skimmed through subsequent newspaper articles that detailed the sensational murder trial of Ruth Ellis. The jury concluded that if she had wanted to get away with killing her husband, she was clever enough to come up with a better alibi than a domestic argument, which would immediately focus suspicion on her.

I looked back at the pictures of the rooms in Delphos, trying to imagine the argument, Ruth stalking off in the middle of the night to end up at a hotel, Thurman going to bed, never to awaken again. According to the newspaper articles, someone had poured an accelerant along the foundation in several different places, igniting all of them to ensure that the mansion burned to the ground. The damage was not quite that extensive, but the remaining structure had to be torn down. To this day, nothing had been rebuilt on the site of Delphos.

I found one article that crossed the line from factual reporting to speculation. The writer was fascinated with questions of insurance, both life insurance for Thurman Ellis, and insurance on the mansion. He appeared to share McCarthy's philosophy on journalism, as in asking a slew of obnoxious questions to ferret out all the intimate details. This reporter had interviewed lawyers at Flint, Perkinson and Hubbard, claims adjusters at Founding Fathers Insurance, as well as John Ellis and finally Ruth herself. His analysis of these interviews ran for seven paragraphs, and included a detailed family tree of the Ellis line starting with Charles Ellis who built Delphos in 1897. The mansion passed down in a direct line to the eldest son in each generation, and was worth at least 3.5 million dollars. It was insured against fire, with an insurance payout estimated at just shy of five million dollars, once the furnishings, jewelry, and art were taken into consideration. All insurance payments went into the estate of Thurman Ellis, bypassing Ruth, who was on trial for murder at the time that the claims were settled. Likewise, Thurman's life insurance payment reverted to the estate, for fear that a murderer might benefit from her crime. When Ruth was acquitted of his death, she chose to leave the estate intact for her heirs, and moved to Laurel Springs to live with her sister Priscilla at Compton Hall.

I absorbed this information, reflecting on the fact that no arsonist had ever been identified. A quick check of the newspaper archives revealed that there were no news reports since the conclusion of Ruth's trial. I wondered if that meant that the police still thought she had done it, even if they couldn't get a conviction. Or maybe they had transferred the case to the cold case file, which was humorous in a twisted kind of way.

I closed the computer with a sigh. I didn't know what I had learned, beyond the facts that Thurman Ellis had died in a house fire and Ruth had been acquitted of his murder. But I already knew that.

I piled up the books I had pulled off the shelves. Mrs. Wirdle had dropped off another one, *Who's Who in Pennsylvania*. I paged through the Compton section, which had a long section on Major Samuel Compton and smaller paragraphs on his more anonymous descendants. Priscilla and Ruth were the sole surviving members of the Compton line, which would die out when they passed away. Presumably they owned Compton Hall, the family homestead. I wondered if Priscilla was legal owner as the older sister, or if Ruth had part or full ownership given the fact that she had a husband and sons. Either way, I wondered if John Ellis would inherit Compton Hall at their passing.

I flipped to the Ellis section. *Who's Who in Pennsylvania* was not interested in relating scandal. Thurman Ellis's death was merely mentioned as an "accidental death in a house fire," and no mention was made of Ruth's trial. A paragraph on John Ellis detailed his wedding to Collette Flaherty in 1990, and listed his occupation as banker, like his great-grandfather Charles. Evidently he had no children. I looked for the corresponding paragraph on Robert. There was none.

Suddenly I felt like I needed to know what happened to Robert Ellis. Priscilla had mentioned him a couple of times, in such a way that led me to think that some tragedy had befallen him. Mrs. Wirdle had just said something about after all that had happened, John was in line to inherit Delphos rather than Robert, the eldest son. What had become of Robert?

I flipped my computer open again and searched for Robert Ellis in Pennsylvania. The name was too common to allow me to zero in on Ruth's son. I went to the Philadelphia *Inquirer*'s website, but I needed the password again to access the archives. I gave a sigh of frustration—my forte was historical fashion design and construction, not historical research on the computer. I got up in search of Mrs. Wirdle.

She sat at her desk, scrolling through something on her desktop computer. I got enough of a glimpse to see that she was playing poker, of all things. I could scarcely contain my amusement.

"Excuse me, Mrs. Wirdle, could you get me back into the Philadelphia *Inquirer*'s website?"

She frowned as if I were a pesky fourth grader asking a question that I should have figured out for myself. "You should have gotten all the information you needed the first time."

"I know." I tried to keep my tone contrite, in the hopes that she would favor me with her assistance. I felt like I was channeling McCarthy, master of the art of winning people over. I smiled apologetically. "I realized that I wanted to look up Robert Ellis, to see what happened to him. There's no mention of him in the *Who's Who* book that you found for me."

Mrs. Wirdle stood up and dusted her hands briskly. "Of course not. Robert Ellis is not a notable person in Pennsylvania."

I walked with her back to my table. "Whatever happened to him?" She turned to me, incredulous. "You don't know the story of Robert Ellis?"

I shook my head. "Can you tell me?"

She leaned over my laptop and keyed in the password again. It would be simpler for us both if she wrote it down on a piece of paper for me, but I could tell that wasn't going to happen.

"Robert Ellis was a wild child. He grew up in Philadelphia, but he and his brother would spend the fall semester in Laurel Springs with their aunt Priscilla while their parents traveled. I remember him coming in here during school hours, trying to persuade me that he was doing research for English class when it was obvious that he was only looking for a warm place to hang out while skipping school. This was when he was ten or eleven years old, mind you. When he was a teenager he found other, more unsavory, places to go."

She stood up, folding her arms on her chest. "Poor Priscilla Compton tried to keep him in line, but she had no idea how to control him." She let that statement hang in the air a moment, as if to say that she herself could have whipped young Robert into shape if only Priscilla had consulted her. "Whenever he went back to Philadelphia to live with his family, he would engage in epic battles with his father over friends, grades, his truant behavior: everything that means something in the life of an adolescent. Things came to a head when he graduated from high school. Yes, he did graduate, partly because he was a gifted scholar, and partly because his father's prominence ensured that he be given however many second chances he needed to complete his high school diploma. But Robert wasn't appreciative of his father's efforts on his behalf. He walked across the stage at graduation, went home, and had a monumental fight with his father. It ended with Robert collecting his belongings and his father's car keys, and disappearing. It was easier to disappear in 1979 than it is today. Robert Ellis vanished without a trace."

She searched in the *Inquirer* archives page and brought up an article dated June 10, 1979. She stood beside me as I zipped through the article. The reporter touched on Robert's juvenile delinquent past and the fight on graduation night that brought police to Delphos late at night. Neither Ruth nor Thurman would speak with the press, and the police couldn't comment since Robert was still a minor, so the reporter could only speculate as to the cause of the disagreement. But the results were obvious. Thurman and Ruth couldn't stop the publication of photographs of the smashed windows along the front of the house. Mrs. Wirdle pointed to a photo of a cracked garden gnome on the floor of the living room surrounded by splintered glass. "This picture won a prize at the Chester County Fair later that summer. Juanita Featherow wanted to win a more prestigious journalism prize, but she had to settle for purely local recognition."

A glance at the photo credit confirmed that it had indeed been taken by Juanita Featherow. I looked up at the librarian with awe. "Did you know her too?"

She bristled. "I told you, knowledge is my calling. Of course I knew her." Her lips curved in a secret smile. "I know you too, if it comes to that, Daria Dembrowski. You acted in all the plays in high school, even though you never got the leading role. Your brother played basketball and hung out with a rough crowd, smoking marijuana on street corners. He took off for Hollywood after college, but now he's back in town with no screen credits to his name. He could have gone the way of Robert Ellis, if it comes to that, but he didn't." She paused triumphantly. "Please give him my regards when you get home this evening."

I could only nod, feeling like the woman at the well in the Bible when Jesus told her everything she'd ever done. I had no idea this ancient woman was keeping tabs on me and my family to this day!

Finally I found my voice. "Do you know what caused that big fight between Robert Ellis and his father?"

Her elation faded. "His parents never spoke about the incident. I did hear that they hired a private investigator to find him, but that individual was unsuccessful. Then three years later the car turned up in New Jersey, crashed into a ditch, but there was no trace of Robert. His parents had him declared legally dead, although his body was never found. Thus his younger brother John was in line to inherit Delphos when it went up in smoke."

"Thank you for all your help, Mrs. Wirdle. I'll remember you whenever I can't find the answers to my questions." And I meant it.

I left the library with a lot to think about, but no more time to spend on it. I needed to deliver Ruth's gown, and find out if there was any more sewing I needed to do for the TV filming. It wasn't until I was already out the door and halfway home that I realized I should have asked Mrs. Wirdle what she knew about Professor Burbridge's death. She was such a font of knowledge, otherwise known as a busybody, that I felt sure she could tell me something I didn't know about the professor. Next time.

I grabbed a quick lunch at home, after carefully checking to be sure that nothing untoward had happened to the house while I was gone. The only thing I found was Aileen, fast asleep on the living room couch with Mohair curled up on her shoulder. I backed out of the room without making a sound.

After lunch I bundled up Ruth's red gown and slung my bag over my shoulder. I made sure to bring along a tape measure and other sewing implements, in case Cherry persisted in wanting me to make a period costume for Louise.

I sent a text to McCarthy during the bus ride to Compton Hall—"Let me tell you about Robert Ellis...."—and then switched my phone to "Do Not Disturb." I enjoyed tantalizing the guy, I guess.

Chapter Fourteen

The bus let me off down the street from Compton Hall. As I approached the house, I saw Priscilla dozing in her rocker on the porch. I decided not to disturb her.

I saw Jamison Royce working by the side of the house. I waved and walked over to speak to him. He was on his knees by the flower border, digging small holes a few inches apart from each other.

"What are you doing?"

He sat back on his heels and looked up at me. "You sound like that TV woman, always asking me what I'm up to. I expected you to shove a camera in my face."

I laughed. "She does that to me too. Actually, I have a question for you. I was wondering if you have any more of Priscilla's Japanese maples, or did they all go to the dump?"

He turned back to his digging. "All gone. Why, did you want another one?"

I nodded. "I picked up a couple the other night and planted them by my front porch. But someone came by, in broad daylight, even, and tore them up and set them on fire. It broke my heart to see those lovely trees all burned up."

"Bummer." Royce picked up a flat of petunias and started pressing them into the holes he'd dug. "Sorry I can't help you, but I carted that whole load off to the dump. They'll be shoring up the landfill by now." He shrugged and kept working his way down the row. The sun shone on his peculiar work hat with the flaps pulled down to cover his ears. I didn't see how he could stand to wear that hat on these hot summer days. Maybe he was particularly sensitive about going bald, or had some kind of problem with his ears. But I was not Randall, so I resolved not to call attention to his unusual headwear.

"Okay, thanks for letting me know. Say, do you know where Miss Ruth is, by any chance?"

He shrugged again, still busy with his petunias. "Haven't seen her," he grunted.

I left him alone with his plants.

As I walked away, I reflected on how odd it was that Jamison Royce felt no sadness or distress of any kind over the fate of those beautiful Japanese maples. The news that they had been burnt to a crisp didn't touch him at all. For a man whose life was devoted to caring for plants, he showed a surprising lack of devotion to them. Maybe it was just a job to him. I thought of the fierce passion that Mrs. Wirdle brought to her job as a librarian, asserting that knowledge was her calling. She had dedicated her whole life to the public library, and would certainly never retire until she was physically unable to look up one more title or shush another patron. I wondered how long Jamison Royce had been in the business of caring for plants.

I pulled out my phone and typed in "Laurel Landscape Arts," but came up with nothing. I tried a couple of different searches to try to locate his business online, but was not able to find it. *He must promote his business through word of mouth or local advertising only.* That was unusual these days. I wondered how Priscilla had found out about him. Of course, online advertising would be unlikely to reach Priscilla Compton, that lover of a bygone way of life.

I found myself chuckling as I walked up the front porch steps. Priscilla still dozed in her chair, so I left her alone.

The furious voice of Carl Harper assaulted me as I passed the open kitchen door on my way inside. I peeked in just to check—yup, he was on his phone. He made no attempt to tone down his volume, so I could reasonably conclude that the call was not private, right? I paused in the doorway to listen.

"Listen, you have got to go through with this job! If they decide to come after us, it's not me that's gonna take the heat. Your neck will be on the chopping block. Got it?" He paused a moment to listen. "No! I won't put up with that! If you back out, I will make your life a living hell." Another pause while the caller shouted something at Harper. I could almost make out the words. Harper hollered back, "Go to hell!" and threw his phone across the room. I ducked out of the doorway and practically ran down the hall to get away from him. In his present mood, I doubted that my glib conclusion that his conversation was not private would mollify him in the slightest.

But what did it mean? Harper was in contact with someone—in cahoots, one could argue. This someone was reluctant to go through with a job, and Harper feared that "they" would come after the two of them. Could that job be a hit? Was Harper soliciting another murder, and his cohort was reluctant to pull the trigger? Maybe he was talking about Noah! I pulled out my phone and turned it back on to find thirteen texts from McCarthy, as well as a missed call from him. But I didn't have time for McCarthy right now.

I started typing a text message to Noah, and then abandoned it and dialed his number. I let it ring ten times, but it never went to voice mail. I took that as an ominous sign, and texted him to call me right away. I closed my eyes, willing my phone to ring, but nothing happened.

Several deep breaths later, I concluded that I would just have to go about my business while waiting to hear from Noah. I shook out Ruth's red gown and draped it over my arm. "Ready or not, here I come," I whispered to myself, and headed up the stairs to find Ruth to deliver her dress.

Ruth's bedroom door was ajar. I knocked firmly. There was no answer. Since the door was open, I decided to go on in and leave the gown on the bed or over a chair, and be done with it. I pushed the door wide.

Ruth lay crumpled on the floor, her gold-tipped cane flung far from her outstretched hand. I ran to kneel beside her, my heart thudding. She was barely breathing—at least she wasn't dead. But she wasn't conscious, either. I stood up without touching her and ran to the doorway. "Help! Somebody, help!" I pulled out my phone and dialed 911, feeling a bewildering sense of déjà vu as I advised the dispatcher that I needed help for an elderly woman who was unconscious on the floor.

Randall appeared in the doorway while I was still on the phone. He took in the sight of Ruth crumpled up on the floor, and knelt beside her unresponsive form.

I finished my call and knelt down beside him.

"You called 911?" His face was unusually pale. I hoped he wasn't going to faint on me.

I nodded. "The paramedics are on their way. They told me not to touch her unless I needed to." I could hear the sirens coming already.

A moment later, a team of paramedics hustled into the room, followed by both Carl Harper and Jamison Royce. The two men started at the sight of Ruth unconscious on the floor. They both edged back out of the room to whisper together in the hall outside. I stood off to one side, shivering as I watched the paramedics working on Ruth. Randall stood silent by my side, clearly moved by the gravity of the situation. All of a sudden he put his hands on my shoulders and drew me close to him. I leaned back against his chest and closed my eyes, drinking in the comfort of the moment. Just for an instant it was as if we were still together, still a couple, still in love.

But that wasn't reality.

I eased myself out of his embrace and took a step or two away from him. "I'd better go tell Priscilla what's going on." I ducked out of the room before Randall could say a word.

I ran down the stairs, cursing myself for taking the chicken way out, but not knowing what else to do. I didn't want to think about Randall right now.

I headed for the front porch, where I'd last seen Priscilla dozing in her favorite rocker. Incredibly, she was still there sleeping, despite the flashing lights from the ambulance and fire truck that were pulled up to the front door. How could she still be asleep? Suddenly fear gripped me, and I ran to her side. I shook her shoulder gently, calling her name. I couldn't believe my relief when she opened her eyes and said, "Is there something you wanted, dear?"

I took a deep breath, trying to calm the beating of my heart before delivering the bad news. I took her hand in both of mine. "Ruth fell in her room upstairs. She's unconscious. The paramedics have to take her to the hospital."

Priscilla stared at me, a disconcerting stare, as if she were having trouble focusing in on my face. "But Ruth is taking a nap, my dear."

I pressed her hand. "No, she's unconscious."

Priscilla frowned, an expression I'd never seen on her face before. "She said she was going to take a nap. Are you sure she's not just sleeping?"

"I'm sure. See, the paramedics are bringing her out now."

I helped her to her feet, and we stood together by the porch railing to watch Ruth being loaded into the ambulance on a gurney.

"She wasn't just sleeping, was she?" Priscilla's mournful face tugged at my heartstrings.

I put my arm carefully around her shoulders. "No, she wasn't. But the paramedics will take good care of her. I'm sure she'll be okay." I wasn't sure of any such thing, but Priscilla looked so forlorn that I had to say something hopeful.

Together we watched the ambulance doors closing. It drove off with a blare of sirens.

Priscilla lowered herself back into the rocking chair. She swayed gently back and forth in her rocker, like she had throughout my entire childhood.

She focused in on the children across the street making a fort for their dolls with tree branches.

"Look, my dear. Those girls must have torn those branches off my Japanese maples. I wish they would leave the poor trees alone."

I looked. Indeed, the branches looked like they came from Priscilla's Japanese maples. The two little girls probably gathered them up from the street or the side of the house, or asked Jamison Royce for them. "I bet you miss your Japanese maples, Miss Priscilla."

Priscilla craned her neck to look at the garden in the front of the house. "All the maples are gone," she said, in a voice of incredulity. "How could those tiny girls have done that?"

"You had Jamison Royce take them out, remember? For the TV show?" I sure hoped that she remembered, and that she had authorized their removal in a moment of lucidity. I would hate to think that this entire TV show renovation nightmare was done without the informed consent of the owner of the house!

"Oh, yes," Priscilla said, her voice vague and uncertain. "I suppose he will put them all back when this whole thing is over."

"I suppose so." Though of course he wouldn't put them back. Those trees were turning to mulch at the dump right now. But if I had anything to say about it, Jamison Royce would plant new Japanese maples in their place.

Priscilla leaned back in her chair and gave a tremulous sigh. "Ruth will hate it at the hospital."

I forced a gay smile. "Oh, you know Ruth. She'll probably start bossing all the nurses around, insisting on different food and telling them to stand up straight and address her as 'ma'am.'"

Priscilla's face broke into a delighted smile. "That's Ruth, all right. You'll go visit her there, won't you, my dear. I would go, but I don't think I can make it. Say you'll go see her for me!"

What could I say? "Sure, I'll go visit her this evening. I'll let you know how she's doing. Shall I fetch Louise to come sit with you for a while?"

She nodded, a faraway look in her eyes. "Ask her to bring some letter paper. I might want to write a letter to Robby."

She might be better off calling John. I wondered if someone at the hospital would contact him, or if I should ask Louise to do that. I left Priscilla on the porch and went in search of Louise. Odd that she hadn't shown up when the ambulance and paramedics were here for Ruth.

I expected I'd have to search high and low for Louise. I started with her bedroom. The door was closed, but I could hear someone moving around inside. I knocked, and then pushed open the door without waiting for an answer. Louise was bending over her bed. She had two hard-sided suitcases open on the bed, and was feverishly shoving wadded up clothes into them. I stopped in the doorway.

"Louise. What's going on?"

She whirled to face me. "What are you doing here? Get out of my room."

I stepped inside and closed the door behind me. "Are you going somewhere?"

"Don't come near me!" Louise clutched a sweater to her breast like a shield. "If you come one step closer, I'll scream bloody murder."

I stopped and held out my hands, hoping to calm her down. "I'm not going to hurt you. What's the matter? Why are you packing like this?"

Her frantic eyes scanned my whole body, and then she suddenly turned back to the bed. She must have decided that I wasn't a threat. She shoved clothes into the suitcases faster than ever.

I watched her in some confusion. Clearly something had upset her badly. I could only imagine that Ruth's situation played into her distress, if she even knew what had happened to Ruth. I watched her closely as I said, "Could you come down and sit with Miss Priscilla for a while? She's upset after what happened to Ruth."

"Upset, is she? Of course she's upset! She thinks she'll be next." She flung open a desk drawer and searched through the papers inside.

"Which is why she needs you, Louise. You take care of her and will be there for her if something happens." I'd always thought that the saddest part about growing old was watching the people around you, your peers, falling ill and dying. The fear that you might be next must haunt all elderly people.

Louise paused in her frenetic packing to throw me a look of scorn tempered by fear. "I won't be here. I'm leaving. I won't be next, I'm telling you that right now!"

I stared at her. "What are you talking about?"

"I'm talking about murder. What else?"

"Murder?"

She threw her armload of clothes down on the bed with a grunt. "Murder. Here, in this house. First Professor Burbridge, and now Miss Ruth. There's no telling who will be next. But it's not going to be me!"

I shook my head, baffled. "Ruth wasn't murdered. Last I saw, she was alive, and I'm expecting she'll stay that way, since she's been taken to the hospital. She fell. That's what happens to old people."

Louise turned to face me, both hands on her hips. "Oh, you're so smart, are you, missy? Well, let me tell you about that Ruth Ellis. She walks with a cane so she doesn't fall. Other than that, she's in perfect health and her doctor says she'll live to be a hundred. She's so ornery that she'd never just keel over from a heart attack or a stroke. She was on that floor because somebody tried to kill her. Just like Professor Burbridge. I'd bet my life on it." She leaned on the top of one suitcase, trying to get it to close. "Well. They're not going to get their chance at me. I'm getting out of here."

I stared at her, the image of Ruth on the floor floating before my eyes. Was there anything suspicious about the way she was lying, or any blood or evidence of a blow to the head like with the professor? I couldn't think of anything. But Louise's words had the possibility of truth in them, all the same. She had been right about the professor, suspecting that his death was more sinister than a simple heart attack. Could she be right about Ruth as well? Had somebody tried to kill her?

"If this is true, what do you think happened?"

"Poison. I'd bet my week's wages that she was drugged with something to make her fall asleep. She was standing up when it hit so she fell over. If it was a big enough dose, it could have killed her straight out. Who would think twice about an old lady over seventy dropping dead one day? But that ornery old lady didn't actually die. It would be interesting to hear her side of the story. But I won't be sticking around to find out." She clicked her other suitcase closed and dragged both of them off the bed. "I'm out of here."

I caught her arm. "You can't leave. If this is true, Miss Priscilla needs you here to protect her."

"You stay and protect her. I'm leaving to protect myself."

I positioned myself between her and the door. "Louise, think. If this was attempted murder and you leave now, the police will surely suspect you. You could have easily poisoned Ruth. If you leave, you will look guilty."

"Are you saying you think I did it? How dare you!"

"No, I'm saying the police will think you did it, and they'll start looking for you. Is that what you want, to get arrested by the cops?"

Louise sank down on the bed. "I want to save my life, that's what I want."

The sight of her terrified face unnerved me. I didn't know what to tell her.

"How about this? You call the police and tell them your suspicions. Then you can leave after that, and they can keep Miss Priscilla safe."

"So who's going to keep me safe? You?" She picked up her phone even as she talked. "You realize, of course, that the murderer is most likely in the house, right now. No one who doesn't belong here has come in or out of the house all day."

Chapter Fifteen

I ran down to check on Priscilla while Louise placed her call to the police. Priscilla still sat in her rocker, gliding gently back and forth, back and forth. With her long white hair bound up in a chignon at the base of her neck and wearing the lavender gown that I'd made her, she was the very picture of an eighteenth-century grand dame. I wished McCarthy were here to do a portrait of her.

I paused in the doorway and pulled out my phone. He'd stopped trying to contact me after those thirteen texts and one missed call. He must have figured, correctly, that I knew he was trying to get in touch with me and would respond at some point. I started keying in his number, and then I hesitated. Did I really want him here when the police arrived to question the entire household yet again on the suspicions of a nearly hysterical caregiver? Now that I was out of the room and free from Louise's presence, I felt more and more dubious about her suspicions. Poor Priscilla, who was already upset about Ruth's condition, would be even more discombobulated at the suggestion that someone had tried to kill Ruth. Couldn't she be spared that, especially if the suspicions were unfounded?

I went back upstairs to find Louise just ending her call.

"What did they say?"

She tucked her phone into her pocket in disgust. "They took my name and number and listened to what I had to say. They said they wanted to check with the hospital and see how Miss Ruth was and talk to her before they sent someone over here. They needed more evidence that a crime had actually been committed." She sat down heavily on the bed. "They said they'd be by later today or maybe tomorrow to talk to me. Sounds like I can't leave after all. Even if I quit my job, I'll still need to be here to talk to the cops. I might as well keep collecting my paycheck through this whole thing." She glared at me, as if I were the root of all her problems. "You got your wish."

"Tell you what. If you stay here and protect Priscilla in case there's any danger, I'll go to the hospital and see what Ruth has to say about what happened to her. I told Priscilla I would visit her."

Louise nodded, accepting defeat. "Come back here after you talk to Ruth."

I stopped to say goodbye to Priscilla on the way to the bus stop. "I'm going to check on Ruth now. I'll let you know how she's doing."

She grasped my hand. "Thank you so much dear. Tell Ruth I'm thinking of her."

As I walked down the driveway to the bus stop, I saw Randall come out of the house. He headed for his car without noticing me. He carried a bulky bundle in his arms. No one could mistake it for a briefcase—it was wrapped in a cloth and he carried it with both hands as if it were quite heavy. Just what was Randall carrying out of Compton Hall?

I almost accosted him to ask that very question, but the sight of the Number Two bus approaching made me change my mind. If I missed this one, I would have to wait another forty-five minutes for the next bus. I abandoned Randall to his bundle and climbed the bus steps.

It was a twenty-five-minute ride to the hospital. I sat in one of the side seats, ignoring the young guys in the back who sat with their legs spread out into the aisle, laughing and talking about their hot girlfriends. I needed to sort things out in my mind.

Images of Ruth lying on the floor and of Louise's terror flickered through my mind, but my most pressing thoughts were of Randall. What was he thinking, putting his arms around me like that? Surely he didn't harbor any romantic feelings for me, after all this time? He was engaged to a beautiful woman, for crying out loud. I wished, fervently, that Randall would finish up his job, go back to Philly, and leave me alone.

The bus let me off in front of the hospital just past five thirty. I didn't know what the visiting hours were or what Ruth's condition might be. I hesitated outside the main entrance. Not much time had passed since I found her sprawled on the floor. What were the chances that she would even be conscious? I shook off my intrinsic dislike of hospitals and let the doors swish open to admit me.

The hospital reception area was quiet. The walls were a pale green color—"hospital green" in my mind. Only half of the admissions desks were manned at this hour. I walked down the hall past the pictures of mountain laurels done by the high school drawing class, and entered the elevator for the third floor. Assuming that Ruth was settled into a room, this is where I would find her.

I checked in at the nurses' station, and was directed to room 318. The nurse didn't tell me anything about Ruth's health status or how long I could stay. I didn't even have to establish a relationship with the patient or a reason for visiting. That lack of vigilance made me uncomfortable. How weird would it be to be unconscious in a hospital room and have any old person walk in?

But I didn't need to worry. Ruth was not unconscious, and she wasn't alone. Her son John sat by her bedside, scrolling through his phone while she spoke to him. Neither one of them noticed me standing in the doorway.

I ducked back out into the hallway, feeling an unexpected rush of relief at the sight of Ruth's face. She was still quite pale, and she lay back against her pillows in a posture foreign to the ramrod-straight woman that I knew. But she was alive, and looking much better than I had feared.

I gathered myself, and knocked on the open door. "Excuse me, Priscilla asked me to stop by to see how you were doing, Miss Ruth. It's good to see you're looking better."

She turned her head to look at me. "I gather my sister did not come with you."

I walked into the room and stood awkwardly by the foot of the bed. "No, she asked me to come on her behalf. She's worried about you."

"Hmm I expect it was a sorry sight to see me being hauled out of the house on a stretcher. I imagine the neighbors were out in force, enjoying the spectacle."

John reached over to pat her thin hand with his pudgy one. "Now, Mother, you mustn't worry about appearances."

She pulled her hand away from him. "The last time I worried about appearances, I was on trial for my life."

John threw me a glance of consternation. "Well, we don't need to talk about that now, Mother."

Ruth followed his gaze. "I'm sure she knows all about it. Don't you?"

I shrugged. "I read about the trial in the newspapers. That's all. But your son is right, that's not what I came here to talk about. I just wanted to see that you were okay, so I could tell Priscilla."

Ruth locked eyes with me in a penetrating stare that belied her prone posture.

I steeled myself to return her gaze without flinching or looking away. Then I smiled. "I'll be happy to tell her that you're almost back to your old self."

Incredibly, Ruth smiled back at me, if you could describe her grimace as a smile. "John, could you please leave? Go have a drink in the cafeteria and come back in fifteen minutes. Not a moment sooner."

John glanced from me to his mother, clearly at a loss. Even in a hospital bed, Ruth was a force to be reckoned with, and he looked like he'd spent his lifetime reckoning. He got up and shuffled out of the room.

"Sit down," Ruth commanded.

I sat.

"So. My sister is worried about me. As are you, I gather?"

"Priscilla said you would hate being in the hospital. She just wants you to be okay."

"And you?" Again that penetrating stare.

"I want to know what happened, in your room. Did you fall over something, or have a heart attack? I'm guessing it wasn't a stroke, since your speech is so good."

She reared her head up in surprise. "The nurse didn't tell you? I took an overdose of sleeping pills. I imagine she thinks I tried to do away with myself. Funny thing is, I don't remember taking any pills at all."

I looked at her, frail and vulnerable in that hospital bed, but with a will of iron. "Where did the pills come from, then?"

She glared at me. "Where, indeed? Maybe you could tell me."

I struggled to keep eye contact with her. "I don't know. Do either you or Priscilla ever take sleeping pills?"

Shifting her gaze to the photograph of a tropical sunset on the wall, she said, "Sometimes Priscilla has a hard time sleeping. She does take Seconal, on occasion." Her hands plucked at the thin blanket covering her. "Louise Pritchard dispenses all her medications, but Priscilla controls the Seconal, since she might need it late at night when Louise is gone."

"Did the nurse tell you what medication you overdosed on?"

She glared at me like I was an idiot. "Seconal, of course. You see where this is going, don't you?"

"You think Priscilla gave you an overdose of sleeping pills? But why? She couldn't possibly want to harm you. She loves you."

Ruth clenched her jaw a moment before answering. "You may have noticed my sister's, well, shall we say, 'peculiarities'?"

I nodded. "You think she's suffering from some kind of dementia?"

"Not in the slightest! She has always been sweet, unsophisticated, somewhat vague. It has nothing to do with old age; it's who she is. I've never considered it to be dangerous in any way. But now..."

We sat in silence for a moment. I didn't know what to say. Mostly I was floored that Ruth would confide in me in this way. But I had no idea how to help her.

She must have seen that, for she gave a sharp sigh, followed by, "Well."

I nodded. "Yeah."

She locked eyes with me again. "Not a word of this to anyone, do you understand? I'll not have my sister hounded by police or psychiatrists or anyone else trying to make her out to be a menace to society."

I returned her gaze as best I could. "Professor Burbridge was murdered in your house. People are going to think your situation is related. Louise already thinks someone tried to murder you."

"Does she, now?" Ruth stared out the window as she considered this. I watched her jaw clench and her eyes go hard as she made her decision. "When life gets to be overwhelming, sometimes the only way out is to take matters into your own hands."

It took me a moment to realize what she was saying. "You want people to think that you tried to kill yourself?"

She lifted her chin in determination. "Wouldn't you?"

I bowed my head for a moment. "But what if people think that you tried to kill yourself because you killed Professor Burbridge and you don't want to be charged with his death?"

"Maybe I did kill Professor Burbridge."

I looked at her closely, my heart starting to thud. "Did you?"

She scoffed. "No, of course not. Why should I kill him? I didn't kill my husband, either, if it comes to that."

I opened my mouth to reply when we both heard the door handle rattle, signaling John's return. She held a gnarled finger to her lips. "We do this my way."

I nodded. What else could I do?

When John entered the room, Ruth was telling me, "So tell her I should be home by tomorrow or the next day."

I stood up. "I'll do that. I'm glad I got to spend this time with you, Miss Ruth. I know Priscilla will be happy to hear that you're going to be okay." I backed out of the room, avoiding any eye contact with John.

I almost ran in my haste to get out of the hospital. I was barely in time to hop on the bus that would take me back to Compton Hall. The bus was mostly empty, probably due to it being the supper hour. I found a spot in the back, stretched out my legs, and considered the remarkable conversation I'd just had.

Clearly Ruth thought that Priscilla had inadvertently poisoned her with sleeping pills. Just as clearly, she intended to cover up this suspicion to protect her sister from prosecution. I doubted that the authorities would go after Priscilla in this case, especially if Ruth refused to press charges. But I didn't know if there was a risk of the mental health professionals becoming involved. Again I wondered if someone held power of attorney for Priscilla.

But what about Ruth? Would she get caught up in some kind of mental health safety net, with people taking unnecessary action in order to keep her safe from herself? Would she risk losing her autonomy, especially since she had a son down the street to take charge of her?

I gasped out loud. Maybe that was the whole plan. Maybe John had slipped Ruth the pills in order to incapacitate her, either partially or totally, so that he could take over her affairs. I could scarcely imagine it when I reflected on the browbeaten man I'd just observed, obeying his mother's every command. But I couldn't forget the fact that Ruth's and Priscilla's wills had been taken from Randall's law firm. Was John making sure of his succession rights before taking his chance at bumping off his mother, or at the very least putting her in a situation where she stood to lose her legal rights? I felt like I needed a lawyer to help me figure all this out, but the only lawyer I knew was Randall, and I certainly wasn't going to ask him. But I also knew Marlena Hernandez. Maybe she and I should have another lunch together. But first, I needed to talk to McCarthy about what he'd learned about John Ellis.

I considered the next issue. If John was the one who had fed the sleeping pills to Ruth, then he obviously posed a danger to her. And I had just left the two of them together in a private hospital room!

Chapter Sixteen

My head was swimming by the time I got off the bus and walked to Compton Hall. I didn't know which way to turn. It was time to call in reinforcements. I pulled out my phone and typed in the number. The phone rang five times before he answered.

"Sean, are you busy right now?"

"Right now? She ignores my messages for the past four and a half hours, and then when I've just started in on a photo shoot of this glorious sunset as seen through the wrought iron fence encircling the Philmont estate, she calls and asks if I'm busy right now."

I tried to keep the smile out of my voice. "Okay, I can wait ten minutes for the sun to finish setting. Then can you meet me at Compton Hall? A bunch of things have come up."

"Aha! The nosy seamstress is onto something, is she?"

"She is indeed, but she needs some perspective from the obnoxious photographer, who is totally living up to his name at this moment."

He laughed. "I'll be there once the sun goes down."

I couldn't help chuckling as I stowed my phone. If nothing else, McCarthy was always good for some comic relief.

Buoyed by the thought of conferring with McCarthy in just a few minutes, I walked up to the front porch. Priscilla still sat there, this time toying with some food on a wooden tray perched on her knees. There might not have been any place for her to sit down and eat inside.

I sat down beside her. "I talked with Ruth, who is doing much better. She was awake and ordering everyone around, just like I said. She asked me to tell you that she should be home in a day or two."

Priscilla smiled at me, her vague smile that made me wonder if she had taken in anything that I'd just said. "The sunset is quite lovely, isn't it, my dear. The red fades into pink on the edges just like a painting on a Chinese fan."

"It is lovely. I have a friend who likes to take pictures of the sunset with his camera."

"Isn't that nice." She nodded and pressed my hand.

We sat in silence for a few minutes before I got up. "I'm going to pop inside and say hi to Louise."

She smiled and nodded, and picked at her salad. "Oh, could you ask her about my silver tea service, my dear? I noticed it wasn't on Great-Grandmother Rachael's side table yesterday. I can't help thinking about Francisca's stolen silver, you know."

I didn't, but I didn't have time to worry about silver at the moment.

I ran inside and scanned the downstairs for Louise, then ran up the stairs to the third floor. I found her in her bedroom, slowly unpacking the suitcases she'd packed so hurriedly earlier. She looked up eagerly when I knocked and entered.

"Did you talk to Miss Ruth? What did she say?"

I stood in the open doorway. "I saw Ruth. She was awake and alert, showing no signs of having had a stroke or heart attack. She told me it was an overdose of sleeping pills."

I didn't get any further. Louise slapped a hand on her leg. "I knew it! Somebody tried to kill her."

I held up both hands, hoping to slow her down. "It was kind of confusing, but I gathered that Ruth took the pills herself, on purpose."

"What? She tried to kill herself? I don't believe it! That ornery old lady would never take the cowardly way out like that. I could see her handing you a gun and ordering you to shoot her, but quietly taking a handful of pills?" She shook her head until her earrings rattled. "I don't think so."

I marveled at how perceptive Louise was, for all her rough demeanor. If she could see through this fabrication, what must she think of me in spreading it? "Did the police come by here to talk to you?"

She grunted, distracted by my diversion. "They never showed. They wanted to talk to Ruth first. Did they stop by while you were at the hospital?"

I shook my head. "The only one there was John." A thought struck me. Louise, longtime member of the household and skilled eavesdropper, might know a lot about John. "What can you tell me about John Ellis?"

A calculating look came over her. "What do you want with John?"

"I don't know, he just seemed kind of distant when I saw him with Ruth. He was looking at his phone while she was talking to him. Does he really care about her?"

"Does anyone really care about that witch?" Her hands flew to cover her mouth. "Did I say that out loud?"

I laughed, hoping to encourage her to talk. "Does he spend much time here?"

"Oh, he's in and out. He takes care of the old ladies' legal issues, so he has to get them to sign checks and things. He's always checking out the art or the silver or whatnot. He's probably looking forward to the time when it all belongs to him."

"I wonder what he thinks about this whole renovation thing for the TV show."

She laughed. "I'm sure he's all for it, as long as we win the million dollars. That'd be something to add to his inheritance, wouldn't it?"

I was sure it would be. Of course, that would be an argument for John to leave his mother alone until after the TV show aired and the vote was taken to reveal which property would win the million dollars. I shook my head sharply, marveling at how easy it was for me to cast John in the role of a murderer.

My phone dinged with a text from McCarthy. I checked it and turned to Louise. "My ride is here. So you'll be sticking around, right?"

She nodded. "Yes, I'll keep my eye on Miss Priscilla. Are you happy? You'll be back in the morning for the TV wrap-up, right?"

I paused with my hand on the edge of the door. "Right, the final filming. Oh dear, I was supposed to talk to you about making you a period gown. It's too late now."

She shrugged. "I'm not planning to be on TV. I'll just duck out of the way when the film crew comes through."

"Okay. See you tomorrow." I waved and scooted out the door. I felt a strong sense of letdown. I usually prided myself on my ability to come through with extras on my sewing jobs. This one felt like a failure.

I waved goodbye to Priscilla as I ran down the front steps and hopped into McCarthy's car. "Can you take me back to the hospital? Fast!"

"Hi, Sean, how are you?" His falsetto immediately made me laugh. "I'm fine, you?" he went on in an unnaturally deep voice. His eyes twinkled at me, even as he shifted into gear and peeled out from the curb.

I leaned over to give him an exaggerated hug. "Hi, Sean. Thanks for picking me up," I gushed. "You're so awesome—I don't know what I'd do without you."

He pushed me away in mock revulsion. "All right, all right! So what's at the hospital, anyways?"

I settled into my seat and double-checked the seat belt. "Ruth is in the hospital. She ended up with an overdose of Seconal, which is a medication that Priscilla takes." I clapped a hand over my mouth. "I wasn't supposed to tell you that. You can't tell anyone where the pills came from—promise me! If any of this gets published in the newspaper, Ruth will absolutely kill me."

He looked at me, bemused. "Suppose you start at the beginning, cruise through the middle, and come to the end in due time."

I almost clutched his arm, despite the fact that he needed both hands to drive. "You have got to promise me that you won't breathe a word of this to anyone. I mean it, Sean! Swear you won't tell anyone what I'm about to tell you."

He frowned. "I don't usually swear to something until I know what I'm getting myself into. I'm a big fan of the First Amendment: freedom of speech, freedom of the press, and all that. I will tell you that there's a long tradition of anonymous sources in journalism. But I can't promise not to say something until I know what I'm promising not to say."

I folded my arms and looked out the window, feeling like a petulant child. "Then I can't tell you."

McCarthy slowed the car to a respectable speed nearing the actual speed limit. "Daria, what if I promised not to tell anyone and then you told me that you were about to massacre all the lions in the zoo? If I couldn't talk you out of it, then, yeah, I would tell someone, even after I'd promised not to. What good would my promise be then?"

I felt my lips twitching, even though I could tell he was taking this seriously. "But I'm not going to massacre all the lions in the zoo."

"No, thankfully you are not a lion massacre-er, if that's even a word. But if you were and I promised not to tell and then I did tell, how could you ever trust me again? Wouldn't we be better off if I didn't promise at all?"

"But that's what I'm talking about. Trust. If I can't trust you to keep a confidence, then I just can't tell you anything."

He sighed. "I don't go around publishing everything you say to me. Really, I don't." He pulled into the parking lot at the hospital. "So do you want to fill me in on what's going on with Ruth, or should I just wait in the car for you?"

Provoking man! "I guess you should just wait, if you can't guarantee that you won't publish her whole story." I got out of the car and leaned on the open window for a parting shot. "I would have expected more of a code of journalistic ethics from you."

McCarthy threw up his hands. "This is an ethics code. I don't make promises I don't intend to keep. You can't get much more ethical than that."

"Well there it is! You 'don't intend to keep' my confidences. I can't trust you."

He shook a finger at me. "That's not what I said and you know it."

I turned on my heel. "Don't bother waiting. I'll take the bus home."

McCarthy smacked the steering wheel with the palm of his hand. "Fine!" He peeled out of the parking space before I had time to regret what I'd said.

But I didn't regret it. I fumed all the way up to the third floor of the hospital. I felt absolutely justified in not telling him Ruth's whole story. He as good as said that I couldn't trust him to keep it confidential. I was glad I hadn't told him about Major Compton's betrayal of his own troops. McCarthy would have published that tale for sure.

I paused in the third-floor hallway, trying to collect myself. I wasn't completely sure what I was doing there in the first place. Acting on a hunch, I guess. I wanted to be sure that Ruth was safe.

I peeked in her room to find her alone and asleep. Could I be sure that this was a natural sleep? I tiptoed into her room and listened to her regular breathing. I laid a finger on her wrist to feel her pulse, and compared it to my own. As far as I could tell, everything was normal. I backed out of her room, wondering what I was so worried about. But what if someone tried to harm her in the night? There was no kind of security—again I was able to just walk right into her room.

I backtracked to the nurses' station, and found a young nurse barely out of her teens filing a mountain of paperwork at the desk. I put on a stern expression and slapped my hand down on the counter, channeling Ruth as I spoke. "I just stopped in to visit my grandmother, Ruth Ellis, and I was shocked that I could just walk right in on her without anyone asking me who I was. Don't you know that there was a murder in her house just last week? What if I was the murderer? Isn't there any security at all around here?"

The nurse dropped her pile of papers. "I'm so sorry. We do have someone at the security desk downstairs from nine o'clock until seven in the morning. If you had come in a little later, you wouldn't have been able to just walk right in."

I frowned at her. "Well I can't hang around all evening waiting for nine o'clock to come. Can I count on you to keep watch over her? Make sure no one goes into her room who's not supposed to be there?"

"I'll do my best, but I do have other patients to take care of."

I heaved an aggrieved sigh. "All right, I guess I can stay for a few minutes." A quick glance at the clock told me that it was only twenty minutes before nine. "I'll just be in her room, then."

The nurse nodded, and bent to pick up her fallen paperwork. I walked back to Ruth's room, wondering if I was wasting my time or not doing enough. If Priscilla had accidentally poisoned Ruth with her pills, there was no threat here at all. But if her son John had tried to kill her, then added security wouldn't help, because no night nurse was going to keep a son from visiting his aged mother.

I sat listening to her breathing, and wished that I had been able to confer with McCarthy. I'd told him I needed some perspective, and I fervently wished I could have gotten that from him. He should have just promised not to tell anyone about Ruth's story!

By the time nine o'clock rolled around, I had made peace with the idea of leaving Ruth alone at the hospital, protected by security downstairs and a rookie nurse upstairs who didn't want to get chewed out again by the critical granddaughter of a human dragon. I said goodbye to the nurse with stern instructions to check on Ruth every fifteen minutes, and went out to catch the bus home.

I'd timed it right so I didn't have to wait long. I found a front seat in the nearly empty bus, and pulled out my phone. I tried again to reach Noah, with no success. I was really starting to worry about the guy. I leaned back against the bus seat and closed my eyes, taking a deep, calming breath. I had done everything that I could do right now. Ruth was sleeping, safe in the hospital. Priscilla was at home with Louise to take care of her. All I still needed to do was discover who killed Professor Burbridge, find out if Ruth's overdose was an accident or attempted murder, figure out why someone was targeting my house with malicious vandalism, and deliver a wedding gown to my ex's fiancée. No worries.

The bus let me off at the end of the block, close on to ten o'clock at night. I felt a strong sense of apprehension as I approached my house. What would I find on the porch this time? All the windows were dark, giving the house a forlorn look. I tried to remember if Aileen had a gig tonight. If so, she wouldn't be home until long after I'd gone to bed. Pete, of course, was working his long days. I marveled at his ability to function on so little sleep.

I took my phone out to light my way up the porch steps. I swept the light from side to side to make sure that I wasn't about to step on something nasty. As far as I could tell, the porch was clear. The only thing I saw was a bunch of dirty dishes sitting on the metal table, and some empty plastic cups scattered around. Aileen must have been entertaining her bandmates. Well, she could clean that up. I unlocked the front door and let myself in.

The house was dark, and Mohair meowed and rubbed against my legs when I came in. She must have been lonely. I scooped her up and scratched her in her favorite spot under the chin. She purred her approval.

I carried her through the dark front hall and into the kitchen at the back of the house. I hung up my keys on the hook under the mirror by the kitchen table, and deposited Mohair onto the table. I didn't normally let her sit on the table during meals, but I felt like she needed some extra loving since I was spending so much time at Compton Hall. Plus, I needed her warm, nonjudgmental presence.

I felt especially low this evening. I had failed to come through with a period gown for Louise. True, she had initially refused to consider dressing up for the TV show, but I could probably have talked her into it if I had persisted. But I didn't. Tomorrow Cherry would ask me for Louise's gown, and I would have to confess that there wasn't one. That didn't look good for business. I was still trying to launch my historical sewing business, and a lot of my success would rely on word of mouth from satisfied customers. As I sat at the kitchen table with my warmed-over soup and my cat, I didn't know if the TV show *My House in History* would count themselves among that group. Not an uplifting thought!

Then there was that argument with McCarthy. I couldn't say that this was the first disagreement we'd ever had. He came by his nickname, "obnoxious photographer," naturally. We had had a number of encounters in the days after I'd first met him. The fact that I suspected him of murder at the time didn't make for a trusting relationship, of course. But this argument felt different. This time I couldn't trust him because of who he was. He wasn't willing or even inclined to make a change. In fact, he considered his position to be honorable. He'd said, "You can't get much more ethical than that." That didn't satisfy me at all. I felt like we were looking at something through opposite sides of a window, so that it was impossible for either one of us to see what the other one saw. How could we go forward together if we were facing in opposite directions?

I pushed aside the half-eaten bowl of soup and laid my head down on the table. "Maybe I could get a do-over?" I mumbled to Mohair.

That's when the doorbell rang.

My mother always told me not to let the doorbell or the telephone dictate my actions. "If you're busy, you don't have to answer," she would say, while blithely ignoring the jangling ring of the telephone. "Just because they want to talk to you doesn't mean you should talk to them." I could never seem to follow this sage advice, even after ten o'clock at night. I gave Mohair one last caress, and nipped into the hall to answer the door. I peeked through the leaded glass to see who was standing outside, but the wavy glass obscured my vision. I eased the door open. There on the stoop stood Randall.

He put up a hand to keep the front door open, but he didn't push on it or attempt to force his way into the house. "I stopped by to see how you're doing, Daria. I know you got a shock this afternoon."

I narrowed my eyes at him. Here he was being all compassionate again. What was going on?

He smiled his slow, sensual smile. "Can I come in?"

I stepped out on the porch and shut the door behind me. "Let's sit out here. It's a nice night." Indeed, the moon was peeking out from behind a bank of clouds, bathing the yard in moonlight and shadow. Mohair had followed me out and curled herself up on the front mat. The faint scent of burnt brush was the only thing that marred the peaceful atmosphere.

Randall sat down on the porch swing and patted the seat beside him. I hesitated, and then scooped up Mohair and sat down next to him. I stroked Mohair's soft fur and felt her purring vibrate against my legs. Nothing like a contented cat to help you relax!

Randall pushed ever so slightly with his feet to set the swing in motion. I kept my hands busy smoothing Mohair's fur along her head and ears, over and over.

"Pretty scary to find an old woman unconscious on the floor, isn't it?" Randall sounded genuinely concerned. "Is she all squared away at the hospital?"

I tensed, and tried to cover it with a cough. Was he fishing for news about Ruth? "I stopped by to see her. She's well taken care of."

He nodded, and swung the swing back and forth. "I'm glad she's going to be all right. How about you?"

"Me? I'm fine. What's another person lying on the floor, give or take? At least she wasn't dead."

He relaxed against the swing cushions and stretched out his arm along the back. His hand dangled close to my shoulder. "Still, it makes you think about your own mortality. Life's short, and all that. It gives me an opportunity to reflect on my life." He turned to look at me. "Know what I mean?"

I studied the tips of Mohair's ears. There was a soft tuft of fur on each one. I wondered what she was thinking about, if anything other than the peacefulness of the moment. Did cats reflect on their lives? Did I want to reflect on mine?

Randall's hand slipped down to rest on my shoulder ever so gently. For some reason that I was reluctant to explore, I didn't shrug it off.

We swayed in silence punctuated by Mohair's purrs. He and I used to sit like this, in this very swing, on balmy moonlit nights like tonight. I remembered one night in particular, early in our relationship, when he had brought me a box of chocolate-covered caramels, my favorite. We had sat and swayed and eaten our way through the entire box, talking about our hopes and dreams and plans for the future. It had all seemed so easy and straightforward then. Now I couldn't envision my future with anyone, much less with the enigmatic man sitting next to me.

Randall eased me into a side-armed embrace. I felt so forlorn at the moment that I didn't resist. He laid his other hand on Mohair's neck and stroked her gently. "I feel like there are some things in my life that maybe I could fix." He left that thought hanging between us, and continued to stroke and sway.

I leaned my head against his shoulder, and his hand came up to caress my hair.

"What went wrong between us, Daria?"

"Apart from the fact that you withdrew all our money and took off?" I pulled away from him. "Or was it the part about you trying to isolate me from my friends and family?" Mohair stretched out her claws and dug into my leg, disturbed by my sudden movement.

Randall bowed his head. He kept his arm flung across the back of the swing. "I guess I didn't treat you very fairly, did I? I'm sorry."

An apology? In all the time I'd known Randall, he had never apologized for anything. He really was taking stock of his life! I picked at Mohair's claws, gently extracting them from my skirt. "I accept your apology."

His arm went around my shoulders again, and I let it. I felt a confusing whirl of emotions. I'd been nursing anger and resentment toward Randall for six months now. All of a sudden that bitter place in my heart seemed to lighten up a little. I had never considered the possibility that our acrimonious estrangement was something we could fix.

Randall stroked my shoulder with his fingertips. I could feel my body responding to his touch. I didn't know if he was hoping to end up getting physical, but I knew I couldn't let that happen. Maybe we could fix our differences enough to actually become friends, but that was as far as it could go. He was engaged to be married to someone other than me. That was the bottom line, as far as I was concerned. I eased out from under his arm and hoisted Mohair off my lap. "It's getting late, Randall."

He slid away from me and stood up. He held out a hand to me. I took it. "Here, let me help you with these things." He stacked up the plastic cups and gathered up some of Aileen's dirty dishes.

"Oh, don't worry about that. Aileen can get it." But his hands were already full, and he stood expectantly by the front door. I shrugged, and scooped up Mohair. I opened the door and let Randall follow me to the kitchen.

I leaned against the wall between the mirror and the white kitchen table, watching him putter around with the dirty dishes and the trash. It was a familiar sight that called up memories of domestic contentment, if I forgot about the increasing arguments of our later years together.

"Tomorrow's the big day, with the final filming," he said, busy washing his hands at the sink. "Are you looking forward to it?"

I forced a smile. "Oh, sure. I hope the house shines for the broadcast."

He wiped his hands on the hand towel hanging on the oven door and came over to me. "Well, there will be one little seamstress lighting up the show." He eased Mohair out of my arms and dropped her on the kitchen table. He put his hands on my shoulders and ran them down my arms before encircling me in a full embrace. "I can't wait to see your face on national television."

I turned my head away, so his lips grazed my cheek. "Randall."

I didn't get any further.

I heard a clatter in the kitchen doorway, and the sharp exclamation "Oh, hell no!"

Randall sprang away from me, a look of panic washing over his face. I tore my eyes away from him to see Aileen stalking into the kitchen in full intimidation mode. She was dressed in skintight black leather pants with purple zigzags streaking down the legs, paired with a purple silk corset tied together with brass chains. Her jet-black hair was gelled into spikes all over her head, dusted with purple glitter. Her habitual black makeup was augmented with purple accents. She gripped a guitar in one hand and the other fist rested on her hip. In her six-inch heels she towered over both Randall and me. "What the hell is this?"

Randall scuttled backward to put a little more space between himself and Aileen. He looked like he couldn't have spoken even if his life depended on it.

I picked Mohair back up and cradled her close to my chest. If she felt my heart pounding double-time, she made no sign. "Randall, this is Aileen, my renter. Aileen, Randall."

Aileen glared at him. "Yeah, I know who this is. Mr. Love 'Em and Leave 'Em in Poverty. I know your whole story, buster. And don't think you can come sneaking around trying to get into our house, because we are all on the lookout for jerks like you."

"Randall was just leaving." I grasped Aileen's arm and drew her into the kitchen so Randall could have a way out.

He zipped past her and made a beeline for the front door. I followed, with Aileen stalking behind me. She loomed over my shoulder as I let him out and locked the door firmly behind him. I turned to face her.

Both fists were on her hips now. "Did I seriously just see you kissing that lowlife?"

"Um, no." I walked back into the kitchen and sank down on a chair. Mohair meowed and settled into my lap, stretching her claws and kneading my skirt. "But who knows what would have happened if you hadn't come home when you did. He came by to see if I was okay after finding Ruth on the floor. He was being awfully nice about the whole thing."

Aileen sat down at the table next to me. "Wait, you found another body? What is it with you, girl?"

"No, this time she wasn't dead. Ruth Ellis had fallen in her bedroom. She's at the hospital now. She's going to be okay."

Aileen frowned, a truly terrifying sight if you didn't know her. I did, so I kept my cool. "Did a murderer help her on the way down?"

I sighed. "I don't know if it was on purpose or an accident. She got an overdose of sleeping pills, only she didn't take any sleeping pills, or at least she didn't mean to."

"Maybe she tried to kill herself."

I shifted Mohair off my lap and stood up. "Maybe. I don't know. The important thing is that she's going to be okay."

"I'd say the important thing is for you not to eat or drink anything when you're in that hellhole of a house."

I couldn't agree more.

I had a hard time sleeping that night. I couldn't close my eyes without seeing Randall's face close to mine, a look of compassion and more in his eyes. But when I fell asleep, I dreamt of McCarthy snapping my picture with a cocky grin on his face. I jerked awake, my heart pounding, at the sound of someone entering the house. It took a few minutes for me to realize that it was only Pete. Good thing I didn't confront him in the dark again. He'd be sending me off to the funny farm. I fell back to sleep chuckling at my silly fears, that didn't seem silly at all if you stopped to think about them.

Chapter Seventeen

Morning dawned bright and clear—a fine day to film the final segment for *My House in History*. I put on a white peasant blouse and calf-length swirly skirt that might approximate a period costume if the camera didn't focus on me directly. I packed jeans and a T-shirt in my shoulder bag, in case Cherry preferred me to look completely modern since I wasn't wearing an authentic eighteenth-century gown. Either way, I resolved to enjoy the process and not fret about what I hadn't accomplished.

I had a quick breakfast by myself in the kitchen. Aileen was still sleeping, and Pete was already gone for his marathon workday. I hadn't even had the chance to tell him about my adventures yesterday. Although, maybe all the details could wait. Pete had a tremendous amount of respect for McCarthy, a departure from his almost universal dislike of my boyfriends in high school. I suspected he'd take McCarthy's side in this argument, and I didn't feel like taking on the two of them. Plus he would surely frown on my unexplainable encounter with Randall last night. Aileen had let it go, which continued to surprise me. Pete would be harder to convince that nothing untoward was going to happen.

I took a deep breath and told myself out loud, "Nothing bad is going to happen." Mohair looked up at me with a plaintive meow. I filled her bowls and gave her a quick caress. Then I threw my bag over my shoulder and reached for my keys.

They weren't there.

I thought I had hung them up on the hook last night like I always did, but maybe not. I'd been in such a sorry state after that argument with McCarthy combined with my feelings of professional failure. Maybe I had dropped them in my bag instead.

I dumped out the contents of my bag and sorted through everything, but my keys weren't there. A quick search of my room and workroom upstairs came up with nothing. I scanned the floor, in case I might have dropped them. No keys. Finally I gave up and sent a quick text to Aileen: "I can't find my keys. If you go out, leave the back door unlocked." She would get the message in the next few hours, since she rarely surfaced before ten or eleven in the morning. I turned the knob so the door locked behind me, and ran for the bus.

I called the hospital from the bus and asked to speak with Ruth. I had to resort to my stern imitation of the lady in question before the nurse would let me speak to her.

"Who is this?" Ruth's barking voice sounded as robust as ever.

"It's Daria Dembrowski. I'm headed over to Compton Hall and I wanted to be able to tell Priscilla how you're doing."

"I am languishing here in a bed that is hard as a board while being prodded and poked by nurses who are young enough to be my grandchildren. I wouldn't consider it to be a party."

I tried to keep the smile out of my voice. "Do you know when you'll be discharged?"

"They're sending in the staff psychologist to examine me first. I expect they'll require me to go to confession and receive absolution before they will let me go."

"Well, I hope you pass all their tests. Do you need anything?"

"I need an excessive dose of patience, which has never been my virtue." She muffled the receiver, but I could still hear her say, "No, I am not finished with my conversation. He will simply have to wait."

"I'll let you go," I hastened to say. "I'll tell Priscilla that you're doing as well as could be expected."

"Diplomatic, aren't you? You can also tell my son John that I will call him to pick me up when I am discharged, which I am sure will be very soon."

I guessed that that last phrase was directed at the nurse or whoever it was who was in her room pressuring her to get off the phone. I hung up, satisfied that Ruth was weathering her hospital stay in her own imperious fashion. I felt a pang of sympathy for the nurses.

I hopped off the bus and walked the rest of the way to Compton Hall. I scanned the vehicles in the driveway as I approached. Blazing among the other vehicles was the bright yellow Mustang of Sean McCarthy.

I didn't know who invited him, but I didn't really want to confront McCarthy today. Maybe he would want to apologize first, and we could just move on. Maybe he'd thought things over and would promise not to tell. I chuckled ruefully. Probably not.

I walked into the front hall, surprised by the quiet that surrounded me. I'd expected a lot more hustle and bustle from the camera crew on their last day of filming.

I poked my head into the kitchen, which was completely empty. The newly restored hearth showcased the antique bricks that Carl Harper had salvaged. He'd even installed a cast-iron rod with a kettle dangling from it. I wondered if the fireplace was safe to use or if it was just for show. At any rate, the entire room looked like a bona fide eighteenth-century kitchen.

I wandered down the hall, wondering where Priscilla might be. I had expected to see her on the front porch. I peeked into her bedroom, where I found Louise tidying things up.

"What's going on, Louise? I thought the final filming was today."

She turned toward me and shook out her duster over the wastebasket. "They didn't tell you? They had to postpone it, on account of Miss Ruth not being here. Cherry specifically wants to film the two old girls together. She has to wait for Ruth to get discharged."

"Sounds like she'll get out today."

"If that ornery old lady knows that she's holding up the show, she'll take her sweet time about coming home."

I doubted that. It sounded from my conversation with Ruth like she wanted to get out of the hospital as soon as possible.

"Since we've got another day, I can make you an eighteenth-century gown."

"You can*not*! In one day?"

I gave her my most winning smile. "I can move pretty fast if I have to." I pulled a tape measure and notepad out of my multipurpose shoulder bag. "Let me just get your measurements."

Louise grumbled, but she let me take her measurements. "I'm expecting you to destroy these when you're finished, got it?"

I nodded. "I'll eat the paper, like a spy. What color do you like?"

"I don't care. I don't have a favorite."

We settled on dark blue, and I packed up my things. Time to head out to the fabric store again.

As I came down the staircase, a flash exploded in my eyes. I blinked away the echoes of light to see the grinning face of McCarthy, of course. "Looks like I came by for nothing."

I shrugged. "The newspaper will just have to wait one more day, like everybody else."

"Waiting on Ruth Ellis, I understand. Feel like telling me what's up with her yet?"

You could always count on McCarthy to get straight to it. "Feel like promising not to tell anyone yet?"

He shook his head with a big smile on his face nonetheless. "Sounds like we're at an impasse. But that doesn't mean we can't talk about other things, does it?"

"Actually, we can't. I have another gown to make, and I need to get to it." His goofy grin melted my heart. It was almost the same thing as an apology. "Although...you could take me to the fabric store again."

He laughed out loud at my suggestion. "She doesn't want to talk; all she wants is a chauffeur."

I took him by the elbow and steered him toward the front door, "That's what Aileen always says. You make Aileen feel used at your peril, you know."

"I can only imagine. You're a braver person than I am." He opened the door and waved an arm with a flourish to usher me through.

I swept through the door, to pull to a stop on the front porch. While I was inside, Priscilla had resumed her habitual seat in her rocker. Her knitting needles flashed to the beat of her rocking. I went over to her, leaving McCarthy standing by the porch railing.

"Good morning, Miss Priscilla. I'm sorry the filming got postponed today. I'll bet you're ready for all this disruption to be over."

"As you say." She gave me her vague, sweet smile. "How is Ruth this morning, my dear?"

I reached out and took her hand. "Ruth is doing as well as can be expected. She's hoping to come home today."

Priscilla nodded with an elfish smile on her face. "Good. I do miss her when she's not around. And how are you, my dear? Is this your young man?"

McCarthy grinned at me from his spot on the railing.

I returned the smile, realizing that he was listening carefully to my answer. "This is Sean McCarthy, photographer for the Laurel Springs *Daily Chronicle*. He's the one I was telling you about, who likes to take pictures of the sunset. He was here last year for the Laurel Springs House Tour."

McCarthy approached and reached out a hand to Priscilla. "Very nice to see you again."

She took his hand with her bony fingertips. "Of course, the photographer. I do enjoy your pictures in the paper. You did the one with the robin perching on a tree branch covered in snow, didn't you?"

His face broke into a smile. "Yes, I did. That was two years ago. I'm amazed that you remember it."

She patted his hand. "You'd be surprised what we old folks remember, my dear. I think you did all those lovely pictures of Francisca Toumay's silver, didn't you? She had such a spectacular collection, before she died."

I gave McCarthy a sharp look. Photographing silver seemed like a stretch for him. But he nodded. "Those photos were for the house tour as well. They turned out to be useful to the police when the silver was stolen from the estate after she died."

"Dear Francisca. She loved to be surrounded by all that silver. I'm sure it broke her heart to look down from heaven and see it all gone missing."

I pictured an old lady looking down from the clouds, seeing her beloved silver being stolen and not being able to tell anyone where it was. Was that how heaven worked?

Priscilla chattered on. "Will you come back and take pictures of the filming tomorrow? It should be an interesting time, I imagine. I do hope Ruth will be feeling up to it."

"I'd love to be here." McCarthy assured her.

We waved goodbye to Priscilla and got into his car.

"It's amazing that Priscilla remembered your specific photographs. I always thought her memory was dicey."

He revved his engine and pulled out of the circular drive. "Well, that robin was something special. I'll show you sometime. Then it sounds like she knew Francisca Toumay pretty well. It was a shocking thing when her silver was stolen between her death and the estate sale. There was one piece that I remember in particular: a silver platter made by Paul Revere himself. It must have been worth upwards of half a million dollars. I did get some beautiful pictures of it."

I checked the tightness of my seat belt when he accelerated around a corner. "Nice job finessing an invitation to come take photographs of the filming tomorrow."

McCarthy grinned. "Nothing like the homeowner's permission to give me legitimacy. You'll stand as my witness, right?"

"I'm sure you've got this—you don't need anyone to back you up."

He laughed and zoomed on to the mall. He dropped me off at the door before circling around the parking lot to find a spot. "I can take you home if you're fast, but I have a job at noon."

I can be fast on demand if it means I won't have to take the bus home. I chose Louise's dark blue fabric in record time, and was in the cutting line when McCarthy came into the store. But it didn't matter in the end, since the woman in front of me had seven bolts of fleece and as many bolts of flannel. We were in for the long haul here.

"What's going on at noon today?" It sounded better if I asked it that way, instead of saying, "Who are you meeting for lunch?" I didn't want him to get the impression that I was keeping tabs on him in any way. I'd suffered through enough of that with Randall.

"There's a panel discussion at the university about the impact of history on modern-day financial markets. A friend of yours is part of the presentation, as a matter of fact." He picked up a spool of thread and tossed it back and forth between his hands. "Noah Webster. Maybe you could introduce me afterward?"

"So I'm going with you, am I?"

He shrugged. "I figured you couldn't pass it up, right?" He elbowed me gently. "Nosy seamstress!"

I laughed, and dodged past another laden customer who was about to cut in front of me. I thumped my fabric bolt down on the counter. "I'm next. Twelve yards, please."

Ignoring the woman muttering behind me, I said to McCarthy, "Why, yes, I'd love to go with you."

* * * *

The panel discussion was just about to start by the time we arrived. The university library had rows of chairs lined up facing a long table set with three tabletop microphones. I paused in the doorway to take stock of the scene. A sparse crowd had gathered, mostly older folks for whom this presentation was probably the high point of their day. I noticed Mrs. Wirdle seated near the front, in pursuit of knowledge as usual. She sat next to a man wearing a classy gray felt fedora, even inside the library. Something about the set of his shoulders looked familiar, although I couldn't place him. This wasn't unusual—when you lived in a small town you were used to seeing the same people over and over, and you would recognize them even when you didn't know them.

Noah sat at the front table, along with a middle-aged man wearing a blue suit and a necktie covered with bright green dollar signs, and a woman swathed with jangly scarves who spoke with an Australian accent. I wasn't at all interested in the topic, but I could have listened to her talk all day long.

McCarthy prowled around the edge of the room, snapping pictures for the paper. The discussion lasted for forty-five minutes, and then the panel opened the floor for questions. After close to an hour in the warmth of the room the crowd was practically comatose, and questions were few. The presentation concluded well in time for the handful of students present to make it to their 1:00 classes.

I hung back while McCarthy greeted the other two presenters and took a few posed shots of them for good measure. Then I joined him when he introduced himself to Noah.

"Noah. I've been trying to get in touch with you."

He glanced sideways at McCarthy and said, "So nice to see you, Daria. Thank you for coming."

McCarthy shot me a swift glance, ever attuned to the nuances of any conversation.

I groaned inwardly. I needed to talk to Noah, to find out how his conversation with the police had gone. But he evidently didn't want to talk in this setting. I couldn't very well ditch McCarthy to get Noah to myself. McCarthy called me nosy, but I knew that he would never rest until he got to the bottom of whatever he was curious about. I guess it was up to Noah to keep McCarthy from publishing Professor Burbridge's research for all the world to see.

"Noah, I'd love to talk with you more about this topic. Can we get together to talk?" I smiled at McCarthy, resigned to accepting him as a witness to our conversation. "Maybe the three of us could go get some lunch or something."

Noah glanced from me to McCarthy and back again. Then he nodded. "We could go to the Station again. I have a class at two forty-five, but I'm free until then." He turned to greet a couple more members of the crowd.

McCarthy drew me aside. "Something's up, my seamstress sleuth."

I nodded with a conspiratorial wink. "You are about to be let in on the secrets of history."

"Are you telling me that you'll trust me with said secrets?" He said it lightly, but I could sense a bit of tension behind his words.

I tried to play it off with a shrug. "I don't have much choice. You're the chauffeur, after all."

He laughed. "I promise I'll behave myself as befits a proper chauffeur."

"That'll be the day."

Noah led the way to the Station. The cozy coffee shop was comfortably crowded even though the lunch hour was over, but we had no trouble finding a private table. We ordered sandwiches and settled down for a talk.

I saw the man in the gray felt fedora sitting at a table by the counter. Fedoras were my very favorite style of hat for men. I wondered what

McCarthy would look like in one paired with a matching overcoat. More like a classy private eye than a chauffeur, I imagined.

Noah seemed uncomfortable with McCarthy's presence. He straightened the condiments on the table and fussed with shimming up the teetering table with a folded-up napkin, all the while avoiding eye contact with either one of us. Finally I leaned over and laid a hand on his arm. "Noah, relax. Tell me what's been going on since I last saw you."

He glanced sideways at McCarthy again, and took a big bite of his ham and cheese sandwich, rendering himself speechless.

I couldn't help rolling my eyes in frustration. "McCarthy's a good friend of mine, Noah. He knows all about the professor's death and the fact that you might be at risk as well."

Although I intended to reassure him, my words had the opposite effect. Noah gulped and almost choked on his sandwich. He coughed and sputtered for a few minutes, trying to catch his breath.

McCarthy gave me the barest wink. "I remember one time when I was at risk. I was traveling with a circus for a couple weeks, photographing the elephants as they went about their daily routines." He leaned back and grinned at me. "This was before I washed up in Laurel Springs on the local beat. I'd gotten on the wrong side of the lion tamer after I made the mistake of chatting with his very attractive girlfriend. I didn't think much of it when he threatened me, until the night we had all the tents staked out in an open field bordered by woods. I was awakened in the middle of the night by the sound of an enormous animal snorting just outside my tent. I was petrified. Finally I whacked up the courage to take a peek out the tent flap, sure that I would see a lion waiting to maul me." He paused a beat. "What do you think I saw?"

I looked at Noah and shrugged. With McCarthy, it could be anything.

Noah blinked, and looked at the sandwich in his hand as if he'd forgotten all about it. "Was it a lion?"

McCarthy's eyes twinkled. "I peeked out that tent flap to see a white-tailed deer looking at me with those big doe eyes you always hear about. It snorted right in my face, sounding like the fiercest predator alive. I almost knocked the whole tent down trying to get away from it."

Noah and I both laughed, tickled by the picture of McCarthy cringing away from a harmless deer. McCarthy grinned, clearly satisfied with the success of his story. "I packed up my gear and took off the next morning. All I could think of was, next time it's gonna be the lion."

We laughed some more, so hard that several heads turned to look at us. I fought to control myself.

Noah wiped his eyes on his shirtsleeve. "I'm sorry, I shouldn't have doubted you. I was getting hang up calls, but now they've morphed into threatening calls. It's a man, but it's definitely not you. I guess I just needed to hear your voice more."

This surprised me, but nothing could faze McCarthy. "Yeah, no, I don't make it a habit to place threatening phone calls. Too much room for misinterpretation."

"What does the man say?" I wasn't sure I really wanted to hear it, but at the same time I wanted to know what Noah was up against.

He shrugged. "It's disgusting. There's a lot of profanity, and 'I'm coming to get you' kind of stuff."

"That's awful," I said.

"Have you called the police?" McCarthy pulled out his own phone, clearly ready to do just that.

"No, I haven't called anyone. I... It could be a prank or something. I don't want to overreact."

"Noah, your professor is dead and we don't know why. Calling the police about threatening phone calls is not overreacting." I tried to put as much conviction into my voice as possible.

"No!" Noah grabbed McCarthy's hand to stop him from dialing his phone. "I don't want to talk to any police. I can handle this without them."

McCarthy laid his phone down on the table, lifting both hands away from it. "What have you got against the police?"

Noah put his head in his hands. "I'm afraid of the police. I'm afraid they'll look at me as a suspect. I'm the only one who knows about Professor Burbridge's revolutionary research. Now that he's gone, I could publish his conclusions under my own name and no one would know any different. It would be a fantastic career move for me. I could walk into any history department in the country. I have a lot of student loans, so I need a good job once I finally get my dissertation. There are lots of ways I could profit from Burbridge's death. Why wouldn't the police see that as motive for murder?"

"Well, maybe they would," I said. "All the more reason to tell them about the threatening phone calls. You can't threaten yourself, so those calls point to someone else as the murderer."

"What if they don't believe me? What if they think I made up the threatening calls to throw the scent off myself? Look, I don't want to talk to the police. Okay?"

I sighed and bit my tongue. There was clearly no convincing him.

"So what is there in Professor Burbridge's research that would put your life at risk and cost him his?"

Noah looked at McCarthy in surprise. "Daria didn't tell you about Major Samuel Compton and the Battle of Laurel Springs?"

McCarthy shot a quick glance at me. "Not really. I understand he was a hero and the whole town loves him."

"Well, let me tell you—"

I cut him off, my heart starting to pound. "Noah, you do realize that McCarthy works for the newspaper, right? He's always on the lookout for a scoop for the front page."

McCarthy's jaw dropped. He stared at me in silence. I could hear the ticking of the clock across the room, ticking to the beat of my heart's thudding. The seconds dragged on as he stared at me with that look of stunned disbelief on his face. I couldn't stand to look at it. He usually covered up his feelings with a joke or a clever tale, so the sight of naked emotion on his face was more than I could take.

Noah's words died on his lips. He looked from me to McCarthy and back again. Then he scrambled to his feet. "Excuse me, I have to use the restroom." He disappeared in a flash.

Still McCarthy said nothing. He broke eye contact with me, and focused on the table in front of him. One hand came up to cover his mouth. I could see his jaw muscles working.

"Sean."

He looked up and said in an unsteady voice, "Have I ever...?" He looked away again, biting off whatever else he was about to say. He got up and walked out of the café.

Chapter Eighteen

I snatched up my shoulder bag and ran out after him. "Sean!"

He was striding across the quad, both hands shoved in his pockets, head down. I had to run to catch up to him.

I fell into step with him, and we walked in silence for a few minutes. We reached the edge of the quad, and he swung around and started back the way we'd come. Still not a word. I held my tongue until his pace slackened a bit. "Sean, I'm sorry I upset you."

He came to a stop and turned to face me. "Wow, you took me by surprise back there. I had no idea you considered me such an untrustworthy bastard that you have to warn people about me."

"Stop. That's not what I think."

"That's exactly what you think."

"Don't be ridiculous. I just wanted him to know that you work for the newspaper, so he could make up his own mind about how much he wanted to tell you."

"He knows I work for the newspaper. He just met me taking pictures of his presentation for the newspaper. I guess what he didn't know was that I have no kind of integrity or sense of journalistic ethics whatsoever, so I can't be trusted not to print every damn thing I ever heard. But you let him know that. Thanks for setting the record straight." He started walking again, faster than ever.

This time I let him go.

I stood frozen in the middle of the path, watching him stride off as if the lion really was coming after him. I'd never seen him this upset. The worst part was, it was all because of me.

I spied an unoccupied bench under an oak tree. I went and sat down, chagrined to note that my legs were a little shaky. I truly hadn't expected McCarthy to react so strongly to my comment to Noah. I thought he might make some joking remark about my not trusting him, but I had no idea he would think I was maligning his integrity.

I had never really considered McCarthy in terms of integrity. He was a charming, obnoxious photographer who loved to go around snapping pictures of everything he laid eyes on. That was how I'd always experienced him. He was a lot of fun to be with, and he could be kind in a lackadaisical sort of way, but I would never have guessed that he valued integrity, of all things. You learn something new every day.

I guess I owed him an apology, if he'd ever speak to me again for long enough for me to make it. I heaved a mighty sigh. I'd prefer not to have to grovel quite so soon, but my fabric was in his car, and I needed to make that dress today. I stood up and walked back toward the parking lot.

I was almost there when I remembered Noah. Poor guy, first we'd erupted into a fight in front of him, and then we'd both abandoned him at the café. Plus our fight centered around his story of Professor Burbridge's research. He might even feel responsible for the altercation. I heaved another sigh of resignation, and turned back to retrace my steps to the Station.

Noah was gone by the time I got back. It looked like he'd left in a hurry—his lunch was unfinished and his napkin lay on the floor. I couldn't blame him. If it were me, I wouldn't want to stick around to face an awkward conversation with either one or both of the recent quarrelers. I'd have to contact him later and apologize for our rudeness. But first I had a more important apology to make.

I walked back to the parking lot, hoping that McCarthy was waiting there for me, while at the same time dreading the conversation we would have to have. When I saw his bright yellow Mustang in the lot, I didn't know whether to feel relief or apprehension.

But he wasn't inside. I scanned the area—no McCarthy. I stifled a feeling of annoyance. I really needed to get started on Louise's gown, and all this drama wasn't helping in the slightest. At the same time I felt like I'd been reprieved from an awkward conversation.

I waited at least ten minutes, pacing up and down the sidewalk and wishing I'd never heard of Major Samuel Compton. I thought about calling McCarthy, but decided to just leave him alone. I checked the time to see that the bus was due in a few minutes. My fabric store bag lay on the backseat of the car, tantalizing me. On the off chance that it was unlocked, I tried the car door. It opened right away.

I grabbed the bag and ran for the bus stop, just in time to catch the bus home. I settled in my seat and sent a text to McCarthy: "I'm taking the bus home." I pressed Send before I thought about how that must sound to him. I followed up with "No worries."

He responded within a minute: "I'll take you home. Don't mean to leave you stranded."

I texted back, "I'm already on the bus. It's all good." But I knew it wasn't. I was probably making things worse by leaving like this, but I just didn't have time to engage in a long, drawn-out discussion about integrity and trust. I had an entire eighteenth-century gown to cut out and assemble before tomorrow morning!

McCarthy's response was "K." That was all. I stared at the phone screen for a long time, hoping there would be something more, but there was nothing.

I toyed with the idea of texting, "I'm sorry," but I didn't. There was nothing worse than carrying out or resolving an argument by text message. There would be time later to talk and make things right between us. I pushed all thoughts of McCarthy out of my mind, and concentrated on the steps I would need to take to get Louise's gown under way.

The bus let me off in my downtown neighborhood. I hurried down the sidewalk and hastened up the porch steps, intent on forgetting about anything other than my sewing. The front door was locked.

Belatedly I remembered that I'd misplaced my keys. I didn't bother ringing the doorbell. I knew Pete was gone, and guessed that Aileen was as well, since there was no driving beat or howling emanating from the basement. Still, I double-checked to see if her car was parked along the curb. No red Ford with flames blazoned across the hood. I traipsed around to the back door, hoping that Aileen had left it unlocked like I'd requested. Nope! I was stuck breaking into my own house.

I knew the window over the kitchen sink had no latch, and the back door had no deadbolt. I jiggled the door handle while I fished in my bag for something to pop the lock with. I didn't want to ruin a credit card or my driver's license, which did serve as an ID even if I never used it to drive with. I ended up with the cardboard backing of the notepad I always carried in my sewing stuff. It fit into the space between the door and the door frame with no trouble. I slid it down and caught the latch on the third try. With a little twisting, the lock released and I flung the door open. The entire process took no more than five minutes.

I felt a flush of accomplishment, proud of my new skill at breaking and entering. At the same time I reminded myself once again that I needed to get a proper deadbolt installed on this door. I went inside and closed the door behind me.

I reveled in the quiet, so rare since Aileen moved in. I was especially glad she was gone right now, so I could use the washer in the basement without needing earplugs. I dashed down to the basement, started the fabric in the washer, and then went upstairs to get ready to cut out an eighteenth-century gown. That's when I heard it.

Footsteps sounded on the third floor above my head. Someone was walking around in Pete's room.

It could be Pete, of course, but instinct and logic told me that it wasn't. Pete was working those sixteen-hour days, and today was no exception. I didn't expect him home before bedtime. Plus, the tread didn't sound like him. Who else could be walking around upstairs?

I heard the scraping sound of wood grating on wood. It took me a minute to realize that it was the sound of the door to the attic opening with a wrench. Whoever was up there was sneaking into my attic.

I tried to picture the attic space, which was accessed by a panel door in the wall under the eaves in Pete's room. The space wasn't very big, but there was room for a certain amount of storage amid the exposed wooden beams. I tended to use the basement for most of my storage needs, but there were a few things stashed away in the attic: things like my grandmother's pewter mug collection that was neatly packed into two matching crates, or the whole bookshelf of children's books that neither Pete nor I could bear to part with. Then there were the boxes of school papers that I'd saved for no reason other than the countless hours of work I'd put in to them, and a few paintings that I'd been given but couldn't stand to look at on a daily basis. I couldn't think of a single valuable thing in the attic that would draw a burglar to it.

The stealthy footsteps continued to pace around the attic, as I considered what to do. Should I call the police, without knowing for sure what I was dealing with? Suppose it really was Pete, home unexpectedly and maybe looking for some kind of prop in the attic. Alternatively, it could be an arsonist, back for a second try after failing to burn the house down with my Japanese maples. He could even now be pouring gasoline all over the attic floor.

There was only one way to find out. I slipped out of my room and tiptoed up the stairs to the third floor. I positioned myself behind the doorjamb of the unoccupied room across the hall from Pete's, where he kept his weight bench and a scattering of magazines around a flabby beanbag chair. I had a good view of the attic entrance through Pete's open door.

I stood there holding my breath for what seemed like at least four hours, although it couldn't have been more than ten minutes. Then I saw a person emerging from the attic. It wasn't Pete. It was a man dressed all in black with a ski mask pulled over his head. He clutched a bulky bundle that looked like some kind of heavy object stuffed into a pillowcase. He turned to pull the attic door closed, fumbling to get the stiff panel in place.

If I were Aileen I would have tackled him at that moment. But I was me, so I just watched, trembling, while he dusted off his hands and picked up his bundle once more. He turned and paced across the room, bypassing Pete's computer and the pile of loose bills and change that lay on his dresser. He paused in the doorway and looked around carefully before stepping out of the room. I shrank back against the wall, holding my breath. If he saw me here there was no place for me to run. I would have to fight him. It didn't take a fortune-teller to predict who would win in that battle.

Lucky for me, he didn't see me. He walked quietly down the stairs, and I crept down after him, hoping to see where he was going. He headed straight down, bypassing the second floor completely. He made no attempt to check in my bedroom or sewing room, or in Aileen's room. Clearly he had come to steal the object in his arms and that was all. What could that object be? I racked my brain but couldn't figure out what he could have taken from the attic, or how he could have known it was there for the taking.

The intruder paused at the front door and pulled the ski mask off his face. He smoothed his hair, preparing to waltz right out my door as if he had every right to be there. As once he had. It was Randall, of course.

A cascade of emotions washed over me at the sight of him. I felt anger, and a little bit of fear, but mostly an overwhelming sense of shame and betrayal as I watched him drop my missing keys onto the window bench to the side of the front door. How could I have been so gullible as to be taken in by his show of compassion last night when all the time he was acting on his own devious agenda? That whole story about wanting to fix what went wrong between us was only a ruse to get inside my house to lift my keys from where they were hanging below the mirror in the kitchen. He'd caressed me in that very spot, leaning in to kiss me while he snagged my keys off their hook behind my head. Then he'd used those keys to let himself in to steal something big and bulky from out of my attic. Well, he wasn't going to get away with it!

I sprang out of the doorway where I was lurking and hollered at the top of my lungs, "What the hell are you doing sneaking around in my house?"

Randall dropped the bundle with a cry. He swung around to face me, a look of fear on his face. It disappeared when he saw that it was only me, and not Aileen. He scooped up the bundle once more. "I just stopped in to retrieve my property that I left here back in January. Thanks for the loan of your keys."

"You left something in the attic when you moved out? What kind of a lame story is that? I checked the house from top to bottom after you split, and you had taken everything with you."

He laughed, holding the bundle behind his back. "Yeah, I cleaned out everything, because I knew you'd sell off anything I left behind. But you didn't find this, because I hid it. I didn't have any use for it then, but now I do, so I came back to pick it up." He pulled the front door open. "See you around, Daria."

I lunged and made a grab for the bundle while his back was turned to walk out the door. The bundle fell to the floor with a clatter. Randall yelled and swung around to push me away from him with such force that I fell hard on my bottom. I reached out and pulled the bundle open to reveal a large brassy object. It looked like a platter, big enough to hold a Thanksgiving Day turkey.

Randall snatched the platter away from me, wrestling the wrappings out of my grasp. He shoved my shoulders, pushing me down again even as I tried to stand up. I lunged for his leg, but he sidestepped away from me. "Forget about it, Daria," he yelled, and ran out the front door.

By the time I scrambled up off the floor to give chase, he was gone. I ran down the sidewalk in one direction, only to hear a car accelerating from the opposite direction. I threw up my hands in defeat, and returned to the house.

I started to call the police, but then I hesitated. Randall would either say he was simply picking up his own property from the house he used to inhabit, or he would hide the platter and claim that I'd fabricated the entire story just to make him look bad out of some desperate need for revenge. He might even exploit last night's camaraderie to prove that anything I said against him stemmed from my unresolved feelings for him. I groaned out loud. He even had Aileen as a witness to our close embrace.

I laid down my phone. He was going to get away with it, like he got away with everything he ever did to me.

I sat down on the window bench and dropped my head in my hands, letting the intense feelings of bitter frustration wash over me. I wished that it were nighttime, so I could crawl under the covers and cry myself to sleep. But it was only three thirty in the afternoon, and I had a gown to cut out.

I pulled myself up off the window bench and made my way down to the basement, leaning on the stair railing as if I were as old as Priscilla. I shook out the fabric and tumbled it into the dryer, then climbed back up the stairs. I walked stiffly, sore from landing on the hardwood floor. Maybe I could finger Randall for assault. I enjoyed the picture of him standing up in court, pleading no contest to the charge of pushing down a defenseless woman who was head and shoulders shorter than him. Of course, he was quite at home in court and he would never plead no contest to anything, so who was I kidding? Maybe I could sic Aileen on him, with Pete backing her up. The two of them could put him in the hospital for sure. But then they'd be the ones pleading no contest to assault. Would it count as assault if you beat up a jerk who deserved it? Probably.

Just the thought of Randall getting his comeuppance made me feel a little bit better, even though I knew it was only a fantasy. I went back upstairs to prepare the pattern for Louise's dark blue gown.

I spent the rest of the afternoon adjusting my pattern and cutting out the gown. My preferred method was to cut on a cutting board laid out on the floor, so I could spread the fabric out all the way. It was really hard to do that today. I had to keep getting up and stretching the sore muscles in the small of my back. Once again I cursed Randall for interfering in so many different aspects of my life.

Aileen popped into my room just as I finished cutting the fabric for the skirt. "I've got dinner on, come on down." She disappeared before I could politely decline.

I stood up and stretched, and decided that I needed some company bad enough that I could deal with whatever bizarre food Aileen had in store for me. Still, it was with some trepidation that I went downstairs and sat down at the kitchen table.

Aileen stood in front of the smoking oven, dressed in a multicolored one-piece bodysuit spangled with red metallic discs that matched her dangly earrings. She pulled out a casserole dish with a flourish.

I groaned inwardly. You could put anything in a casserole and try to pass it off as palatable food. At least it didn't smell too bad. I grabbed a hot plate to save my table before she plopped the casserole down.

She lifted the lid, revealing mashed potatoes mixed with mandarin oranges and cheese puffs and topped with what looked like grated zucchini peels. Before serving up, she grabbed up a huge bottle of hot sauce and slogged it over the entire dish.

I could see a round of antacids in my future.

Aileen thumped my plate down in front of me and loaded up her own. She took a big bite and mumbled around her fork, "Bon appétit."

I took a dainty bite and followed it up with a big gulp of water. "What's the occasion tonight?"

She shrugged, swallowed her massive bite of food, and wiped her mouth. "Maybe I'm worried about you stepping out to dinner with a former lover turned world-class jerk."

I tried another tiny bite. "No worries on that score. If I never see him again, it'll be too soon. He was using me yesterday, just like he used me the whole time we were together." I laid down my fork and covered my mouth with my napkin to hide my trembling lips.

Aileen nodded, as if she'd known exactly what I was going to say. "I could've seen that coming a mile away."

"Well I didn't." I didn't really want to talk about it, but at the same time I wanted somebody to make me feel better about the whole mess. "While he was cozying up to me in the kitchen yesterday, he was stealing my keys off their hook. He used them today to get in and take something out of the attic—a big tarnished platter. I've never seen it before: he said he'd left it here before he split."

Aileen stared at me, her laden fork halfway to her mouth. "That lowlife stole your keys to break into our house? Did you call the cops?"

I shook my head. "I got the keys back and I didn't recognize the platter so I can't say he stole it from me. It just makes me so mad that he came on to me like that, and I bought every bit of it. If it hadn't been for that argument with McCarthy, I wouldn't have been in such a vulnerable state of mind."

Again Aileen stared at me. "You had an argument with McCarthy? What was that like?"

I sighed. "Yesterday I told him I couldn't trust him because he wouldn't promise not to repeat something I was going to tell him in confidence. He tried to convince me that not promising was the ethical way to go. Today I told Noah Webster not to trust McCarthy because he takes pictures for the newspaper and is always after a scoop. That really pissed McCarthy off." I looked down at the food on my plate, pushing it around with my fork. "I think I really hurt his feelings. I questioned his integrity."

"Damn!" Aileen let the one word hang between us while she shoveled down another few mouthfuls. Finally she spoke. "Integrity." She stood up, holding her hand over her heart. "'Nothing is at last sacred but the integrity of your own mind.'" She sat back down, unfazed by my look of amazement. "That's where you hit him."

"You're right. I feel terrible." I got up and gathered up my mostly untouched food. "Where do you get this stuff, anyway?"

"'This stuff' is Ralph Waldo Emerson. Nothing like the classics." She finished off her last bite of casserole and picked up her plate as well. "Of course, the question is, does McCarthy have integrity or not?"

"Yup, that's the question." I dumped the dishes in the sink. "I'll wash up later. I need to finish this gown."

I practically fled up the stairs, pursued by Aileen's question. Did McCarthy have integrity? I settled down to my sewing machine and forced myself to consider it. What did I know about McCarthy, really?

Aileen once told me that what you see is what you get with McCarthy. I'd seen a few things recently. At Randall's law firm, he went out of his way to be persistent and obnoxious and then set up a conflict in which Randall's dad would emerge the victor, all in order to keep a secretary from losing her job. He let a waitress goad him into challenging her pool shark boyfriend knowing that he would surely lose, and then he let her enjoy ribbing him about it. He didn't hesitate to confess a humorous and rather embarrassing story of being afraid of a white-tailed deer if it would help make a grad student feel more comfortable. He showed no self-consciousness about any of these incidents, seeming to enjoy the humor in his own predicaments. What did this all say about integrity? What did it say about Sean McCarthy?

What you see is what you get. I'd always seen a man with a good sense of humor who was a joy to be with. I'd never really thought about his honesty or trustworthiness. Had he ever let me down? Had he ever, in fact, printed something intimate or compromising about me, or even something that I'd requested that he not print? Had he ever violated a confidence?

The answer was no. He never had. I had no basis whatsoever for my assertion that I couldn't trust him. All I'd accomplished was to show him that he couldn't trust me to form my opinions about him based on the man he was rather than my own prejudices about newspapermen in general. Who was lacking in integrity here?

I let the bodice I was sewing fall to my lap and dropped my head in my hands. I knew what I had to do. I reached for my phone. I had to make this right. I dialed McCarthy's number.

The phone rang and rang until it finally went through to voice mail. I left a message. "Sean, I need to apologize to you. I was a jerk. Call me." I texted him the same message, and then went back to my work.

McCarthy must have really been upset, because he never responded to either text or voice message. I called a second time, but hung up without leaving another message. I guess I needed to give him time to get over his hurt feelings.

I stayed up well past midnight working on Louise's gown. I took all kinds of shortcuts, leaving seams unfinished on the inside and sewing even the hems by machine. The only thing that mattered at this point was speed and a finished product, with no regard for quality. It was my least favorite way to sew.

Pete poked his head in when he got home. "You're still up?"

"Duh!" I didn't know why people always asked such silly questions. Of course I was still up; he could see that. "I have to finish this gown by tomorrow. I only just cut it out this afternoon. I don't even get to fit it—Louise has to wear it first thing tomorrow morning." I rubbed my aching back. "I'll be so happy when this filming is over!"

Pete settled down on the edge of my desk. "I thought you were excited to be a part of it."

"Yeah, that was before they kept piling on more and more projects. Creeping disclosure, that's what I'd call it."

"I guess the professor's death didn't help matters, huh? Did the police ever find out who did it?"

"Did you read anything about it in the newspapers? No! Of course they don't know who did it. Every time I go into that darn house I'm looking over my shoulder, wondering which one of them is a murderer. It's horrible."

Bless his heart; Pete didn't snap my head off at this point. He was probably too tired to take me on. "Sounds like a real drag. I'm sorry."

"Plus, I had a big fight with McCarthy this afternoon, after a smaller fight yesterday. He won't even call or text me back when I'm trying to say I'm sorry." I looked at him beseechingly, as if he could solve all my problems for me, like a helpful big brother. Of course he couldn't.

"What did you guys fight about? Please tell me it wasn't Randall."

My head snapped up. "What is that supposed to mean?"

"Aileen told me you were kissing him last night. I told her she was full of it, but she insisted."

"You told Aileen she was full of it?" I said, momentarily diverted.

He shrugged. "I tell it like I see it."

"And she lets you. That's the amazing part."

"Well, she does call me Moron. If she thinks she's telling it like she sees it, I guess I'm in big trouble."

I couldn't help laughing, but it was short lived. "Yeah, Randall was here last night, coming on to me when I was feeling low after arguing with McCarthy. No, I did not kiss him. It turns out that he was using me to get ahold of my keys. He let himself into the house today and fished a big platter out of the attic."

"Wow, I was not expecting you to say that." Pete rubbed his eyes with both hands. "We don't have to stay up all night again to keep him out, do we?" I stared at him. "Oh, my God. It was Randall trying to get in that night. I should have checked to see if he had a bump on his head where I threw that box down on him. He was trying to break in to get that platter out of the attic. That no good..." I threw my pincushion across the room, scattering pins everywhere.

Pete made no move to help me pick them up. "Do you think he's behind the eggs and the mice and the fire too?"

"I wouldn't put it past him." I jabbed the pins back into the pincushion.

"Well that's good, in a way. He got what he wanted, so he'll leave us alone now. Right? What's up with this platter?"

"I don't know. I didn't recognize it. He said he hid it here when he split, and now he had a use for it so he came and got it. That jerk! If he had just asked to come in and get something he left behind, I would have let him."

"Would you?" Pete never hesitated to ask the tough questions, even when he was exhausted.

"Well, maybe not. I don't know. I hope you're right, that he won't be back. I probably won't be able to sleep anyway." I shook the dress. "Of course I won't even get the chance. I'll be up all night long finishing this dress."

"Not me." Pete stood up and yawned, stretching both arms over his head. "I gotta get to bed, so I can get up again in five hours." He said goodnight and left, only to pop his head back in a minute later. "Don't give up on McCarthy. He's a good guy."

"You telling it like you see it again?"

He nodded with a smile. "You bet."

Chapter Nineteen

I was wrong about the all-night prediction. I finished Louise's gown at 3:45 a.m., so I was able to get a few hours of sleep before I had to get up for the final day of filming. I was so tired when I finally lay down that I went straight to sleep with no thought for either Randall or any other unknown intruder.

Saturday morning was rainy and windy. The front windows rattled from the rain. I wondered if it would affect the filming at Compton Hall. It did make my wait at the bus stop an exercise in endurance. I clutched my shoulder bag close, hoping to keep Louise's dress dry.

When the bus let me off down the street from Compton Hall, I scurried as fast as I could up to the house. I noticed an unusual number of vehicles in the drive, which made sense for the wrap-up.

I headed straight upstairs to give Louise her gown. If I was lucky, I would have a few minutes to pin up anything that didn't fit perfectly.

I found Louise in Priscilla's room, tidying up. I called out a cheery greeting. "Hi, Louise. I've got your gown for you."

She turned and frowned at me. "I can't believe I have to wear this silly dress. It'll make me look like some kind of prissy parlor maid."

I bit my tongue to keep from blurting out the fact that I had stayed up until the wee hours of the morning just so she could wear that dress. I merely helped her into it in silence. It fit perfectly, which was some consolation. "There. You're ready to step back in time with Miss Priscilla."

Louise grumbled, but I didn't care. I was just pleased to have fulfilled my obligations in the end. "So, is the filming taking place this morning? Did Miss Ruth come back from the hospital yesterday?"

"Oh, yes, she's here, that ornery old woman. She's in the living room, raising Cain like she does. You'd think a little poisoning would set her back a bit, but no. She's queen of the roost, like always."

I smiled inwardly, looking forward to seeing that "ornery old woman." I gathered up my bag and headed back downstairs.

The living room was packed with people, cameras, and filming equipment. I got a glimpse of Ruth in one of the wingback chairs and Priscilla in the other, both dressed in the eighteenth-century gowns I'd made them. Cherry hovered between the two chairs, offering advice to the makeup artists who worked on the sisters' faces. It looked like the makeup artists were ignoring Cherry completely.

I wormed my way into the room a bit, until I could get a closer look at Ruth. She looked a lot better than she did when I visited her in the hospital, although the color in her face could have been due to makeup. But her bearing was as straight as ever, giving no indication that she had been bedridden only a day earlier.

Priscilla smiled at her own reflection in the handheld mirror, enjoying the process of having her makeup applied. Little wisps of her long white hair escaped from her loose bun to curl gently around her face. The nicely pressed ruffles on the ends of her sleeves waved gently when she reached out to accept a tissue from Cherry to blot her lips.

I took a closer look at the sisters' gowns. When I saw the two of them side by side like that, it was obvious to me that Ruth's gown had been made quickly, with a much simpler pattern and little thought for detail. Nothing to do about that now. I hoped no one else would notice the difference.

I was about to slip back out of the crowded room when I felt a tap on my shoulder. I turned to see Martin Sterling, a reporter from the Laurel Springs *Daily Chronicle*, standing behind me. He beckoned me to follow him into the hall.

I knew Sterling, a small, thin man with short dark hair who often worked on assignment with McCarthy. They made a good team: Sterling with his soft-spoken manner asking the tough questions, and McCarthy with his exuberant charm taking the photographs. I guessed Sterling was here today to write a story to accompany McCarthy's pictures of the event. I couldn't imagine that there would be many hard questions today.

Sterling drew me into the hall away from the hustle and bustle in the living room. His dark eyes were drawn with concern. "Have you seen McCarthy?" he asked. "He told me to be here at eight o'clock, but it's nine thirty now and he hasn't shown."

I shrugged. "You didn't have a fight with him yesterday, did you?"

"With McCarthy?" He laughed, momentarily diverted from his worry. "I can't even picture that. No, it's just not like him to be so late without a word. I've been calling and texting, but no response."

I bit my lip. Evidently I was the only one in the world who had ever had a fight with McCarthy. Did I bring out the bad side of him or something? "Maybe something happened to delay him."

Sterling frowned. "That's what I'm afraid of."

A chill ran across my spine. Sterling was right; McCarthy was a very punctual kind of person, especially when it came to his assignments. He'd once told me, "With photography, timing is everything. If you get there late, the shot is gone." I couldn't think of a time when he'd been late or hadn't responded when I tried to contact him.

Until now.

"You don't suppose he's had an accident or something? He does drive like a maniac."

Sterling nodded. "True. But I've checked the police scanner, and there's nothing about any accident with injuries. If it was a fender bender, I'm sure he'd let me know. That's the weird part. We've got a code to alert each other if there's some kind of trouble brewing, but he didn't hit the code."

Was McCarthy in some kind of trouble? I pushed down a mental picture of him lying unconscious somewhere, unable to hit the code, whatever that meant. McCarthy was a very capable person, who could easily cope with all kinds of trouble. But there was a murderer out there. The killer could be here at the house, even as we spoke. The image of Professor Burbridge's inert form sprawled on the library carpet filled my mind. Had McCarthy fallen victim to the same fate? My hands went cold at the thought. I pulled out my phone and dialed his number one more time. Still no answer.

"Sterling, there's a murderer still at large." I struggled to keep my voice level. "We think it's someone associated with the renovation of Compton Hall. Should we call the police and tell them McCarthy's missing?"

Sterling whistled. "Someone associated with Compton Hall, as in, someone here in the house right now?"

I nodded, not trusting my voice.

"Okay. I'll spin over to McCarthy's apartment and see if he's there or if there's any sign of him. You can fill in the cops." He was gone before I could even thank him.

I tried McCarthy one more time, and when there was no answer I called the police. The dispatcher took down all my information, and clicked her tongue when I told her McCarthy's name. "Sean McCarthy. Sure. You don't need to give a full description—we all know him here. You sure he's not just off doing something else? We don't normally pursue a missing persons case when the person is only an hour and a half overdue."

"I'm not sure of anything. I've been trying to reach him since yesterday afternoon, so it's not just an hour and a half. But the thing is, he could have run into the person who killed Professor Burbridge. He could be..." I couldn't say it. I choked down my growing fear. "He could be in trouble."

She assured me that the police would take my report seriously, and hung up. I had to be satisfied with that. I stowed my phone and turned to see Ruth standing behind me, her sharp eyes homed in on my face. She had heard every word.

"Talk to me," she commanded, leading the way to her bedroom. She walked slowly, trying to maneuver her cane around her long, flowing skirt. I knew better than to try to help her.

"Sit." She pointed to a bedside chair and sat down on an armchair by the bedroom fireplace. She sat stiffly, her back not touching the back of the chair. Both hands clenched the head of her cane. "What do you know about the murderer?"

I slumped down in my chair. "Nothing. I just haven't heard from McCarthy, who was going to be here this morning and he's not. He's a photographer from the newspaper who was supposed to take pictures today. His colleague from the paper doesn't know where he is. I'm afraid...I'm afraid he may have run into the murderer. He could be..." No, I refused to consider it. He was just running late, and maybe his phone was dead or something. He'd laugh at all the fuss I was causing, if he would ever speak to me again, that is. "It's probably nothing. I'm just on edge after everything that's happened here."

Ruth frowned. "It's never nothing."

That chill hit me again, but I pushed it away. "How are you feeling this morning, Miss Ruth? I'm happy to see you here."

Her frown grew deeper. "Inane pleasantries will not divert me from talk of a murderer."

"I'm not making inane pleasantries. I'm saying I'm glad you're looking so well after somebody tried to kill you. Okay?" As soon as the words left my lips I wished I could take them back. I imagined that Ruth Ellis was right up there with Aileen on the list of people you didn't want to argue with. But her response surprised me.

"Well. You've got a bit of spunk, haven't you? So, about this murderer."

I took a deep breath. "I don't know a whole lot. It has to be someone involved with the house and the renovation, because the police said there was no evidence of forced entry. Everyone involved with the renovations is here right now, so the murderer is in the house at this moment."

"There's a sobering thought. So we go through them, one by one."

I nodded. "Okay. There's Carl Harper. He's got a terrible temper and a bunch of heavy metal tools. He could have easily hit Professor Burbridge over the head with a wrench or something, although I'm pretty sure one of his bricks was the murder weapon. Plus he's had a number of strange phone calls that sound like he's up to something."

Ruth's lips twitched. I could almost picture her smiling in amusement. "You've tapped his phone, then?"

"No, he talks really loud when I'm walking past. He's always shouting, in fact. I'm kind of scared of him."

"Hmm. Who else?"

"There's Jamison Royce, the gardener. He didn't blink an eye when I told him that the Japanese maples I'd rescued from the dump got torn up and burned. He's a gardener but he doesn't care about plants. I looked up his business and it's not listed online. So there's definitely something shady about him."

Ruth looked me over with growing respect. "Your detective business isn't listed, either. I mistook you for a seamstress."

I laughed. "McCarthy calls me 'nosy seamstress.'" The mention of McCarthy wiped the smile off my face. This discussion was no joke. "All right, who else?"

I swallowed hard, and then said it. "There's Ruth Ellis, who came home to Laurel Springs after being acquitted in the death of her husband. She had an argument with Professor Burbridge the day he died. Burbridge was seen stalking out of the room muttering, 'I will not be silenced.' Soon after, he was silenced, permanently."

I expected an explosion, but Ruth merely regarded me with a deep frown on her face. "How did you come by this information? From the police?"

I shook my head, chagrined to find my hands shaking. "I saw Professor Burbridge come out of the living room and head for the stairs. I heard what he said."

"And did you hear what was said inside the room?"

"No. I heard raised voices, yours and his. I couldn't tell what you were saying."

"All right. I will tell you. Professor Burbridge presented my sister and me with his groundbreaking research into our ancestor, Major Samuel Compton. I imagine you've heard of him?"

"Yes. In fact, I know about the professor's research. I've talked with the graduate student who helped him with the research."

"Ah. You failed to include that person on your list of suspects."

I ducked my head sheepishly. "I'm not through the whole list yet."

"All right. So I don't have to tell you the details of this revisionist history. I imagine I also don't need to tell you how this revelation could affect the fortunes of the Compton family, which has prospered from the adulation paid our heroic ancestor. If it came out that our family had perpetrated a fraud on the town all these years, and in fact our esteemed forebear was a traitor who caused the deaths of the ancestors of our neighbors, then my sister Priscilla could become a pariah in this town. I do not intend to allow that to happen. In addition, we are in the midst of an expensive and very public renovation of the property. How fast do you think the television show would drop Compton Hall at the slightest whiff of scandal? I have no illusions about winning a million dollars, but I do expect the producers to restore this house to its livable modern condition when all this nonsense is finished.

"So Professor Burbridge came to tell us that he planned to release his findings to coincide with the television show's finale, if you can believe it. I told him in no uncertain terms to cease and desist. He refused, and stormed out. That was the last time I saw him alive. But I did not kill him. Neither did my sister, whom I notice you also left off your list. Or maybe you haven't gotten to her yet?"

"Of course Priscilla didn't kill him! She's the sweetest person imaginable. She wasn't upset about the professor's research, was she?"

"She wasn't angry. She was shocked at the suggestion that the major could have been a traitor, of course. Priscilla doesn't recognize the existence of evil in others. She sees nothing but good in everyone." She pressed her lips together for a moment. "The presence of a murderer in our midst has been very hard on her."

I bowed my head, reluctant to ask the next question. But we needed to get to the bottom of this. "What about the sleeping pills? Do you still think that was Priscilla?"

Ruth's frown deepened, a feat I wouldn't have thought possible. "I prefer to focus on the professor's murder at the moment. Who else is on your list?"

"Okay. There's Noah Webster, Professor Burbridge's grad student. He worked with the professor on this groundbreaking research and knew all about it. He knew the professor was looking for fame and fortune with this historical coup. He could have killed the professor to get there first. But I'm sure he didn't."

"What makes you so sure?"

"Well, you and Priscilla knew about the professor's work, so you could easily dispute his claim that it was his own." Of course, that would give Noah a motive to poison Ruth, wouldn't it? I hastened to defend him. "He's a nerdy history guy with a heart of gold. He couldn't hurt a fly, I'm sure of it. Plus he wasn't in the house until after the professor died."

"I'm not convinced by these arguments. But we'll lay that aside for the moment. Anyone else?"

I heaved a deep sigh. "There's Randall Flint, the lawyer who has been appraising the valuables in this house. He's my ex-fiancé, and I just realized that he's the one who has been vandalizing my house for the past week. He had left something in the attic and stole my keys to get it out. He's a jerk."

"Being a jerk does not give him a motive for murder."

"Right. I forgot to tell you. Besides his research into Major Compton, Professor Burbridge was researching a cheating scandal at Oliphant Law School during the time that Randall was a student. Burbridge was also looking into the contractors' union that Carl Harper must belong to. That gives both Randall and Harper a motive to silence Burbridge to prevent his research from becoming public."

Ruth scowled. "Is that all?"

I took another deep breath. I didn't know how this next name would be received. "There's John Ellis, who has the same motives as his mother to keep the professor's research from seeing the light of day. I don't know if you know that your will and Priscilla's was stolen from your law firm during a break-in. Maybe that was John?"

"Of course I know." Ruth rubbed her temples with both thumbs. "Have we come to the end at last?"

I nodded.

"All right. We have a varied cast of characters. Too many of them have legitimate motives for murder." She paused at my involuntary gasp. "Don't be ridiculous! I'm not saying those reasons would legitimize murder. I'm saying these people have motives that cannot be discounted. We cannot narrow down the list through consideration of motive alone."

"I see." As far as I could tell, the professor's research, whether it was his research into Major Compton or his research into the two different scandals, was the direct cause of his death. The only suspect who had no connection to the professor's research was Jamison Royce. What motive did he have to murder Professor Burbridge? Could I take him off my list?

"I have an idea." I wasn't sure if it was a good idea or not, but we had to do something. "What if you make an announcement that you have a momentous historical revelation based on Professor Burbridge's research that you're going to divulge at the end of the day's filming, to be broadcast on the nationwide TV show? The murderer will certainly object to such a revelation. We can both watch closely and see who is threatened by this announcement."

Ruth narrowed her eyes at me. "And are you watching me closely at this moment? If I reject your idea, does that prove to you that I am the murderer?"

I smiled at her, clenching my hands in my lap to stop their shaking. "I've taken you on as an ally. If I thought you were the murderer, I wouldn't have done that."

"Aha. I suppose I have done the same, although I could add another name to your list. There's Daria Dembrowski, who was the first one to find Professor Burbridge's body. She has gone out of her way to be kind and accommodating to Priscilla Compton, perhaps in hopes of receiving some kind of favors from her. This has extended even to the point of going to visit Priscilla's difficult sister Ruth in the hospital."

I had jumped to my feet at Ruth's suggestion that I might have an ulterior motive for being kind to Priscilla, but by the time she got to the end, I couldn't help laughing. "I hope you don't really think I'm trying to get something out of Priscilla."

For an instant Ruth's face softened. "No, I don't. You have been genuinely kind, as well as uncommonly perceptive. I trust that you are not a murderer."

Her word "trust" took my breath away. She knew so little about me, yet she could trust that I was safe. But I had told McCarthy, whom I cared about, that I couldn't trust him. A lump rose in my throat. Where was McCarthy now? Would I get the chance to tell him that I was wrong?

I shook off a growing sense of dread. He was probably downstairs snapping pictures right now, wondering why Ruth was taking so long to come down. "So? Should we try it?"

Ruth planted both hands on the arms of her chair and pulled herself to her feet as an insistent knock sounded at the door. She picked up her cane and thumped it down in front of her. "Let's go flush out a murderer."

Chapter Twenty

It was Louise knocking at the door. "They're waiting for you downstairs, for the filming." She didn't say, "Hurry up, will you?" but she managed to convey a sense of urgency nonetheless. I wondered how long she'd been standing at the door, listening, before she knocked.

Louise was decked out in her period gown, which looked even more rushed than Ruth's did. It wasn't like you could see the stitching or the buttons didn't line up or anything like that. It was just a lack of detail that made the gown disappointing in my eyes. It looked like something you could find on sale in a house museum gift shop for $79.99: just a simple bodice and long skirt to make a history tourist feel like she could briefly touch the olden days. Maybe this production was nothing more than that. I followed Louise and Ruth down the stairs, hoping that my sewing business survived once my creations were broadcast nationwide.

Ruth held her head high, a ruse that almost concealed the slowness of her steps. My initial assessment that she was fully recovered from her medical ordeal may have been overly optimistic. Still, there was nothing hesitant about her speech when she entered the living room.

She thumped her cane on the floor. "I have an announcement to make, before the filming can begin."

Priscilla still sat in her wingback chair by the fireplace, her skirt spread about her to great effect. The makeup artists had worked their magic. Her face was artfully made up to minimize her wrinkles and highlight the sweetness of her smile. She held out a hand to Ruth, blithely disregarding Ruth's announcement. "Ruth, dear, you look lovely. Come, sit by me."

The rest of the household stood around the room, dressed in their best clothes, looking almost universally uncomfortable. Carl Harper seemed lost with no tool in his hands. Jamison Royce shifted from foot to foot, still wearing his unusual cap with the earflaps. John Ellis leaned on the back of his aunt Priscilla's armchair, his sharp eyes on his mother. Randall lounged against the window frame, hands in his pockets. His eyes met mine momentarily, but I looked away. Randall and his misdeeds were the least of my concerns right now.

I scanned the rest of the occupants of the room; the camera operators, lights people, makeup folks, Cherry and Stillman directing the whole operation. No sign of a newspaper photographer or his reporter sidekick. I slipped out into the hallway for a quick check around, but he was nowhere in sight. Where could McCarthy be?

I hurried back to the living room in time for Ruth's next words.

"I want you all to know that I plan to make a momentous disclosure at the end of our day of filming today. In memory of Professor Burbridge, whom we all mourn, I shall reveal the essence of his original research into the life of my ancestor, Major Samuel Compton, as well as some other historical inquiries he was pursuing." She closed her mouth with a snap, seemingly unfazed by the buzz that greeted her words.

I kept my eyes on the four suspects who stood around the room: Harper, Royce, Randall, and John. I saw looks of surprise and interest, but couldn't gauge whether any one of them was threatened by Ruth's announcement. Maybe I just needed to let events unfold.

Cherry and Stillman signaled to begin the filming. Evidently their plan was to follow each contractor in turn through the house, focusing on the elements that that person was responsible for. They began by leading Carl Harper off to the kitchen, leaving the rest of us in the living room with instructions to remain on-site.

I started to follow the cameras to the kitchen with some idea of listening in on Harper's responses to see if I could tell if he was nervous about Ruth's impending disclosure. I didn't get very far. Martin Sterling whisked through the front door and caught my eye. I almost ran to his side.

"Any sign of McCarthy at his apartment?"

He shook his head. "His newspaper was still in the box, so he didn't pick it up this morning. I went up and tried the door, but it was locked and nothing looked funny there."

I plucked at his sleeve. "Did you go in? Maybe he had some kind of an accident inside."

He nodded. "Yeah, I went in. Good thing no one else was home, 'cause I made a fair amount of noise breaking in. Guess I'll owe McCarthy for some repair bills when this is all over. But he wasn't there. No breakfast dishes, or wet toothbrush or washcloth or anything. I'm guessing he didn't go home at all last night."

"Where else would he have gone?" As soon as I said it, I was struck by the obvious and unacceptable answer that he'd gone to spend the night with someone else, someone who was not me. I couldn't think of a particular person whom McCarthy would turn to for solace and more, but women loved McCarthy. They all did. He could have ended up at the home of any number of women in town. Who was I to say he shouldn't? I blinked a few tears out of my eyes and concentrated on Sterling's next words.

"Where was the last place you saw him? I saw him at the *Chronicle* first thing in the morning yesterday, but not after that."

I took a deep breath, trying to get my emotions under control. "I went with him to his assignment at the university at noon. We had lunch afterward at the Station, where he and I had an argument. Last I saw him he was walking on the quad, upset with me. He did respond to a text a few minutes later, but nothing after that."

"Did he drive to the university?"

I nodded.

He pulled out his phone, and then shoved it back into his pocket. "I'll head over there, see if his car is still there. I guess the paper will have to do without a feature on Compton Hall's shot at the limelight."

I started to say I'd go with him, but I realized that I couldn't leave Ruth alone to carry out our plan to expose a murderer. "Last I saw it, his car was parked in the lot next to the library. It was unlocked. Text me what you find." I gave him my number.

Sterling nodded and whisked back out the front door.

I returned to the living room to find that Cherry and Stillman were done with Carl Harper. They were focusing on Jamison Royce, who talked easily about the plants he'd added to the garden. It looked like the rain had let up, so they could go outside and take some shots of the dripping garden.

I fidgeted and paced for the next hour and a half. If I had been a suspect, my actions would have given me away as guilty. At some point my phone dinged with a text from Sterling. "Car's at university. No sign of McC. I'm calling police."

I read this message over and over, trying to make sense out of the words. McCarthy had never left the university. Not in his car, at any rate. That tense little text message exchange that I had with him about how I was getting home may have been the last communication he had with anyone. At least I didn't have to worry about him spending the night with an unknown woman. I just had to worry about whether or not he was still alive.

I pushed this thought away in horror. Of course he was still alive. I needed to see him, to apologize and make things right between us. It wouldn't be fair if I never had the chance to say I was sorry for the way I treated him. It didn't matter if he forgave me or not. I couldn't bear it if the last conversation I ever had with McCarthy was a fight that I had started.

I put my hand over my eyes and tried to think. If he never left the university, then he must still be there. Maybe he'd gone back to talk to Noah again. I dialed Noah's number, but there was no answer. Did the guy ever answer his phone?

I texted Sterling back. "Find Noah Webster. History grad student. He had lunch with McCarthy and me yesterday. Maybe he knows where to look."

He responded right away. "Got it."

I couldn't stand being inside for one more minute. I slipped out of the living room, not caring whether or not I would be the next one interviewed. I walked out the door and paced up and down the driveway.

There were so many vehicles in the driveway that I could barely move. I couldn't help looking for a bright yellow Mustang, even as I knew that it sat at the university, unoccupied. I remembered Noah's comment that he had read little Eli Fuller's letters over and over, hoping that maybe this time the end would come out differently. Where was Noah right now?

I paused next to Jamison Royce's pickup, and tried Noah one more time. No luck. Was he missing too? I leaned my forehead on the passenger window, and closed my eyes. Oliphant University was a few short blocks away. I longed to search it, classroom by classroom, instead of leaving that job to Sterling. But I couldn't abandon Ruth after she had set our plan into motion. I sighed and opened my eyes to push myself up off the door of the pickup. I wasn't really trying to spy into Royce's truck, but the object on the passenger seat caught my attention. It was a classy gray fedora.

It was identical to the gray fedora that I had admired at Noah Webster's presentation, worn by a man who looked vaguely familiar to me. I tried to remember what it was about him that triggered that recognition. Something about the way he sat, in front of me. He was a big man, but unremarkable aside from his classy headgear. As I recalled, he didn't have a beard, like Royce did.

Could that man at the presentation have been Jamison Royce? I'd seen the gray fedora twice: once at the presentation and then at the Station afterward as McCarthy, Noah, and I talked about the import of Professor Burbridge's research. Was Jamison Royce spying on us? What interest did he have in the professor's research? I couldn't think of a single reason why he would feel threatened by historical revelations about Major Samuel Compton.

Of course, it could be a different fedora altogether, and I was wasting my time even thinking about it. Somehow I doubted that that was the case.

I looked over at the garden to see that the TV folks had finished up with Royce. I walked back inside, wondering who was next.

Apparently Cherry had called a lunch break. The front hall was deserted. All the men had left, leaving Priscilla and Ruth alone in the living room. Priscilla smoothed her long skirt and smiled at me as I came in. "Such an exciting day, my dear. I'm almost too wound up to eat. John has gone out to fetch us some sandwiches."

Ruth sat next to Priscilla. She held an unopened envelope in her hand with a look almost of dread on her face. "Daria, will you come with me for a moment?" She pulled herself to her feet and spoke to Priscilla. "We'll be back in time for the sandwiches."

She led me without speaking to the kitchen, and had me close the door behind me. She put a hand on the heavy wooden table as if she lacked the strength to stand without support. She indicated the envelope. "Louise just handed this to me. She found it on the bathroom counter."

The envelope had Ruth's name scrawled on the front. "It's the response to your announcement." I held out my hand, but Ruth kept hold of the envelope. She ran her finger under the flap and tore it open. It contained one sheet of paper. She read it in silence, her face paling by the time she got to the end. She handed it to me without a word.

It was a short note, handwritten with block lettering. The message was frighteningly simple: "Meet me in the basement if you want to see your son alive again. Come alone."

I handed it back to her. "It's a trap. Priscilla said John went out to get sandwiches."

She frowned. "How do I know that's where he is?"

Before I could answer, she pulled out a cell phone and dialed. I was still marveling that she was so up-to-date with technology when she clicked off her phone in frustration. Did no one in this town ever answer their phones?

"I suppose I have to go, to get to the bottom of this nonsense." She straightened up and gripped her cane like the warrior that she was.

But I wasn't going to let her do this. "You can't go alone. You're only just back from the hospital. I'll go with you."

"You'll do no such thing. This has nothing to do with you. You'll stay here and get yourself on camera and cover my absence."

She almost had me there. But I knew she wasn't up to confronting a murderer. Not that I was either, but that didn't matter. "You can't go down there, Ruth. You'll never make it down the stairs in that long dress. You know I'm right."

She gritted her teeth. "I'm not going to send you down there to be killed."

"No, listen. Whoever it is doesn't know that I've read your note. When I go down to the basement with a load of wash to stick in the washing machine, they'll just hurry me on my way. I can see what's going on and come back up, while you call the police to back us up. Nobody's going to get killed." I headed out the kitchen door. "Where can I get a quick load of laundry?"

Ruth pointed out the linen closet, and I shook out a few sheets and gathered them into my arms. "I'll be at the top of the stairs keeping an eye on you," she said as we headed for the basement stairs.

I was dressed in a calf-length full skirt, which might give me trouble on the narrow wooden stairs to the basement, but I refrained from mentioning this to Ruth. I could hear her cane tapping behind me as we walked toward the head of the stairs.

So could the murderer! Whoever was waiting in the basement would hear that cane tapping above their head. They would know where Ruth was. I stopped with her right behind me. "You can't come any further, Miss Ruth. Whoever's down there will hear your cane. You should go back and stay with Priscilla."

"Did I hear my name?" Priscilla shuffled around the corner, clutching a bouquet of lilacs in both hands. "The girls across the street picked these for me. Such sweet little things. Can you help me find a vase, my dear?"

I shot Ruth a look, and hurried back to the kitchen to root out a vase for Priscilla. Ruth followed slowly, thumping her cane a bit more than usual.

I found a crystal vase that would fit the lilacs, and placed it on the table for Priscilla. She made an attempt, and then held out the bouquet to me. "Would you do it, my dear?"

I laid down my bundle of laundry, and eased the lilacs into the vase. I turned to wash my hands in the sink, but the sink was no longer there. I gave a sharp sigh and wiped my hands on my skirt. I turned back to the two sisters to see Priscilla holding the folded-up note from the murderer.

She read it before Ruth or I could snatch it away. She dropped it on the floor and clasped both hands together, almost in an attitude of prayer. "It's Robby!" she cried. "Robby is alive again. I knew he would come back to us some day. Didn't I tell you, Ruth?"

Ruth and I just stared at her, mystified. I picked up the paper and read it again, aloud. "Meet me in the basement if you want to see your son alive again. Come alone." Priscilla had spent years wishing to see her nephew alive again. In her own vague way she was misinterpreting the words to mean what she hoped it could mean.

Ruth leaned on the table again. She passed a gnarled hand across her face. "Daria is going to go down and see him, Priscilla. She'll tell us how he's doing. Let's go sit down in the living room and wait for her to come back." She led the way out of the kitchen. "Come with me."

I waited long enough to be sure that Priscilla was going with Ruth, and then I gathered up my laundry and walked toward the basement stairs. My heart was pounding, but I held my head high. As long as I didn't make a mistake, I would be fine. I would put in my laundry, see what was going on, and get out of there. Nothing bad was going to happen to me.

My phone dinged right at the top of the stairs. I shifted the sheets to one arm and snatched my phone out of my pocket. The text from Sterling said, "Can't find Webster. Waiting for police to come and search."

Police. I didn't know if Ruth was still planning to call the police. I texted Sterling, "Tell police to come to Compton Hall. Now." But I couldn't wait any longer. I opened the door to the basement and turned on the light.

I half expected the light to not work, but it came on with no problem. A quick glance showed nothing amiss in the basement. I clutched my sheets in one hand and the railing in the other, and made my way down the stairs. It wasn't until I got to the bottom that I saw him.

He stood in the corner at the bottom of the stairs, out of sight of the upper doorway. At first glance I thought he was John, but he wasn't. He was a big man, clean-shaven, with his bald head uncovered. He'd left his fedora in the van, and the hat with the earflaps lay on the floor at his feet. Now that I could see his ears for the first time, I noticed the distinctive long earlobes that distinguished the Compton family. I didn't know how he could have shaved off his beard so quickly, since I'd just seen him talking in front of the camera in the garden. It was Jamison Royce, only it wasn't. I'd never met him, but I knew I was looking at Robert Ellis. Robby was alive again.

Chapter Twenty-One

I tried my best to play it off. "Oh, my goodness, you scared me! I wasn't expecting anyone to be down here." I paused to stare at him a moment, for form's sake. "It's Jamison, isn't it? You look so different without your beard. I wasn't expecting you to shave it off so quickly." I brushed past him on the way to the washing machine. "I just need to get this laundry into the washer."

If I had dropped my sheets and run up the stairs, I might have been okay. But in the moment it took me to load up the washer, Robert sprang into action. He grabbed my arm and spun me around to face him. "You're in the wrong place at the wrong time, dearie. I'm expecting someone else to come down for a little chat. Now you're going to have to wait until I'm done with my business." He pushed me down and grabbed a sheet to wrap around me.

I screamed and kicked out at him from the floor. If he thought I was going to be an easy victim, he had another think coming! I scurried away from him and fumbled in my pocket for the mini sewing kit I'd brought along to deal with any emergencies during the filming. When I'd said "emergencies," I was thinking split seams, not murderers in the basement. I pulled out the tape measure and flung it around his ankles and pulled tight. He fell heavily to the floor.

I scrambled to my feet and backed away from him. "Where's John?" I scanned the basement but couldn't see anyone else down there.

Robert laughed and pulled himself up. "Johnny's not here. He's off somewhere, buying sandwiches for his mommy." Then he stopped, staring at me. "So. You saw the note. You came down looking for John. My mother sent you in her place."

I held myself straight, heart thudding. He didn't have any weapons that I could see. "Ruth didn't send me. I chose to come."

"To do laundry? Or to be a hero?"

I didn't have an answer for that one. "Did you kill Professor Burbridge to keep his research from coming out?"

He edged toward me, cutting me off from the stairs. "I asked him nicely to reconsider, but he refused. If my mother hadn't already chewed him out, I might have been able to persuade him. But she had to take him to task and put him on the defensive." He bent down and picked up a hammer that was lying on the floor. Hefting it in one hand, he pounded the head into his other palm.

Now he was armed, and certainly dangerous. I pulled out my phone and snapped a picture of him. With the flick of a finger I sent the picture to whoever was on my text message at the moment. "I just sent a picture of you to the police department. No matter what you do to me down here, they'll know it was you. I caught a good image of the hammer, just so you know."

Robert paused, clearly rattled by this statement. McCarthy would be proud of me, using photography to save my life.

McCarthy! I gasped out loud and flashed my phone a dozen times in his face. "What have you done with McCarthy?" If I kept moving in a circle, keeping him at a distance, I could work my way back to the stairs.

He blinked the light out of his eyes. "That mouthy photographer? I shut him up."

"No!" I screamed. I almost threw my phone at him, but I knew I might need it. I shot a frantic glance behind me, looking for something, anything, to hit him with. What had he done to McCarthy? Tears streamed down my face. I didn't even think about the very real danger to my own life. McCarthy!

Robert came slowly toward me, hammer twitching. "I picked up your nerdy friend too. He's doing a job for me. When the job's done, they'll both be reunited with the late professor."

Noah. Noah was still alive, held somewhere by Robert. Again I glanced around the basement, but there was no one there. No one but Robert Ellis, bent on shutting me up too.

I took another step backward, trying not to let him back me into a corner. I stumbled over something on the floor and almost fell. I reached down to grab it, whatever it was, so I would have something to throw at him. It was the kitty litter box.

I snatched it up and flung it full in his face. It smelled terrible. With all the renovations going on, Louise must have neglected to clean up after the cat. I blessed her for her negligence.

Robert cried out and scrabbled at his face, dropping the hammer in the process. I caught it up, but restrained myself from hitting him with it. Instead I pushed past him and ran for the stairs. He made a grab at me, but missed. I clutched my skirt in one hand and the railing in the other, and darted up those stairs faster than I'd ever run in my life. I almost knocked Ruth over at the top.

She stood there, leaning on her cane, with a couple of policemen right behind her. They had obviously just arrived. Another minute with Robert down in the basement, and I would have been rescued.

She caught my arm to keep me from crashing right into her. The cops pushed past us both and proceeded down the stairs, weapons drawn and at the ready.

"Are you all right? I heard you scream." She looked frightened, more vulnerable than I'd ever seen her before.

Priscilla came into the narrow hallway behind her. "Was it Robby down there, my dear?"

I took Ruth's arm and led her out to the front porch, away from the clamor in the basement. She didn't pull away from my hand. "Let's sit down on the porch. You too, Miss Priscilla."

When they were both settled and I stood before them, I said, "Yes, it was Robby. He's not dead." I paused while disbelief swept over one sister's face, and pure joy over the other's. "He was masquerading as Jamison Royce. He must have used a fake beard, so you wouldn't recognize him."

"I haven't seen him in thirty years." Ruth made no attempt to hide the quiver in her voice.

"He looks a lot like John," I said.

At that moment, John himself came up the drive, a fast-food bag clutched in his fist. "What's going on, Mother?"

I left them then to try to make sense of their bizarre family reunion.

I went upstairs to the bathroom, thankful to find that Carl Harper had not touched this little room. I washed the stink of kitty litter off my hands and splashed my face, removing the traces of my recent tears. I dried my hands in a daze. I didn't know what to do, or what to feel. "McCarthy," I whispered to my reflection.

My phone dinged.

I snatched it up, hoping against hope that it would be him. It wasn't.

"Are you okay?" ran the text from Sterling. "What's with the guy with the hammer?"

It must have been Sterling who had received my photo of Robert. I texted him back, "It's all good now. Any luck?"

He responded, "Cops came but then left in a hurry. No progress."

I sighed, and stowed my phone in my pocket. I stepped out of the bathroom, and dragged down the hall, past the library. I stopped and stood in the doorway, staring at the carpet where Professor Burbridge had lain. His research had caused all this trouble. I hoped it never, ever got published.

I caught my breath. That was Robert's ultimate goal, to keep the professor's research from becoming public. But the professor's death didn't kill the research. How could Robert ensure that Burbridge's research would never come to light?

He would have to erase the professor's work from any place that it was stored. Robert had said Noah was doing a job for him, and when the job was finished Noah would die. Had he set Noah the task of removing all traces of the professor's research from his files, both physical and digital? If so, where would Noah be doing that job?

I started to run, running right out the door and down the driveway to the sidewalk. Oliphant University was only a few blocks away. I couldn't keep up the pace the whole way, but I got there in record time. I panted up two flights of stairs in Old Main to get to the history department.

Professor Burbridge's office was still roped off with police tape. I didn't care. I grasped the doorknob and pulled with all my might. The door was locked.

I rattled the knob until I thought it should fall off in my hand, but it didn't. I heard thumps and muffled sounds coming from inside. I burst into an empty classroom and ripped through the teacher's desk, coming up with a manila envelope and a fancy bookmark as the best possibilities. The envelope was too big to fit between the door and the doorjamb, and the bookmark was too flimsy to budge the lock. Finally I folded the bookmark in two to give it greater heft, and thrust down with all my strength. The bookmark buckled, and the lock released at the same moment. I threw the bookmark on the floor and flung open the door.

Noah sat at the desk, tied to the desk chair with a necktie shoved in his mouth as a gag. I scarcely gave him a thought. In a metal chair next to him, tied and gagged in a similar fashion, sat McCarthy. He wasn't dead! Robert had shut him up with a gag.

I flew to McCarthy and untied the necktie and pulled it out of his mouth. The tears were flowing again as I held his face in both hands, drinking in the sight of him. "I am so sorry, Sean! I never should have said I didn't trust you. I didn't think I'd ever see you again, to have the chance to take it back."

He worked his jaw a few times, and then said, "Hey. Hey. It's okay. You're here to save the day, right? I knew I could trust you to find us in the end."

I laughed and cried and pulled at the knots holding him until they finally came loose. He rubbed his wrists and flexed his ankles while I struggled to untie Noah. When Noah was finally freed I turned back to McCarthy. He caught me in his arms and pulled me into a close embrace. I held him tight and laid my head on his shoulder. "You got here in the nick of time," he whispered into my tousled hair. "I really have to go to the bathroom."

I left McCarthy and Noah to sort themselves out while I called Sterling to tell him all was well. He arrived a few minutes later. I saw the relief wash over his face when he laid eyes on McCarthy. He slapped McCarthy's shoulders, and then the two men embraced.

"Hiding out behind the police tape, were you?"

McCarthy sat down on the edge of Professor Burbridge's desk, his leg dangling down. "Noah brought me back here to show me the professor's research."

Noah's face reddened. "I know I wasn't supposed to cross the police tape, but I didn't want to let Burbridge's work go to waste. I hope the police don't charge me for trespassing or something."

"I'll deal with them," McCarthy said. "So we were deep into it when the door flew open and Jamison Royce came in. He pulled a gun on us and had me tied up before I knew what was happening to me. He held the gun on Noah and told him to delete all of Professor Burbridge's research from his computer, and anyplace else it might be online."

He rubbed the stubble covering his normally clean-shaven chin. "I could tell that I was expendable—there was no reason for Royce to keep me alive. I just kept telling him that he needed me to keep Noah calm so he could perform his tasks, that if he killed me Noah would be so freaked out that he wouldn't be able to delete the professor's research."

"That was actually true." Noah's face was red again. "I was freaked out by the whole thing. If it wasn't for McCarthy, I would have been a total mess."

"After a while Royce got tired of listening to me and shoved that horrible necktie into my mouth."

I went to stand beside him, putting my arms around his neck. "He told me that he shut you up. I thought he'd killed you." I hid my face in his shoulder.

McCarthy stroked my hair very gently. "I'm sorry," he whispered. He cleared his throat, and then said nothing at all.

Noah took up the tale. "I worked on it all day and into the night. It went really slow because my hands were shaking so much that I kept making mistakes. It's hard to be efficient with a gun pointed at your head. Of course, I had no incentive to work quickly, since I knew Royce wasn't planning on letting us go." He sat back down in the desk chair. "I've pulled a lot of all-nighters in my academic career, but this was the absolute worst. Generally you're trying to finish a project on time to get a good grade. When I finished this project, I was going to get a bullet to the head. Even worse, I was erasing the work of a man I admired and respected, work that got him killed. It was awful." He closed his eyes for a moment, and then he shook it off. "Of course, what Royce didn't know is that Burbridge, being the suspicious person that he was, had all his work backed up on a hard drive that he kept in a locker at the pool. He swam laps every day after work, and had a faculty locker assigned to him. I haven't had a chance to check, but I'm pretty sure it's still there, untouched. Even if he'd killed us, Royce wouldn't have succeeded in killing Burbridge's research. You can't kill knowledge."

Suddenly McCarthy jumped up from the desk, jerking free from my embrace. "Where's Royce now, Daria?"

"As far as I know, the police have him. He's not really Jamison Royce, by the way. He's really Robert Ellis, oldest son of Ruth and Thurman Ellis. He disappeared after high school and just reappeared. He was trying to preserve his family's fortunes, with the goal of inheriting them, I suppose."

I didn't get any further. My phone rang. It was Aileen.

"I can't believe you did it again. You've got a client at the door and you're not here."

"Who is it?" I couldn't figure out who I'd scheduled to come during the final day of filming. Although, that day was supposed to be yesterday. "Today's Saturday, right?"

Aileen snorted. "Get it together, Daria. It's the bride from the other day. She says she's come to pick up her wedding dress. You want to just tell me where it is and I'll hand it to her?"

That was the first time Aileen had ever offered to help me out with my sewing business. It felt like a momentous occasion. "Thanks, but I need to see her. She needs to try it on one more time, and she needs to pay me." I checked the time. I could catch the bus home in about ten minutes. "Could you ask her if she'll wait?"

She groaned, and hung up. I'd take that as a yes.

I turned back to McCarthy. "I gotta go. Catch you later?"

He took both my hands and squeezed them tightly. "Want me to take you home?"

I returned the squeeze. "You probably have to talk to the police. You're a missing person, remember? Call me when it's all over."

I hurried out the door in time to catch the bus home.

Fiona was waiting in my fitting room when I got home. I was thankful that she was alone. I summoned up as much cheeriness as I could. "I'm sorry I'm always late when you get here. But your gown's all done and your wedding's not till next Saturday, so it's all good."

She smiled and held out both hands to receive the gown I handed her. "Go put it on, and I'll button you up the back."

While Fiona dressed, I brushed my hair and freshened up in the bathroom. Hard to imagine that I'd been fighting for my life not an hour ago.

Fiona's gown fit perfectly. The hem broke at the tip of her toes, exactly. She twisted and turned and admired herself in my big three-way mirror. "Randy will be so amazed. He told me he's so glad you're the one who made my dress for me."

Yeah, right. He just wanted the chance to get back into my house. I bit my tongue and merely smiled.

Fiona chattered on while striking a few poses in front of the mirror. "Randy's so sweet. He gave me a special gift yesterday, for our wedding. It's a beautiful silver platter. It took my breath away. Here, let me show you." She picked up her purse and pulled out her phone. After a few swipes she displayed a photo of an impressive silver platter. The camera had picked up the intricate detail of fluting around the edge, decorated with swirls and curlicues. "It's pretty old. Randy said that when he got it, it was almost black from tarnish. It took him hours to get it to shine like this."

Almost black. I caught my breath. I'd seen that brassy platter, spilling out of a pillowcase that Randall had filched from its hiding place in my attic. I hadn't thought anything of it beyond the sense of violation caused by him breaking into my house. It hadn't occurred to me that what I was seeing was a silver platter hidden beneath a layer of tarnish. I hadn't asked the obvious question: Where had Randall gotten an old silver platter from in the first place?

My hands went cold as the obvious answer hit me. "Could you text me that picture, Fiona? I love old silver, and that's the most beautiful platter I've ever seen."

She shrugged and pressed buttons on her phone. "Isn't he a sweetheart?"

I couldn't bear to tell her. If I were right, the police would pick up Randall in time for her to postpone or cancel her wedding. She'd have a narrow escape, but it wouldn't be me, the jilted ex-fiancée, who had ruined her bright future.

I felt guilty about taking Fiona's money, but I knew I had earned it through my work. Her gown was stunning—no one could dispute that. I covered it carefully in plastic and handed it to her with as much of a smile as I could manage. As soon as she was gone, I called McCarthy. I needed to see one of his photographs.

McCarthy listened patiently as I blurted out my story. He gave a low whistle as I reached the end. "Those photos were published in the *Chronicle* last May. If you go to our website, you can find them. I'm almost done with the cops here. It's your old buddy Carson. Shall I send him over to you when we're done?"

"I'll let you know." I hung up, and searched the website of the Laurel Springs *Daily Chronicle*.

I couldn't remember the woman's name, so it took me a few minutes to call up the photos I wanted. When I finally found them, they took my breath away. Priscilla was right; McCarthy had taken fantastic photographs of Francisca Toumay's antique silver, including the one piece that was made by Paul Revere himself.

It was a big silver platter, decorated by the master with swirls and curlicues running around the fluted edge. McCarthy had picked up the soft shine of the silver. His photo was far more artistic, but the platter was identical to the one in the picture Fiona had shared with me with such fond pride.

McCarthy had said the piece was worth half a million dollars, but how could Randall sell it without someone recognizing it? So he had decided to gift it to his bride as a wedding present. I laid my phone down in amazement. Maybe he really did love her.

Chapter Twenty-Two

I spent the rest of the afternoon at the police station. I got chewed out for leaving the crime scene at Compton Hall, and lectured for taking off for a fitting instead of debriefing with the police after releasing McCarthy and Noah. I thought they were going to charge me with not showing proper respect for police procedure or something, but they calmed down when I mentioned Fiona's silver platter. In the end, they sent me on my way with the hope of hearing the rest of the story if I called in later.

I walked home from the police station, enjoying the moment of respite in a hectic day. The downtown sidewalks hummed with the weekend crowd of window-shoppers, kids on their skateboards, and couples out on a dinner date. Nobody gave me a second glance. That felt odd—couldn't they see that I'd escaped both death and heartbreak this afternoon? I could scarcely believe that the stress hadn't left a mark.

When I got home Pete and Aileen sat at the kitchen table, eating some kind of unidentifiable slop that smelled like a mix between boiled cabbage and frosted cinnamon buns. Aileen waved at the empty chair. "Come join us."

I just shook my head. I surprised them both by giving each of them a huge hug. "McCarthy's picking me up for dinner. It's a great day to be alive!"

Pete chuckled. "I guess you made up with him."

I scooped up Mohair and gave her a big kiss. "Actually, we haven't technically made up yet. But I rescued him from a murderer, so that's gotta count for something." I left them both staring and ran upstairs to shower and dress for dinner.

I put on a tea-length flowing dress in a pale blue floral print, paired with a cream-colored shawl that I'd crocheted out of the finest-gauge yarn possible. I slipped on my favorite pair of dressy sandals, and brushed my hair until it shone. I was ready to step out on the town with my guy.

McCarthy sat in my chair at the table when I got downstairs. I could tell from the absorbed looks on Pete's and Aileen's faces that he was telling them the whole story of kidnap and the apprehension of a murderer. Better him than me.

McCarthy broke off when he saw me. His eyes lit up and he jumped to his feet. He'd dressed for dinner as well, throwing a sport coat over his customary white button-down shirt and exchanging his jeans for a pair of gray twill pants. He extended a hand to me. "So Daria came bursting through the door to save the day, and the rest is history."

I dropped a little curtsy and reached over to snag my keys off their hook under the mirror. I took McCarthy's hand and waved goodbye to Pete and Aileen.

McCarthy led me to his car. "I thought you might like to check on the Compton sisters before we eat."

I hadn't had any lunch and I was pretty near starving, but I did want to see how Ruth and Priscilla were faring.

As if he'd read my mind, McCarthy said, "I got us reservations for seven thirty, so we'll have time for a short chat."

The driveway was empty when we arrived. No sign of any contractor's van or lawyer's smart vehicle. The TV vans bristling with technology were also long gone. Priscilla sat on the front porch, quietly rocking the way she had throughout my childhood. Ruth sat beside her, ramrod straight and clutching the head of her gold-tipped cane. Peace had returned to Compton Hall.

Priscilla's lined face lighted up when she saw us. "So nice to see you, my dear, and your young man. Do sit down and talk for a minute."

I sat in the rocking chair next to her, and McCarthy leaned against the porch rail. "You must be exhausted after everything that happened today," I said.

Priscilla nodded. "The filming took much longer than I expected. The poor cameraman had to keep filming the same scene over and over again." She indicated McCarthy's camera dangling around his neck. "Do you have that same problem when you take pictures for the newspaper?"

He smiled. "I take multiple shots of whatever I'm photographing, and then I pick the best one. It can take a long time. But it's usually worth it."

"Oh, I'm sure you're right, dear. I don't think I'll win the million dollars, though. I think there was too much drama even for the reality show."

Ruth rolled her eyes. "Cherry was intrigued by the reappearance of a long-lost son, but when he turned out to be a murderer, she backed off."

"Poor Robby," Priscilla murmured.

Ruth held her head high, her face grim. "He confessed to the murder of Professor Burbridge. He also confessed to setting that fire seven years ago. He had hoped to kill both his father and me, but I foiled his plan by leaving that night. Then he hoped that I would be convicted for my husband's death, but I was acquitted. So he seized the opportunity during the renovations to try again. He put those sleeping pills in my tea, of course." She pressed her lips together and looked away.

Priscilla shook her head. "He must have lost his mind. So sad."

"He heard my argument with Professor Burbridge through the open window." I could tell this recitation was paining Ruth, but she seemed to need to get it all out. "He'd gotten the idea that he could inherit the Hall once I was dead, and the professor's research threatened that plan. I don't know what he intended to do to John, or Priscilla."

"Robby would never hurt me," Priscilla said. "Dear boy."

Ruth looked down at her hands clenched around the head of her cane. "Probably not."

McCarthy flicked a glance at me. "Have you two ladies had dinner yet? Daria and I would be happy to have you join us."

Not really, but I smiled nonetheless.

"Oh, no, we couldn't intrude on your date, my dear. John is coming to take us to dinner." Priscilla leaned forward and patted me on the hand. "We can't eat at home until that nice Carl Harper gives us back our modern-day kitchen. He'll be back next Wednesday, once he finishes this other job that's been causing him so much trouble."

"What other job?"

The three of us all concentrated on Priscilla. She waved a hand. "A member of his crew was replacing a kitchen floor with wooden flooring. The whole floor was done when he realized that he'd put it in wrong, with the planks going crosswise instead of lengthwise, or something like that. It was a simple mistake, but the poor man had to rip it all out and put it in right before the client would pay for the job. Poor Carl was very upset, because he lost a lot of money on the job. I can't tell you how many times I heard him fussing about it over the phone."

"Me too." I shook my head, thinking that I should have mentioned Harper's phone conversations to Priscilla earlier. I could have taken him off my list of suspects.

McCarthy checked his watch. "We should be going." He waited while I gave Priscilla a gentle hug.

"I did hope you would win the million dollars," I said.

"Oh, no, my dear. I'm not at all sorry. If I won, poor Louise would have to learn how to cook over an open hearth. We couldn't keep on going out to eat like this every night. The million dollars would be gone by Christmas."

I laughed and gave Ruth a hug as well. I felt her stiffen so I kept it very short. "Thanks for helping me flush out a murderer. I'm just sorry it turned out to be your son."

She nodded, twisting the handle of her cane between both hands. "My husband used to tell the boys to strive to grow up to be like their honorable ancestor, Major Samuel Compton. Robert may have taken that advice a bit too far, as it turns out."

"Seriously." I picked up my shoulder bag and turned to go. "If either of you ever need another eightcenth-century gown, please call mc."

"Of course, my dear," Priscilla said with a smile.

"I don't foresee the need for any future gowns, but if I ever need a detective, I know where to look." Ruth gave me a genuine smile that meant more to me than the check for payment that she'd pressed into my hand.

McCarthy threw me a curious glance as we walked down the porch steps. "Looks like you tamed the dragon there."

I nodded. "She's got a soft underbelly like most dragons do, or so I'm told." I waved to Louise, who lingered at the bottom of the steps, finishing a cigarette. She tossed the butt into the flower border when she saw me.

"Didn't I tell you those pills were attempted murder? We're all lucky to get out of this alive."

"You called it," I said. "But you're sticking around, right?"

She dusted her hands on her pants. "Looks like it. Miss Priscilla could hardly be expected to manage without me." She looked McCarthy over. "I see you're off the missing persons list."

I stared at her. "How did you know McCarthy was missing?"

She shrugged, with the closest thing to a smile that I'd yet seen on her face. "It's a big house, chock full of doors with keyholes."

I laughed. "I'm glad Priscilla and Ruth have you to watch out for them."

McCarthy opened the car door for me. I slid into the seat and rummaged through my bag for my phone. I got the answering machine. "Rats, the police department is closed for the weekend. I wanted to find out if Randall got arrested."

He zoomed away from the curb and hurtled down the hill toward town. "Don't tell me the nosy seamstress is looking for revenge?"

I put on my most innocent face. "Who, me?"

McCarthy pulled into a parking spot adjacent to the Commons. He picked up his phone.

My stomach growled at that moment. "Dinner?" I said.

"I just need to make one quick call." He dialed, and then covered his phone with the palm of his hand. "I've got a contact in the police department. Riley can tell me what's up with Randall."

I got out of the car and strolled up and down the sidewalk while McCarthy sat and talked with Riley. I didn't want to hear a lengthy one-sided conversation; I just wanted McCarthy to give it to me short and sweet.

At last he hung up and got out of the car. I turned to walk along the Commons without delay. He fell into step beside me.

"You were right; Fiona had the missing platter from Francisca Toumay's estate—the one that was made by Paul Revere. Police recovered a number of other pieces that most likely came from Compton Hall. They suspect that there were many more that had already been fenced. There's been a rash of thefts from the estates of half a dozen people who have died in this area in recent years. The police are reviewing those cases for links to Randall."

"Wow. I lived with a silver thief." I couldn't believe it, but at the same time I knew it had to be true.

McCarthy clicked his tongue. "When confronted, Randall initially claimed that he'd gotten the Paul Revere platter from you as an engagement gift."

I cried out in dismay at that, but he only chuckled. "That tactic got him exactly nowhere with Fiona. It only highlighted the fact that he'd never mentioned that the two of you were engaged, and that he was low enough to try to pin the crime on you. Riley says she pulled off her diamond ring and handed it back to him, right there in front of the police officers."

"Poor Fiona. I never told her, either. I'm as bad as he is."

McCarthy took my hand and swung it lightly as we walked. "Never in a million years."

I squeezed his hand gratefully. "Where are we going for dinner?"

"You'll like it. Trust me." His eyes twinkled at me.

I punched him on the arm. "I said I was sorry for not trusting you."

He rubbed his arm as if I'd slugged him with a two-by-four. "True, but you were under the influence of extreme stress, so I'm not sure that it counts."

I rolled my eyes. "I'll say it again if you want me to."

"Wait until we get seated." He waved his arm with a flourish to indicate the entrance to La Trattoria. "Best new restaurant in town." He slipped past the dozen or so people milling about outside and went up to speak to the hostess. I waited for him to say, "Reservations for McCarthy," but instead he said, "Hey, Janice. Daria and I are here for our seven-thirty reservation." He held out his hand and drew me to his side. "Janice is a big fan of *My House in History*. She can't wait to see the episode on Compton Hall." He turned his attention back to Janice. "Daria made all the historical gowns. You'll love them."

Janice smiled at me. "I wish I could sew like that." She ushered us to the coziest table in the place.

I settled my napkin in my lap and watched McCarthy order us some wine. It all felt somehow familiar. With a start, I remembered that whenever Randall and I would eat out, he would turn on the charm for the waitstaff, just like that. But Randall was nothing like McCarthy. When I was with Randall, I never knew where I stood. With McCarthy, I didn't need to wonder. Everything about McCarthy was genuine—I could put my trust in that.

I picked up the glass of wine he poured for me. "Time for me to say it again, Sean. I'm sorry I said I didn't trust you. There's no one I'd rather trust than you." I put the wineglass down and reached out to take his hand. "Really, I mean it. You've never let me down. I don't know why I thought you ever would."

He squeezed my hand. "And I'm sorry for taking off in a huff like that. I shouldn't have taken it so personally." He rubbed his thumb across the back of my knuckles—an incredibly sexy touch. "I guess it hurt because I care what you think about me."

"You know what I think about you. You're an obnoxious photographer—my favorite obnoxious photographer in the whole wide world."

He laughed. "I'll take that. And you are a nosy seamstress, who always manages to figure it all out in the end. You're the sweetest nosy seamstress I've ever met in my life." He raised his glass in a toast. "To trust, whatever that means."

I raised my glass to clink with his. "We'll figure it out. Trust me."

If you enjoyed *Historically Dead*, be sure not to miss the first Stitch in Time Mystery

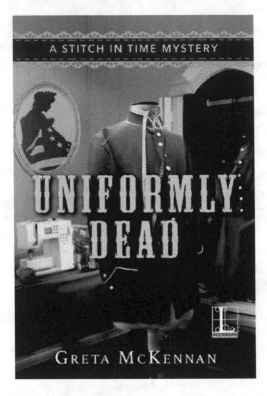

Historical seamstress Daria Dembrowski has her work cut out for her as she searches for a killer's pattern....

Daria has come up with a brilliant new plan to expand her seamstress business beyond stitching wedding gowns—historical sewing. And with Civil War reenactors setting up camp in her hometown of Laurel Springs, Pennsylvania, she has plenty of opportunities, including one client portraying a Confederate colonel who's a particular stickler for authenticity.

But soon the small-town peace starts coming apart at the seams as an antique doll is stolen from a Civil War exhibit and the cranky colonel is found impaled by his own bayonet. When Daria's brother is suspected of the theft and a bridal client's fiancé is accused of the murder, Daria is determined to untangle the clues to prove their innocence. She needs to get this case sewn up fast, though, before the murderer reenacts the crime and makes *her* history.

Keep reading for a special look!

A Lyrical Underground e-book on sale now.

Chapter One

My first meeting with Colonel Windstrom was a disaster. He marched into my fitting room—previously the formal dining room of my Federal-style house—as if it were a military headquarters. A hefty man, his tread shook the floorboards, jiggling the bolts of cloth leaning on the built-in shelf along the inside wall and toppling a rag doll on the mantel. He narrowly missed knocking into my antique spinning wheel. He took no notice of the books on the Civil War I'd carefully selected from the library, or the framed portrait of a Union soldier that I'd borrowed from an old lady at church. His bluster disrupted the cozy atmosphere I tried to create with my ruffled white organdy curtains and the hot cider simmering on the sideboard.

"I'll need coat and breeches from the gray wool," he instructed me, without even a *"hello."* "The shirt of white cotton broadcloth. Mind the stitches now. Anything that shows has got to look authentic." He pulled on his long, "authentic" moustache and scowled. "General Eberhart won't tolerate any Farbs in his outfit."

"Yessir, no Farbs," I repeated, wondering if a Farb was some new kind of Velcro. "You can count on me." I brandished my measuring tape to reassure him of my competence.

Colonel Windstrom glared. "Ms. Dembrowski, you don't even know what a Farb is, do you?"

I drew myself up to my full five feet, three inches. It was the first time I'd ever faced down a colonel, of any description. "Actually, no," I said. "But you can be sure I won't be using any Farbs on your uniform."

Colonel Windstrom's laugh startled me. His pudgy face turned bright red and he snorted through his nose. "Do you know a thing about reenacting?"

he barked. "A Farb is someone who doesn't care about history or an accurate portrayal of the period. He just wants to go out on a sunny day and shoot off some cannons. He'll make his uniform out of polyester if he feels like it." Colonel Windstrom wiped his face with a grimy handkerchief. "You obviously need to learn a thing or two about Civil War reenacting," he admonished me, as if I were seventeen instead of twenty-nine. He strode out the door without a backward glance.

I rolled my eyes at my cherished silhouette of Betsy Ross that hung above the mantel. Betsy Ross had been my hero ever since I did a project on her life in the fifth grade. I sewed a miniature felt flag and a mobcap for my presentation and pretended to be the illustrious seamstress. Even if no one could prove that she designed the first flag of the United States, she continued to inspire me as I focused more on historical projects in my sewing business, A Stitch in Time. I wondered how many belligerent patrons Betsy had to put up with in her day.

I hated to admit it, but Colonel Windstrom was right when he said I should learn more about reenacting. I got my first lesson later that very evening.

* * * *

I didn't often do house calls, unless I was working on drapes or upholstery, but this time I made an exception. I'd never seen a Civil War reenactors' encampment before, and I wasn't going to miss this one. If I was lucky, I might get a few more uniform orders before the mock battle at the end of the week. I'd be well on my way to establishing myself as the premier historical seamstress of Laurel Springs, Pennsylvania.

I got off the bus on the outskirts of Turner Run Park. The reenactors had taken over. Normally the serene river valley, nestled between two wooded bluffs, hosted a few dog walkers or the Laurel High School cross-country team on a training run. Today rows of canvas tents filled the valley floor. Laid out in straight lines as if on a grid, they illustrated the kind of military discipline required from a commander who would not tolerate any Farbs in his outfit. Men squatted around campfires scattered among the tents. The smell of wood smoke mingled with the unmistakable odor of gunpowder. The scent reminded me of the Fourth of July—an ironic association for a camp filled with Confederate soldiers bent on dissolving the Union. The men all had beards and long moustaches, and wore homespun shirts or tattered uniform coats, with muskets and rifles propped carelessly by their sides. My heart beat a little faster as I approached these mock Civil War soldiers. I felt like I was taking a step back in time.

I glanced around the groups, wondering how I would find Colonel Windstrom, when all of a sudden I heard my name.

"Daria!"

I peered through the campfire smoke to see a beefy soldier waving at me. "Hey, Chris." I knew Chris Porter through my work on his fiancée's wedding gown. With the wedding coming up next week, I needed all the time I could get.

Chris lumbered to his feet and came over to me. He held out his arms and pivoted slowly around. "What do you think—Confederate soldier extraordinaire?"

My lips twitched, but I didn't laugh. Obviously General Eberhart wasn't paying enough attention, because Chris was a Farb if there ever was one. His coat looked more like a Halloween costume than a period piece. I didn't even need to feel the fabric—I could see the unmistakable sheen of polyester. His cheerful face was bare of beard or moustache—not because he was too young, but evidently he just chose not to grow one.

"This is such a rush, Daria! I get to march with rifles with real bayonets and everything. How cool is that?" Chris plopped down on a log. "You wanna come sit by the fire?"

"Just for a minute." I sat down carefully beside him. "I'm here to see Colonel Windstrom." I blinked smoke out of my eyes. "I didn't know you were a reenactor."

"A buddy told me about it—he said they needed more soldiers. People keep quitting or something. So I snagged a coat and here I am. I'm taking a whole week off work to get the full experience."

"A whole week, with a wedding just around the corner? What does Marsha have to say about that?"

He shrugged. "She's got all the wedding preparations in hand, between herself and her mom. There's nothing for me to do." He tossed another log on the fire, dodging a spray of sparks. "So you're making a coat for Colonel Windstrom, eh?" Chris didn't even try to suppress his smirk. "What do you think of our fearless leader?"

"Fear-inspiring, more like. I'm not sure I'd want to hang around here all day listening to him criticize everyone."

Chris nodded. "True, he can be kind of a downer. Yesterday he pulled all the infantry aside for a lecture. He told us that if we weren't shopping at YeOldeReenactors.com, then we were Farbs and not worthy to be in this outfit."

I laughed. "YeOldeReenactors.com? Sounds like a cross between a New England sweet shop and eBay for history buffs. So are you shopping there?"

Chris gave me a sidelong glance. "'Course I am—what do you think? Wouldn't want to stand out as a Farb, now would I?" He smoothed his shiny polyester coat with a wicked grin.

"Got it." I indicated the less-than-authentic coat. "Where did you get this, anyway?"

He leaned in close to whisper behind his hand. "There's a little costume shop on Baker Street, right next to the Keystone Playhouse. They sell leftover costumes from past shows. The Keystone did the musical *The Civil War* two years ago, and they wanted to get rid of the old costumes. I lucked out."

I mentally filed this information, ever on the lookout for leads for my sewing business. Maybe the Keystone would need a seamstress with historical expertise someday.

"There's a lot of interest in the Civil War these days," I said. "You know there's a Civil War movie filming in town right now. Do you guys have any interaction with them?"

"I dunno, they might want to film some of our skirmishes for background shots or something." He shrugged. "I just go with the flow."

A line of gray-clad soldiers marched past us, muskets held at the ready. I scanned their uniforms, looking for reassurance that I was on the right track with Colonel Windstrom's. Their coats came in a wide variety of colors: gray, butternut, and even some faded Union blue. "I don't get it, Chris. How come you guys are Confederate soldiers? There weren't any Southern troops in Laurel Springs, were there?"

"Nah, Laurel Springs was straight Union. But you can't have a battle with just one side, now, can you?" He lowered his voice to a dramatic whisper. "In actual fact, Daria, we're the bad guys."

Chris could never be the bad guy. He was one of the nicest people I had ever met. He worked in construction and remodeling —always a lucrative business in a town full of homes dating back to the early nineteen hundreds. The recession had slowed business a bit, Chris had told me, but he didn't think he'd get laid off. "I'm not worried," he'd said—three words that seemed to sum up his cheerful personality.

"So how come you're not wearing a hoop skirt?" Chris said. "I'll bet you could whip up a ball gown in no time."

I waved a persistent wisp of smoke away from my eyes. "I wouldn't need a ball dress to hang out with you soldiers, unless I just wanted to watch." I remembered a picture I'd come across in my research that showed women in long dresses and parasols standing on a hill watching the Civil War soldiers skirmishing down below. "If I wanted to fight for the glorious cause, I'd dress as a man, and you'd never know as long as I didn't get wounded or captured."

Chris slapped his knee in delight. "You got that right! In fact—"

Suddenly shouts and curses erupted from a tent about fifty yards away. I jumped and scooched a little closer to Chris.

"Who the hell has been messing with my stuff?" A stocky soldier stomped out of the tent, clutching a haversack in one hand and a small wooden box in the other. "You guys may think you're funny," he shouted, waving both arms for emphasis. "If I find out who did this, I'm taking him straight to the general!"

I leaned forward to look at the haversack dangling by its strap from the soldier's hand. A splash of red paint marred the flap of the small canvas bag. Dripping red letters spelled out the word *FARB*. The box bore the same message. I looked anxiously at Chris.

He shrugged. "Some guys want everyone to believe that they're really Civil War soldiers. I guess you could call them fanatics. They're messing with the guys who don't live up to their standard of perfection."

I reached out to touch Chris's polyester coat. "Are they messing with you?"

"Nah." He shrugged. "What can they do to me? I'm not worried."

I looked again at those red letters, paint dripping like blood, and shivered.

The commotion didn't faze Chris. He merely stood up, brushed some dirt off the seat of his pants, and led me to a cluster of larger, more imposing tents. "I think Colonel Windstrom's in a briefing with the general, but I'm not sure."

A smooth-faced sentry stood in front of the colonel's tent, musket held at the ready.

"Are these things loaded?" I said to Chris, waving a hand at the gleaming musket.

He looked me straight in the eye. "Of course, ma'am. You never know when the enemy might strike."

I shot him a sharp glance. "Are you trying to be funny?"

"We're supposed to stay in character at all times," he whispered with a grin. "I try to keep up appearances when the brass are looking."

I shook my head as Chris spoke to the sentry. The sentry was short, clearly a teenager. He wore a gray kepi pulled low over his eyes, so I couldn't see much of his face. No beard or moustache covered his strong jaw. Sandy curls peeked out from the back of his cap—he wore his hair long like boys did in the 1860s.

Chris turned to me. "Colonel Windstrom is busy, Daria. Private Rawlings is going to talk to the sergeant."

I was about to protest, when the sergeant stepped out of the tent. A tall man with a dark brown beard and moustache, he wore a tidy gray uniform coat over dark gray trousers and shiny black boots. He moved with a quiet military grace that came straight out of *Gone with the Wind*. When I held out my hand to introduce myself, he took it gently and bowed down to lightly kiss the back of my hand. No one had ever kissed my hand before, not even in jest. It didn't matter that I wasn't dressed in silk and petticoats—he saw me as a Southern belle. I could feel a sappy grin creep over my face as he lifted his eyes to mine. He had deep brown eyes, so dark you could barely see the pupils. They were eyes to get lost in.

The sergeant smiled, his whole face lighting up. "I'm Sergeant Jim Merrick," he said. "Pleased to make your acquaintance, ma'am."

"I'm Daria Dembrowski." I could feel the blush rising on my cheeks. "I'm making a uniform for Colonel Windstrom. I just needed to take a few more measurements."

"I won't hear another word!" a voice thundered from inside the tent. I jumped with a slight gasp. Sergeant Merrick smiled apologetically. "The colonel is busy at the moment. May I show you around until he's ready?" He held out his arm and tucked my hand into the crook of his elbow. I said goodbye to Chris, who headed back to his fireside with a cheery wave.

Jim Merrick walked me slowly through the tents, pointing out the cook tent, the infirmary, and even the photographer's quarters. "We have a camp photographer traveling with us for a few weeks," he said. "All the men want to have formal portraits taken to send to their loved ones back home."

It took me a minute to realize that I was talking to a Civil War soldier, not a twenty-first century man playing dress-up. This reenacting stuff would take a bit of getting used to. But I could play along. "So, it's the middle of the Civil War, huh? Where's back home to you?"

Jim flashed me a brilliant smile, obviously delighted by my willingness to get into the spirit of the game. "I hail from Tift County, down in Georgia," he drawled in a southern accent worthy of Clark Gable. "I'm a wheelwright, by trade. When this war is over, I hope to take up that useful pursuit once more."

I nodded slowly, chewing the inside of my cheek to keep from laughing. "A wheelwright? So what's that? You make wagon wheels or something?"

"Or something." Jim glanced down to see if I was really interested. "I work with wood, constructing the hub, spokes, and rim of the wheel, which is then reinforced with iron by the village blacksmith. Henry Fleisher and I work as a team, back home in Tifton."

"And the loved ones, back home in Tifton? Is there a Mrs. Merrick waiting at home for you?" I didn't usually ask such personal questions right off the bat, but the game seemed to allow it.

"Indeed yes," he replied. He reached into his pocket and pulled out a worn leather wallet. He fished through it to extract a tiny daguerreotype of a young woman, which he held out to me. "My dear Susannah, that is, Mrs. James Merrick."

I bent over the little picture, admiring the striking features under the modest ruffled bonnet. With her high cheekbones and dark, arching eyebrows, Mrs. James Merrick was a beautiful woman. A fitting partner for the attractive sergeant by my side. I caught myself feeling an absurd sense of disappointment, as if it mattered to me whether or not Jim Merrick had a gorgeous wife at home. I shook myself mentally. "She's very lovely."

He tucked the picture back into his wallet. "Yes, she is." He extended his arm to me again with a half bow. "Shall we continue our tour?"

Jim steered me away from a smoky campfire on our way back to the officers' tents. I noticed a small tent off by itself under some trees. I didn't see a campfire near it, like with all the others.

"What's that tent over there?"

"Hmm? Oh, that? It's the isolation tent." He gave me that apologetic smile again. "You need discipline in any army, you know."

"You're kidding. What, it's like the box in movies, where you lock up the guy for..." My words faltered. I could tell by the look on his face that that's exactly what it was. "Wow," I said. "So is it pretend, or are you really disciplining guys in there?"

Jim gave just the hint of a small, mysterious smile.

We returned to Colonel Windstrom's tent, and Jim murmured to Private Rawlings, who nodded curtly.

"The Colonel will see you now," Jim said. He removed my hand from his arm and held it for a moment, his deep brown eyes fixed on mine. Then he bowed over my hand and once again kissed it ever so lightly.

My heart pounded. I dropped a little curtsy, wishing I had worn a ball gown, or at least a pretty sundress, instead of my faded blue jeans. Maybe another day...

Jim turned and walked away, leaving me to enter the colonel's tent alone.

It took a moment for my eyes to adjust to the dim light within. Colonel Windstrom's tent was crowded with a cot and chipped washstand in one corner, a trunk and traveling chest of drawers in another, and a large folding table surrounded by several camp chairs crammed into the middle. The stuffy smell of warm canvas intensified the claustrophobic feeling of the enclosed space.

Colonel Windstrom was in a foul mood. He stood in the center of the tent breathing heavily, his face a deep, unhealthy red.

"Ms. Dembrowski," he barked.

"Hello, Colonel Windstrom," I replied. "I, uh, I realized that I neglected to take your neck-to-waist measurement. If you'll permit me?" I pulled out my tape measure and squeezed behind him. "If you'll just stand up straight and hold your arms at your sides?" Of course, that was the way a military man *would* stand. I hastened to take the measurement and jot it down in the notepad I always carried in my sewing bag.

"Thanks. Sorry to bother you."

"How is the uniform coming?" Colonel Windstrom asked, a frown darkening his face. I wouldn't want to be disciplined by him, that was for sure.

"Great," I said with a big smile. He didn't need to know that I had yet to cut it out. "It'll be ready for your final fitting on Tuesday. I'll bring it here, if you like."

Private Rawlings poked his head into the tent. His face was white. "Excuse me, sir, there's been another disturbance."

"Not again!" Colonel Windstrom exploded. He snatched up his kepi and shoved it on his head, whirling for the tent opening. His eye fell on me. "Are we done?" he snapped.

"Yes, sir. I'll see you Tuesday at two."

And he was gone.

I folded up my measuring tape and ducked out of the tent. I was ready to get out of there. As I walked away, I could hear the colonel launching into Jim Merrick, berating him for a lack of leadership and failing to properly control the men. I covered my ears and walked faster. I didn't want to hear another word.

* * * *

The next morning, as I laid out the gray wool fabric on the floor to cut, a gentle breeze stirred the muslin curtains in my workroom. I did my cutting and sewing in a vacant bedroom on the second floor of the three-story house that was all I had left from the wreck of my last relationship. I loved the place, originally built in the mid-nineteenth century as a two-story Federal-style home. Over the decades, various owners had added a third floor with whimsical dormer windows and a deep front porch. The lacy Victorian gingerbread molding along the roofline clashed with the austere brick façade, but I didn't care. I loved poking around, looking for hidden passageways in nooks and crannies. My biggest find was a trapdoor in the basement leading to a cramped chamber below. Local lore held that it had been used as a station on the Underground Railroad.

I spent three happy years in the house, as my wedding shop flourished downtown and I started to reap the rewards of entrepreneurship. Then I met a charismatic law student and fell head over heels in love. I encouraged him to move in with me to save on the high cost of law school, and worked hard to support us while he passed the bar and began his legal career as a junior partner in his father's law firm. I envisioned marriage and a lifetime of happiness. What I didn't realize was that he was interested in me not as a fiancée, but as a means to finance his law school education.

When he cleaned out our joint bank account, left for New York on a weeklong business trip and never returned, I was left with a mountain of debt. I had to close the wedding shop and sell off my entire inventory to pay the bills. All I had left was my beautiful, quirky house and a lot of bitter memories.

Under the circumstances, I was happy to have a roof over my head, even though I had to share it with an impossible renter. Still, the lead guitarist in a metal band was a sight better than a domineering boyfriend best known for his disappearing acts. But I didn't want to think about loss and betrayal on this beautiful sunny morning. I pushed the dismal thoughts aside and surveyed my serene workroom.

A varnished wooden door stacked on two chests of drawers served as a desk to hold my new Bernina sewing machine. Grandma's antique Singer treadle machine occupied the place of honor between the two tall windows. My orange-striped cat, Mohair, lay curled on my worn easy chair, watching my every move. Everything seemed so normal and ordinary that it was hard to believe that I hadn't imagined the Civil War camp with its shouting and tension.

A loud knock on the front door interrupted my thoughts.

I hurried down the stairs yelling, "Just a sec!" Could it be Marsha? Her fitting wasn't until tomorrow morning. I'd heard of nervous brides, but that would be ridiculous!

I checked my hair in the mirror over the fireplace in the front hall, smoothing a few stray wisps into the bobby pins pulling my hair back from my face. I always wore my thick brown hair in a severe bun when I was working. It was hardly flattering, but how could I cut out a Civil War uniform with my hair falling into my eyes?

I peeked through the leaded glass of the front door. If it was Marsha, I would have to confess that I hadn't touched her wedding gown since her last fitting. With any luck, she wouldn't lose confidence in me.

Instead, standing on my doorstep, large as life, was my older brother Pete. I threw open the door.

"Daria!" Pete grabbed me into a big bear hug.

I pushed him away. He looked awful. He'd lost a lot of weight since I'd last seen him, His face was drawn and pale, with something weird about it that I couldn't quite put my finger on. He wore a plaid flannel shirt unbuttoned over a T-shirt, worn jeans, and an old Phillies cap.

"What are you doing back home?" I said. "I thought you and your movie camera were set up for life in Hollywood."

"Nice place you've got here." Pete eyed the rosy wallpaper and the sturdy hardwood floor. "Can I come in?"

I held the door open wide. "You can come up and chat, but I have to work. Want some tea? Something to eat?"

Pete shook his head and followed me up the stairs. "You always have to work. You're the workingest woman I know. What is it this time, a pregnant bride and her whole entourage?"

I gave him a sharp look. Did he know Marsha?

"So why aren't you in Hollywood?" I countered. "Did you finish filming, what was it, *Raiders of the Lost Park*?"

Pete laughed. "*Park Raiders*. It folded, and we all got fired. The producer decided he was bored with the whole thing, and the director was crazy. He was convinced we were all out to get him." He took off his hat and ran his hands through his wild brown hair. He needed a haircut, or maybe some of my bobby pins. "I'm so glad to be out of it. It's such a drag to work for a boss who's paranoid. But you know, Hollywood's not the only place to work in the movies. There's so much going on in Pennsylvania right now. I've got a union card that opens all kinds of doors. I just walked into an epic film on the Civil War."

His eyes flicked from the library books strewn on my desk to the gray fabric on the floor, and his face lit up. "Is that what you're working on— costumes for *God and Glory*?"

"I wish." When I had first heard the movie would be filmed in Laurel Springs, I thought it would be the perfect way to break into the historical sewing business. But the film came with its own union shop, and unlike

Pete, I lacked that all-important union card. I was left with the Civil War reenactors and their tailoring needs.

Kneeling on the floor, I finished pinning on my makeshift pattern and held my breath as I made the first cut. So much of sewing was ripping out and starting over, but it was really hard to change what had already been cut.

"*God and Glory*," I said. "Where do they come up with these titles?"

Pete straddled an old wooden chair that I'd picked up at a garage sale. Dark shadows smudged below his eyes. A memory shot through me, of Pete lying on the couch in the tenth grade, wiped out by mono. He didn't look much better now.

"When did your movie fold?" I demanded.

"Oh, it was the day after Halloween. Trick or treat!"

"But it's June fifth," I cried.

Pete cut me off. "Don't fuss, Daria. I've been out of work for seven months, okay? There's a recession on, in case you hadn't noticed. But I've landed on my feet here in Laurel Springs. Camera operator on *God and Glory* is good enough for me." He took a deep breath. "But there is one small detail." He grinned his crazy, pleading grin at me. "I need a place to stay. You've got this huge old house—got a spare room for your big brother?"

"Hmm." I pretended to consider him. "Can you provide any references?"

It wasn't necessarily a stupid question. I hadn't seen him since he left to follow his Hollywood dream six years ago. We'd talked on birthdays and Christmas, but not much more. A lot could change in six years.

He dropped to his knees and clasped his hands in mock supplication. All of a sudden, I knew what was different about his face. His nose was crooked, bent along the bridge up between his eyes. He must have broken his nose in Hollywood—unless someone had broken it for him. It gave him a slightly desperate look that was intensified by the sharpness of his cheekbones. He looked like a panhandler down at Centennial Park.

As if he'd read my mind, he stretched out his arms. "Come on, Daria, give a guy a break. I don't want to have to stay with Dad."

That did it. "Okay, okay. You can have the third floor bedroom. But be forewarned, you'll have to deal with the renter from hell." A thump and a muffled groan came from the room next door. I looked up from my cutting and rolled my eyes. "There she is now."

Pete sat cross-legged on the floor. "What's the big deal?"

I bent over my fabric again. "Aileen's the lead singer in a metal band, the Twisted Armpits. They practice in the basement. Loudly." Slamming noises emanated from the next room. "She's recovering from a gig at the

Hourglass Tavern last night. The band played till two a.m., evidently. She's just now getting up. Drives me crazy."

"So why put up with her?"

I heaved an overly dramatic sigh, and waved my naked left hand in his face. "Maybe you didn't notice, but there isn't anyone else lining up to share the house with me. I've got to make ends meet somehow, in the midst of this recession that you so kindly reminded me of."

Pete contemplated the fading tan lines on my ring finger. "What happened to what's-his-name, that lawyer guy you were with?"

"Good ol' what's-his-name. His name was Randall. It was Randall for the past four years." I took a breath, concentrating on the pattern pieces. It wasn't Pete's fault that he couldn't remember Randall's name. He'd never even met the guy. With any luck, I'd forget his name too. "But he's gone." I didn't feel like going into specifics at the moment. I didn't want to admit to Pete that Randall had conned me from start to finish. The hurt was still too raw, too new.

Pete didn't press for details. "So you never got to wear that white dress down the aisle, huh?"

The dress was gorgeous—rich white satin with an off-the-shoulder neckline and tight bodice flowing down to a flaring A-line skirt. I'd spent every evening for two whole months sewing lace and seed pearls on by hand. The dress was tucked away in a garment bag at the back of my closet. "Did you get an invitation? Or did you think I just skipped that part?"

"Obviously I didn't think much about it at all," Pete confessed with a grin. "I figured you'd get married someday, and I'd have to make a speech or something, after spending the night out on the town with your boyfriend." A teasing note crept into his voice. "At least it won't be old what's-his-name. He sounded like a loser—definitely not the guy for my little sister."

"I'll tell you about it sometime. You know all those lawyer jokes? They were thinking of Randall when they made them up."

Pete's laugh was drowned out by Aileen's dramatic entrance. Her door flew open with a crash that rattled the house, shaking my "Home, Sweet Home" cross-stitch right off the wall. She stomped out of her room and stopped in my doorway, glaring at Pete. He stared right back, his mouth dropping open.

Aileen always had this effect on people. Nearly six feet tall, with spiky black hair streaked with pink and black makeup that never really washed off, she was used to causing a stir. She thrived on attention, soaking it up like a dry plant drinks in water. If people didn't stare, she'd probably shrivel up and turn into an ordinary person like the rest of us. This morning she wore a black T-shirt with obscenities splashed across the front and a pair of lacy black panties.

Pete gulped and gave it his best try. "You must be the rock star," he said.

"You must be the moron," Aileen shot back. "I thought the men were going to stay downstairs," she said to me.

I pasted on a smile. "Aileen, this is my big brother, Pete. He's going to move into the third-floor bedroom."

"Like hell he is," Aileen snapped. "I'm gonna get some breakfast." She stomped off toward the stairs.

"Charming girl," Pete said lightly. "Has a real way with people, wouldn't you say?"

"Oh, stop. She pays her rent. Like I said, I can't afford to live here by myself." I scrambled to my feet and faced my brother. "If you can cover her share, six fifty a month, I'd gladly kick her out."

Pete picked up my pincushion and fiddled with the pins and needles. "Uh, yeah, I'm sure we'll get along great, once she gets to know me."

"That's what I thought." I crossed my arms and glared at him. "You will chip in for groceries, or you won't be staying here."

"Yes, ma'am. I'll clean the bathroom and take out the trash, and I make a killer lasagna." He stood up and folded his hands meekly in front of him like a good little boy. "You just say the word."

I laughed in spite of myself. "Come on, let's give it another try. Maybe some food will have mellowed her a bit."

We walked into my high-ceilinged kitchen. Aileen sat at the table, eating powdered sugar donuts straight from the bag.

I sat down across from her. Pete hovered in the doorway.

"How was the gig?" I asked.

"It was awesome," she mumbled through her mouthful of donut. "Three guys got into it and smashed a couple chairs and dumped a pitcher of beer on the waitress." Puffs of powdered sugar punctuated each sentence. "You like music?" she shot at Pete.

"Yeah, sure. I'm a big Springsteen fan."

Aileen snorted and stuffed another donut into her mouth.

"Pete's just moved back home." I ran my fingers along the vine pattern stenciled into the table edge. "He's been in Hollywood for almost six years."

She humphed and wiped her sugary hands on her shirt. "Big Hollywood dude, huh? What'd you come back to the boonies for?"

Pete shrugged. "Guess I didn't make it in Hollywood. Pennsylvania's the place to be in the movies right now."

"He's got a job as a camera operator for a movie here, *God and Glory*," I said. "It's about the Civil War."

Aileen grinned at me. "You're gonna get your fill of the Civil War." She scraped her chair against the floor and stood up as if she owned the place. "Alright, Moron, you can stay. For now."

"You can call me Pete. I don't answer to 'Moron,'" Pete said mildly.

Aileen clomped out of the room, waving her long black fingernails behind her. "Whatever."

About the Author

Greta McKennan is a wife, mother, and first-time author, living her dream in the boreal rainforest of Juneau, Alaska. She enjoys a long walk in the woods on that rare sunny day, reading cozy mysteries when it rains, and sewing the Christmas jammies on her antique Singer sewing machine. She is hard at work on the next novel in her Stitch in Time Mystery series featuring seamstress Daria Dembrowski. Visit her on the web at gretamckennan.com.

Printed in the United States
by Baker & Taylor Publisher Services